MADE

OF

STARS

MADE OF

OF

STARS

JENNA VORIS

VIKING

VIKING
An imprint of Penguin Random House LLC, New York

First published in the United States of America by Viking,
an imprint of Penguin Random House LLC, 2023

Copyright © 2023 by Jenna Voris

Viking & colophon are registered trademarks of Penguin Random House LLC.

Visit us online at penguinrandomhouse.com.

Library of Congress Cataloging-in-Publication Data is available.

Printed in the USA

ISBN 9780593525210 (hardcover)

ISBN 9780593622117 (international edition)

1st Printing

LSCH

Design by Lucia Baez • Text set in Aldus Nova Pro

For Sarina,
who wished on every star
and every window with me for years

PART ONE
Shot in the Dark

You've read the story of Jesse James,
of how he lived and died.
If you're still in need;
of something to read,
here's the story of Bonnie and Clyde.

—Bonnie Parker,
"The Trail's End"

CHAPTER ONE

✳ ✳ ✳

The young ones died first.

Blood pooled between the stones and crawled across the floor with delicate phantom hands. Shane felt it sink into his bones the longer he lay in the cell. How long had it been since he tasted pure, unrecycled oxygen? Since he felt the steady weight of a weapon in his hand? His finger twitched as he imagined the shock of a rifle against his shoulder, the silent shot in the open vacuum of space.

You're not going to die here.

Shane rolled over, wincing as his shoulder twisted painfully. He'd popped it back into place after the fight yesterday, but the skin was still swollen and tender. His hands ached, too. He tried not to think about why, but the memories always overcame him in the end.

A pulse slowing under his fingers. The other man clawing at the floor, broken nails scratching down the dusty walls. Shane had always thought killing would be harder, that it would take a certain kind of person to wrap their hands around another's throat and squeeze until there was nothing left, but it had been over by the time the warden arrived, before the droids swarmed and the prisoners rioted. Killing was the easiest thing in the world. And Shane wasn't sorry.

He exhaled, grimacing at the sharp pain in his chest. They kept it cold in solitary. Add that to the list of things these people would pay for. He'd come for them all eventually—every officer, every warden, every droid. Everyone who funded a place like this. *You're not going to die here.*

Shane's last thoughts before the dark claimed him again were of his hands, pale and trembling without something to hold, and that man's vacant, lifeless stare.

CHAPTER TWO

✳ ✳ ✳

Three months of planning and Ava had still managed to underestimate the cold.

She shivered as she followed a masked officer through the twisting corridors of the Opian prison moon. They had made it through the first security checkpoint without so much as a whisper from the alarms, but another officer stopped her before she reached the second. He yanked her into a corner between a damp, icy wall and a security droid, and Ava had to remind herself that *this was normal* as his hands closed around her waist.

This was Chess. This level of security was expected. Still, she had to force herself not to flinch, to focus on the camera embedded in the droid's flat, metal face and instead think about all the ways she could take this officer apart while his hands skimmed up her legs. He got as far as her left thigh before finding the protein bar tucked in her stocking. His face twisted into a mocking grin.

"Not allowed."

Ava tried to snatch it back, but the officer shoved it into his own pocket before giving her a pat on the back that lingered a bit too long between her shoulder blades and pushing her through the second checkpoint.

The officer in front of her now wore a thick padded jacket

and boots in addition to a mask across the bottom half of his face. Ava had to clench her jaw to keep her teeth from chattering as they walked. *What do the prisoners wear? How many freeze to death alone in these cells?* She tried not to think about what three months in a place like this might have done to Shane. The frigid climate on their home planet, Nakara, meant she wasn't usually cold, but Ava didn't think this chill was entirely due to temperature.

The officers tried to block her view of the cells as they walked, one after the other in a shifting wall of black fabric and polished weapons, but it wasn't necessary. Ava had stopped looking after she saw a girl slumped against the rough stones, eyes half-open as her fingers twitched in time to their footsteps.

"Are you a friend of his?"

The officer's question was too loud. Ava tensed as he looked over his shoulder, lowering her gaze to the floor. "Yes."

What she could see of the man's face relaxed, and satisfaction heated her bones. This was why Shane had hired her, after all. This was why she wore pretty dresses and wove moonflowers into her long, dark hair and blushed at every question. Because she was a good actress, good enough to make it if she'd been born on any part of Nakara other than barren, wasted West Rama. Because she was *harmless*.

When the officer spoke again, his voice was almost kind. "Can I give you a piece of advice?"

Ava nodded as they stopped in front of a thick, steel-plated door. He could give her all the advice he wanted if he looked the other way in that room. "Of course."

The officer removed his glove and pressed one finger to the

scanner laid into the wall. "That boy is nothing but trouble. Everyone on this moon is trouble."

Ava did smile then, and she was glad his back was turned. She ran a hand down the front of her dress, tracing the sharp edge of the pistol still tucked beneath the fabric, cold against her skin.

He didn't know the first thing about trouble.

When the door clicked open, she used the time it took for the officer to put his glove back on to find the cameras—one in every corner. That was fine. Jared said he'd deal with those. He should be in the system by now; she just had to buy him time. Then the officer stepped aside and Ava's next breath caught as she locked eyes with Shane.

Three months.

Had it really only been three months? Ava could see his ribs against the thin fabric of his prison shirt, see the way he stood with one arm pressed against his side. *Too thin.* They had shaved his hair too, so only a thin buzz remained across his pale scalp, but Shane still straightened when he saw her, eyes widening in surprise before his face split into a painful-looking grin.

"Hey, baby, how's it floating?"

Same voice, same confidence, same wry smile. Ava grimaced. "You look like junkmatter."

She reached out a hand, but the officer caught her wrist before she could touch him. "That's close enough."

It took every ounce of Ava's self-control not to snap his fingers. She pretended to shrink away, hands shaking as they fell back to her sides. He didn't need to know it was from fury, not fear. *Harmless.*

Then she heard it—a faint *click*.

The cameras. Jared said anyone watching from the prison's control towers would see the room exactly as it had been seconds before, their images frozen in time. She had two minutes, but the only person Ava had to fool was the officer himself.

And Shane, who hadn't been expecting her, who had no idea what she was planning, who could barely stand.

Ava pushed the thought away. It didn't matter; they would make this work. She took a tentative step forward and silently begged Shane to play along. "I've missed you. How are you doing?" It was a stupid question. Purple bruises masked most of Shane's face and now that she was closer, Ava could tell he was keeping the weight off his left ankle, too. She swallowed her unease and added, "I tried to bring food, but they found it."

She said that part loud enough for the officer to hear, to let him think the game was over.

Shane's confusion only lasted a second longer. His face smoothed into an easy grin, eyes flicking toward each camera as Ava took another step. "That's fine. You were all I wanted anyway, baby."

Ava resisted the urge to roll her eyes. That was a bit much, even for him, but it worked for what she had to do next. Slowly, she lifted her hands to the front of her dress and unfastened one button. "Really?" she whispered. "That's *all* you wanted?"

Shane blinked, color deepening on his bruised cheeks as she opened another button, then a third. Ava glanced over her shoulder to find the officer suddenly very interested in a spot on the floor. She undid another button, finally revealing the barrel of the gun stashed down the front of her dress, and Shane's expression shifted into cool understanding. This time, when he reached for her, the officer didn't intervene.

Because she was a simple, harmless girl caught up with a boy from the wrong side of town.

Ava slid her hands across Shane's chest as he lowered his face into the curve of her neck. She could feel him shivering under her fingers, and her next words caught in her throat as one of his hands groped at her chest, grabbing the barrel of the gun.

"There's a droid at the first security checkpoint," she breathed, and Shane's answering nod was almost invisible. He slid the weapon into the front of his pants and Ava stepped back, hurriedly buttoning her dress. Every few seconds she threw nervous, purposeful glances over her shoulder at the officer, who still had his gaze fixed on a crack in the floor, but it was Shane who spoke first.

"All that and I don't even get a kiss?"

Ava's hands stilled on her collar, and when she glanced up, Shane looked like he was fighting the urge to laugh. *He thinks this is funny*, Ava realized. Here he was, barely able to stand, and he still wanted to embarrass her.

Unbelievable.

So instead of blushing and turning away like she knew he expected, Ava smiled, grabbed Shane's face with both hands, and kissed him right on the mouth. He let out a pained grunt at the sudden movement, but she ignored him, and when she pulled back, the officer seemed to decide that was the last straw. "Time's up."

Ava patted Shane's cheek and stepped away. "Bye, *baby*."

The last thing Ava saw before the door closed was Shane's grin, wicked and cutting as he lifted a hand to his lips.

The man behind the visitor's desk handed Ava her bag and fake ID as she signed out, but her heart was still hammering as she stepped outside and picked her way through the docks. Their Cruiser was easy to spot, clunky and out of place among the shiny patrol vehicles. The ship wasn't particularly fast, but the boxy model and nondescript paint job blended with the commuter traffic on almost every planet. Shane never would have stolen a Cruiser—they weren't flashy enough for him. But Shane hadn't been there when they needed a new ship. And given the circumstances, Ava thought she'd done a decent job.

Jared was already sitting in the front, feet propped against the dashboard. He scrambled up when Ava hauled herself into the ship. "Did you see him?" he asked without waiting for her to sit down. "What did he look like? What's going on?"

His fingers danced nervously over his skin screen and the sound of fingernails on glass raked down Ava's spine. She shuddered. "Bad."

"How so? What—?"

"It was *bad*, Jared!"

He flinched and Ava immediately regretted snapping. "Sorry," she murmured, running a hand across her face. "I'm sorry. It was bad."

There was a moment of frosty silence before Jared leaned forward, tucking his chin against her shoulder as they waited together. Ava had debated pushing him out the air lock half a dozen times over the last three months, but she was glad he was here now. She wouldn't have made it this far without him. Jared was only fifteen—two years younger than she was—but he was the best hacker she'd ever met, and he still had the skin screen to prove it, despite ditching the Nakaran military years ago.

Ava wound the chain of her necklace around one finger until the small, rectangular charm landed in her palm, gleaming silver in the harsh light of the docks. They shouldn't linger here, especially in a stolen ship. The flow of traffic on and off Chess was almost as strictly regulated as the prison itself, and any minute someone would notice she was still here.

And that a prisoner was making his way toward the exit, shooting down everything in his path.

She checked and rechecked the Cruiser's landing gear, trying to ignore the weight of each passing second. Then, when nothing happened, she checked it a third time before pulling the mirrors forward to reapply her lipstick. It was still smudged from kissing Shane. That was going to be a lecture for sure—he didn't like surprises. She glanced back toward the entrance, certain she would see him dashing across the docks, but the doors were still firmly closed.

He's taking too long.

How long did she wait before calling it and leaving Shane inside? What if he never made it past the guard in the visitor's room or the droid at the checkpoint? Ava reached down and started the Cruiser, wincing at the sharp rattle of the engine. *Just a few more seconds . . .*

"What's the holdup?"

Jared jumped, scattering wires and spare parts over the floor, as another voice echoed across the docks. He turned panicked eyes toward the approaching officer as Ava jammed a finger into his chest.

"Do *not* speak," she hissed. Then she turned and plastered on a smile. "Hi, Officer, is there a problem?"

He didn't smile back. "What's the holdup?"

Ava could only make out his eyes, narrowed over the top of his mask. Shane always said the people who worked on Opia's prison moons hid their faces because they didn't want anyone to know what they were capable of. She remembered his bruises, the girl from the cell, and it was an effort to keep her smile from slipping. "Nothing, Officer, we were just leaving. You know these old Cruisers take forever to start."

The officer ignored her and peered into the back, where Jared was running his hands through his nest of white-blond curls. "What's your business here?"

Ava risked a glance toward the controls. Three switches. That was all it would take to get them in the air. As long as she was through the prison checkpoint before the alarms sounded, she had nothing to worry about.

"Hello!" The officer snapped his gloved fingers in front of her face, and Ava wondered how long it would take to break his hand. Could she do it before he called for backup? Before he reached for the assault rifle strapped across his chest?

"I'm sorry," Ava gasped. Her eyes blurred with fake tears. "We were visiting a friend."

"Who?" The officer's gaze didn't soften. He didn't even flinch. When she didn't answer, he reached a hand toward his ear, and Ava barely had time to open her mouth before he pressed a finger to his portable comm and said, "Air control, this is—"

He never finished the sentence.

One second, he was standing in front of the window and the next he had tipped forward, blood blooming across his chest as he choked on a strangled cry. Jared yelped and Ava shoved the body to the ground, already feeling for her own weapon. Her hand had barely closed around its barrel when she saw Shane limping hurriedly across the docks.

He came to a stop outside the ship, and Ava watched him glance at Jared, who still cowered in the back, before his gaze slid over to her. She opened her mouth, three months of practiced conversations blurring together the longer they looked at each other, but Shane held up a finger before she could say anything at all.

"I cannot *believe* you stole a Cruiser."

CHAPTER THREE

***

"Cyrus! Watch your six!"

The enemy dreadnought appeared out of nowhere. Cyrus threw himself to the side, gloved hands tightening over the controls of his own Falcon fighter as he watched the rest of the ship materialize: five miles of steel-plated armor and deadly heat cannons. *Who was guarding the jump point?* He pressed a finger to the comm in his ear as the dreadnought cruised overhead, lithe enemy Falcons dropping in its wake. "Cornelia, where are you?"

The only answer was the faint hiss of static.

Cyrus swerved as the oncoming swarm of fighters opened fire, one after the other. He accelerated forward, stomach dropping through the floor, and tried the comms again. "Cornelia?"

"Are you planning on dealing with that cannon anytime soon?"

It was Lark's voice that crackled through Cyrus's headset then, not Cornelia's. "I'm having a wonderful time up here," he continued, "truly, but I'd love to get home before our retirement benefits kick in."

Cyrus rolled his eyes. Like that was *his* fault? But he kept his voice light in case any commanding officers were listening and said, "On it. See you there."

"My hero." Lark's sarcasm was clear, even across the empty void of space. "Whatever would we do without your unmatched skill, your unwavering bravery, your—"

Cyrus switched off his comm, plunging his Falcon into a brief, blessed silence. Of *course* Lark didn't want to deal with the cannons himself. They were huge. Why would he risk it when he could swoop in at the end, after Cyrus's ship had been blasted out of the sky, and claim the final victory for himself? Cyrus craned his neck for any sign of his squadron but saw only stars glinting faintly in the distance.

They had been on the way back to Opia when the dreadnought appeared. Now they were surrounded, pushed into a lone corner of the Valentina System, half a jump point from the nearest planet. Cyrus hadn't even finished breakfast. But this was what he lived for: the thrill of the chase, the desire to prove himself, the tingle across his skin as he flipped his comms back on and dodged another oncoming Falcon. He fired back instinctively, each shot sending another enemy ship spinning. Satisfaction flared warm in his chest. *This will look good on a report.*

"Nice!" Cornelia's voice echoed in his head as Cyrus made it through the first wave, and he faltered.

"Where are you?" he asked, scanning the sky for the familiar glint of her ship.

"Already here, Cy. Starboard!"

And there she was, a brilliant streak diving for the dreadnought's exposed side. Falcons were made for speed and so was Cornelia. She dropped her missiles one after the other, the force of the blasts tearing one of the cannons from the dreadnought's hull entirely. But when she circled back for the second cannon, she missed by almost a foot.

Cyrus bit back a grin. Cornelia could fly better than almost anyone at the Academy, but she was a lousy shot. "They're right in front of you. How did you miss?"

"Shut *up*."

He could practically see her exasperated expression, the same one she'd had since they were kids.

"I mean, they aren't even moving," Cyrus added, watching her double back. "How hard can it be? Do you need me to—?" He broke off as something tore past his window. "Cornelia, look out!"

But it was too late. The enemy Falcon opened fire and Cornelia had nowhere to go. The bullets sliced through her ship one by one. She cried out once before tumbling back, and in the second it took Cyrus to watch her fall, the enemy Falcon circled around. Three bullets lodged under his feet with solid, definite *thunks*, and he yanked the controls to the side so fast his own ship rolled, narrowly avoiding the rest of the attack.

Get it together.

Cornelia was gone—he would think about that later. Right now, Lark was hovering around the main engine, ready to fire as soon as Cyrus took out the remaining cannon. They had to work quickly, before the other Falcons came back to finish the job. Cyrus let his hands steady, listening to the hum of the engine through his seat, familiar as his own heartbeat. Then he dove.

He followed Cornelia's original flight path, dodging enemy Falcons and bits of debris as he went. The remaining cannon screeched as it wound up to fire again, and Cyrus felt the roar deep in his bones. "Lark?"

"I'm ready!"

Cyrus blew out a breath, whipped his ship around, and unloaded the entirety of his arsenal straight into the cannon's gaping mouth. To his right, Lark turned his attention to the main engine as the rest of their squadron fell into place behind him. The shock of each impact rocked Cyrus side to side, his Falcon creaking from the force. *More time.* He needed to give his team more time.

There was a high-pitched groan, a split second of silence, and then the dreadnought exploded.

The blast tore Cyrus's hands from the controls. His Falcon rolled, stars blurring overhead in a twisted black vortex until he couldn't tell which way was up. He couldn't grasp the trembling control wheel. He couldn't *think.* Then one by one the stars flickered out. The ship steadied and Cyrus was left staring at a blank, pixelated screen. An automated voice blared through his pod.

"Simulation complete."

He had time for one shuddering breath before his door slid back and blinding, blue-tinted light cut across his vision.

"You distracted me!"

Cyrus blinked as Cornelia yanked him to his feet. He took off his gloves, shaking out his left arm as his skin screen flickered back to life. It was hot from running the simulation, and Cyrus could feel the glass embedded in his forearm radiating energy through his flight suit as it disconnected from the servers and linked back with the wires under his skin. The rest of his team clambered out of their pods, but Cornelia was still glaring at him, arms crossed, toe tapping on the worn cement. How she managed to look down on him when she was an entire foot shorter was a mystery Cyrus had been trying to solve his entire life. He shrugged. "You should have been paying attention."

He should have been paying attention. Those Falcons shouldn't have been able to sneak up on him, much less land three shots.

"I got that cannon for you," Cornelia pointed out. Pieces of her bright red hair still clung to her neck as she removed her helmet. "You're welcome for that, by the way."

Cyrus tucked his own helmet under his arm and glanced around the training center lobby. There were more people here than when they had started the simulation an hour ago. Fresh-faced first-years jostled for a position on the stairs, upperclassmen leaned over the railings, and senior officers stood at the front, arms folded across their uniforms. Despite their varying ages and ranks, they all seemed to gravitate toward the center of the room, and Cyrus felt a thrill spark under his skin as he recognized General Pelara Noth among the crowd.

Her sleek, graying hair was pulled back in a low bun, uniform pressed and spotless against her white skin. Cool, stark perfection. The superintendent of Opia's Air Force Academy didn't have room for error, but Noth wasn't the kind of officer who mingled, and Cyrus knew her presence in the training center now could only mean one thing.

"I think you got it," Cornelia whispered, following his gaze across the room.

Cyrus didn't want to think about how much he hoped she was right. After that simulation, it didn't seem possible. He could still feel the bullets hammering into the hard exterior of his ship, one mistake after another.

"What?" Cornelia chewed on a nail, brow furrowing as she surveyed the room. "I don't see how it could be anyone else."

She still had blue polish on one hand, chipped and messy. Because only Cornelia could get away with violating dress code so openly. If she didn't fly as well as she did, Cyrus thought someone would have kicked her out of the Academy ages ago.

The rest of the cadets gathered in the center of the room without being told and Cyrus joined them, eyeing his squadron with renewed unease. He wasn't the only pilot with a good record. There was Essie, with their near-perfect aim and sharp eye. Lark, who constantly found ways to remind Cyrus that *he* was actually ranked first in simulated flight times. Cornelia, who once ran a sim in a thirty-year-old Star Rover as a dare. Cyrus knew them all, had lived and worked and fought with them for the last four years. There had been more in the beginning.

Not everyone made it to eighteen at the Academy.

"Congratulations, cadets." General Noth turned in a circle, and Cyrus straightened at the sound of her voice. "You survived your last sim as Academy students. How does it feel?"

A few of the younger soldiers clapped, but Cyrus didn't move. It felt like a trick question. Anticipation pulsed under his skin, somewhere between dread and excitement, as he tried to remember if Noth usually came to congratulate the graduates. His mind came back frustratingly blank.

"I know graduation isn't until tomorrow, but we always like to give out a few of our own awards before your families arrive. After all, you've been physically, mentally, and emotionally tested since the day you arrived on campus. Isn't it time to celebrate?"

Lark elbowed Cornelia in the ribs. "Emotionally tested, huh?" he muttered. "That's one way to put it."

Cornelia didn't look at him. "No one cares about your love life, Lark. You are *not* that interesting."

A few of the cadets snorted as Lark tried and failed to look annoyed, but Cyrus couldn't relax. Lark might love the attention of a roomful of officers, and he might be able to get away with holding it, but they were still in class. There were still rules Cyrus couldn't break. But even Noth was grinning as she waved Lark back in line.

"As you know, cadets are ranked by combining academic standing, simulated scores, and merits," she said. "Graduates will receive their final rank tonight, but we like to take a minute to honor the year's valedictorian cadet ourselves—a student who has been an example to us all from the day they walked through our doors."

Cyrus's nails dug into his calloused palms. When Noth spoke again, her voice was another enemy Falcon, sharp and deadly and aimed right for the center of his chest.

"It is my absolute honor to introduce this year's valedictorian cadet, Cyrus Blake."

It wasn't until Cornelia poked him in the ribs and whispered *"That's you!"* that Cyrus fully registered the sentence. *Valedictorian cadet.* He remembered to salute just in time, and to his surprise, General Noth mirrored the action.

"Congratulations, cadet." She looked him up and down, eyes glittering in the fluorescent light.

Cyrus wondered if that was supposed to be encouraging. He risked a glance over his shoulder and found Lark's brow furrowed with annoyance. Most of his classmates were smiling, but Cyrus watched a few exchange puzzled glances, saw apprehension echo itself on the faces of his commanding officers, and knew what they were thinking. The valedictorian cadet was supposed to go to someone like Lark, someone whose family name was plastered on Academy buildings, who had photos of grandfathers and great-grandfathers hanging in the alumni hall.

General Noth seemed oblivious to the tension as she raised her voice to address the room again. "You should all be very proud of yourselves. But please celebrate responsibly tonight," she added, eyes narrowing on the line of waiting cadets. "If any of you embarrass me, I'm giving you asteroid duty."

Then she left, flashing a wink in Cyrus's direction on her way out, and his response caught in his throat at the familiarity of it. Like they were friends, even equals. It wasn't until the rest of the officers filed out behind her that Cyrus realized he hadn't said a word.

"I *knew* it was you!"

Cornelia threw her arms in the air, and Cyrus grunted as all five feet of her slammed into his chest. Her exclamation broke whatever spell General Noth had cast on the training center and the rest of his classmates trickled forward, patting each other on the back. Lark let out the longest, most dramatic sigh Cyrus had ever heard.

"Congratulations, I suppose. I still think your time was a fluke, considering *I* took out the engine."

Despite the sim helmet, Lark's golden hair was still frustratingly perfect, slicked to his scalp with an amount of hair gel that made Cyrus immediately wary of open flames. Still, he didn't have the energy to argue. He was less than twenty-four hours away from never seeing Larksarid Belle again. "Do you want to try and beat it?" he asked, jabbing a thumb over his shoulder at the simulation pods. "We could go again."

Actually, Cyrus thought he *should* run the sim again, to pinpoint where he'd gone wrong.

Lark glanced at the pods, like he was seriously considering it, then shook his head. "Wouldn't want to make you cry on our last night."

"Of course you don't." Cornelia grabbed Cyrus's hand, fingers slipping into the familiar spaces between his. "I'm so proud of you, Cy. You'll get the best assignment for sure. Where do you want to go?"

Lark rolled his eyes so impressively Cyrus half expected them to fall out of his head. "They'll probably send you to one of those prison moons. Hey"—he straightened—"did you hear Chess had a breakout last night? You'd fit right in since those officers are also, apparently, incompetent and—"

Cornelia laughed. "You want to talk about incompetent? You almost shot me thirty seconds into the sim. It's literally our last day!"

"Okay, but I *didn't.*"

Cyrus was only half listening as Cornelia threw out more guesses. Maybe he'd join Atmosphere Patrol and fly along the edge of the system. Maybe he'd run security for the planetary leader, live in a towering building in the capital, and take important meetings. Cyrus tried to pay attention but the itch lingered in the back of his mind, clawing down his spine to his boots, where he could still feel those three bullets slamming into the bottom of his ship.

Mistake. Mistake. Mistake.

He should have gotten through the sim unscathed. A proper valedictorian cadet would have. Cyrus glanced at the pods again. It wouldn't take long. He needed one more run, one last time behind the wheel.

Cornelia's fingers tightened around his. "Stop it," she whispered. "I know what you're thinking."

Cyrus scowled and yanked his hand away. That was easy for her to say. Cornelia had stopped being the girl from the Port City gutters when she flew literal circles around their commanding officer on day one. She would be assigned somewhere she could fly and no one would think of grimy piers and smoking factories when they looked at her, because girls from Port City didn't end up top of their class at the Air Force Academy and boys like him were never supposed to be valedictorian cadets.

But he was here now. He had made it, and as Cyrus exhaled, he felt some of the tension melt off his shoulders, where that same nagging itch still buzzed. Only now it felt like a voice, a warning whisper in his ear.

You're ready, it seemed to say. *Let's go.*

CHAPTER FOUR

✳ ✳ ✳

"**Y**ou're *serious?*"

Jared was pacing back and forth behind Shane's seat, footsteps too loud in the open bay of the Cruiser. He hadn't stopped moving since they'd fled Chess with three separate squadrons in pursuit. Shane had lost them in an asteroid junkyard hours ago, but Jared was still looking over his shoulder, flinching at every passing satellite. He leaned forward when Shane didn't answer, and tried again. "You really think that's a good idea? Because what if—?"

"I can eject him if you want." Ava propped a foot against the dashboard and flipped the page of her magazine. "There's a lever in the back."

Jared stiffened, like he couldn't decide if Ava was joking, then sighed. "Fine. Go ahead, plan another job. It's not like we just *broke you out of Chess.*"

The words hung in the air with a dangerous finality. *We broke you out of Chess.*

Shane had never really let himself think about the possibility of serving his full sentence. Thoughts like that tended to snare people, to drag them under when no one was looking. They wanted him on that moon for sixteen years, but he'd barely survived three months. Three long, brutal months where he had plenty of time to think about what they would do the second he got out.

Behind him, Jared inched across the dusty floor until he was sitting cross-legged next to Shane's seat. "A government building?" he asked, voice creeping higher with every word. "You want to rob— I know we've done it before and it was really great, excellent times—but given the circumstances, don't you think—?"

"What circumstances?"

Shane could feel himself shaking in time with the Cruiser. He wanted Jared to say what he was so obviously thinking. That he thought Shane was weak. That he *couldn't* do it. That Chess had changed him somehow, shattered something that couldn't be fixed by an odd job or a risky heist. But this plan, this idea of a plan, was going to work. It had to. He was going to fly right into the Nakaran capital and fly out with someone else's money.

Because he wanted to. Because he could.

Jared was the one who looked away first. "Sorry," he muttered. "But do you really need to go home, too? We could refuel anywhere; West Rama's the first place they'll look for you."

Shane clenched his teeth. Like he didn't know that. Of course it was dangerous, but this was how they worked. Every few jobs, he and Ava would fly through West Rama, dropping whatever extra cash they managed to score at their parents' doors. It was routine by now, and Shane wasn't stopping because a few officers on a foreign prison moon thought they owned him.

"Ava wants to visit her mother," he said. "It's been a long time."

It wasn't technically a lie, but Shane didn't meet Ava's

questioning gaze. He would visit his family, too, but not because he wanted to. He was their only source of reliable income, and Shane didn't want to think about what his absence had done to the farm. He had never been gone this long before.

Did his parents know where he'd been?

The thought was cold. A thief in West Rama was nothing. All of Shane's friends could pick locks by the time they were ten, and most parents pretended not to notice when their children stayed out too long and came back too late. But those boys didn't get hauled off to Chess because the wrong officer caught them at the wrong time.

Jared shifted closer, his bony knee knocking against Shane's ankle with each movement. "So not only do you want to rob a government building," he said tentatively, "but you also want to risk our lives for your parents?"

"*Stars*, Jared." Ava put down her magazine. "Don't be so dramatic. No one's risking anything. Just because you don't have a family to check on doesn't mean we don't."

"And no one's looking for Ava," Shane added. "We'll take advantage of that while we can—have her do a supply run and find another ship."

"They might be looking for me. I'm dangerous."

The corner of her mouth lifted, and Shane had to look away as the memory of her kiss seared through him. She had done that on purpose, for no reason other than she thought it was funny. Maybe it would have been, once. Maybe three months ago he would have kissed her back, but now he was exhausted. The bruises on his face throbbed along with the engine, his muscles ached from flying this far in a stars-forsaken Cruiser, and the last thing he wanted was to let Ava know she'd rattled him.

He didn't get rattled.

Shane braced himself as he guided the ship through the last stretch of bone-shaking turbulence into Nakaran airspace. He'd done this countless times, knew every bump and turn. When they slammed out of the jump point, space dust spilling in their wake, Nakara loomed below, a desert storm spewing clouds of sand into the atmosphere.

Home.

Nakara sat at the very edge of the system under a constant veil of dust and sand. With limited sunlight and a climate too cold for most plants to survive, the Nakaran capital and most major cities lived under the protection of glossy, temperature-controlled domes. They allowed life to flourish in the manufactured warmth, but in West Rama, the desert city Ava and Shane both called home, that luxury didn't exist. People survived on root vegetables and desert herbs, whatever they could grow themselves outside of the dome's protective embrace.

The planet's real income came from the rich axium deposits below its surface, the miles of mines and tunnels that kept their people employed and other planets happy. When Opian ships landed on Nakara centuries ago looking for something to fuel their dreadnoughts and sprawling factory cities, no one had been able to fight them off. Opia was a weapon disguised as a planet, honed to take and conquer and steal. Nakara traded time in the mines for the food and supplies they desperately needed. It was an agreement they said would benefit everyone.

Now Shane watched the dome flicker over downtown Rama as he merged with local traffic on the surface, light fading as the city settled into dusk. He used to wonder what the domed cities felt like, who he could have been if he'd gone to sleep every night with the reassurance that there would always be light when he woke. But he felt the cold now, a crushing weight that deepened the farther they flew. It thrust him back to a night-cloaked cell, reminded him of cold hands and sharp steel. Shane's fingers tightened on the controls. How long would he feel the blood coating his skin? How long would he see the bodies of those who didn't make it?

Ava shifted in her seat, and the sound dragged him back to reality. Shane released a tight breath. He couldn't do this now, not so close to home. Not when they had a job to do. Usually, Shane could hear the familiar roar of the trains from the road, but tonight, the streets of West Rama were quiet and still. Even the streetlights wavered, like everything was low on fuel.

"How long were we gone?" he asked. The silence was too consuming to be comfortable.

"Six months," Ava whispered. "We did that job over in Melesink and then you were . . ."

She trailed off, the unspoken words clear. *Six months.*

"The Opian supplies should be here by now." Shane knew he was thinking out loud, but he couldn't stop. "Why does this town look like they haven't seen a fuel cell in weeks?"

Ava didn't answer. Even Jared was silent. Shane tried not to let his unease show, but there went his plan to steal a ship from West Rama. If the trains didn't have fuel, nobody did.

He parked a few streets down from Ava's house and released

the side door. Something in his chest unfurled as he inhaled his first lungful of frigid Nakaran air. Rationally, Shane knew this city was nothing. He knew the entire planet was slowly sinking into the desert, one bad storm away from disappearing, but he was *here* and the lingering smell of damp sewage was nothing compared to how good it felt to breathe.

Ava was halfway out of the ship before Shane opened his eyes. "Wait!"

He grabbed her wrist, fumbling with the storage compartment under his seat. Their stash was still there, bags of coins stuffed under the floorboards, and he almost laughed. If their positions were reversed, Shane would have taken the money and left Ava and Jared to rot on Chess.

No, you wouldn't. He would have left Jared, maybe, but not her. Never her.

Shane realized he was still holding Ava's arm and released it immediately. "Here." He shoved a bag in her direction. "Tell your mother I miss her. She's devastated by my absence, I'm sure."

Ava's eyes widened. She didn't even laugh at his weak attempt at humor. "Are you sure?"

Shane knew what she meant. They never gave away money, but he owed her more; he owed her everything. This was the best he could do right now. "Just take it, Castor."

This time, Ava did. "How long?"

"Half an hour." Shane flipped the Cruiser back into drive. "We have a job, remember? Don't do anything stupid."

One of Ava's eyebrows lifted. "I survived three months on my own, Shane."

Her gaze was so direct Shane was momentarily convinced he'd be the one to do something stupid before Jared leaned forward and cried, "On your own? What am I, space dust?!" and the moment vanished.

"Half an hour," Shane repeated. "Don't be late." He slammed the door and accelerated so quickly Jared tumbled across the back. "Seat belt, Jared."

His family's farm was a neighborhood over, on the other side of a river crusted with brown ice. Shane brought the Cruiser down between two dunes and cut the engine. It spluttered into silence with a grating rumble he decided to ignore. "Stay here," he told Jared. "Watch the ship. I'll be back."

Shane's knees buckled as he hit the sand and he had to grip the side of the Cruiser to remain upright. Ava had wiped the blood off his face as they flew and he had found a clean shirt in their extra supplies, but the Cruiser only had a small bathroom in the back. No shower, no way to wash the feeling of Chess off completely. He knew he couldn't hide the bruising entirely or disguise the bones pressing against his pale skin, but as long as no one looked too closely, it would be fine.

He'd broken out of Chess. He wasn't scared of his family.

The windows were as dark as the street, cold and empty as Shane approached the shabby farmhouse. No water gurgled from the well in the back and even the root garden was dry. He lifted a hand, then hesitated. This was supposed to be his home, but something felt different. Something had changed.

You changed.

Shane pushed the thought away and knocked. There were a few heartbeats of aching silence before the door flung back and he was face-to-face with his older brother.

"Shane!"

He tried not to cry out as Glen pulled him into a crushing hug. There was another scurry of movement before their mother appeared in the doorway, and Shane watched the same combination of relief and outrage flicker across her face before she threw her arms around him as well, tugging him over the threshold. "Where have you *been*?" she gasped.

Shane patted her on the back as best he could. When she pulled away, he noticed her hair was gray and new lines creased her broad forehead.

"I've been around." Shane felt her eyes narrow on his bruised face and tilted his chin so she couldn't see the worst of it. "Working jobs, saving money."

"What sort of jobs?"

She lifted a hand to smooth back his hair and Shane flinched instinctively, arms flying up to shield himself. He realized what he'd done too late and tried to disguise his growing panic by brushing at Glen's shoulder. This had been a bad idea. He should leave, get out before he ruined this, too. But before Shane could think of an excuse, his father rounded the corner.

The last few months had hunched his shoulders and whitened his hair, but his eyes were the same—an ashy gray so piercing Shane felt it all the way down to his frozen toes. His father considered him before folding his arms and saying, "You look like you need a hot meal."

Glen and his mother wavered in the hallway a second longer before slipping into the kitchen. Shane wished they would stay. Under his father's watchful gaze, he was painfully aware of every misshapen bruise, his shaved head, the gun tucked against his too-sharp hip bone. His mouth twisted, and Shane didn't have to wonder. He knew. And the judgment wasn't fair.

Heat sparked under his skin despite the desert chill. He had spent his entire life at the edge of West Rama, living through fuel shortages and wearing Glen's old shoes. He dug his family out of sandstorms until his fingers bled, waved off offers to join the men on the rails or the Nakaran military. The men in this town lived and died within the same three blocks, memories lost to the sand as soon as they took their last breath. That thought didn't seem to scare anyone else, but it had scared Shane. He'd told himself he would be different.

He would get out and he would do it his way.

Slowly, Shane reached into his pocket, pulling out the second bag of coins. It was an effort for him to stand still as he watched his father's gaze narrow on the bruises ringing his wrist. Then, without a word, his father took the coins and tucked them into his own jacket pocket.

There weren't a lot of things money couldn't fix.

"We don't have the fuel for anything hot right now—what about leftovers?" his mother called from the kitchen.

Shane turned, grateful for the distraction. "What do you mean, you don't have fuel?"

He slid into a chair and immediately wished he hadn't. He didn't like how his back faced the open kitchen, like he was asking for someone to jump him, to steal his rations, to drag him into a corner until the guards thought to check. They never thought to check.

"There's a fuel shortage in Rama," Glen said. "And in the capital. Our supplies came a few weeks back, but it wasn't much. Apparently Opia had a bad year."

Shane's jaw tightened. Opia's bad year hadn't prevented

them from keeping Chess stocked with soldiers and droids. It hadn't prevented them from opening new mines in his absence and continuing to suck Nakara dry. His mother slid a plate of sandwiches across the table and Shane felt his stomach churn. They looked congealed around the edges, but he didn't care. He hadn't seen this much food in months. He was halfway through the second one before he thought to slow down. When he looked up, juice dripping over his chin, he found his family staring down at him, wearing identical expressions of concern.

"Shane?" His mother spoke first. "Where were you?"

Shane dragged the back of his hand over his mouth. "Working."

"Working where?"

Resentment prickled over his skin. *Do they want the money or not?* "Around."

"Are you—?"

She broke off, mouth half-open, and it was another second before Shane felt it, too. A hum in the air. The rattle of dishes in the cabinets.

He leapt up and hobbled to the window in time to watch an enormous black warship roar overhead. It flung sand in its wake, clouding the windows, but Shane saw the sharp, triangular brand stamped against the side of the ship. The same one stitched on the pants he still wore.

Chess.

Shane was achingly aware of his family behind him—his father's fingers tight on Glen's shoulder, his mother's hand clamped over her mouth. Shane swallowed his panic, forcing it all the way down as he leaned one arm against the window.

"So," he said as casually as he could, "what's for dessert?"

CHAPTER FIVE

✳ ✳ ✳

One year earlier

"Stop it, you look *fine*."

Ava scowled as Sayra slapped her hand away from her hair and forced a glass of rootwine into it instead. The fermented liquid stung her throat, but Ava didn't care. She had just finished a shift and knew the diner's ashy smell still clung to her skin. There hadn't even been time to change before Sayra dragged her downtown, and she wasn't in the mood to mingle.

"I can't stay," Ava said, raising her voice over the music. "I have things to do."

Sayra shook her head. "No, you don't. Come on, you have to meet Katia, at least."

Ava surveyed the writhing crowd before them. She couldn't pick Katia out if Sayra paid her. Everyone on this planet looked the same—graying hair and thin, translucent skin from lack of sunlight and nutrients. But Ava could always tell who was lucky enough to live under Rama's protective dome, because the veins latticed beneath their skin were blue, not black, and when they laughed, Ava thought they looked like they meant it. Even manufactured sunlight had its perks.

"Ava Castor." Sayra folded her arms. "How many people do you know here?"

Ava rolled her eyes. "Literally just you. This was your idea."

"*Exactly*. So no one knows who you are and no one cares that you smell like diner food."

"Wait, I do?"

Sayra's manicured fingers tightened around Ava's shoulders. "What's wrong?" she asked, and for a second, Ava thought she genuinely wanted to know. "Is this because of your new boyfriend?"

"No!" Ava pulled away, but she knew she'd spoken too quickly.

Is Dominik here? Was that why Sayra brought her? She hadn't spoken to him since yesterday, which was apparently not something people in relationships were supposed to do. They were supposed to like each other. They were supposed to care. But sometimes Ava didn't think she'd mind if Dominik Parker disappeared from the planet altogether.

"I like him," Sayra said, pouring herself another drink. "His family's rich, aren't they?"

Ava nodded. "They sell sunlamps."

"You don't have to sound so bitter."

You're lucky. That was what Sayra meant. *You're dating a nice boy from a domed city who'll whisk you off to a palace made of sunlamps, where you'll have beautiful babies who won't know what it's like to get cold in the desert.*

Ava sipped at her drink to avoid answering. Dominik Parker was the kind of boy who made her want to put her fist through his teeth, just to see if he'd break. Because he was tall and handsome, and for a while, she had really thought he was her ticket out of here.

But Dominik wasn't leaving Nakara. He would probably never leave Rama. Why would he? His family had more money than Ava's entire neighborhood, and the market for sunlamps was booming. He had no reason to leave, and she had no desire to stay. She hated the cold, the desert, the constant grit of sand under her feet. Sometimes she hated her mother for falling in love with a Nakaran miner and leaving her sunny home planet of Veritas behind.

I could have been an actress on Veritas, Ava thought bitterly. Here, she was a waitress.

"You drive people away when you look at them like that," Sayra muttered.

Ava scowled. "Like what?"

"*That.* Would it kill you to smile? We're at a *party*. Here." She shoved her glass into Ava's hands. "I'm going to find you someone to talk to. Please try not to pout at everyone while I'm gone."

Ava didn't have time to protest before Sayra tossed her glossy blond ponytail over one shoulder and disappeared into the crowd, leaving a trail of citrus-scented perfume in her wake. Only dome kids paid to smell like fruits they would never see, let alone eat. Ava turned her back on the dance floor, shifting Sayra's drink from hand to hand. She usually loved parties, but something about Rama always set her on edge. Like even if the city couldn't say it out loud, it knew she didn't belong.

"Hey, waitress, can I get another drink?"

Ava turned and found a boy lifting an empty glass in her

direction. He wore a faded shirt that looked several years out of style, and he'd tied half his hair up in a knot, the rest brushing his collarbones as he grinned at her. She must have looked murderous, because his smile faded almost immediately. "That was a joke," he said. "Because you're wearing that apron?"

Ava glanced down, and her face heated at the sight of the dirty apron still wrapped around her waist. How long had she been walking around like that? She ripped it off and tossed it into a corner, but the boy caught her arm as she tried to slip past him onto the dance floor.

"Wait!"

What happened next wasn't really his fault; Ava had spent too many years fending off unwanted advances from stingy customers at the diner to not have developed an instinct of her own. She seized his wrist, twisting as hard as she could, and it wasn't until he let out a pained gasp that she remembered where they were. Probably not the impression Sayra had in mind. Ava released him immediately.

"I'm sorry."

The boy shook out his hand, expression still twisted with pain. "No, that was my fault. *Shit*, where did you learn that?"

Ava folded her arms. "I'm a waitress."

It didn't matter if she knew most of the people who came through Swiss Diner. Everyone was unpredictable after a few glasses of rootwine. The older girls had taught her the basics during her first week—how to go for the eyes, where to bite so it left a mark, how to come away with evidence under every fingernail. It wasn't much of an explanation, but the boy nodded. He was still looking at her with thinly veiled amusement, but there was something else there, too. Admiration. Apprehension. Like he was wondering how many bones she could have snapped if she wanted to.

Good, Ava thought. Fear was always better than pity. She didn't think Dominik would look at her like that if he knew what she was capable of.

This boy, though, handed her a fresh glass of wine. "Swiss Diner, right?"

Ava glanced at her discarded apron. "That obvious?"

"It's the only place worth going around here. Excellent drinks, decent menu." He paused before adding, "Prettiest waitstaff."

"Of course," Ava said. Maybe she had apologized too quickly. "How often does that line work?"

The boy shrugged. "Like four times out of ten."

"Those aren't great odds."

"Better than nothing."

His profile was strong and sharp in the flickering light. Ava looked away before she could linger on the way his lips curled when he called her pretty. "What year are you?" she asked. "I haven't seen you in class."

The boy shook his head. "Don't go to school."

"Really?" Ava couldn't help the flicker of surprise. He couldn't be much older than she was. Everyone went to school, even the West Rama kids who worked two jobs. It was one of the only places to get a hot meal in the desert. "Why not?"

"I have better things to do."

"Like what?"

"Are you trying to get me in trouble?"

The words were hushed, secretive. The party, the people,

even the thumping pulse of the music faded and Ava forgot her training. She forgot the warnings, the stories of boys who seemed too good to be true. They always were. But this one had the most interesting eyes Ava had ever seen—a pale gray so soft it blended into white.

"What about you?" He sounded like he was humoring her. "Why are you in school when you clearly have it made as Swiss Diner's most valuable hostess?"

"I'm going to be an actress."

It had to be the wine making her brave. He was so close Ava could smell him—damp desert earth and something sharp and snappy, almost electric. She expected the boy to laugh when she said that, like her friends did, or shake his head and smile, like her mother. Instead, he nodded, like it was the most logical thing in the world.

"An actress." He wasn't much taller than her, so Ava didn't have to look up as he took another step and said, "Good. You look like you should be famous."

Something about his voice made her response catch in her throat. Before she could speak, Sayra melted back out of the crowd. She threw an arm over Ava's shoulders. "I've been looking for you," she said too loudly. "Your *boyfriend's* here."

She gave the boy a pointed look, and Ava remembered the party around her. The music, the people. The thought of Dominik somewhere in the crowd. "I have to go," she said. This was safer, anyway. "It was nice to meet you."

The boy reached out, then froze, like he was still thinking about what she could do to his hand. "Can I get your name?" he asked. "To follow your film career, of course."

Ava's face warmed. She bit back a grin and said, "Ava," at the same time Sayra said, "*No.*"

But he heard.

"Ava." It sounded like he was turning the name over in his mouth. "That's pretty. I'm Shane."

Now

Ava's kitchen smelled like smoke.

She could taste it as she walked up the front steps and pushed at the unlocked door. Guilt rooted in her chest when it swung open easily. Of course her mother forgot. She had always been scattered and distant, sick from radiation most days, and Ava had left, just took off across the system in a stolen ship. She would leave again, as soon as Shane came back.

Maybe that made her a bad person.

Her mother was asleep on the couch, tucked against the worn cushions. Ava sank to her knees on the floor, and something in her chest loosened at the familiar sight. *Six months.* Her mother always looked less frazzled in sleep. Ava could almost see the resemblance between them. Her mother had grown up on the watery planet of Veritas, tanned and healthy from the perpetual sunlight on the white sand beaches. She had the dark, thick hair and brown skin of the islanders, but decades of living in West Rama had turned her as gray and lifeless as the rest of the planet.

"Mom." Ava rested a hand on her mother's shoulder. "It's me."

It took her mother a minute to wake, blinking like she

couldn't quite remember where she was. Then her gaze cleared and she sat up. "Ava!" she gasped. "What are you *doing* here?"

Guilt flared again, hot in her chest, and Ava had to bite her tongue to keep it from spilling over in the form of endless apologies. When Shane had hired her, she'd told everyone she had been accepted to an acting program in Melesink—a domed city on the other side of the planet. The lie had been innocent enough; Ava had every intention of going as soon as they had the money, but one stolen ship turned into three, then six, and then she lost count. The coins piled up, but it was never enough. The ships needed maintenance. She had a sick mother to care for. Shane felt responsible for his farm, no matter how vehemently he denied it.

They needed more, and opportunities like that didn't come in West Rama.

"School's out." Ava forced a smile. *Put that fake acting program to good use.* "Thought I'd stop by."

"So you're back?" The hope in her mother's voice was crushing.

"No. I have a job in Melesink. A good job." Ava pulled the bag of coins out of her pocket. "I didn't know things were still this bad here."

Of course she hadn't known. It wasn't like she'd bothered to check.

Her mother waved a hand. "I get by. Dominik comes every once in a while." She paused a second too long before adding, "You should let him know you're back."

Ava grimaced. She would rather bury herself in the desert. She'd never actually *told* Dominik she was breaking up with him, but he probably put it together the day she vanished without saying goodbye.

Her mother clicked her tongue. "He's a nice boy, Ava, I like him. But you've met plenty of nice boys in Melesink, I'm sure."

Ava wondered what her mother would say if she knew the last person Ava had kissed had been Shane, bloodied and bruised in the middle of a high-security prison moon. "Shouldn't the Opian supplies be in by now?" she asked, suddenly eager to change the subject. "It's so cold. Is there a reason they're late?"

"Late?" Her mother's brow furrowed. "They dropped the supplies weeks ago."

Ava glanced around the room. *Weeks?* The smell of smoke lingered, but now that she thought about it, the stove in the corner looked unused. If the supplies came weeks ago, why was the house so dark? Why were ships sitting abandoned on the street?

Why did West Rama feel like it was made of ghosts?

"It wasn't much," her mother added. "Opia had a bad year, apparently."

Ava's nails bit into the rough skin of her palms. She was willing to bet the domed cities weren't suffering like this, regardless of how bad Opia's year was. Because they made things worth paying for, because they could stockpile supplies, bask in the glow of synthetic sunlight, and turn their backs on the outside world whenever they wanted.

"What are people doing, then?" she asked. "How are they getting to work without fuel?"

Her mother twisted a strand of hair between her fingers. "A lot of us are out of work at the moment."

"Us?"

"I'm fine. Don't worry."

But it took her mother too long to haul herself to her feet. Ava gripped her arm and wondered if the medical supplies had run out, too, if there were fresh radiation burns under her mother's clothes. That was something no one had told her about leaving Veritas. The Nakaran atmosphere was thin, the change usually too abrupt for outsiders to handle for long. The domes blocked the most harmful rays for those inside, but everyone else either adapted or died. If her mother hadn't been so consumed with grieving a man who had been dead almost as long as Ava had been alive, she might have left Nakara while she still had the chance. Now this house was all she had, their combined wages barely enough to cover daily expenses.

"I pick up shifts at the diner," her mother continued. "The pay's decent, but this . . ." She clutched the bag of coins in a trembling hand. "Thank you. I don't know what I did to deserve you."

Ava squeezed her eyes shut, and when she opened them again, the room swam. Maybe she should tell her mother everything. Their city was fading, and she had been halfway across the system, breaking into prison moons and stealing Cruisers for fun. *But why shouldn't you?* The voice in the back of her mind was low and dangerous. *You hate it here. You never asked for this.*

Why should she deal with the consequences of other people's mistakes when she and Shane were doing so well on their own?

The rumble of an engine cut through the silence before Ava could speak. First it was one, then two, then six roaring overhead, rattling the dishes in the cabinets. An icy fist closed around her chest as three jet-black warships landed in the open desert across the street. Ava yanked the curtains back across the window, heart hammering. Chess. They had come for Shane, for *her*.

Her mother craned her neck as neighbors poked their heads out of doors, watching the officers and droids file into the streets, but Ava didn't linger. She crossed the room in three strides. She only had one number memorized, and Shane picked up on the second ring.

"I know," he said before she could speak. "Can you see them?"

"Six Catapult warships," Ava muttered. "Three on my street. Lots of officers. Some droids."

Shane was quiet for a long minute. "Stay there. I'm coming."

"No! They're *here*, Shane, I'll come to you."

"They'll catch you before you get half a block."

Ava scanned the ships through her window, forcing her panicked thoughts to still. She had been in charge while Shane was gone. She might not have Jared's mastery of tech or Shane's skill with a ship, but she was a survivor, too. Outside, black-clad officers pounded across the cobblestones. Ava watched her neighbors pull their curtains tight at the sight of the droids and the hulking ships behind them. The ships that were now sitting empty on the sand.

Ava's breath caught. "Shane?"

"I'm here."

Something about his voice calmed her ragged nerves. "Grab Jared and anything we need from the Cruiser."

"Ava, I don't—"

"Shut *up* and listen to me!"

She could feel Shane's surprise on the other end, same as when she'd kissed him. Someday, he'd get used to this.

"What are you going to do?"

Ava glanced over her shoulder to where her mother still peered through the curtains at the massive warships, and grinned.

"I'm getting us a new ride."

CHAPTER SIX

***

His mother had cried during graduation. Cyrus could tell because she was doing a terrible job of holding it together when they met in the parking lot after the ceremony.

It had been almost a year since he'd seen her in person, but Cyrus was relieved to find that while he felt light-years away from the boy he'd been, his mother remained unchanged. Wide, smiling face, brown curls, strong hands. She even wore the same lilac dress, the only one she owned that was nice enough for a crowd like this.

"Where do you go now?" she asked, holding Cyrus at arm's length so she could look him up and down.

He shrugged. "I don't know. We get assignments this afternoon. I'm hoping for something in the capital," he added. Because that's what the valedictorian cadet was supposed to say. Truthfully, Cyrus had no idea what he wanted. After four years of strictly regimented education, the idea of freedom, no matter how limited, was unthinkable.

His mother smoothed the sharp folds of his collar, but Cyrus leaned back, angling himself away from her touch and his family's ancient Cruiser. That thing should have died years ago but here it was, still dripping oil onto the pavement below. It didn't belong here, among his classmates' shiny ships, but his mother didn't seem to notice.

"Five more years," she whispered.

Cyrus nodded. Five years of service in exchange for an education they wouldn't have been able to afford otherwise, for opportunities that didn't exist in Port City. It wasn't a hard choice, but he knew she was thinking of his father and the years he spent commuting back and forth to the manufacturing plants. The Opian government had promised him a job, too.

Instead, he got a decade of hard labor, a broken arm that never healed right, and a disease that rotted his lungs from the inside out.

Cyrus pushed the thought away. "I'll be fine."

His father never left Port City, but Cyrus already had. He had a uniform and an assignment card waiting for him, and he wasn't going back now. Not after everything he'd sacrificed.

"I know." His mother cupped his cheek in a calloused hand. "I'm so proud of you, Cyrus. Your father would be, too. And tell Cornelia to be careful, okay? I miss her."

Cyrus exhaled, grateful for the change in conversation. "I'll pass it on."

"I'm serious." His mother poked a finger into his chest. "I've seen how she flies around in those ships. Remember what happened to the roof?"

Cyrus bit back a grin. "She knows what she's doing."

"Tell that to my roses."

She patted his cheek one last time and climbed into the front of the Cruiser. Cyrus hesitated as he watched her strap into the pilot's seat. Something about this felt final in a way the graduation ceremony hadn't, a goodbye that was freeing and terrifying all at once. He never wanted to go back home, never wanted to think about that place again, but there had been something comforting about knowing he *could*.

His mother turned and extended a finger toward him through the open hatch. "Find a window."

"Make a wish," Cyrus said automatically, finishing the last half of the expression. He wrapped his finger around hers. It was an old rhyme, the beginning of a childhood story he couldn't remember the name of, but the familiarity of it soothed his racing pulse.

"Remember to write." She squeezed his hand once. "I love you."

Then his mother sealed the exit hatch and started the Cruiser. It roared to life with a growl so loud half the parking lot turned in their direction and Cyrus shrank back, away from the watchful eyes and the implication something like that could belong to him. "I love you, too."

The last thing he saw before turning his back on the past was the ship falling into the flow of traffic and his mother's hand pressed against the window.

"You should have gone out more. You wouldn't be this hungover if you'd gone out."

Cornelia nudged his shoulder as the two of them walked into the Academy's aircraft hangar and Cyrus resisted the urge to rub at the headache throbbing above his left eyebrow. It had been there since he watched his mother leave. "I'm not hungover," he insisted. "And that's the worst advice you've ever given. Including the time you said salmon was my color."

"Salmon is everyone's color if they're not a coward." Cornelia waved a hand, and Cyrus saw that her nails were red today.

"Whatever, nobody here has any taste. Stars, I can't wait to leave."

Neither could he. Yesterday's anticipation stirred in the pit of his stomach as Cyrus watched the senior officers make their way through the hangar, transferring assignment details to the waiting crowd of cadets one at a time. *What if you can't do it?*

"Stop that." Cornelia brushed his shoulder again. "I can hear you thinking."

Cyrus resisted the immediate urge to pull away. They weren't supposed to touch in uniform, and he hated that Cornelia could still read his mind, even now.

"I'm fine."

"I *know*." Cornelia grinned and looped her arm through his. "Wow, what are you going to do without me? Die, probably," she said before Cyrus could answer. "That's pretty obvious now that I'm thinking about it."

Lark shoved his way between them before Cyrus could answer, pushing himself to the front of the line. "Get out of my way, Blake."

Cyrus stumbled, and when he straightened, all thoughts of rules and regulations had vanished. Lark's hair was as perfect as ever, his uniform spotless even though Cyrus had *just* watched him steal three powdered pastries from the officer's lounge on the way in. Because that was the kind of thing Lark could get away with.

"I hope he gets asteroid duty," Cornelia muttered as Lark shouldered his way toward one of the senior officers. "It would be *so* easy to knock him off, make it look like an accident . . ."

"Don't give his future partner any ideas." Cyrus tugged at the sleeves of his jacket. Why did Lark's look so much better than his?

Now that he was thinking about it, everyone's uniform looked better than his. Sleeker. Darker. More important. They were all dressed the same and still Cyrus couldn't shake the feeling that this was all an elaborate ruse. He caught a glimpse of General Noth across the hangar and turned away.

One day, she was going to realize she had made a mistake, that he wasn't the soldier she believed him to be.

"Did you hear she's leaving the Academy?"

"What?" Cyrus looked down and found Cornelia following his gaze.

"Noth. I'm surprised they didn't say anything at graduation."

"How do you know?"

"I know things."

Cyrus snorted. "You eavesdropped."

"I *happened* to overhear! But I'm serious; she got promoted. She's moving to the capital to work with Planetary Leader Derian or someone else equally fancy."

Cyrus glanced back across the hangar, but Noth was already gone. "I thought she liked the Academy."

"No, she likes being in charge," Cornelia said. "And telling people what to do. I mean, same, but somehow she's getting paid for it." Then her expression fell. "Oh no. Look."

She pointed over Cyrus's shoulder and he turned in time to watch one of the senior officers tap his skin screen against Lark's. Whatever assignment unfolded on Lark's forearm must have been good, because he broke into a wide, unabashed grin Cyrus didn't think he'd seen before. The expression softened the sharp lines of his face, made him seem more like someone Cyrus wouldn't mind spending time with.

Cornelia tipped her head back toward the ceiling. "Why do good things happen to the most insufferable people?"

"Right." Cyrus forced himself to look away from where Lark was still scrolling through his letter. "Insufferable."

When it was their turn, he let Cornelia go first. He needed his hands to stop shaking before he showed them to a senior officer, but Cornelia thrust out an arm, shifting back and forth in her boots as a colonel Cyrus didn't recognize touched his screen to hers. She scrolled through the letter in a single flick. "I got atmosphere patrol!"

If their superior officers weren't watching, Cyrus might have broken uniform rules to hug her right there. At-patrol was always reserved for the best pilots; it was perfect for her. "I told you!"

"Congratulations, Lieutenant." The colonel gave Cornelia a stiff-fingered salute and Cyrus realized with a jolt that *he* was a lieutenant now, too. *Second Lieutenant Cyrus Blake.* It sounded important.

He took a deep breath and extended his arm toward the waiting officer. There was a tiny vibration as the document transferred to his screen and the buzz lingered in his fingers when he swiped it open. The colonel inclined his head. "You should be very proud. From what I've heard, you earned it."

Cyrus looked up, a response stuck somewhere in his chest, but it was too late. The colonel had already moved on to the next person in line.

Cornelia lifted a brow. "Read it!"

Cyrus swallowed and lifted his arm, scanning through the letter until he found the part that mattered.

SECOND LIEUTENANT CYRUS BLAKE
Assignment: Capital Security, Opian satellite stations
Commanding Officer: General Pelara Noth

Cyrus had to read it three times before the words sank in. *Capital security.* That was good. No, it was better than good; it was *excellent.* It was a reputable position, an important one. And with Noth as his commanding officer, he'd be right in the center of any political action. Maybe he *had* fooled her.

Maybe he'd fooled everyone.

"Are you serious?" Cyrus turned to find Lark hanging over his shoulder, reading his assignment word for word. "You have her, too?"

"Back off, I—" Cyrus froze, stomach plummeting as Lark's words sank in. "What do you mean, *too?*"

Lark extended an arm. The same message was displayed against his pale skin, and Cyrus's gaze narrowed, tunneling in on Lark's perfect hair, his infuriatingly immaculate uniform. Next to him, Cornelia muttered something that sounded suspiciously like a prayer.

This had to be a mistake.

Lark was still smiling, but Cyrus could feel the frustration crackling in the air between them. "You sure about this, Blake?" Lark asked. "You know the general is going to Nakara, right? Think you can handle that?"

"Go away!"

Cyrus didn't think his self-control would hold during a flight to the Opian capital, let alone to the far reaches of the system. He didn't want to think about Nakara at all, and he definitely didn't want to think about it with Lark. Why was Noth even making a trip that long? And how did Lark know about it already?

Because they trust him more than they trust you. They always will.

He watched Lark stalk back into the crowd before turning toward Cornelia. "I'm . . ."

"Going to murder him in his sleep?" Cornelia nodded. "I didn't think that was a question."

"No." Cyrus shook his head. "Lark could murder me and no one would care, but if I did anything, I'd be blacklisted, court-martialed, kicked off the mission . . ."

He waved a hand to indicate the list went on.

Cornelia pressed her lips together, but Cyrus could tell she was smiling. "I think you're making that up."

"I'm not."

"I *really* think you're exaggerating."

"Whose side are you on?"

Cyrus was only half joking as he eyed Lark's retreating back. Maybe he should go now, get to their ship first so he could sit with the pilot and relegate Lark to the back where he belonged. "Do you think he's making it up?" he asked. "About Nakara? There's no way he'd know that, right?"

Cornelia shrugged. "Nepotism's one hell of a drug, baby. Maybe we should try it."

"You're right. Let me resurrect our fathers. I'm sure they'd be thrilled."

Cornelia laughed again, and when Cyrus looked down, she was close enough that he could see every freckle on her face. She leaned her head against his shoulder. "You know you're my best friend, right?"

Cyrus swallowed over the lump in his throat. He did; she had told him at least twice a week for the past twelve years. "I know."

He didn't notice her arms sliding around his waist until it was too late, and Cyrus glanced around to make sure the other officers were occupied before hugging her back.

The night they got their Academy acceptance letters, the two of them had climbed Cornelia's fire escape, desperate to leave the clinging heat of the streets below. It was always hot in Port City, the exhaust from the ships mixing with the noxious fumes of the manufacturing plants, but Cyrus still didn't know why she liked the roof. It wasn't like they could see through the layers of smog.

"I'm going to be someone someday," Cornelia had said after she hauled herself over the last few rungs of the ladder.

Cyrus remembered lying down beside her, watching her hair spill across the stones like liquid fire. "What do you mean?"

"I mean I'm going to be a real person. I'm going to *do* something. Something really spectacular."

Cyrus always loved this game, the *If you could be anybody in the world, who would you be?* game. "Something spectacular?" He turned the word over in his mouth. "Like what?"

When Cornelia looked at him again, every light from the bustling street below was caught in her eyes. "You'll see."

Now Cyrus's throat ached, and for a second, he couldn't get the words out. "You survived Port City," he whispered eventually. "At-patrol's not going to kill you." He felt Cornelia laugh into his jacket and added, "I'll message you every day. You'll be fine; you're the best pilot I know."

"You're right." Cornelia pulled back, nodding solemnly. "And you're going to freeze to death on Nakara."

Cyrus squeezed her hand. Maybe he'd see her in the capital tomorrow. Maybe they'd run into each other next year. The uncertainty made it harder.

"Find a window," he said.

"Make a wish," Cornelia answered automatically.

The same expression Cyrus had shared with his mother, the one every Port City kid grew up reciting. Some people wished on stars, but they always used windows. The smoke was too thick to see much beyond that.

"I'll actually be able to see the stars up there," Cornelia added, like she couldn't quite believe it. "Real stars, Cy. Not simulations. What should my first wish be?"

Cyrus grinned. "Something spectacular."

He gave Cornelia's hand one last squeeze as she pulled away to join the new group of at-patrol recruits already gathering in the corner of the hangar. She didn't look back.

"I don't think I've ever seen you hug anyone, Blake." Cyrus didn't see Lark until it was too late. "Really. Is that what happens when they crown you valedictorian cadet?"

He tried to throw an arm around Cyrus's shoulders, but Cyrus shoved him away. "Don't touch me. And don't call me that."

Lark's eyes widened. "I'm sorry, is it *Colonel* Valedictorian Cadet? Or should I say *General*, because Noth picked you? Oh, wait!" He put a hand to his chest. "She picked me, too, didn't she? Funny how that works."

He patted Cyrus on the back with enough force to send him stumbling, and set off across the hangar. Cyrus watched him go, his frustration growing every second. He could probably deal with a trip to Nakara, but a trip with Lark?

With one last glance over his shoulder, Cyrus strode in the opposite direction, toward where he knew Noth's warship waited. If Lark froze to death in a foreign desert, he could probably make it look like an accident.

CHAPTER SEVEN

✳ ✳ ✳

Pain sliced through Shane's shoulder as he stalked across the room, away from the sound of Chess warships on the other side of the window. "I have to go."

"Now?" Glen blinked. "You just got here."

"Sorry to disappoint."

Adrenaline tingled down his spine, but Shane's mind was clear. *You're not going back.* He needed to sink back into the skin of Shane the thief, Shane the runaway, all the things he'd been before, but his mother blocked his path before he made it to the door.

"What's going on?" Her grip was firm. "Let us help."

Glen nodded so enthusiastically it reminded Shane of Jared. "Stay. We need you."

That might be the first honest thing his family had said since he walked through the door. Shane searched for a thread of sympathy but found only cold, empty disdain. Maybe Chess had taken that from him, too.

"You need me?" He couldn't keep the rough edge from his voice. "Is that what you tell everyone who leaves? There's *nothing* for us here."

"Shane." His father's voice was a warning, but Shane didn't care.

His family could stay in West Rama if they wanted. They could waste away here, but he was getting out before the desert found a way to bury him, too. He pushed the front door open. "What do you want me to do? Tend the garden? Work in the mines? What kind of a life is that?"

His mother recoiled like he'd slapped her, but Shane kept going, stumbling off the porch as a bitter gust of wind cut through his clothes. "I'm not going to sit around waiting for someone to take the house or burn through the last of those fuel cells. You should be ashamed you're still here."

Shane thought Glen might have said something else. He might have heard his name, but it was too late to turn back now. He was already gone, limping as fast as he could across the sand. It wasn't a clean break, but it wasn't supposed to be. His family would be less likely to follow if it was messy.

People who followed him tended to get hurt.

"Jared!" Shane rounded the edge of the dune and pounded a fist against the hull of the ship. "Let's go! Get everything from the back."

Was it his imagination or was the distant roar of an engine getting closer? He was running on pure adrenaline now, mind spinning.

Jared's face appeared in the window above him. "What? Why?"

"Just do it!"

Shane hauled himself into the ship and shoved everything he could reach into his own bag: the extra fuel can, his dirty prison shirt, Ava's makeup. He winced as the weight settled across his bad shoulder. *What else?* A spare energy bar, oxygen masks in case the air lock popped, an old toolbox rattling with loose screws. He jumped back to the ground as the first warship appeared over the dunes.

It was dark, sleek as a sand beetle, and Shane felt himself freeze. He pulled Jared under the Cruiser, heart pounding as the ship roared closer. *You're not going back.* How many of those leering prison guards would he have to kill? How many ships would he need to destroy? Shane didn't care. He'd do it.

But when the doors hissed open, the warship was empty except for a lone figure waving frantically from the pilot's seat. *Ava.* Shane couldn't hear what she was shouting until he pulled himself through the door next to her.

"They're right behind me!" she cried, sliding over to let him have the controls. "We have to *go!*"

Jared tripped into the back and Shane had barely fastened himself into the pilot's seat when four identical Catapults appeared over the horizon. Because stars forbid they get a second of peace. Shane glanced at Ava out of the corner of his eye. "Hope you got a good one, Castor."

Then he pushed everything forward.

The ship cut through the night like a blade, swift and deadly, and Shane blew out a long breath. He had always wanted to get his hands on a ship like this. A shot grazed over their left wing as he turned, and there was a loud cracking sound in the distance as their pursuers opened fire.

"They're firing at us!" Jared squeaked. He clutched his bag to his chest, knuckles white. "They're firing at us! They're firing at us! They're—"

"Shut up!"

Shane glanced at their rear cameras in time to watch the warships drop into a familiar attack formation. Maybe this would be fun after all. He'd never flown an Opian ship before, much less a Catapult, but the mechanics were probably the same as the Cruiser. This one was two levels of sleek black steel and armored walls. "It looks like there's a weapons bay downstairs," he told Ava without taking his eyes off the sky. "Can you handle it?"

She snorted and pushed herself out of her seat. "I broke you out of Chess, Shane."

"And now an entire moon is after us."

"Told you I was dangerous!"

Another shot, another streak of light through the dark. Shane swerved and Jared groaned as the force of the turn threw him across the back. The bottom of the ship vibrated as Ava fired back, a steady *pop, pop, pop* in the night.

Shane let himself look at the cameras again. The Catapults were still there, matching him turn for turn, and he pushed the ship forward, faster and faster until the city fell back. As West Rama's dusty roads gave way to smooth, rolling dunes, Shane realized this could work. Those officers might have firepower, but they were used to the paved streets and rigid rules of Chess.

This was *his* home, and he knew the desert better than most.

"Got one!" Ava's voice crackled through the intercom, and Shane glanced back in time to watch one of their pursuers spiral to the ground. The Catapult hit the sand with an explosion that rattled his seat, but Jared's whoop of celebration was cut short as the next round of bullets slammed directly into their hull.

The ship lurched forward and Shane temporarily lost control of the wheel. He fumbled, gritting his teeth as they slowed enough for the remaining Catapults to gain the ground they lost, cannons blazing, sirens blaring. *You're not going back.*

Shane yanked the controls to the right so hard they rolled and Jared tumbled across the back, slamming into the opposite window.

"Seat belt, Jared!"

It was so dark Shane couldn't see anything other than the sand rushing under their hull. No protection. No shelter. They were a lone target in the middle of the night. The desert was supposed to save them, but here they were, a stolen, steel-plated gift for Opia to devour. *You're not going back.*

"Shane!" Jared peeled himself away from the window and pointed. "Look!"

Shane turned, fingers already itching for his weapon. If there were more of them, if they were surrounded . . .

But it wasn't a ship barreling toward them across the sand.

When the first dust storm ripped through West Rama years ago, Shane thought the world was ending. The Opian mining methods had stripped the desert of its natural defenses, leaving the border cities exposed to the unpredictable elements. Shane remembered clinging to his bed every other night as the wind roared and the house shuddered. Now people were used to it. Shops closed, windows were boarded up, and no one went into the desert.

No one but him.

Shane pushed the ship faster, reveling in the slick speed. "Ava," he yelled into the intercom. "Get up here!"

It took her a minute to emerge. "What are you doing?

They're—" Her eyes widened as she caught sight of the spinning clouds of dust and debris barreling toward them over the dunes. "Shane . . ."

It might have been the beginning of a warning, but Shane wasn't listening. His head pounded, body trembling as he pushed them faster. "Sit. Both of you."

For once, they listened. Shane tilted the nose of the Catapult up, letting their pursuers think he was circling back, away from the dust storm and its devastation. One by one, they followed. He had just enough time to wonder if those officers had ever seen a storm like this, if they knew what sort of damage lay inside, before he pulled sharply to the left, directly into the roaring cloud.

Ava gasped and then he couldn't hear anything over the wind. An updraft closed overhead, pulling them away from the ground and Shane felt his stomach drop at the speed of it. His fingers ached. His ears popped. Sand splattered the windshield until he couldn't see or hear anything over the deafening roar. If the Catapult hadn't been Opian made, he thought it would have cracked apart in seconds. Ava's knuckles were white on her knees, Jared had gone deathly still, and it was all he could do to keep them steady. He didn't look to check if they were being followed. He couldn't see that far.

For all Shane knew, they were the only ones left in the world.

The wind softened slowly, imperceptibly, and then it was gone. They shot forward into the eye of the circling storm. It took a minute for the feeling to return to Shane's fingers, and when it did, he nudged them toward the open sky.

Jared slumped forward. "You're insane," he muttered, face

ashen as he ran his hands through his hair again and again.

But Ava shook her head. "No. You're brilliant."

When Shane met her gaze, he felt something spark under his ribs, so different from the ice that had gripped his chest over the last three months that he didn't know what to say. He turned away before it could linger.

Because this was it. This was their new life. It might have been easy to avoid Nakaran officers before, to hide out in asteroid motels and laugh at the idea of being found. A stolen Cruiser was nothing. A holdup at a corner store was nothing. But Chess was something, and Shane didn't think those officers intended to give up. They would hunt him across the system if they had to, because they didn't *lose* prisoners. And they would revel in the opportunity to break someone like Ava, he was sure of it. Every single one of those officers would try. Maybe she'd last longer than he had, maybe they would snuff her out on the first day, but the thought of her behind bars was enough to send cold panic racing down his spine.

If he weren't such a coward, if he didn't feel like he would crumble on his own, he would leave her while she still had a chance, drop her in the capital after the next job and go.

"Shane." Ava's voice was low, and for a second, Shane thought she could see every terrible, selfish thing he'd never said out loud. "What's wrong?"

"Nothing." It was the automatic response, but his brain felt like it was running on fumes. Sooner or later, it would shut down. "Yes," he added when Ava opened her mouth again. "We're still going to the capital. At the very least, we need a ship that isn't the most recognizable vehicle in the entire system.

Between this and the Cruiser, you're on thin ice, Castor."

"I'm sorry." Ava propped both feet on the control panel. "I think what you meant was *Thank you for saving me again, Ava. I don't know what I'd do without you.*"

Shane ignored her, focusing instead on the plan unfolding in the back of his mind. He would still take them to the capital. Robbing a government building was reckless, yes. They were out of practice, but the old Shane wouldn't hesitate. He couldn't quite remember the boy he'd been three months ago, but if this wasn't a way back to him, Shane didn't know what was.

Next to him, Ava leaned forward in her seat, dark hair falling over one shoulder. They were flying high enough for the moon to paint every strand in silver, for the stars to catch in her eyes as she twirled her necklace around one finger.

Thank you for saving me again, Ava. I don't know what I'd do without you.

Shane might have said it out loud if Jared hadn't chosen that moment to lean forward, knees pressing against the back of Shane's seat despite the ample room in the back.

"I'm not an expert," he said in a way that made it clear he thought he was, "but based on the atmospheric conditions of this region and the pressure of the western winds, another storm isn't out of the question. If we're heading to the capital, you should know the desert's isothermal—"

"Jared." Ava's voice was silky. "I love you dearly, but if you say one more word, I will dump your body out the air lock."

Jared looked so offended Shane actually laughed. The sound felt foreign in his throat, and it wasn't until it happened again that he realized he hadn't laughed in months. There hadn't been a chance to. But he was back, he had a crew, and they were going to rob the Nakaran capital. Shane watched Ava bite her lip, unable to keep her own grin from spreading, and then they were both laughing as Jared scowled, knee bouncing up and down against the back of Shane's seat.

CHAPTER EIGHT

One year earlier

Ava never meant to cause trouble. It was always something that seemed to happen when she was around. Her mother used to tell her she just needed to think about making better decisions, but Ava was beginning to wonder if she even knew what that meant. Because why else would she let Shane Mannix walk her home from the party?

West Rama was deserted this late at night. The only light came from the pale pulse of the dome at their backs, the sickly glow that sucked the life from everything it touched. It darkened the hollows in Shane's cheeks and cloaked his long, white hair in shadow. Ava knew she looked the same. Out here, she was as dull as the rest of this town.

"How do you know Katia?" Shane asked after they walked a few more blocks in silence.

Ava kept her eyes on the ground. Every magazine she stole from Sal's corner store said that avoiding eye contact made girls look *aloof and mysterious*. "Katia?"

"The host," Shane said. "Of the party. The one we left."

Ava shook her head. "I don't. My friend Sayra does."

"Ah, yes. The girl who made up a fake boyfriend so you wouldn't have to talk to me."

"He's not fake."

"Okay. So where is he?"

This was definitely a bad decision. Ava searched for something to say, anything to make Dominik feel as exciting as the boy next to her, but Shane's presence was making it hard to think. "He's busy," she said eventually. "He works."

Shane's mouth twitched. "Does he? Big-city boy with a big-city job. You must be proud."

He's making fun of you.

Ava lifted her chin and almost forgot her no eye contact rule. "He has his own Cruiser. And a house in the dome. As soon as we graduate, we're taking that ship and going somewhere far, *far* away from here."

She didn't know why she felt the need to defend Dominik, of all people. He wasn't taking her anywhere, but Shane looked like the kind of boy who had adventures. He didn't go to school, and he walked like he expected the entire city to bow before him. Ava wanted him to think the same about her.

"And you want to go with him?" he asked.

They stopped under one of the lamps, shadows stretching long, and Ava looked up for the first time since leaving the party. Shane's gaze was so direct she almost forgot how to breathe. "I'm getting out of here as soon as I graduate."

"That's not what I asked."

There were pockets of space so thick not even light itself could escape, places that pulled everything toward their singular path of destruction. That was what Shane felt like—the empty void of space, and Ava was a lone ship teetering on the brink of him.

He opened his mouth again, but whatever he'd been about to

say was cut off by the sharp click of armored boots against pavement. Ava whirled, squinting as an officer strolled into view. He had his cap pulled low over his eyes and a patrol droid scuttling in his wake. She recognized him from downtown Rama, one of the men who sat outside the station and looked a little too long at the girls walking to class. *Officer Ryer.*

"If it isn't our good friend Shane Mannix." His voice was too loud against the quiet street. "What do you think he's been up to?"

The droid's screen flashed and Ava took a step back. She didn't like patrol droids. The cameras embedded in their head combined with the long, thin projection screens made them look like sneering cyclopes, twisted nightmares crafted from new-age tech. She glanced at Shane and found his face contorted in thinly veiled fury.

"What do you want?"

Ryer raised a bushy eyebrow. "Can't I check in?"

"You check in on me three times a week. You come by the shop, make the customers nervous, make my boss wonder if I'm worth the trouble."

"Pity. It's hard to hold a job around here. Why are you out so late?"

"I was at a party."

"A *party.*"

The droid's screen flashed again before it said in a slow, even voice, "There are several parties in the area."

"See?" Shane gestured to the droid. "Thanks, Tim."

"That's *not* its name." Ryer folded his arms. "Anything reported missing?"

Shane gave an exasperated sigh as Tim's screen flickered. "One ground Cruiser. Reported half an hour ago."

"Interesting."

"No, it isn't. And I'd never steal a *Cruiser*," Shane added. "I'm honestly offended you're suggesting it."

Officer Ryer's hand lingered at his belt, too close to his weapon. "So how did you get to your party?"

"I took the train."

Ava glanced into the deserted alley over her shoulder. Ryer hadn't acknowledged her, hadn't even glanced her way. With any luck, he wouldn't remember her at all and she could fade away, leaving Shane to deal with whatever this was on his own. The two of them were obviously familiar. Maybe he'd been in trouble before, but he wasn't a thief. Not tonight, anyway.

Ava wasn't willing to bet beyond that.

She stepped forward before she could change her mind and forced every ounce of her meager stage training into what she said next. "He didn't steal anything."

Ryer whipped around, eyes narrowing. Even the droid faltered, but Ava didn't back down. She had seen every classic movie the library had to offer, read every romance novel and magazine she could get her hands on. Those girls never backed down.

"He didn't steal anything," she repeated. "I swear, I've been with him all night."

Ryer raised a brow. "All night?"

It wasn't hard to make herself blush, to duck her head and turn into the girl he so clearly thought she was. "Please. He's walking me home. I don't know my way around here."

Lie. She probably knew this area better than any of them, but Officer Ryer wasn't looking at her stained dress or shoes that were clearly West Rama made. He was too busy watching her shoulders hunch and her chin tremble as fake tears brimmed in her eyes.

"We went to a party." Ava sniffed. "And I didn't even want to go, but my friend said I'd have a good time, and my mother always says not to walk through West Rama alone because you'll get jumped faster than you can call for help, and maybe I should have listened, but—"

"All right!" He threw up his hands. "Stars, you don't have to cry! I'm just doing my job. Do you want my advice?" he added, glancing over Ava's shoulder to where Shane still stood.

No. But Ava blinked up at him and said, "Yes, sir."

"Don't let him walk you home again." Ryer's pale eyes hardened until they were the same color as the desert ice. "He's nothing but trouble."

Then he sidestepped her and jabbed a finger into Shane's chest so hard he stumbled. "There's been a cell on Chess with your name on it for years, Mannix. Don't let me catch you out this late again."

He stalked back the way he'd come, droid rumbling over the stones at his side.

"I don't have a curfew!" Shane called after his retreating back. "You can't make up laws for me!"

Ava heard the droid say, "The boy is correct," before the pair vanished around the corner.

She exhaled and swiped the back of her hand across her face until her cheeks were dry. That was almost too easy. "What?" she snapped when Shane didn't move.

His gaze shifted, something between amusement and hunger, but he shook his head. "Nothing."

"Officer Ryer is a bastard," Ava said, rubbing her hands down
her arms as they continued walking. "And I hate droids."

Shane laughed, a low, raspy sound that made her shiver in
the dark. "They're all bastards. Do you spend a lot of time lying
to patrol officers?"

"Maybe."

"The same amount of time you spend breaking people's
hands?"

"If he's stupid enough to believe I care what happens to you,
he deserves to have his ship stolen." Ava hesitated before adding, "Did you actually steal it?"

Shane was quiet long enough to raise the hair on her arms.
"Would it make a difference if I did?"

Ava was surprised to find that it wouldn't. Dominik didn't
steal ships. Dominik didn't feel anything like this.

"I'll leave you here, then," Shane said as they reached the end
of the street. "I'm in the next neighborhood over."

"Oh." Ava bit her lip. "I was—"

"Are you looking for a job?" Shane's question was sudden,
and Ava thought she caught a flicker of admiration before his
face cleared.

"What sort of job?"

Shane closed the distance between them, lowering his
face toward hers, and for a wild, heart-pounding second, Ava
thought he was going to kiss her. She thought she might let
him. Then the corner of his mouth quirked, and he whispered,
"The kind that would take you far, *far* away from here."

He pressed something into her hand and when he pulled

back, Ava wasn't entirely sure where she was. Shane grinned as he backed down the street. "I leave in three days, Ava Castor. It would be a pity not to see you before then."

Ava unfolded the paper as he disappeared into the night. A comm number. She crumpled it in her fist and turned down her street. Maybe there wasn't a job at all, just an elaborate scheme to get her alone. Wasn't that the number one thing she told the new girls at work?

Don't trust the pretty ones. Don't trust the ones who make you promises.

Dangerous. The word whispered across her skin, borne on the desert breeze, and Ava shivered. She liked dangerous. She liked exciting. West Rama was neither of those things. Shane on the other hand . . .

"This is how the girls in those movies die," Ava said to herself.

She jumped onto her front porch. Saying it out loud broke whatever spell Shane had cast over the neighborhood, and everything came back to life. The groan of the wood under her shoes, the screech of the lizards hiding in the sand, the dry rustle of wind through the plants. Calling Shane would be a risk, but to go as far as meeting him again? Definitely not a good decision.

Well, Ava thought as she closed the door behind her, *when have I ever been known to make those?*

CHAPTER NINE

*** ✳ ✳ ✳ ***

The water pooled like blood under Shane's fingers.

He gripped at the wall as it gathered on the bathroom floor, soaking his clothes, cold under his bare feet. When he closed his eyes, he was back in that solitary cell. It had been cold there too, like the icy water pounding against his back now. *You're not there. It's not real.*

The masked officers used to take turns dragging prisoners into the courtyard at the end of the hall. Sometimes they wanted information. Sometimes they were bored, but Shane always knew when someone had been taken because he'd wake up to wet stone, the smell of iron thick and choking.

Not there. Not real.

Someone knocked on the bathroom door, too loud, too sudden, and Shane slipped as he lunged out of the shower.

"Are you done?" It was Ava, her voice muffled over the roar of the water.

He tried to open his mouth, but his jaw was clenched so tight even that small movement ached. There was something in his throat, blood on his hands. *No, it's water.* He was floating somewhere between Chess and this hotel, and his clothes were soaked, clinging to his ribs like an empty promise. Ava couldn't see him like this.

She knocked again, cracking the door when he didn't answer. Shane caught it, but not before he watched Ava's eyes widen at the sight of his wet clothes. "Are you—?"

"I'm fine." But the words cracked on the way out. He tried to close the door, but Ava was stronger than he remembered. Or he was weaker. Shane didn't know which was worse. He shook his head. "Get out."

"Shane, you don't have to—"

"I said get *out*."

The last word ripped out of him, and Shane slammed his palm into the bathroom wall, inches from the doorframe. Ava's jaw tensed at the sound, but she didn't move. Then the pain splintered in, a fraction at a time. The stinging in his palm, the aching bruises on his hands, the scars healing across his back. He sagged against the wall and Ava stepped into the bathroom, closing the door behind her.

"Sit." She pointed at the sink, face twisting as she picked her way across the wet floor. "It's freezing in here. What's wrong with the water?"

The water? Shane couldn't remember. Everything had been fine when he turned on the shower. But it had been cold, so cold it shocked him back to Chess. Embarrassment roared in his ears then, momentarily drowning out the sound of the water as Ava adjusted the temperature. It only took a second for steam to start curling across the mirror.

"Let me see."

Her grip was soft as she turned his wrist over, brushing the bruises on each knuckle. Shane watched her mouth twitch and realized she might already know how he'd injured his hands.

She might know about the body he'd left on Chess. There had been others since, but that was the one he saw when he closed his eyes.

"I killed someone."

The words were out before he could stop them. Half confession, half challenge. He always felt like Ava could see into the darkest parts of his soul, places even he didn't bother looking for too long, but he needed her to look now.

So that when he left her in the capital tomorrow, she would know it wasn't her fault.

But Ava just nodded, turning his hands over in his lap. "Did they deserve it?"

Yes. Shane couldn't bring himself to say it out loud. He didn't need to. Ava squeezed his hand once before letting go.

"Good."

When he looked up again, she was so close he could see every one of her eyelashes. They shadowed the tops of her cheekbones each time she blinked, and he reached up without thinking, tucking a stray curl behind her ear. Something was thrumming in his chest, right under his ribs. Then he blinked and it was gone.

The bathroom was a cell, and this time, it was Ava's blood on his hands.

Shane shot to his feet, pulling himself out of her grip, and the moment vanished, drifting away in a cloud of steam. It was too familiar. Maybe that would have been fine before, but this was now. His legs ached as he stood, but they were steady as he stripped off his dripping shirt, angling so Ava couldn't see the worst of the scars.

"I'm fine," he muttered. "Get out."

For a second, Ava looked like she wanted to say something else. Then she seemed to think better of it and slipped back out the door.

By the time he showered and changed, the lights were dim, curtains pulled against the last rays of domed sunlight. Jared was passed out on the floor, using one of Shane's old shirts as a pillow. Hopefully, he had managed to pull the information they needed before falling asleep. They still had a job to do. Shane stepped over him and found Ava already curled in the middle of the bed. He sighed. Three months ago, he would have pushed her out and taken the bed for himself, but now he was too exhausted to do anything other than nudge her to the opposite edge of the mattress.

She rolled over as he slid under the worn sheets next to her. "Shane?"

"What?"

She reached without opening her eyes, patting across the mattress until she found his hand. "I missed you."

Shane fell back against the pillows, edges of the room already darkening as sleep overcame him. *I missed you, too.*

The first time Shane woke he was sweating, blinking back shadows of half-formed officers and looming warships. He rolled over as the images faded, and clutched a lumpy pillow to his chest.

The second time was worse. He sat up, clawing at the sheets because there was someone holding him down. Someone had followed them; someone was coming and there was nowhere to run.

"Shane."

Ava's grip on his shoulders was firm. She hovered over him in the dark and it only took a second before hot, unrelenting embarrassment broke through the haze of sleep.

Shane pushed her away. "I'm fine."

There was a moment of silence before Ava pulled back, and Shane felt ice crack over his chest as she settled on the opposite edge of the mattress. The distance between them was a void and he reached out, searching for something to tether him back to this moment.

"I'm sorry."

For a minute, he was afraid Ava hadn't heard. Then her hand snaked toward him under the blankets. "It's okay," she whispered. "You're okay."

And somehow that was enough.

The third time Shane woke, he knew they had slept too late. The domed light outside their window was bright and he could already hear traffic moving in the street below. He turned, reaching for the clock on the table and found Ava curled against his side. She was still asleep, head resting on his shoulder, fingers tangled in the fabric of his shirt like she expected him to vanish in the night.

If Shane were smart, he would have done that ages ago, before they found themselves here. But right now it was quiet. He closed his eyes, allowing himself one more minute of calm as he rested his chin in Ava's hair. Maybe it was the early hour, but the memory of her kiss wouldn't leave him alone.

They had never crossed that line, no matter how much it blurred and faded, no matter how much they used to joke about it. It had been funny before, a faraway future for someone else to enjoy, but Shane knew Ava had climbed into his ship that first day because she wanted to leave West Rama. If someone else waltzed into her life and whispered wonderful, glamorous things in her ear, she would leave him, too.

The thought was enough to sour the moment and Shane pulled away, spilling out of bed as Ava startled awake. "Get up." He nudged Jared with a foot as he passed. "It's late. Do you have my notes?"

Jared's answering groan was muffled by the carpet as he rolled face-first into their leftover room service.

Ava pushed herself up. "What time is it?"

"Late." Shane tapped at the wall screen until he found a local news program. "Let's go, Jared. I need those blueprints."

Jared sat up and pressed his arm against the screen, yawning as they waited for the information to transfer. Sometimes, Shane thought that screen was Jared's best quality. He had tried over and over again to track one down, but it wasn't the kind of thing he could find on the black market. He still didn't know how Jared had managed to remove his device's tracker without damaging the screen when he left. Military deserters were always easy to spot, with the chunk of arm that went missing when they tore out their screens, but somehow Jared was here, smiling and whole. Too smart for his own good.

Shane pulled back the curtains as Jared worked, blinking at the burst of light. Their hotel was high above the bustling downtown streets, a few blocks from the Nakaran Capitol building. *One more job.* That was all he needed. He would stuff his pockets, drop Ava and Jared among the crowds, and just fly.

What does freedom feel like? Shane couldn't remember.

When he turned to face the room again, the sketches and blueprints Jared had pulled from the city planner's office blinked on the left half of the screen, partially covering the newscaster's face.

"Okay. Here's the plan."

Jared's fingers stilled. It wasn't until Shane watched him steal a glance in Ava's direction that he realized it had been a while since either of them had taken his orders. What if they didn't want to? What if they didn't *need* to?

But Ava just hugged her knees to her chest and nodded. "We're listening."

"The Capitol building is six blocks east," Shane said, hoping his relief wasn't too evident. "They don't allow tour groups, but you can still tour the Interplanetary Relations building next door. Which works for us since the two share a service alley."

Jared drew two fingers across his arm and an aerial shot of the alley expanded on the screen. That was the easy part. The distance between the doors was only a few feet.

"Jared and I will enter the relations building as tourists and use that alley to access the Capitol itself," Shane continued. "At noon, Planetary Leader Cordova has a meeting that will leave his personal office open and empty for about twenty minutes. I'll be in and out before he knows we're there."

"You want to rob Cordova?" Ava lifted an eyebrow. "I mean, yes, dream big, I love that, but sneaking into the Capitol is a bit different than robbing the *planetary leader*, Shane. Why does it have to be him?"

Shane shrugged. "Because it's fun, Ava darling."

Because Planetary Leader Cordova had to approve every

prisoner transfer off Nakara. At some point, he had looked at Shane's file and agreed that a stolen ship was worth sixteen years on a foreign moon.

"There's a government safe in his office," he continued, ignoring Ava's lingering gaze. "I've seen the security footage. His staff uses it to store money and important documents, but Cordova's the only one with access codes."

Ava folded her arms. "I see. And you want to say you cracked the impossible safe. How are you even getting into the embassy? You'd need to sneak away from the tour, find your way to the alley, avoid whoever's guarding the Capitol, break into Cordova's office, *and* leave without getting caught."

"Like I said. Fun."

Shane motioned for Jared to flick through the rest of the images. He didn't understand the technical parts of the plan as much as he pretended to, but they didn't need to know that. "It'll be fine. Jared has access to the cameras."

Jared looked up. "I do?"

"What? You can't do it?"

"No." Jared sighed. "I can. You never asked, but don't worry, I'll add it to my list of *very important tasks*."

"You've been a terrible influence, Ava. He never used to ask this many questions."

"Don't blame me!" Ava held up her hands as Jared scowled. "I can't control him, either."

"Fine." Shane turned back to Jared. "*Thank you*, Jared. You'll black out the cameras like you did last time so we can move through the halls undetected."

"He won't be able to black out whoever's guarding that alley,"

Ava pointed out. "It's the Capitol, Shane, there are going to be at least three different kinds of officers."

"I know. You'll take care of them."

Ava's frustration was clear from across the room, but Shane didn't care. She hated playing bait, especially for officers, but she was so good at it he never felt bad for long.

"You'll also need to get a ship," he added. "You won't have much time, but bring me something nice, will you, like a Lincoln? Something with a good radio and reclining seats—"

"Why does she get to steal the ship?" Jared interrupted. "You never let me do that!"

"Because I like her more than I like you, Jared," Shane said. "And because she snatched a Catapult from Opian officers yesterday. When you do that, I'll let you steal whatever you want."

Jared folded his arms. "She also stole a Cruiser."

Shane glanced across the room to find Ava still chewing at her bottom lip, winding the same strand of hair around her finger again and again. "You don't have to do this, Shane," she said. "Your face is probably on every watch list in the system. It's a huge risk."

It was. There was no way around that, but Shane didn't have another option. He needed this. It wouldn't erase the last three months. It wouldn't stop the nightmares or flashbacks, but it would be something *he* planned. Something that made at least one of the responsible parties pay.

Jared swiped the images back onto his skin and the face of the Nakaran newscaster appeared on the wall over his shoulder. Shane was already packing up the room in his mind. He was ready to go.

"Shane."

He didn't look back when Ava spoke again. He was done explaining himself; he didn't care how risky she thought it was. But she shifted toward him, hand outstretched. "Shane."

"What?" He whirled, expecting another lecture, but Ava pointed wordlessly.

CHESS BREAKOUT flashed across the bottom half of the wall screen, and Shane grimaced as his mug shot appeared next. Not his best angle. At least he looked different now—three months on Chess had sucked the color and fullness from his face. His hair had been longer, too, and *much* better looking.

"Well," he said, fighting to keep his tone light. "Can you blame them? I'm valuable, probably the most important person they had. Of course they would—"

Shane broke off as another picture took its place. This one was blurry, pulled from a security camera, but it was clearly Ava, glancing over her shoulder on her way out of the visitor's center. His throat went dry. *No.* No one was supposed to know about her.

He had to open his mouth three times before any sound came out. "It's fine. No one can tell it's you."

"I can," Jared said. "You wear that dress all the time."

"So we'll burn it," Shane snapped. "It's fine. You're fine. Everything's fine."

But it wasn't. He was supposed to be in control, but that one blurry photograph knocked everything out of reach, because any job that ended with Ava in custody wasn't worth it. But when she looked at him, her eyes were shining, almost mischievous.

"Looks like you're not the only wanted man around here. What are you going to hold over our heads now?" It took Shane a second to realize she was joking, that she thought this was funny. Ava turned to Jared and asked, "How much do they want for me?"

Jared squinted at his screen. "No reward yet. You're wanted for questioning."

That was something. Shane exhaled and forced himself to mirror Ava's easy expression. "That's embarrassing, Castor. Try to keep up."

"Whatever." Ava rolled her eyes. "If we do our jobs right, they'll be offering half a planet for me next time."

She slid off the bed and started packing their meager supplies. *Half a planet.* Shane didn't like how much the thought excited him. He didn't like how much it scared him, either. When Ava passed him again, he caught her arm. "I'm serious," he muttered. "You'll be fine."

"I know." Ava grinned, and the sight of it made Shane's pulse quicken. "I trust you."

She opened the bathroom door, doing one last scan for forgotten items, but Shane wasn't paying attention. *I trust you.* That didn't make him feel better.

Because out of all the reckless, irresponsible things he'd ever asked Ava to do, trusting him was one of the worst.

CHAPTER TEN

✳ ✳ ✳

L ark, it turned out, was not lying about Nakara.

"It's a diplomatic visit," General Noth had explained the first day they boarded her ship in the Academy aircraft hangar. "I know, I know," she added when neither of them spoke right away. "It's very last minute and very inconvenient, but it won't take long. And I am sorry to make you do this so soon. Nakara usually requires a bit more . . ." She trailed off, as if searching for the word. "Preparation. But you know how things are in the capital."

Cyrus didn't, but Lark had smiled like he and Noth were both in on the same joke, so he nodded anyway. *Of course* he knew how things were in the capital. *Of course* he understood the ins and outs of interplanetary politics.

But now, when the doors of General Noth's ship hissed open to reveal a barren Nakaran street, Cyrus wished he'd asked more questions.

Even within the city's protective dome, the air was freezing— the kind of cold that burrowed under his skin and stopped his breath. *Nakara usually requires a bit more preparation.* That was an understatement. Cyrus couldn't imagine anything preparing him for this. He clenched his numb fingers as another gust cut through his uniform and Lark swore, hopping from foot to foot as they waited for Noth to join them.

They hadn't seen much of the general during the flight. Sometimes, Cyrus heard her voice floating up from the level below, muffled by layers of steel, but never enough to make out what she was saying. He had been stuck on the main deck with the rest of their team, in a folded-out bunk behind the kitchen that was entirely too close to Lark, who—despite flight regulations and limited luggage space—had somehow managed to fit an entire salon of hair products into his carry-on. Cyrus had broken down after the first night and messaged Cornelia, Help, I don't know if it's better to kill him or myself at this point.

She wrote back immediately. Jump out of the air lock. I've heard that's quick. Now she sent a different suggestion every morning. Yesterday's was Can you poison his tea? The day before was a graphic description of how to strangle Lark with his own jacket.

Cyrus had almost considered it.

It was one thing to pass Lark in the Academy halls or run simulations together under the watchful eye of their commanding officers. That was never real—false pleasantries and half-hearted teamwork to get them through the day. Cyrus didn't know if he trusted Lark to watch his back without the promise of a good grade or shiny medal, and he certainly didn't want to test that here, on a planet that felt designed to kill him.

There was a rustle of movement from the back and Cyrus straightened as General Noth emerged from belowdecks. Her coat was buttoned up to her throat, falling in sleek lines down to her knees. Even if he didn't know her titles, Cyrus thought Noth's command of a room was hard to miss. It was a strange feeling—the fact that he was at her side instead of at her mercy. Four years at the Academy hadn't fully managed to shake his inherent distrust of people like her, the ones with perfectly pressed uniforms who always looked down the bridge of their nose at the Port City kids selling wares on the piers.

She pointed at the two of them without stopping, then continued down the ramp into the street. "With me. Let's go."

Cyrus felt Lark waver and seized the opportunity, pushing his hesitation down as far as it would go. He fell into step beside Noth, tracing the outline of his weapon under his coat, and felt a brief flicker of satisfaction when Lark had to jog to catch up. He had run plenty of security drills at the Academy, but this wasn't a simulation. This was real, and Cyrus felt every bit of training flood his veins as he ran through the familiar checklist. Scan the street. Keep an eye on the sky. Pay attention. Sand slipped inside his shoe as he walked, scraping against his ankle with every step. The whole city was covered in it—the streets, the windows, the *people*. Here they were inside a protective, temperature-controlled dome, and even the government buildings were dusty.

Cyrus looked up, gaze catching on the transparent outline of the dome above the buildings. The sky beyond was dark—he could see that even through the synthetic sunlight—but every star stood out in stunning clarity. They didn't have stars like that on Opia. Or maybe they did. Cyrus couldn't remember a time when his sky hadn't been hazy with yellow smog. *Make a wish.*

He turned his collar against the wind and pushed the thought away.

But there was an eerie familiarity to this city he couldn't place, not until the three of them marched through an alley lined with boarded-up buildings and discarded trash. Only then did the realization hit him, fracturing through his chest like ice. This was Port City. A version of it, anyway. This was a place people wanted to *leave* and somehow, after everything, he had ended up right back where he started.

Cyrus fixed his eyes on General Noth's back and didn't look away until she led them down a narrow alleyway between two Nakaran government buildings. "Wait here." She pressed a button laid into one of the walls. "This won't take long."

Lark's brow furrowed. "We're not coming?"

For once, Cyrus understood the question. His instinct to follow Noth's orders warred with his own wariness of letting her walk into a foreign building alone. If she were anyone else, he might have protested, but with Noth standing against the slick marble, light from the dome shadowing her face, he realized why she got her promotion. She was never meant to stay at the Academy, hidden away and out of sight. She was always supposed to be here, making decisions in the middle of the action.

The corner of her mouth lifted as she watched Lark hesitate. "I appreciate the concern, Lieutenant, but I assure you, there's nothing to worry about. These visits never take long. Just stay here; no one in or out until I'm back."

Then the door opened behind her and Noth stepped inside.

Cyrus let out a long breath as the door fell back into place. *Stay here. No one in or out.* Out of all the things she could have asked them to do on their first day, this seemed harmless. He could do it. But it didn't take long for Lark to start fidgeting, fingers tapping along the worn bricks.

"Who do you think she's meeting with?" he asked. "Is this a

regular thing? Should I invest in winter uniforms? Do we *make* winter uniforms?"

Cyrus ignored him. He couldn't relax, even with Noth gone, but Lark just tilted his head back, taking in the buildings on either side of them like he wasn't in the middle of an assignment. "I would have no idea this was the Capitol if she hadn't told us. There should be more security, right?" When Cyrus ignored him again, Lark rolled his eyes. "Come on, Blake, she's not here. No one's going to get you in trouble."

That was easy for Lark to say. He'd never been in trouble in his life. Cyrus turned his back, fixing his gaze directly on the door in front of them. Which Lark, unfortunately, took as an invitation to keep speaking.

"What do you think people even do for fun around here? It's *freezing*. And it's hard to breathe, isn't it?"

The thinner atmosphere *was* difficult to breathe, but Cyrus didn't care enough to discuss it with Lark. His skin screen buzzed, and when he pushed back his sleeve, he found another message from Cornelia. Stabbing him would be messy but I think it would be fun in the moment.

Lark groaned and pretended to slide down the wall. "You're killing me, Blake! How are you less fun here than at the Academy?"

Cyrus didn't look up. That's good, he typed back. Off the top of your head, do you know how long it takes people to freeze to death?

"Okay." Lark held up a hand. "Fine, let's play a game. First rule, I ask you a question. Second, you have to answer with more than one word."

"Why?" Cyrus asked before he could stop himself.

"Because," Lark snapped, "I want to bash your head against this wall, and this will let me know if I'll miss you or not!"

Cyrus's hands curled in his pockets. He didn't want to give Lark the satisfaction of a response. He didn't want to give General Noth a reason to question him. Everything felt so fragile, and he hadn't worked this hard for it to fall apart on day one.

Lark folded his arms and leaned against the building on the other side of the alley. "Where do you think that goes?" He nodded toward a second door Cyrus hadn't noticed before. "Want to check it out?"

Cyrus tensed. "Do *not* open that."

"Oh, relax." Lark's fingers landed on the worn handle. "Aren't you a little bit curious?"

Something about his voice lifted the hair on Cyrus's neck. "This might be hard for you to believe," he said through gritted teeth, "but not everything exists for your entertainment."

"Not with that attitude it doesn't." Lark kicked at the door, and the answering *thump* echoed down the alley. "Come on. Give me one good reason—"

"*Because*, Lark!" Cyrus cried, composure momentarily forgotten. "Sometimes there are consequences for your actions! *Stars*, you don't know everything!"

"There it is!" Lark jammed a finger into his chest. "I like this energy, Blake. What else?"

Cyrus flinched, heat blossoming across his face. "I'm going to *murder*—"

"I wouldn't say the *M* word on a diplomatic mission. People don't really like that."

Lark rested an elbow against the wall and grinned. Cyrus always thought he looked like he was carved from something sharp and unforgiving, but just like back in the Academy hangar, Lark softened when he smiled. It would have been nice if it wasn't so infuriating. Cyrus had just opened his mouth to tell Lark how little he cared for people's opinions on murder when another voice cut through the alley.

"Officers?"

Cyrus's hand flew toward his weapon. He had been so busy letting Lark get under his skin he had forgotten their only job—watch the alley. But he relaxed when he saw the girl approaching them now; she didn't look like a threat. If Cyrus had to guess, she wasn't much younger than he was. Seventeen, maybe. She wore a faded red dress with her dark hair tied away from her face, and even though she didn't look Nakaran, she barely shivered as another blast of frigid wind soared through the alley. Too comfortable to be anything but local.

"Hello?" She spoke the system language, eyebrows lifting when they didn't respond.

"I . . . Sorry, can we help you?" Lark asked, slipping into the same language after another moment of hesitation.

The girl beamed. "Oh, perfect, I thought you only spoke Opian. I have a ship back there that won't start. Can you help?" She glanced over her shoulder before adding in a whisper, "Between you and me, the law enforcement around here is junkmatter."

Lark relaxed, hand falling away from his weapon. "Well, that's not exactly a secret; everything around here's junkmatter. No offense," he added.

But the girl shook her head. "No, you're right. It's *so* embarrassing, but my ship's right outside. I promise it won't take long?"

"Sure." Lark glanced back at Cyrus. "You're good here?"

The girl shook her head before Cyrus could answer. "I'm sorry, I think it needs two people. I can't hold the hood myself, and someone will need to check the fuel gauge." She looked back and forth between them again, brown eyes wide and pleading. "Please, my mom's going to *kill* me if I'm late again."

Cyrus hesitated. They were supposed to watch the door. Those were the orders. But hadn't he just sat through a graduation ceremony where he'd promised to help those in need? *Honor, loyalty, dedication.* What was the point if it didn't extend here, even to the small things? He glanced over his shoulder again. They could watch the door from the sidewalk, just for a second. After all, there was no other way into the alley, so anyone who wanted to enter the Nakaran Capitol still had to go through him and Lark. It wasn't technically breaking the rules, but it still made him uncomfortable.

"Okay." He cleared his throat. "What do you need?"

The girl's ship was parked a few steps away—an older model of the same ground Cruiser they had back home.

"What are you doing all the way out here?" she asked as Lark popped the hood. "Long flight, isn't it?"

"Just checking in," Cyrus said quickly. He didn't trust Lark not to spill their entire mission if this girl smiled at him long enough. Which was ridiculous, because he was pretty sure Lark didn't even *like* girls. But Lark liked attention more than anything, and right now, attention was wearing a red dress and laughing at his jokes.

Lark nodded. "Right. Checking in. What about you?"

"My dad works in Interplanetary Relations." The girl pointed to the smaller building next to the Capitol. "All the way at the top. He usually works late, and he forgets to eat if I don't remind him. I swear, men are going to die out if they don't learn to cook."

"Don't say that." Lark grinned. "Who would fix your ship?"

The girl laughed, resting a hand on Lark's arm, and Cyrus decided he was never letting Lark live this down. "Come on," he said. "Let's do this; we need to go."

"Sure." The girl reached through one of the open windows and unlocked the doors. "Thank you *so* much, Officer . . ." She trailed off, squinting at Lark's badge.

"It's lieutenant, actually," Lark said. "But call me Lark. This is Cyrus."

She reached for Cyrus's badge anyway, turning it toward the light. "Lieutenant Blake. I'm Blanche. It's nice to meet you."

Lark had just stuck his shoulder under the hood when a loud screech split the air. Cyrus jumped, whirling to make sure the alley was still secure.

"What are you doing?" A Nakaran woman, arms overflowing with shopping bags, ran toward them from across the street. "Get away from my ship!"

Lark's mouth opened in a way that might have been funny if everything wasn't slowly turning to ice. Cyrus watched the girl's smile fade as she stepped back, and he barely had time to grab his rifle before she bolted. Lark started to follow but Cyrus took aim, his breath steadying as he found her in the crosshairs, caught the flash of her red dress across the street. It would be a clean shot, an easy one. His finger stilled on the trigger right as Lark swore, and Cyrus blinked, concentration momentarily broken. By the time he looked back, she was gone.

"My rifle!" Lark gasped. He turned in a circle, frantically patting the front of his jacket. "She . . . she took it!"

Cyrus looked down to check that his own weapon was still clutched firmly in his hands. "Are you serious? Lark, that's *military grade—*"

But Lark cut him off, pointing at Cyrus's chest. "Your badge. Where's your badge?"

"What—?" Cyrus touched the front of his uniform, numb fingers brushing over rough fabric. The gold square wasn't there. He sagged against the wall as Lark slammed his palm against the bricks. *Of course.* Of course he was here with Lark, who could talk his way out of anything. Nobody ever lectured the student whose family name had been on the Academy campus library for years. But him?

"What do we do?" Lark asked. All his earlier bravado was gone. Cyrus wondered if the girl had taken that with her, too. This morning, he would have thanked her, but now he watched Lark's throat bob as he swallowed. What was the punishment for losing military property? For abandoning his post on the first day? Was there a warning? Immediate discharge? Maybe Noth would shove them out the back of her ship on their way home and tell everybody they died tragically in the Nakaran desert.

Cyrus stuffed his hands deep in his pockets and tipped his head against the dusty bricks. If he was going to be fired, at least he wouldn't be alone.

He just hated that it had to be with Lark.

CHAPTER ELEVEN

✳ ✳ ✳

"If you smile at one more person, I'm knocking your teeth in." Shane grabbed Jared's bony wrist and steered him into the stairwell. "Walk faster."

They had slipped away from their tour on the second floor without raising alarm, but Shane wanted to get out of the Interplanetary Relations building before someone noticed their absence. Getting in had been smooth enough, but the disguises Ava had stolen that morning were anything but subtle. He was finding it very difficult to use his trusted method of walking fast and looking important when he was wearing a backward hat and flower-patterned jacket.

And then there was Jared, who kept glancing over his shoulder, flashing nervous grins at everyone they passed and saying things like "I love what you've done with the place" to anyone who looked their way.

By the time they slipped into the stairwell, Shane's chest ached from holding his breath. The longer he and Jared walked without interruption, the more his unease grew. He almost wished someone *would* stop them so he could work out some of the adrenaline coursing under his skin. Looking at the plan on paper was one thing. In real life, it felt too quiet and too easy.

They wound their way down to the basement, taking the

stairs two at a time. The door that led to the alley was tucked in the back storage room, and Shane shivered at the sight of another empty hallway. The lack of security felt wrong, like someone running their fingernails across his bones. Maybe he was still used to the strict schedule of Chess, the irrational number of officers. *Had Nakara always been this empty?*

Shane pushed the thought away. He could think about the state of this planet's national security later. Right now they had a job to do. He tugged off the tourist disguise and smoothed the wrinkles from the suit underneath as best he could as Jared stuffed his own clothes in the trash.

"Right on time," Jared muttered. "Ready?"

Shane nodded. "Let's go."

But when he went to open the door, his hand faltered. This was the variable he couldn't control, something neither of them could plan for. If Ava didn't distract whoever was standing guard, or if she failed to steal a ship after, they were as good as dead. They were dead and this room was too small, too dark. Shane felt it close overhead as he struggled to draw breath. *You're not going back.*

"Hey." Jared's hand on his arm was a jarring shock, and Shane pulled away, face heating at the concern in his voice.

"I'm fine," he muttered. "Just do your job."

Then he opened the door.

Shane hated the relief that swept through him at the sight of the empty alley and the Capitol building a few feet away. He motioned Jared outside. Two officers stood in front of the alley, caught in the storm of charm and well-timed jokes that was Ava Castor. Perfect. Jared tapped his arm to the door, eyes blurring as they shifted between his screen and the Capitol's security system. Then one of the officers laughed and Shane recognized the accent immediately. *They're Opian.*

For a minute, he forgot how to breathe. He should have noticed the uniforms, the dark red so unlike anything the Nakaran officers wore. He should have noticed the way they stood, self-assured and commanding on a planet that wasn't theirs. Shane's first thought was that they had found him. They'd found *her*. Because why else would they be here?

His shoe caught on a cobblestone and he stumbled, barely catching himself on the opposite wall as Jared pulled the door open.

As the two of them slid into the empty hallway, Shane felt something shutter in his chest. He was *fine*. He was always fine, and it was going to take more than a few Opian officers to ruin him, especially today. He ran a hand over his face and forced the image out of his head. "Come on."

As they walked, Jared alternated between blocking their image from the cameras and guiding them through the maze of corridors. Every time an employee turned their way, Shane ducked around the nearest corner, forcing Jared to reroute as they went. He knew Planetary Leader Cordova's office was only two floors up, but by the time they stumbled out of the stairwell, his legs were trembling, breath tight in his chest.

"We can take a minute," Jared whispered as they turned the corner. "Do you need to—?"

"I'm fine." Shane tugged his lockpicks from his sleeve. "Three minutes, remember? In and out."

Jared hesitated a second longer before nodding. "In and out. I'll get the cameras."

He slid into a nearby storage closet and Shane put a hand on Cordova's office door. The Capitol locks were electronic, but the offices themselves were still manual and there was something reassuring about sliding the end of the first needle into the lock, turning it slowly, and inserting the second pick. The panic that had shadowed him since Chess dulled, and when Shane heard the sound of the locks releasing, he almost felt like his old self. He ducked inside and crossed the room in two quick strides.

The safe from the security footage was tucked under Cordova's desk. It was one of those fancy Price safes, with three different combination locks and a dead bolt for "extra security." Shane could have told Cordova to save his money. There was no such thing as extra security—not when it came to him. When the safe door swung back, heavy and cold in his palm, he knew he'd made the right call.

Heavy bags of Nakaran coins sat in the corner next to piles of bank cards, interplanetary IDs, and customs tickets. Two watches lay coiled in the back, and when Shane held one up to the light, it cast dazzling patterns across the walls. *Veritian fire crystal.* Just one of those gems was enough to buy him a one-way ticket to a new system. Far away. Filthy rich. He put it down, then shoveled everything into his pockets. Let Cordova try to get anywhere without his passports. Let him feel what it was like to be trapped.

The doorknob outside rattled, catching with a sharp *click* as someone locked the door without realizing it was already open. That moment saved him. Shane slammed the safe shut and dove for the coat closet as the lock clicked again.

"Please, come in."

Planetary Leader Cordova stepped into the room right as

Shane closed the closet door, leaving only a small crack to peer through. Cordova settled himself behind the desk, back unnaturally straight as he watched someone just out of Shane's line of sight.

"Thank you for meeting on such short notice, Planetary Leader."

It was another second before the other speaker stepped forward. Shane didn't recognize her face, but the Opian accent was impossible to miss. Her expression reminded him of the officers who roamed West Rama—hungry and cunning and smart. If it weren't for her coat, still buttoned despite being indoors, he wouldn't have been able to tell she was uncomfortable. Opians were always dramatic about the cold.

"Of course, General." Cordova nodded. "You're always welcome."

The woman smiled. "No need to lie. We both know how little you care for my planet."

"Isn't the feeling mutual?"

She laughed, a soft sound that made color rise in the high, pale lines of Cordova's face, then wandered toward the far side of the room, taking in the sparse decor as she went. Shane thought it might have looked casual to anyone else, careless even, but he had staked out enough jobs to recognize the deliberate way she catalogued every aspect of the office.

"This is a rare one." She trailed a finger down the spine of a leather-bound book. "And in such excellent condition. Where did you get it?"

Cordova's shoulders stiffened. "It was my father's."

"It's beautiful." The general tugged it off the shelf, into her waiting hand. "Opian made, right? Tell me, Cordova, have you spent time down in the mines lately?"

Shane watched Cordova blink at the sudden change in subject. "The mines? Why—?"

"It's sad, isn't it?" She opened the book, thumbing through the pages as she crossed the room with slow, careful steps. "Our planets have been partners for a long time. We send supplies every month. We let your citizens work in our mines."

"*Our* mines," Cordova corrected.

The general's fingers stilled. She was too close to the closet for Shane's liking. "Of course." She smiled. "Your mines."

"What's your point?"

Shane was wondering the same thing. He had memorized Cordova's schedule that morning. He knew exactly where the planetary leader was supposed to be down to the minute, and this meeting was not on the list. So it was either a surprise or something purposefully left off his schedule. Right now, Shane didn't care. He just wanted it to be over so he could take what he came for and leave.

"What's my point?" The general took a step forward. "Cordova, those mines haven't turned a profit in months. Your planet's drying up. It's dying."

"What?" Cordova leaned forward. "How? Every report I've seen says you're harvesting at greater levels than ever before."

"Those reports are mistaken."

"*All* of them?"

The general took another step. She was close enough that Shane could see the sleek pull of her hair, the way every medal on her coat gleamed in the lamplight. If she took one look down at the cracked closet door, he was done. "Yes," she said. "All of them. Our trade agreement is clear, Cordova. You're only eligible to receive Opian aid as long as we're seeing a profit. If there's no axium, there's no reason for us to continue this partnership."

But that couldn't be right. The Opians dug new mines every week, new colonies that cracked the earth apart and dislocated undomed villages. Shane had seen them himself. He had seen Glen's hands, blistered and raw from prying axium out of the ground day after day. If what the general was saying was true, his brother wouldn't have a job. The Opians wouldn't still be on his planet.

Cordova gripped the edge of his desk, fury evident as he searched for a response. Shane didn't blame him. At the end of the day, it wouldn't matter if the general was telling the truth— cities like West Rama relied on the Opian shipments for almost everything. Deliveries outside the domed cities were already few and far between. Even Shane couldn't pull enough jobs to support his family if they stopped entirely.

"You can't break the contract," Cordova said eventually. "The terms of dissolution are clear."

"Can you pull axium from thin air? If so, I'd be more than happy to renegotiate." Impatience clipped the general's words. She paused, letting that sink in before adding, "Of course, there might be another way."

A chill dragged down Shane's spine and he saw this meeting for what it was—a game. A trap. Get Cordova desperate, let him think he'd lost, then offer him a solution on Opian terms. Shane had pulled that trick himself, so many times he'd lost count, but he didn't like that this time, Nakara was the victim. And Cordova was playing right into the general's hand.

"What do you want?"

She grinned, snapping Cordova's book shut in her hands. "Do you know where the largest source of raw, untapped axium is on this planet?" It was clearly a rhetorical question, but she waited until Cordova shook his head before looking pointedly at the floor. "Right below your feet. There's a deposit here, about two miles down. It's fresh, it's new, it's powerful. I have an Opian base down the street; we could get an army here in a day. It wouldn't take long to level the city. We could start drilling by the end of the week and you could keep your trade agreement."

"Level the city?" Cordova pushed himself to his feet. "What kind of proposal is that? How do you even know where the axium is?"

The general arched a brow, like she couldn't possibly be any clearer. "It's my job to know. We can sever the agreement now if you like, and I'll have my people off Nakara by the end of the week. You'll never hear from us again. But I'm trying to help you, Cordova."

Shane could see the resolution in the square line of the general's jaw. She could do whatever she wanted. Maybe she was wondering why she hadn't tried sooner.

Cordova shook his head. "Neither option is acceptable. Where's Derian? I want to speak to her."

"You really want to trouble the Opian planetary leader with this?" The general laughed. "Cordova, those mines are *my* responsibility. She'll tell you to take it up with me."

"So what happens if I say no? You can't destroy the capital and you can't leave. You signed a contract."

"I don't think you want to find out."

Shane watched Cordova bow his head, hands braced on the desk. When he spoke again, it was almost too quiet to hear. "Where else?"

The general's eyes narrowed. "What do you mean?"

"Where else can you drill? There has to be somewhere else. Leave the capital, leave the domed cities, but what about the desert? No one lives out there; surely there's something."

Shane had to press a hand to the wall to steady himself. *No one lives out there.* He had always known how little Cordova cared for the undomed cities, how willing he was to turn his back on the people in the desert. He'd sent Shane to a foreign prison moon without a second thought, but this felt different. A betrayal that slashed through everything this planet was supposed to be.

The general smiled, a flash of too-white teeth. "Interesting."

"There's more land," Cordova offered. "More space. And there are a few cities, yes, but give me some time. They can relocate. The rest of us can't."

The silence stretched, then shattered. Shane watched the general hesitate. The gesture wasn't real, he could tell that much from here. She had probably wanted this from the beginning; the rest of the conversation had just been for show. Then she tucked Cordova's book under one arm and turned.

"Three months. I'll be back in three months, and I expect the deserts open by then. If they aren't . . ." She let the sentence hang in the air, and Shane remembered her words from earlier: *I don't think you want to find out.* "Be a good host and show me out, will you?" she added when Cordova didn't move. "You've wasted enough of my time."

Like this entire meeting hadn't been her idea. Like she didn't hold all the cards even now. Cordova stood like he was caught in a dream, and Shane wondered if he was weighing the implications of this decision, the lives in his hands, as he opened the door. The general swept past him, lips pressed in a tight smile. Shane might not understand the intricacies of interplanetary politics, but he knew a victor when he saw one. It was the same way he looked at unlocked ships and empty convenience stores. Nakara was an easy mark to her, and he was willing to bet that whatever funds were funneled out of the new mines would go directly into her pockets.

The door closed behind them, and he spilled out of the closet, gasping in a long breath. *Get in, get out.* So much for that.

"You said three minutes," Jared hissed when Shane yanked him from the supply closet. "*Three minutes!* Do you know how easy it is to detect malware if you've been in a system as long as I have? We need to go!"

For once, Shane agreed. "Then move."

They started toward the first floor, and Shane forced his mind to steady, to ignore the unease stirring in the pit of his stomach. This was fine. His pockets were full, they were on the move, and he was going to walk out the front door, just like they'd planned. Then he rounded the next corner and almost ran straight into Planetary Leader Cordova's back.

Cordova stood at the top of the stairs with the Opian general, surveying the Capitol lobby. Jared let out a frightened squeak, but Shane willed his expression to remain neutral as he inclined his head in their direction. "Excuse us."

He pulled Jared down a new hallway as something that

looked horribly like recognition flashed across Cordova's face.

"Stop!"

Shane glanced over his shoulder in time to see two Nakaran officers pounding after them. *Took them long enough.* He broke into a limping run, Jared scurrying along beside him. If they could just get out of the Capitol, they could meet Ava. He always had the advantage on the streets. The footsteps picked up speed as they burst into a long, winding stairwell and Shane looked up as more shouts echoed below their feet, louder this time. *The roof, then.*

Shane started climbing. "Jared?"

"I got it!" Jared's fingers slid across his screen. "We're good. Keep going!"

It took Shane two shots to tear open the locks sealing the roof door. An alarm blared through the stairwell as it snapped, and Jared's eyes widened. "They'll weaponize the dome! We'll be trapped in—" He broke off, watching Shane tuck his gun back into his belt. "You got that through security? Without me? How—?"

"Not now, Jared!"

Shane shoved at the door with his good shoulder, and the two of them stumbled onto the roof, twelve stories above the dusty pavement. He turned in a circle, weighing their options. Behind them were armed guards, stampeding through the Capitol like a pack of desert bison. Below them was open air. It wasn't ideal, but Shane was positive he had been in worse situations.

You're not going back. The thought crept across his skin like ice. If it was between the officers behind or the pavement below, Shane knew which he'd choose.

Jared paced back and forth, running his hands through his curls. "What do we do?"

"Hold on," Shane muttered. "Let me think. Let me . . ."

The familiar buzz of an engine cut through the air. A small black ship was soaring toward the Capitol, dodging air traffic as it went. A Lincoln, exactly the kind he had asked Ava to steal. He could fly Lincolns better than anyone, and the doors were notoriously easy to crack. A wild thought bloomed in the back of his mind. *Do you trust her?*

That's what it would come down to, and right now Shane didn't have time to give in to the crushing doubt. *Yes.*

He just hoped she was paying attention.

Guards behind, pavement below. Shane backed up, turning his face into the freezing wind, and a hysterical laugh bubbled in the back of his throat. "Do you ever wish you'd stayed in the army, Jared?" He didn't know where the question came from.

Jared blinked, like he couldn't decide if this was a trap. "I . . . no? I don't think so?"

"Good. Remember you said that. Let's go."

"Go?" Jared squeaked as Shane wrapped a hand around his wrist. "Where?!"

Shane nodded toward the Lincoln vibrating in the air below as the door behind them slammed open and armed guards poured onto the roof. "There."

Then, without stopping to think, he took a few running steps and jumped.

CHAPTER TWELVE

***

L ark had been pacing for the past ten minutes, alternating between cursing himself and cursing the girl who ran off with his very expensive, very dangerous military-issued weapon, and Cyrus could only tell himself that a missing badge wasn't as bad as a stolen rifle so many times before the words lost all meaning.

Guilt churned in his stomach with every step. If their situations were reversed and he was the one without a weapon, Cyrus was certain Lark would never let him hear the end of it. But when he searched for something to say—some clever comment or cutting insult—he came up empty. He would have to add this inexplicable wave of compassion to the list of things he was doing wrong.

They heard the footsteps before they saw the officers. Cyrus barely had time to look up before the Capitol door flew open and a horde of Nakaran soldiers swarmed into the alley. For a wild second, he was certain they were coming for him. Even Lark jumped, hands flying up instinctively as General Noth pushed her way to the front.

"Get the others," she snapped. "And bring me whoever's in that Lincoln."

There was an edge to her voice Cyrus hadn't heard before. He looked up in time to watch a civilian ship soar overhead, back hatch still swinging in the open air. Cyrus caught a flash of red skirts before it slid shut and his stomach turned. The girl from before. What had she done?

What did you allow her to do?

Lark must have had the same thought, because he didn't wait for Noth to ask again. He turned without another word and sprinted across the street, clouds of dust puffing under his boots. Cyrus ran after him, dodging pedestrians and street vendors as he went. The lack of oxygen was even more apparent now that he was moving, but he didn't stop until Lark climbed into the back of their ship, where the single-pilot Falcons sat in storage.

"Lark, wait!"

But Lark released one of the ships and climbed inside before Cyrus could stop him. "Wait if you want to, Blake. You'll miss the fun."

The floor under Cyrus's boots trembled as the Falcon roared to life. He glanced over his shoulder, toward the ship's main deck. Noth said to alert the rest of the team; those were their orders, but Lark was about to take off into foreign airspace unarmed and alone. And somehow, Cyrus knew if Lark's ship went down, he'd be the one taking the blame. He bit back a curse and released another Falcon. "I'm going to kill you," he muttered, pressing a finger to the comm in his ear as the ship sealed itself and pressurized air pumped into the cockpit. "I *swear.*"

"What did I tell you about making threats on duty?" Lark's voice crackled through his helmet. "It's unbecoming. Come on, I have a good shot."

Maybe Lark thought Noth would overlook his missing

equipment if he came through on this. Maybe he thought he'd be safe.

Not if you tell her first.

Cyrus was surprised at the severity of the thought, how it cut through his head. But if he wanted Lark out of the way, this would be the perfect time. He grinned and flipped his visor down.

The smooth roar of the engine caught in his chest as Cyrus thrust the controls forward, and then he was flying, all thought vanishing with the streets below. His stomach was somewhere on the ground, but this was what he had been itching to do since graduation. This was what he was good at. He fell into place beside Lark, a familiar anticipation clawing up the back of his neck.

He could still hear the wail of the city's alarm system from here, piercing and shrill as they plowed through the packed skies. The Lincoln was straight ahead, weaving through towering downtown office buildings, and Cyrus followed, pulse steadying the longer he flew. But as they whipped around the side of a building, Lark let out a frustrated groan.

"They're too low. I can't shoot without taking out half the block."

Sure enough, the Lincoln wove between buildings faster than Cyrus could track, using civilian vehicles for cover. "Cut around back," he decided. "We're faster, let's force them out."

The Lincoln would have to make a break for one of the passageways sooner or later if they wanted to leave the city. There wouldn't be another way out, not after the Nakarans weaponized the dome. Come to think of it, why hadn't they weaponized it yet?

Cyrus jammed his thumb into the emergency radio and found it filled with static, all communication between the dome checkpoints and reinforcements on the ground lost. He bit back a frustrated groan. Either Nakara's radio service was as useless as the rest of this planet, or someone was blocking him on purpose.

"We need them to seal the city."

"No," Lark snapped. "I just need a straight shot."

Cyrus watched him cut across three lanes of traffic and pushed his own ship faster. The force of the acceleration glued him to his seat, but they were gaining fast.

Still, the longer they sped through the streets, the more Cyrus's confidence faltered. He and Lark were Academy-trained pilots, but whoever was flying the Lincoln was masterful. It reminded him of Cornelia during simulations. They found alleys and streets Cyrus didn't see until it was too late. They used buildings as cover, spraying up clouds of sand that blurred his vision. His frustration turned to fury as he tailed them and he could tell Lark felt the same. When the Lincoln whipped around another corner, Cyrus lost them in the momentum of the turn and it wasn't until Lark shouted, "Straight ahead!" that he saw it, too. The ship was climbing fast, heading for one of the open passageways.

"There's your shot!"

Lark was already in motion. His first blast went wide, but his next caught the Lincoln in the back. It stuttered, stalling in midair, and Cyrus accelerated, thumb hovering over his own weapon. He was still several yards away when the Lincoln whipped around and returned fire with more force and precision than Cyrus expected.

He swerved, letting his instincts take over as he dove to avoid the volley of bullets. *Another simulation.* Just like the enemy fighters at the Academy. Then he heard Lark cry out over the comms. "I'm hit!"

"What?" Cyrus twisted in his seat. "Where?"

Cold fear flooded his chest. That was always the thing that killed people first. Cyrus never felt it in simulations, but he felt it now as he watched Lark's smoking Falcon spiral toward the dusty streets.

"It's fine." Lark's voice was strained, like every word was pushing its way through clenched teeth "It's fine, I just . . . need to . . . land."

Cyrus closed his eyes, but he still heard the rocking scrape of Lark's ship against pavement over the comms. "Lark?" he pressed a finger to his ear. "Are you okay?"

For a terrifying second, the only thing he heard was static. Then a groan. "Oh yeah. I'm having a wonderful time. Truly fantastic."

"So that's a yes?"

"That's an *I'm going to kill whoever's in that ship*." There was another crunch of metal that Cyrus assumed was Lark kicking open the Falcon door.

"Great." He glanced up in time to watch the Lincoln soar through the open passageway and vanish beyond the dome. "Glad to hear it. I'm going after them."

"Wait, *what?*"

Cyrus ignored Lark's outburst. The Lincoln was hit; it couldn't have gone far. He could catch them before they made it through the atmosphere.

"Come on, Blake," Lark tried again. "You can't take them alone. They just shot me out of the sky."

"I got it."

"You don't. You have no idea who's on that ship."

If Cyrus didn't know better, he might have thought Lark sounded genuinely concerned. Still, he couldn't return to Noth empty-handed and it was too late to turn back now. He pushed his ship forward and soared through the passageway right as the radio kicked in and someone on the other end yelled, "*Close the dome!*" The city's security system finally locked into place behind him, open air turning into a weaponized wall of sparking electricity.

Lark swore. "Blake, if you die out there, I'm going to *kill you*—"

Cyrus reached up and turned down the volume as the night closed around him. He shivered at the sudden change. Opia always felt alive, a planet on fire, lit by miles of power grids and factories, but out here, the dark had hands. Cyrus felt them on his skin, pressing against the sides of his Falcon. It was terrifying, worse than the empty void of space. At least up there, he knew there had been life once, even if it was light-years away. Out here, there was nothing. The only light came from the sparkling dome at his back and the thousands of stars overhead. *So many stars.* Cyrus didn't know skies could look like this— pulsing and bright and endless.

But there was no sign of the Lincoln anywhere.

He exhaled and released his grip on the controls as the reality of the situation set in. Alone in a foreign desert with no badge or identification. With the dome weaponized, he'd have to fly around to the city's main entrance and beg someone to let him in. *Shit.* Why hadn't he stayed with Lark? Why did he think he could do this? He was less than a week into his first job and he'd already been robbed, shot at, and locked out of the city.

Some first impression.

And maybe Cyrus would have sensed the shift if he weren't busy feeling sorry for himself. Maybe he would have noticed how every one of his instincts came alive at the same time. But by the time he realized something was wrong, it was too late.

Something slammed into the side of his Falcon with enough force to send him spinning. Cyrus sucked in a breath as his head cracked against the controls and he twisted to find the Lincoln directly above him, weapons glowing as it wound up to fire again. He clenched his teeth and shot forward, climbing toward the stars as fast as he could. Black static edged at his vision, the force of the acceleration pushing him back into the seat, but the Lincoln followed. He swerved as they fired again, and felt the heat of it brush his window.

He felt the next impact through his boots as his collision shields flickered, red *X*s across the control screen. There was the panic again, cold in the back of his throat. A crash from this height would be dangerous even with the shields. Without them . . .

Cyrus fired back and smoke bloomed above him. *There!* The Lincoln dipped, losing altitude fast, and he watched sparks jump from the hole he'd blasted in its hull. He wound up to fire again, heart pounding in his throat, but nothing happened. His weapons system clicked, then faltered, then died.

"No." Cyrus could taste the smoke, see it clouding the air in front of his face. *"No!"*

His ship lurched dangerously, scraping along the underside of the Lincoln as they barreled through the night. They were flying together now, on top of each other in a collision course Cyrus couldn't look away from. His Falcon tilted, wing dragging against the hole he'd blasted earlier, and a desperate thought flitted at the corner of his mind as scraps of metal rained into the sand.

Desperation killed people in the Port City gutters. It would probably kill him up here, too.

Cyrus unbuckled and clambered on top of his seat as best he could. The smoke was so thick he could barely see, but the stars outside were crisp and bright, bathing the sand in a frosty glow.

He took a deep breath and made a wish. Then he pulled the ejection lever.

He shot out of the Falcon with more force than he'd anticipated. He reached, straining in midair, and managed to catch hold of the Lincoln with both hands, clinging to the edge of the crater he'd created. It was freezing, colder out here than it had been inside the dome, and Cyrus ignored the slice of metal on his palms as he hauled himself into the other ship and collapsed, shaking, on the icy floor. His Falcon fell away, hitting the sand in a cloud of flame.

It took him a while to remember how to breathe. His chest hurt. His hands hurt. There was an ache behind his eyes that deepened every time he blinked. When Cyrus finally managed to haul himself up, he realized he was alone in the Lincoln's storage bay. Smooth walls curved over his head, leading to a single door on the far side of the ship.

"Blake?"

Cyrus jumped, scrambling to his feet. The voice came again,

a distant whisper in his ear. "Blake, where are you?"

He pressed a shaking finger to his comm and turned the volume up ever so slightly. "I'm a little busy, Lark."

"Where are you?"

"I can't talk right now."

Cyrus ran a hand over the air lock door, squinting into the dark. It was good quality, but this ship wasn't going far, not with the damage he'd inflicted. Whoever was driving would have to land soon, and he'd be ready when they did.

Footsteps sounded on the other side of the wall. Cyrus flinched. He could hear voices—angry voices, shouting—but couldn't make out what they were saying. *How many are there?*

The voices came again, and he heard Lark inhale. "You are *not* on that ship."

"Goodbye, Lark."

"Seriously? You're going to make *me* tell Noth you died? Who do you think she'll blame?"

Cyrus rubbed his numb hands up and down his arms. "Right, I was definitely thinking about how this would impact you."

Should he storm the air lock now? If he had the element of surprise, it shouldn't matter how many were inside. He should be able to subdue them and pilot this ship back to the capital. But none of the Academy simulations had told him what to do after leaping headfirst into an enemy ship.

"Whatever," Lark muttered. "She's going to kill me anyway. Then she's going to bring me back to life so she can discharge me and kill me again."

Despite himself, Cyrus bit back a grin. He'd never heard Lark sound so normal. "Why would she do that?"

"Because I lost my weapon. And because you're about to die in a foreign desert."

Right. There was that.

Cyrus hesitated, shifting his own weapon from hand to hand. "But you crashed," he said. "There are pieces of your ship everywhere. Things get lost."

He felt Lark hesitate, like he couldn't tell if Cyrus was joking. *Cyrus* didn't even know if he was joking because this was the last place he should joke about anything, but something about the feeling of Lark in his ear was comforting.

"Yeah," Lark said eventually. "I lost it. In the crash."

Cyrus nodded. "Exactly. That's a different set of problems."

"A different set of paperwork." Lark hesitated before adding in a rush, "I need you to know I look awful in black so, unfortunately, I won't be attending your funeral. But don't do anything reckless, okay?"

Cyrus started to say that he never did anything reckless, but here he was in the middle of the desert, the capital's dome rapidly fading over his shoulder. He didn't even know who he was chasing. *You never asked.* The realization chilled him as much as the wind. He had followed Lark and followed orders, completely prepared to shoot a civilian ship out of the sky.

Maybe that was why the Academy trained them with simulations and codes—so the real thing felt as easy as pressing a button.

"You still there?" Lark's voice was fading, the signal too weak to follow him this far out.

"Yeah." Cyrus flinched as another icy blast of wind cut through his jacket. "I have to go. See you soon, Lark."

His response was too staticky to hear and Cyrus switched off the comm as the dark closed around him. He felt the Lincoln drop again and steadied himself against the air lock. He couldn't wait out here much longer, not in the cold. Cyrus inhaled and replayed the sound of Lark's voice in his ear as he pried the door open and slipped through the air lock. One way or another he was getting off this ship.

CHAPTER THIRTEEN

***

"If you ever do that again, I'm throwing your corpse off this ship, Shane Mannix!"

Ava slammed her fist into Shane's arm with every word. She felt like a dying engine, unsteady and shaking as they flew farther into the desert. No part of her had recovered from watching Shane and Jared leap from the Capitol roof, from accelerating toward them, scrambling to open the doors as she went.

"Stop!" Shane swatted her hand away. "I'm driving. Let me—"

"No!" Ava hit him again, knuckles aching. "You can't just jump off *buildings*! What if I hadn't been there?"

"You were!"

"But what if I wasn't?"

"Then we'd be dead, and you wouldn't have anyone to yell at!"

Ava groaned and rubbed a hand over her face. "That's not the point! We have to find a new ship now, you know. After everything I did to get this one. Because you couldn't be subtle for five seconds! Were you *trying* to alert the entire Opian army?"

Shane tensed. "It wasn't the *entire* army."

"Oh, you wanted more?" Ava pointed out the window as another piece of their wing broke off, showering sparks into the sand. "Was that part of your plan?"

"I have a plan for everything."

But she was starting to seriously doubt that. The capital's

dome was fading behind them along with the smoking wreck-age of the Opian Falcon. In the distance, the mountains loomed, sharp and jagged against the sky. They needed to get off Nakara, but they'd be lucky if the Lincoln made it to the next town. She could smell smoke and hear the faint trill of an alarm in the air lock. The ship had done a perfectly fine job of catching Shane and Jared in midair, but space travel would be too much at this point. The thought made her angry all over again.

"For the record," Jared said, leaning forward in his seat, "I didn't want to jump off the roof."

"Really?" Shane flipped the Lincoln into autopilot and turned to face them both. "You'd rather be back in the city?"

"I think he'd rather be alive," Ava snapped.

"We *are* alive!"

"Barely!"

Shane leaned back in his seat, gaze sliding across the dash-board as the engine gave a high-pitched whine. Ava thought he was trying to look casual, like their rapidly slowing ship was also part of his plan, but he hadn't stopped moving since Chess. Even now, his fingers tapped against the armrests, an erratic rhythm that sent her pulse racing. There was something dan-gerous behind his gaze, tucked against the sharp corners of his body.

"I don't know what else you want from me," he said. "I think we were pretty successful, all things considered. Did you see the haul?"

Jared nodded. "It was good."

"It was excellent," Shane corrected. "Exactly what we wanted. Now, Ava darling, would you please take care of whoever's about to walk through our air lock? I'm really not in the mood."

He said it so casually that it took Ava a second to realize he was serious. "What?"

Shane waved a hand at the dashboard, where a grainy video of their compromised air lock flickered on one of the screens. Ava had to scan it three times before she noticed the clump of shadows in the corner. Definitely human. She blew out an exasperated breath. They had probably picked up a street kid, a stowaway who was also currently regretting every choice they ever made.

"Fine," she said. "But this isn't over. I want to have a conversation about what sort of risks we're taking in the future. This is ridiculous."

Ava stalked toward the back of the ship and swatted her palm against the control panel. The air lock door slid back with a rough scrape. The cold hit her first, a sudden wall of ice, and she didn't even look at the boy pressed against the wall. She just grabbed the barrel of his gun, pushed it aside, and slammed her other hand into his throat. The weapon clattered to the floor and Ava reached for it, turning it over in her hands. The rifle was clean and sleek, military made. *Definitely not a street-kid weapon.*

She turned and surprise flared hot and fast when she recognized one of the Opian soldiers from the alley. "You."

It was the boy with the stern face and wary eyes, who had watched her too closely and looked like he saw too much. He rubbed his throat, face still twisted in pain, and Ava rolled her eyes. She hadn't hit him *that* hard. "Lieutenant Blake, right? Cyrus? I hope you're not here to get your things back."

She looked him up and down, taking in his ripped gloves, his dirty uniform, the cuts on his face. Stars, had he jumped from that Falcon? Ava turned and walked back to the front, shoving the rifle into Jared's chest as she passed. "There you go. Watch him."

"Me?" Jared let out a frightened squeak, eyes widening as he clutched the weapon. "Ava . . ."

She ignored him. She knew Jared hated guns, but she didn't care. Let him be uncomfortable. She was still mad at him for following Shane off that roof. "How'd you get up here, anyway?" she asked, turning back to Cyrus. "If you weren't here to kill us, I might be impressed."

Cyrus straightened, hands fisted at his sides. "I'm not here to kill you."

"Can you keep it down?" Shane called from the cockpit. "I'm trying to concentrate."

As if in response, the ship gave another ominous shudder and dipped closer to the sand. Jared jumped, hands trembling on the rifle as he pushed it against the boy's chest. "Right," he said. "Sorry. Shut . . . shut up?"

Ava nudged his shoulder. "Take the safety off."

"The what?"

Cyrus looked at the ceiling, and Ava couldn't tell if he was searching for courage or patience. "Just put it down. You're all under arrest, anyway. Let's—"

"Who's arresting us?" Ava asked. "You? No offense, but you're doing a terrible job."

Cyrus continued like she hadn't spoken. "You stole Opian property. You endangered the whole city. You . . ." He broke off, and something behind his gaze hardened. "You shot an Opian officer out of the sky."

"That one's on you," Ava said. "I don't even think you have

jurisdiction on this planet. Why do you care what we steal?"

"That's not—"

"Stop talking." Shane stepped out of the cockpit before Cyrus could finish, one hand braced against the doorway. Ava felt the temperature drop as he limped forward. "Jared might not want to shoot you, but trust me, I'd like nothing more. Get down." He pointed at the floor and waited until Cyrus sank to his knees before rounding on Jared. "The safety is on the bottom. No, the other—there you go. You." He pointed another finger at Ava. "You want to stop taking risks? Fine. You can stay here."

He turned away, and Ava choked back a laugh. She couldn't help it. But Shane's expression didn't change. "I'm serious," he said. "I'll drop you at the next town. Tell them I kidnapped you, or something."

"What?" *Where is this coming from?* She reached out, but Shane pulled away before she made contact. "That's not what I said. Shane—"

"They're after me," Shane hissed, pointing back at Cyrus. "This isn't about Chess. I robbed a government building. We shot down two Opian ships. They're not going to leave me alone, and I can't—" He broke off, and something Ava didn't recognize flickered across his face before he said, "And *you* obviously can't handle it."

"So you're firing me?" Ava couldn't believe he was doing this here, in front of Jared and an enemy soldier. This was the thanks she got for saving his life? "I don't want out. I'm just saying we could be more careful. You got your haul. Let's get off Nakara for a while; you can take a break!"

Shane looked away and Ava saw the dark again, bubbling up from somewhere she couldn't reach. It hadn't always been like this, she was certain of it, but Shane had always been good at hiding, at building walls too slick and solid for anyone else to climb. His gaze darted around the ship, and when it landed on Cyrus again, Ava felt his anger shift.

"I can't leave Nakara. Maybe he should tell you why."

"Me?" Cyrus looked up from the floor as Jared readjusted the rifle against his shoulder. "Can you lower that, please? You clearly have no idea what you're doing."

"Don't, Jared," Ava said before either of them could move.

She didn't know what Shane meant. She didn't know what Cyrus could possibly tell them, but she felt the shift in the air like the second before a sandstorm appeared on the horizon. "Why can't you leave?"

Shane ran a hand across his forehead, and Ava watched his fingers tremble before he stuffed them back in his pocket. "Those Opian soldiers today weren't in the capital for nothing. They want more money from us, more mines, and Cordova signed over half the planet. Just handed their general everything so he could protect the capital city."

Every word came out twisted and sharp. Ava couldn't make sense of it. "The capital?" She glanced between him and Cyrus. "The Opians already have mines. Why do they need more?"

"Because they want it, Ava," Shane snapped. "Because they've always taken what they want, and Cordova's going to let them. He's going to sit in the dome and look the other way while they tear through the deserts, and I know we aren't supposed to care, but . . ." He hesitated. "There are still people out there beyond the domes. Our families live there."

His mouth twisted and for a second Ava saw it—the Shane from before, who smiled easily, who went out of his way to make her laugh, who cared about things more than he wanted to admit. It vanished as quickly as it had come.

"And what if they don't stop there?" he asked. "What if they come for everyone else next? That's what you want, isn't it?" he added, rounding on Cyrus again. "That's why you came."

The last part wasn't a question.

Cyrus lifted his hands. "That's not . . . No, there's been a mistake."

"Clearly."

Shane's footsteps were heavy across the floor. He shifted his weapon from hand to hand as he crouched to look Cyrus in the eye, and Ava felt anticipation gather along the walls. The Shane Mannix she had known wouldn't shoot a foreign officer in cold blood. He might have threatened it, he might have cut off a finger or two, but there was always a line. This Shane, however, thrived on that treacherous, razor-tipped edge. He slid the barrel of his gun under Cyrus's chin, forcing him to look up.

"Tell me why you were on Nakara today. I want you to say it."

Cyrus looked like he was carved from stone, like one wrong move could break him, but his voice was steady. "It was a diplomatic visit. We were—"

"No." Shane's finger tightened around the trigger, and Cyrus winced as the weapon dug into his skin. He was sweating now, moisture catching in his hair. Shane leaned closer. "Why did you meet with Cordova?"

"I don't know, I wasn't inside!"

He's telling the truth.

Ava didn't know where the thought came from, but she was certain of it. Whatever Shane heard inside the Capitol building was beyond them all. So when he raised his weapon again, grip steady and firm, Ava stepped forward and pulled Shane to his feet. He stumbled as his ankle gave out, but she caught his shoulders, forcing him to turn.

"Stop it," she whispered. "I get it, really I do, but let's not do this here. Look at me," she added when Shane's jaw tightened. "He's not worth it."

She could feel the sharp outline of his collarbone under her fingers, the pulse fluttering too fast in his throat. Shane exhaled, head dropping ever so slightly, and if Ava hadn't been so focused on his face or the way he felt under her hands, she might have noticed Cyrus move. By the time Jared cried out, it was too late.

Cyrus drove his shoulder into Jared's chest, sending him and the rifle tumbling across the floor. Ava dove for it, but Cyrus didn't bother. He slammed a fist against the control panel instead, sliding into the air lock as Shane took aim. His shots ricocheted off the wall, barely missing the top of Cyrus's head, and Ava's next breath caught in her throat as she watched him hurl himself back through the hole in the floor and out of the ship entirely.

Shane swore and stalked toward the cockpit, stepping over Jared as he went. "I'm turning around."

Ava peered into the air lock. She didn't want to think about what it would feel like to hit the ground at this speed, but it was too dark to see anything other than the sand shifting across the dunes. The sand that was entirely too close for her liking. "I don't think that's a good idea."

"He saw us," Shane insisted. "He knows what we look like."

Ava remembered their photos on the news that morning and

shivered. "So does half the planet. He's going to freeze to death by the time you turn this ship around."

"He'd be dead right now if it weren't for you." Shane braced both hands on the dashboard, and Ava watched the lines of his shoulders tighten as he added, "You're staying in town when we land."

"I'm not."

"You *are*. You're a liability."

"To who?"

Shane flinched but didn't look at her, not even when Ava came forward to stand next to him at the controls.

She wanted him to look at her. She wanted him to give her *something*, but Shane hung his head, starlight cutting deep shadows across his face. His throat bobbed once. "I'm not going back to Chess, Ava."

"I know."

"You don't." Shane ran a hand through what was left of his hair, tendons in his arm straining. "I mean I'm not letting them take me."

Something about the way he said it snagged in her chest, and for the first time, Ava wondered if Shane actually had a plan when he jumped from the Capitol roof.

"I know," she said again.

"I'm serious, I—"

"Shane!" Ava grabbed his hand without thinking and finally, *finally*, he looked at her. "I know. I'm not going to prison, either, but you are not leaving me here. What do you want to do?"

For all his talk about getting off Nakara, Ava didn't think Shane would actually leave the planet to the mercy of the Opian military. She might not understand exactly what was unfurling around them, but she knew there was nothing for her to go back to, nowhere to look but up.

A pulse fluttered in Shane's jaw as he considered her question. "The Opians will be back in three months to claim the desert. That should give us some time, but we can't take on an army alone."

"Okay." Ava shrugged. "So we hire more people."

To her surprise, Shane nodded. "We could hit their mining ships first," he said. "Destroy the drills and equipment they send over before it reaches the surface. Anything to slow them down. Jared's good with explosives, he could do it."

"Oh, sure," Jared called from the back. "I'd love to, thanks for asking."

Ava had almost forgotten he was there. She looked over her shoulder. "Well, can you?"

"That's not the point!"

"See?" Shane nodded, and Ava thought she caught a whisper of a smile at the corner of his mouth. She looked down at their hands, still curled together on top of the controls.

"We?"

Shane's cheeks flushed. "We'll need all the help we can get."

There was something he still wasn't telling her, something else hidden behind his jagged edges, but Ava didn't care. Opia had the most powerful army in the system. They had waltzed into a capital city that wasn't theirs and told Cordova what they wanted—no notes, no negotiations, no protests. But the idea of taking from people like that, people who thought themselves invincible, was better than any convenience store robbery or bank heist.

Shane's thumb ghosted over her knuckles, and Ava shivered as the sensation ran down her spine. She remembered the feeling of his hands that night in the bathroom: on her face, caught in her hair.

"What do *you* want, Castor?" His voice was hesitant, and Ava caught another glimpse of the boy he'd been. A crack in the wall. Maybe she could pry it open.

She grinned. "I want them to put my picture in the paper with a giant reward."

"Same." Jared raised a hand. "I'm still here, by the way."

Ava laughed and even Shane smiled—a real smile for the first time in days. *What do you want?* He leaned down to check their coordinates, and Ava almost told him the truth. That she wanted too many terrible, selfish things to even figure out where to start. That some part of her would gladly watch West Rama burn, just to be rid of its shadow. That if Shane told her they were running tonight and never coming back, she would take his hand without hesitation.

But right now, Ava wanted to savor this moment as long as she could. Shane's hand in hers. Jared at her shoulder. The open desert stretching before them. If this was what it took to leave Nakara for good, she'd do it.

She turned her face to the window and closed her eyes. *One more job.*

It was always one more job with them.

PART TWO
Shot to the Heart

If a policeman is killed in Dallas
and they have no clue or guide.
If they can't find a fiend,
they just wipe their slate clean
and hang it on Bonnie and Clyde.

—Bonnie Parker,
"The Trails End"

CHAPTER FOURTEEN

***

Captain Amar Nexin wasn't afraid of the dark.

The long Nakaran nights were as familiar as his own heartbeat, memorized over years of living and working alone. He wasn't usually afraid of the quiet, either, but the silence surrounding him now had weight. When the light came, it was all at once, and Amar winced at the sudden ache behind his skull. If he squinted, he could make out the curved bay of a small cargo ship. Blank walls, empty floors, low ceilings. The stars blurred together outside the windows, but in here, Amar was alone.

Then a boy shifted against the doorframe.

His expression was unreadable, but it was the eyes that gave him away. Amar would have recognized them anywhere. *Shane Mannix.* The convict who collapsed mines and blew Opian ships out of the sky. The one whose face was plastered in newspapers and flashed across every nightly broadcast, linked to crimes too terrible and deadly to think about. Amar thought he'd be older.

He had the sleeves of his shirt rolled up to the elbows, and Amar had enough time to wonder if the material was as expensive as it looked before Shane grabbed a chunk of his hair, tilting his head back until he had no choice but to look up.

"Do you know who I am?" He spoke like someone used to

giving orders that people obeyed. "Do you know why you're here?"

Those eyes. How were they so pale and so very, very dark at the same time? Amar's stomach twisted at the vulnerability of his position. But he was a captain. He did not bend. He spat in Shane's face, wincing at the sight of his own black blood.

Shane released him and wiped his face in a smooth, careless motion. Then he drew a knife from the sheath at his thigh, holding the blade so it caught the light. "Tell me who you and Cordova talked to last week, and I'll let that slide."

Amar clamped his teeth together so hard his jaw ached. He wouldn't. He couldn't, not if the planetary leader's life was on the line. *You are a captain. You do not bend.* But Shane asked again, pushing harder with each question.

Did Cordova approve the fleet of Opian warships in our airspace? Does he plan to evacuate the undomed cities? Where is he now?

Each time, Amar shook his head.

"Fine." Shane stepped back and glanced over his shoulder. "Ava darling?"

Amar hadn't noticed the girl. She stood in a shadowed corner next to the door that divided the cargo area from the cockpit, watching them with a bored, distant expression. Had she been there the whole time? Her long hair was braided across the top of her head, and she wore lipstick the bright-red color of Opian blood. She looked up at the sound of her name. "Yes?"

Shane tapped his blade against the edge of the table. "Which finger do you think he can live without?"

Amar knew he cried out as the girl pushed herself off the

wall and plucked his hand off the table. She ran a finger over the back of his knuckles, like she was seriously considering the question. For some reason, the tilt of her head set him on edge more than Shane's threats.

"Wait!" Amar hated the way his voice cracked. *You are a captain. You do not bend.*

Shane paused. "Yes, Captain?"

The title sounded forced, a mocking joke when they both knew who held the power here.

"You have to understand," Amar whispered. "Interplanetary treaties are complicated. There are a lot of people involved and you can't possibly—"

"I'm bored," Ava interrupted. She glanced over her shoulder at Shane. "Make him talk faster."

Shane flipped the knife to his other hand. "Does Cordova know that Opia's sending armed warships into our airspace? Is he allowing that, too?"

"I can't tell you—"

Amar heard the *thunk* of the blade before he felt the pain. His blood was shockingly dark as it sprayed across the table, splattering Shane's hands and Ava's perfectly pressed skirts.

She stepped back, face twisting. "You're ruining my dress."

But her voice sounded very far away. Spots clouded Amar's vision and Shane swam in and out of focus. His pale, translucent skin. The smirk cutting across his face. The knife in his hand.

"Cordova knows about the warships," Amar gasped. "They've been up there for months. It's just surveillance."

Ava snorted. "Surveillance of a planet that isn't theirs? We know why they're here, Captain. Does Cordova plan to do any-thing about it?"

"You don't understand." Amar hated every word pouring from his traitorous lips. "He *can't* do anything. You think he wanted this? We could either give up the deserts or the whole planet; which would you prefer?"

Shane's hand curled in Amar's hair again. "I'd rather give up nothing. Why aren't you sending a distress call, then? If he's that afraid of the Opian forces, why not alert our allies to what they're doing?"

"We . . . can't."

"What do you mean *can't?*"

"Call," Amar whimpered. "The Opian fleets are blocking every signal off Nakara. They're blocking the traffic, too. Even if we wanted to . . . there's nothing we can do. They're coming back, and the more ships you blow out of the sky, the worse it'll be when they're done. Just stop."

That was what he should do now. Stop. Close his eyes and sink into the comforting embrace of the dark. Shane's gaze turned lethal as he stepped back and wiped his knife on his shirt.

"You cannot stop this, Captain. Cordova's a coward and so are you."

Black edged out Amar's vision. His breath came in short gasps and he realized Shane was backing toward the door that separated the two parts of the ship. "You can't . . ." he tried. "You can't leave me here. I'm . . ."

But it was difficult to think.

Shane paused on his way out, glancing over his shoulder one

last time. "Leave you here? What kind of host do you think I am?"

Amar looked from him to Ava. He thought he saw something flicker behind her eyes when she looked at Shane. Then her face smoothed over, and she slipped out of the bay as quickly as she'd come.

"Wait!"

But neither of them looked back as the door slid into place. The only sound was the panicked hiss of Amar's own breath. That, and the soft *whoosh* of the air lock releasing. The last thing he saw before the force of the acceleration sucked him into open space was his severed finger lying on the table.

Then the table was floating, too, and all he saw were stars and blood and black.

CHAPTER FIFTEEN

✳ ✳ ✳

If Cyrus could go back in time, it would be to tell his past self that jumping out of a moving spaceship was actually a really terrible idea.

The high-backed chairs in General Noth's council room were too stiff to sit in any position for long, but the faded bruises on his knees ached each time he moved. So did his ankle and his wrist and something in his hip. Cyrus grimaced as he shifted again, trying to focus more on the conversation happening around him and less on how much everything still hurt, months later. General Noth sat at the head of the table, surveying the room with practiced calm, but he could tell she was annoyed. After two months of working in the Opian capital, Cyrus had learned to recognize the signs of danger—lifted chin, tight lips, narrowed eyes. He learned to see it in the quiet moments, too, when she told him things were fine and he believed her.

Because he had no reason not to believe her.

This time, Noth's frustration was aimed across the table at Opian Planetary Leader Derian.

"Your hesitation is putting everyone at risk," she said, smiling through the edge in her voice. "Every day we wait is another one of our mining ships lost to a rebel insurgency group Nakara obviously can't control. Planetary security is my number one priority, and I don't see how I can guarantee it from here."

"That's unfortunate." Derian tapped a nail against the arm of her chair. "Perhaps I should appoint someone who can."

It was Derian's first time attending one of Noth's security briefings, and Cyrus was beginning to wish she had stayed in her office. He used to wonder what happened in meetings like these. He used to want to be a part of them. The reality was decidedly messier. Every time his ankle throbbed, Cyrus remembered that night in the desert. He might have walked across half the planet that night, but it hadn't been enough to outrun Shane's accusations or his own blistering unease.

Cyrus's skin screen vibrated under the table, and he looked down as a message from Cornelia shifted to the top of his feed.

Who would win in a fight—Noth's left eyebrow or Derian's manicure?

He looked up, trying to catch Cornelia's eye across the table, but she had her gaze fixed on Noth, the picture of attentive innocence. Cyrus typed back without looking.

Eyebrow for sure. That thing's dangerous.

When he had walked into their first security briefing last week to find Cornelia sitting among the at-patrol reps, Cyrus had dropped his bag and hugged her in front of everyone, all thoughts of rules and regulations forgotten. She had hugged him back, but not before rolling her eyes and whispering, "When I said you were going to freeze to death on Nakara, I didn't mean it as a challenge."

At the front of the room, Noth's face smoothed. "Apologies, Planetary Leader. But it's my professional opinion that invading Nakara would be the quickest and easiest way to minimize our losses. The longer we rely on their government, the more people die. It's that simple."

Next to him, Cyrus felt Lark shift in his chair, watching the conversation with pained amusement. They had both listened to some version of this argument multiple times over the last few months, but never in front of the council. Noth was clearly done waiting. They couldn't go three days without another report of an Opian mining ship blasted out of the sky by an insurgency group no one had been able to locate. A group Cyrus hadn't been able to talk about, not even to Lark. Not even to Cornelia. It would mean admitting that all this death and destruction was his fault, too.

By the time his team picked him up in the desert that night, Cyrus had been half-frozen, dragging himself toward the light of the capital's dome step by step. Lark had taken one look at him and shrugged out of his jacket.

"Who was it?" he'd asked, tucking it firmly around Cyrus's shoulders. "Where are they?"

When Noth asked him the same thing, Cyrus pulled Lark's jacket tight around him, took a deep breath, and said he'd gone down with his ship, that he'd lost the Lincoln in the firefight. It was the first lie Cyrus ever told her, and it burned his throat on the way out. Noth had held his gaze for so long he was certain she would call his bluff. Then her eyes softened, and she said, "Well, we're very glad you're still with us," before patting his shoulder and leaving him alone.

Even now, Cyrus couldn't say exactly why he'd lied. Maybe it was the cold. Maybe it was some leftover survival instinct, the same one that told him officers like Noth were never meant to be trusted. It would have been so easy to ignore it, to give her descriptions and tell her who she was dealing with, but that would have meant revealing what Shane Mannix told him that night in the desert. Cyrus didn't believe the words of insurgents and convicts, but he hadn't been able to forget them, either.

His arm buzzed again.

Ok new question: One dreadnought-sized Noth
or 100 Noth-sized dreadnoughts?

Cyrus declined the message. When he looked up again, Derian had her arms folded across her blazer.

"I will not invade Nakara if we can help it. They're our biggest trading partner, General. We need that axium, and I won't start a war over a couple of convicts in a stolen ship. Do you understand?"

Noth drew in a breath, as if readying herself for battle. "I think you need to decide what's more important—a trade alliance with a planet that can't even protect its own assets, or the lives of your people."

Derian's shoulders stiffened. "I asked if you understood me, General Noth."

Derian might be the public face of Opian power, but Cyrus always thought Noth wielded it better. Because everyone knew the planetary leader gave orders from a mansion in the capital, feet planted firmly on the ground. She didn't command a room like this. But this was where the conversation always stalled, Noth adamant about their need to invade Nakara, to regain control, and Derian refusing to approve the order. No mention of a secret meeting with Planetary Leader Cordova, no mention of an attempt to displace Nakaran cities or dig new mines. No hint of anything more brewing. Maybe there wasn't.

Under the table, Lark's knee knocked against his, lingering a second longer than necessary, and Cyrus felt his face warm. His skin buzzed a third time.

> Who would win—Cyrus Blake's inability to break rules or a wild, passionate one-night stand with Larksarid Belle?

He swiped Cornelia's message away before Lark could see it and moved to the opposite end of his seat.

Noth was still watching Derian across the length of the table, expression frosty. She gave a curt nod. "Understood."

"Thank you." Derian glanced toward the at-patrol reps. "Why don't you walk us through the past few months?"

A soldier Cyrus didn't know flicked a map of Nakara onto the wall for the entire room to see. "As of right now, twelve different mining colonies have been attacked by the Nakaran insurgency group." Red dots appeared on the map, scattered across the northwest continent. "Most are permanently damaged. They've made no attempt to contact us or deliver demands, so we have no idea what they're after. They've also hacked our supply shipments and destroyed four mining ships. You've seen the aftermath of that, I'm sure."

The photos clicked by one at a time. Broken shards of glass floated among the stars, gleaming between twisted chunks of metal. Remnants of the massive ships that carried mining equipment, drills, and weapons to Nakara's surface. Cyrus looked away at the first glimpse of a bloated, frost-covered corpse.

"They can hack our supply shipments?" Derian glanced at Noth. "The ones we send to Nakara? This is the first I'm hearing of this."

Probably because the last time the group had commandeered a supply barge, they had gutted the supplies and sent the ship speeding back to Opia with three words coded into the hard drive—Your move, General.

"We don't usually send soldiers with the supplies," Cornelia said. Her nails were green today, catching in the light as she drummed them on the table. "We've never had to. From what we can tell, they're taking what they want and sending the supplies on their way to Nakara. It's the mining equipment they seem intent on destroying."

Derian's brow creased. "Those ships are crewed. How are they getting close enough to plant explosives?"

The officer up front hesitated. "We . . . don't actually know."

"Seems like something you should figure out, doesn't it? Is this the same group who attacked you on Nakara, General?"

Cyrus thought attacked was a bit of an exaggeration. Noth wasn't the one who'd been shot out of the sky, but she nodded anyway, face a portrait of grave concern. "Yes. They aren't exactly subtle." She pointed to the next picture. "That's the leader. Shane Mannix, eighteen."

"Eighteen?" The corner of Derian's mouth lifted. "He's a kid; are you sure—?"

"He's the one Chess has been after for two months," Noth said. "He and Ava Castor almost killed two of my officers in the Nakaran capital. They've left a trail of death and destruction across the system. I assure you they're not kids."

Cyrus felt Lark tense as Shane's photo glared down at them from the wall. It looked old, probably taken the day they dragged him to Chess. His hair was longer and he wasn't as thin, but Cyrus could see something burning behind his eyes even here.

They were the same age, and Shane had already murdered more people than Cyrus could count.

"Why was he on Chess?" Derian asked. "What kind of person are we dealing with?"

Another at-patrol officer scrolled through her notes, nose wrinkling like the mere mention of the prison moon offended her. "Petty crime, mostly. Someone got him for stealing a ship back on Nakara."

"A ship?" Cornelia made a face. "That's it? Who made that call?"

Cyrus tensed, silently willing her to drop the subject. He knew Cornelia was thinking of the Port City officers and the unspoken knowledge that they could also do whatever they wanted as long as they kept it quiet. He had lost track of how many kids disappeared over the years. But how many ended up in places like Chess, frozen and alone because an officer wanted to fill an arbitrary quota?

General Noth's eyes narrowed in Cornelia's direction. "Why he was there doesn't matter. The point is, no one knows where he is now or how many people he employs. The damage they've done—"

"But why?" Derian interrupted. "Why target their own mines? Why sabotage our equipment? You said they have no demands, no ultimatums. Do they want us off Nakara entirely?"

If Cyrus hadn't been watching Noth, he would have missed the way her knuckles whitened on the arms of her chair. "We don't know."

"Do you actually know anything? Or is this all an elaborate guessing game?"

Lark spoke up before Noth could answer. "They were in West

Rama three weeks ago. There's a picture of Ava Castor coming out of a department store." His fingers twitched when he said her name, like he was imagining what it would feel like to wrap them around her throat. "They both have family in town. Maybe we can use that?"

"No." Derian shook her head. "We can't. We don't have jurisdiction on Nakara."

"So you want me to feed this information to Cordova and hope for the best?" Noth snapped. "No one's heard from him for months; he hasn't exactly been helpful." She cut a glance toward the at-patrol reps. "What's the girl's record?"

"Not much," Cornelia said. "Her first appearance on any sort of watch list was for helping Mannix break out of Chess. Allegedly," she added. "That was never confirmed since no one's been able to bring her in."

"You could offer her parents a deal," Lark suggested. "Tell them to let us know next time she goes home?"

Cornelia's gaze sharpened. "Again, we don't have jurisdiction, Lark."

"And they don't have jurisdiction to murder people, but that hasn't exactly stopped them!"

Derian held up a hand. "No, she's right. Unless they appear in our airspace, there's nothing we can do. I cannot allow us to waste more resources or endanger our trade relationship with Nakara." Her gaze settled on Noth. "Understand?"

"Of course."

But Cyrus watched a muscle twitch in Noth's jaw as she inclined her head.

"Wonderful." Derian pushed herself up from the table. "Get

in touch with Cordova, then. Find out if the insurgents have sent him any demands or if he knows anything about their motivations. In the meantime, at-patrol can start sending officers with the supply shipments. Protect our equipment first, then figure out how to get those mines back up and running, but no dreadnoughts, all right? I don't want any warships deployed, nothing that could be seen as a threat."

Cyrus watched Noth's face smooth back into practiced nonchalance at the mention of Cordova and knew with complete certainty that she had no intention of setting up any meetings.

Derian glanced around the room one more time before turning to go. "Let's reconvene next month. You know where to find me if anything changes."

There was a rustle of fabric as her security team melted from the wall. Everyone stood to watch her go, and Cyrus gripped the edge of the table to keep the weight off his bad ankle. Noth waited until the last member of Derian's security team had filed out before looking up.

"You heard her," she said. "Starting this week, we'll send crews with all Nakaran supply shipments. I don't want to mislead you, and I don't want anyone going in blind. It'll be dangerous, no matter where you stand, but that being said, if anyone wants to volunteer, I'd consider it a personal favor."

Despite the warnings, Cyrus felt his pulse jump in nervous anticipation. There hadn't been another opportunity to return to Nakara since that first mission or to figure out what Shane had meant that night in the desert.

"I'll go," he said before he could think better of it.

Every head turned in his direction, but Cyrus held Noth's

gaze, watching her eyebrows lift in surprise. He was always half-convinced she was going to fire him one of these days. For not capturing the gang when he had the chance. For losing them that night. For lying to her even now. But she smiled, her cold mask cracking for the first time all day.

"Excellent. Thank you, Lieutenant. Anyone—?"

"Me!" Lark's hand shot into the air. "I'll go, too."

No. Cyrus's stomach dropped. He needed to do this alone. He needed to find answers, and Lark would make any mission to Nakara about revenge.

Cornelia glanced between the two of them before raising her own hand. "Me too. I—"

"No." Noth held up a finger, cutting her off mid-sentence. "I need at-patrol on surveillance here."

Cornelia slumped back in her seat, expression souring at the clear dismissal, but Cyrus wasn't paying attention. His mind was already turning, working through the different ways he could get the gang alone, how he could fix this.

"I'll assemble the rest of the team myself," Noth said, glancing between him and Lark. "But you two will take the lead on this one. You're the only ones who have direct experience pursuing them, after all. Not many people survive."

Lark was practically vibrating out of his seat. This was where he always came alive—at the intersection of Noth's orders and his own wild ambition—but Cyrus couldn't bring himself to feel the same. Noth caught his eye, and to his surprise, another smile lifted the corner of her mouth. "Don't look so startled, Lieutenant. You were my valedictorian cadet. You're one of our best pilots, and you've been doing great work here in the capital. We trust you."

Cyrus inclined his head as some of that doubt loosened. *Trust.* Hadn't that been all he wanted from day one at the Academy? For a second, he let himself imagine the mission, the *real* mission. Stowing away on a supply barge, confronting Shane Mannix alone, throwing the lies and conspiracies back in his face. *Not true. Never true.*

Cyrus felt eyes on him and realized he had yet to speak, to acknowledge that the general's trust was an honor she could easily rescind. He cleared his throat. "Thank you."

When Noth smiled, it reminded him of razor wire—slick and sharp and deadly. "Excellent," she said. "Let's begin."

CHAPTER SIXTEEN

✳ ✳ ✳

"Let's go, Jared, we don't have all day."

Shane shouldered his empty bag and swung out of the ship, wincing as he landed hard on solid steel. The air lock of the Opian supply vessel was bigger than the one they had raided yesterday, but just as cold. A sharp breeze drifted from the air vents, lifting the hair on his neck as he waited for Jared to open the air lock doors.

"Hold on." Jared's fingers flexed as he worked. "Give me a second. These locks are fancy."

The silence of the supply vessels always unnerved Shane, but he had done this job too many times to waver now. They had it down to the second—tracking the shipments through space, hacking the servers to commandeer the air lock, setting Jared loose on the internal locks. After that, they were free to take the supplies they wanted before rerouting the entire ship to land near whichever undomed Nakaran town they felt like treating that week. It was almost too easy. Stopping the mining vessels was harder. Those ships were stuffed with weapons and equipment and more Opian soldiers than Shane could count, but he had learned to be stealthy, keeping to the shadows while Jared planted the bombs. At the end of the day, it was one less Opian crew hurtling toward the Nakaran deserts. One more night his family could sleep peacefully unaware in their beds. It still wasn't enough.

Shane didn't know if it ever would be. His crew didn't have the firepower to launch a real counterattack against the Opian armies or destroy the dreadnoughts blocking Nakara's airwaves, but they could do this—odd jobs and flashy heists that left Opia scrambling to cover evidence of their decimated ships. Eventually they would miss something. Eventually one of the other planets would notice the commotion and investigate. Shane knew he couldn't continue like this forever, always one step behind, barely keeping them alive, but for now, it was all he could do.

And today's raid was easy. No explosives, no death, just in and out of a supply ship, the same job they'd done half a dozen times this month.

Jared swept his overgrown curls away from his forehead and looked up. "Does anyone want to guess the password?" he asked, fingers hovering over the keypad.

"Oh, me!" Ava raised her hand. She was standing against the opposite wall, rifle braced over her shoulder. "What was it last time? BananaKing69?"

Across the bay, Ares adjusted his own weapon, scowl deepening the longer they waited. He stood next to Henry, the other newest member of their crew, on the opposite side of the air lock. "Hurry up," he muttered. "We're wasting time."

Shane stiffened. He had been thinking the same thing, but it wasn't Ares's job to give orders. He didn't regret hiring outside help, especially not after watching Ares strangle an Opian captain with his bare hands last week, but that didn't mean he liked the company.

"Leave them alone, Ares. We're fine." Clara swung out of the ship and handed Ava an extra bag. "Here. Get me more soap, will you?"

"Sure." Ava shouldered the bag, then paused. "Wait, where did you get that hat?"

Clara grinned, teeth flashing against her brown skin. She patted the back of her head. "From our last supply raid. Do you like it?"

"Of course I do. Why didn't you get me one? I'm *famous* now, Clara. People want to take my picture." Ava braced a hand on her hip. "And I look good in hats. I have the face for it."

"Okay." Shane stepped forward. "That's enough. Clara, back on the ship, please. You know the drill."

Clara rolled her eyes and whispered something to Ava that made them both stifle a laugh. Then she pressed a kiss to Henry's cheek. "Be careful, all of you!"

Shane gritted his teeth as she climbed back into the Lincoln. He hated their nonchalance. He hated that Ava was planning what to wear next time she was photographed, like she was posing for a magazine cover instead of dodging interplanetary soldiers. And he *especially* hated Henry for bringing extra people onto his ship. If Ava didn't like Clara so much and if she hadn't turned out to be a half-decent pilot, he would have dumped them all at a fuel stop weeks ago and never looked back.

"Got it!" Jared hit a few more buttons, and the air lock door whooshed open with a soft hiss. He glanced back at Ava. "It was RevengeDaddy3000."

She laughed, running a hand down Shane's arm as she passed. "So predictable. One day it's going to be *Shane Mannix,*

Please Stop Taking Our Ships, We Are Literally Begging You."

Her fingers lingered at the edge of his sleeve, and Shane shoved his hands in his pockets, pulling away from her touch. "Let's move."

They filed out of the air lock one by one, footsteps too loud in the open corridor. Shane had boarded plenty of supply ships in the last two months, but something about today felt different. He couldn't stop glancing over his shoulder, checking their position again and again. There was Ava behind him, Jared pressed against her side, and Henry and Ares at the rear. Clara remained with the ship, keeping it warmed up and ready to take off at a moment's notice.

Shane paused in the final stretch of hallway, motioning for the others to do the same as he peered around the corner. The main cargo hold was deserted, piles of boxes stacked in neat rows against the walls, but fear tightened in his chest the longer he scanned the quiet room. He had always trusted his instincts. That was how people stayed alive in West Rama, but his instincts weren't what they used to be, not when he kept waking in cold sweats to the feeling of rough hands around his wrists. Living in constant terror meant he could never tell which fears were justified.

"What is it?"

Ares leaned forward and Shane tensed, suddenly aware of the others behind him. Sometimes, he wondered if he should tell them the full extent of what was at stake, what exactly would happen to Nakara if they failed. They had less than a month before the Opian army was set to return, guns out, drills whirring, and no one seemed to care. And here he was, maybe the last person in the system who *did* care, and he was flinching at shadows. Shane straightened and brushed Ares aside. "In and out," he said. "Let's not keep Clara waiting."

Then he stepped into the cargo hold.

Jared slipped out ahead of them, running a hand over the wall until he found the control panel. He had to stand on his tiptoes to reach it and Shane watched him grin as he cracked it open, eyes already darting across the screen. The only light came from the emergency bulbs in the doorways and the open sky outside. The starlight glow caught in Ava's hair as she made her way to the other side of the bay, stopping every so often to sort through one of the boxes.

"This is a good haul," she murmured. "Shane, do you need anything?"

"No." Shane forced himself to relax as he followed her across the room. "Not this time."

He sank down on the edge of a crate next to her as she sorted through the supplies. Even with the quiet, familiar hum of the engine, he couldn't shake the feeling that he was missing something. There were too many entrances off the main cargo hold, too many places for people to hide. There was no way to check them all.

"Here." Ava handed him a folded-up bundle of shirts, pulling his attention back to the supply bins. "Take these. Now you can toss the one you're wearing."

Shane blinked, momentarily caught off guard by the casual conversation. "What's wrong with what I'm wearing?"

"Nothing! But would it kill you to wear a color once in a while? You'd look so good in green."

Shane ran a hand over the fabric in his lap. It felt expensive, silky under his fingers. He didn't care much for fashion, but he liked things that made him feel rich, things he had never been able to afford before. He liked the way it made Ava light up. Some of the earlier tension lifted as he poked through the rest of the box, pulling out cartons of soap, yards of fabric, and boxes of prepackaged electronics. Shane grinned and turned one of the boxes in Ava's direction so she could see the parker sun-lamps logo stamped onto the box. "Looks like these are for you."

"Ew." She wrinkled her nose at the name. "Absolutely not."

"Are you sure? You don't want one for old times' sake?"

"Shane."

But she was grinning, her cheeks flushed a delicate shade of pink, and Shane forgot why he'd been so worried in the first place. The others were still poking around by the doors, but they were far enough away that he could almost pretend they were alone. "Whatever happened to him?" he asked, dropping the lamp back into the crate. "Did he ever leave West Rama? Go somewhere far, *far* away?"

"No." Ava shook her head. "Of course he didn't."

"But you did."

"*We* did."

Shane felt Ava's thigh against his, felt her shoulder rise and fall each time she breathed. He ignored the way she looked at him then, gaze hesitant and searching. He ignored how her hair fell back over one shoulder, exposing the line of her collarbones, and he absolutely ignored the wild, unfounded urge to reach over and twist the end of her braid around his finger, just to see if it was as soft as it looked.

Something creaked in the shadowed corner behind them, and Shane shot to his feet, heart pounding as he reached for his weapon. How long had they been sitting in the open, talking about things that didn't matter? How long had he been looking at Ava instead of watching their backs? The feeling of being watched lingered, but he couldn't even tell if it was real or a figment of his paranoid imagination. Either way he wanted it to stop.

Maybe he would always feel like the world was shifting under his feet. Maybe the fear would never truly leave, even in moments like this when he wanted nothing more than to let it go entirely.

Shane ducked behind a stack of crates and poked his rifle into the corner. His pulse was an uneven rhythm in his ears, but every place he checked was empty.

"Shane." Ava's voice was soft and the hand that landed on his arm was softer still. Shane shrugged it off, but she followed anyway, keeping pace as he circled the far side of the bay. He pretended not to notice her hand hovering in the open space between them. He pretended not to notice her pull back. *Good.* She should leave him alone. People near him tended to get hurt; he wouldn't let himself forget again. Shane had just opened his mouth to tell her to go back to the others when a soft rustle of fabric sounded from the corner and a lone figure slid between the crates, quiet as a shadow.

He noticed the Opian colors too late, the dark-red uniform and helmet. Ava stiffened at his side, but the soldier stepped forward before Shane could move, blocking their escape route.

"Don't."

Three feet. That was all that stood between them now. The

soldier moved through a patch of pale starlight, and Shane heard Ava inhale. He noticed it the same time she did, and it was an effort to remain still as recognition flashed through him. The boy from the desert, the one he should have killed. Slowly, the soldier lifted a finger to his lips, eyes darting across the crates. "I don't want to hurt you," he whispered.

Ava choked back a laugh. "Then put the gun down."

"I can't."

"Why are you even here?" she asked, and Shane thought she sounded surprisingly calm for someone staring down the length of a military-grade machine gun. "*How* are you here? Are you alone?"

The boy hesitated. "They started sending us with the supplies. To . . . deter any illegal activity."

"Well, once again, you're doing a fantastic job."

But Shane didn't miss how he neglected to answer Ava's last question. *Are you alone?*

He took stock of their position—pinned in a corner, pushed behind a stack of boxes, away from the others. No matter what this boy said, Shane was certain he wasn't alone, which meant he had led his crew right into an Opian trap. He stepped forward, angling himself in front of Ava, and watched the boy's eyes widen.

"Don't move!"

"What?" Shane lifted his hands. "I thought we were friends. What was your name? Chris?"

The boy's face twisted. "Cyrus," he muttered. "That's not . . . You need to drop your weapon."

Shane pretended to consider it as he scanned what he could see of the ship. The others were still sorting through supplies on the other side of the cargo hold, too far to signal for help. "No," he said. "I don't think I will."

Cyrus glanced up, and his eyes lingered too long on something over their heads. Shane followed his gaze. At first, he saw only the smooth, rounded walls of the cargo hold. Then a shadow shifted somewhere to his left, and his hands turned to ice. Someone else was here, crouched on an upper balcony Shane hadn't noticed before. He had been so focused on the silent, empty corridors that he never thought to look up. How many Opian soldiers were poised above them now? How many signs had he missed?

How many people will die tonight because of you?

"It's okay," Cyrus breathed. "They won't do anything unless I give the signal."

Ava snorted. "Wonderful. Is that supposed to be reassuring?"

"No. But I don't have long before my comms come back online and they can hear me again, so put your weapon down and pretend we're having a conversation."

Shane could shoot Cyrus first, he was sure of it, but what would happen next? Ava was behind him, pressed against his side, but the others were still exposed on the opposite side of the bay. Clara was back with the ship. What happened to them if he moved first? Shane gritted his teeth and, even though it went against every one of his instincts, slid his gun back into his belt.

"What do you want?"

Cyrus inhaled, the sound too sharp in the cloaking shadows. "That night in the desert," he said. "On the ship. You said something about the general—that she wanted to level your cities, create illegal mining colonies on Nakara. I . . ." He hesitated.

"Are you sure? You're absolutely sure it was her?"

That was it? Cyrus had cornered them to talk politics while his friends circled overhead?

"Yes." Ava moved so slowly Shane didn't notice she had her knife in hand until the cold blade pressed against the side of his leg, half-hidden under his jacket where no one else could see. "You saw the ships on the way here, didn't you? All the soldiers she's sending?"

Cyrus's face was pale under his helmet, a stark contrast with the pressed uniform and heavy weapons. He looked thinner, hollow in a way Shane recognized immediately. That was what West Rama did to people—chewed them up and spit them out. Maybe Opia did, too. Ava's hand was featherlight on his hip, centering him back in the moment. *She can get the others.* Shane risked a glance toward the balcony, searching for any sign of movement. He could draw fire if Ava moved fast enough. Then all she had to do was get to the air lock. There was shelter in the halls, somewhere for them to hide.

Cyrus's weapon dropped a fraction of an inch. "I want—"

He didn't get to finish.

Shane heard it as soon as Cyrus opened his mouth. A series of soft *clicks* over their heads as half a dozen safeties ticked back. The next several seconds froze, suspended in the air like phantom limbs.

Three. Ava's grip was viselike on his arm, nails digging into skin.

Two. Shane watched Cyrus's eyes widen as he stepped back, pressing a finger to his ear.

One. He had just enough time to wrap his arms around Ava and throw them both to the ground before the room erupted.

CHAPTER SEVENTEEN

*** ✱ ✱ ✱ ***

Everything took too long to turn on.

The heat. The smoke. The clang of bullets on steel. Something was burning; Ava felt the sting of it in her throat. She blinked, vision blurring as Shane gripped the front of her shirt. He was shouting something, but she couldn't hear him over the relentless volley of gunfire.

"Ava!" Shane's voice was muffled as he shook her again. "We have to move!"

He pulled her across a pile of broken crates, and Ava saw the blood on his hands, caked under his broken fingernails. A bullet slammed into another stack of supplies, and Shane dove to the side as boxes of canned food exploded across the floor. He tugged his weapon out of his belt and motioned her forward. "Go! Get to the ship!"

The ship. Ava's fingers ached as she dug them into the cold, steel floor. She could do that. They were surrounded here in the open cargo hold, but there was cover in the halls. Glass crunched under her knees as she crawled forward. Their luck had always been tenuous. She'd known it would give eventually, but she never thought it would be like this: torn apart by an Opian soldier she'd been too soft to kill.

Someone coughed as Ava dragged herself behind another

towering stack of boxes, and Jared sat up, brushing dust from his hair. He fell into her, shaking so violently Ava felt it in her bones, and she yanked him against the wall as another shot cratered the box above their heads. Oil dripped across the floor, hot and thick.

Over the last year, she had gotten better at swallowing her panic, sealing it away like Shane did. It wasn't something she practiced, just something that happened after so many high-speed chases through the upper atmosphere. But she never got used to being shot at. The sound of it always reminded her of exploding mines, freak dust storms, and combusting stars. Ava gripped Jared's hand as her vision blurred again. They were not going to die on an Opian vessel in the middle of nowhere.

"The ship," she gasped. "We have to get back to the ship."

Jared nodded, bracing himself to run, and then, as quickly as it started, everything stopped.

The last of the bullets clattered to the floor. Ava watched one roll between her boots, shining in the patches of starlight. *Too quiet.* Somehow that scared her more than the shooting. For a minute, the only sound was Jared's panicked breath and her own thundering pulse. She turned as quietly as she could, peering into the open bay. Across the aisle, Shane motioned her back, finger to his lips. Slowly, he pointed up.

One by one, the Opian soldiers rappelled from the upper balconies, hitting the floor with solid, definite *thumps*. Ava recoiled, pressing herself against the crates as her heart kicked into her throat. *So many.* She could hear their footsteps as they fanned out, poking behind boxes, shoving their way into corners.

They're looking for you.

There was a flash of movement to her right, and Ava turned in time to watch Henry slide behind another pile of boxes as an officer kicked over the crate he'd been crouched behind.

She felt the panic again, cold and heavy at her throat. They were too far from the hall to run without being seen, too close to the soldiers to try anything else. She gripped the hilt of her knife as Jared ran his fingers across the oil-slicked floor. He drew in a sudden breath, grabbing at Ava's wrist as he pulled a twisted clump of wires from his pocket, and she immediately understood what he wanted to do. The knowledge did nothing to calm her ragged pulse.

Jared glanced across the aisle at Shane, wire gleaming between his fingers. Shane's eyes widened, then he nodded once before positioning his weapon between a gap in the crates, tracking the soldiers across the floor. Ava tried not to think about how powerful Jared's explosives usually were as he emptied his pockets, assembling pieces on the floor between them. If they were going down, she wanted to take as many soldiers as she could with her. Make them put *that* in the papers.

She ducked behind another crate as Jared worked, inching closer to the hall. There was a loud *smash* as one of the soldiers kicked through another box, produce splattering under their boots, and Ava flinched. *All these supplies, destroyed.* When she glanced back at Jared, his face was pale but determined. He inhaled, and Ava felt her own chest rise along with his as he leaned forward and pressed a final button. Then he scrambled to his feet and ran.

The Opian soldiers didn't have time to raise their weapons before the explosion knocked the floor out from under them.

The heat of it crawled across Ava's face, searing her throat. She stumbled, but Jared was on her before she hit the ground, pulling her forward as flames licked across the walls. Somewhere behind them an alarm blared, high and panicked.

They crashed into the hallway in a tangle of limbs. Where was Shane? Ava turned, frantically searching for any sign of the others as Jared rounded the first corner. *There.* She caught Shane's outline through the smoke, struggling as an Opian soldier locked an arm around his chest. She palmed her knife, but she barely made it two feet back into the bay before Shane yanked himself free and slammed the butt of his rifle into the soldier's face. The officer fell, clutching their nose, and Ava closed her eyes as Shane fired. That was her mistake.

In the split second she looked away, someone seized her around the waist, pulling her to the ground before she could cry out.

"I'm sorry!"

Ava's head cracked against the floor and she opened her eyes: she found Cyrus pinning her to the ground, face smoke-stained and ashen. She laughed through the sharp pain in her skull. When would this end?

"I should have let him kill you," she snarled, struggling against his grip. If she could get her hands free . . .

"Stop," he said through gritted teeth. "I'm trying to *help*! I need to know—"

"If you don't already know what's happening, you're a bigger idiot than I thought," Ava gasped. The smoke was hot in her throat. "And if you think we're talking *now*, after everything you've done—"

"This wasn't me!" Cyrus's eyes were wild. "I didn't know . . .

They weren't supposed to . . ." He shook his head. "I can help you. No one else has to get hurt!"

That was easy for him to say. He was the one holding the gun.

Cyrus's weight shifted and Ava kicked her leg free. She hooked it around his waist and twisted until she was the one crouched over him. The tip of her knife fit perfectly against the hollow curve of his throat, like it was made for this. But as he looked up at her from the ground, Ava felt a whisper of the same feeling she'd had that night on the ship. There was something familiar here, buried under the uniform and weapons. She knew a survivor when she saw one, knew how people looked when they spent their lives fighting for some distant, golden promise. Something in her chest constricted, and when she opened her mouth again, it felt like the first nail in her inevitable coffin.

"Nakara," Ava whispered. "Meet me west of Whitby Field two days from now. If you make it, maybe we'll talk. If you bring anyone else, I swear—"

Something hot grazed her arm and Ava fell, biting back a cry of pain. Another soldier stalked toward them through the smoke, face a mask of twisted fury, but she recognized it all the same. The other officer from the Nakaran capital, who had fallen for her tricks. She hadn't thought him dangerous at the time, but now his aim was deadly.

Leaving Cyrus sprawled on the ground, she dove into the hallway and flung her knife over her shoulder. It was a wild throw, a messy one, but she watched the blade cut through the smoke and sink deep into the other soldier's thigh. His mouth opened in a wordless cry, but Ava didn't stay to see what happened next. She just ran.

She caught up with Jared at the next corner. His breath was coming in gasping sobs, but his grip on her wrist was viselike. Ava caught sight of Ares ahead of them, but there was no sign of Henry or Shane. *They're coming.*

They had to be.

Clara leapt out of the Lincoln as they spilled into the air lock. "I heard shooting!" she cried. Her eyes were wide, hair escaping from a hastily tied braid. "What's going on?"

Ava let her pull them both into the ship before crumpling to the floor. There was blood on her skirts, in her hair. It was on her hands, and she couldn't remember how it got there. Another explosion shook the air lock, smaller than the first, and the windows rattled. Jared flinched, but Ava wasn't paying attention. She felt Clara's hands, cool and steady on her back, stroking her hair.

"Ava." Her voice was steady. "Where's Henry?"

"He's coming." Ava sat up, wincing at the sharp pain in her side. "They're . . . they're coming."

Shane wouldn't go back for her. Ava knew that. He would cut his losses and get the others out before the soldiers could breach the air lock, but she couldn't move. Footsteps echoed down the hall, pounding closer with every passing heartbeat.

"Enough." Ares shouldered his way into the front. "It's time to leave."

"No!" Clara grabbed at his arm. "No, you can't!"

"Do you want to die here tonight?"

Ava climbed to her feet and planted herself in Ares's path as he shoved Clara away. "Enough. No one's leaving."

His face twisted, and Ava instinctively reached for her knife before remembering she'd buried it in an Opian soldier. It didn't matter; she could kill him without it if she had to.

"Stop!" Jared shoved his way between them before she got the chance. He pointed toward the hall. "Look!"

Ava turned in time to watch Shane limp around the corner. There was blood in his hair and spreading across the smoke-stained fabric of his shirt. She pulled him into the ship with trembling hands, patting across his chest as he caught his breath. It had to be coming from somewhere. If he was hurt . . .

"I'm fine." Shane swatted her away. "Get ready. We need to—"

A bullet cracked against the side of the ship, barely missing the top of Shane's head. Clara ducked. Jared cried out, but Ava felt a rush of chilling calm. She was ending this here. Now. She snatched Shane's gun from his belt, took aim, and fired into the hallway. Shadows moved in the dark, still outlined by the raging inferno in the cargo hold. Somewhere in the smoke, a figure collapsed, then another. Ava's doubt evaporated the longer she stood, focus narrowing on her hands. Another shot, another mark, another kill.

Right now, she didn't care who she hit. She didn't care what help they claimed to offer. One shot for her mother. One for West Rama. One for every kid locked behind bars on an Opian prison moon.

She barely noticed Henry sprint into the air lock.

"Ava." Shane's voice was low in her ear. He gripped her wrist, slowly forcing her to lower the gun. "Stop," he whispered. "We're okay."

Ava inhaled and realized she didn't remember how to breathe. It came out shaky and distant as Shane uncurled her fingers one by one until the weapon clattered to the floor. He scooped it up, sliding into the pilot's seat as Henry gripped the edge of the Lincoln.

Another round of shots rattled the air lock, and Ava ducked as they bounced off the walls. Outside, Henry let out a choked gasp and fell to his knees.

"No!"

Clara lunged forward, hands outstretched, and Ava had just enough time to grab her around the waist before Henry toppled off their ramp, landing in a crumpled heap on the floor of the air lock. Blood pooled under his broken skull, chips of bone caught in his pale hair. She heard Shane swear, and when he looked at her from the cockpit, Ava swallowed the bitter taste in her throat and shook her head. She knew what death looked like. It never made cutting their losses easier.

Shane's expression was unreadable as he turned away. "Seat belts, everyone."

"Henry!" Clara clawed at Ava's hands as the door hissed shut. "No, you can't! We have to help him, please!"

"Jared, get the air lock." Shane's voice was measured as his hands flew across the controls. Jared hesitated, glancing from him to Clara.

"Now, Jared!" Ava snapped.

She hated the sharp crack of her voice. She hated how it made Clara sink to her knees as the engine roared to life under their feet. It made her feel cold and hollow, like the girl from the papers everyone feared. Maybe she had always been that girl deep down. Maybe this was why Shane shut himself away from everyone, including her.

Because pretending not to care was easier when every alternative ended like this.

Ava pressed her face against Clara's shaking shoulders as the air lock released. "I'm sorry," she whispered. "I'm sorry, I'm sorry, I'm sorry."

It was all she could say, and it wasn't enough.

Later, Ava remembered the floating bodies of the Opian soldiers who had been unfortunate enough to be inside the air lock when it released. She remembered Clara clinging to her as they accelerated. She remembered thinking that Henry's body was still back there somewhere, and she hoped more than anything he'd been dead long before the dark claimed him.

Shane took the first jump point too fast and the entire ship tilted under their feet. Jared slid across the floor as Shane shifted gears and turned again. He did that over and over, hopping through jump points until Ava was half-convinced they'd land in another system entirely.

Clara pulled herself free when they entered the third jump, and when she spoke, her voice felt like the edge of a blade. "I'm going to bed."

"Clara . . ." Ava reached for her, but she drew away.

"You wouldn't have left," Clara whispered with a ferocity Ava hadn't known she possessed. "If that had been *him*? You wouldn't even have thought about it."

Ava opened her mouth, but nothing came out. She watched Clara make her way downstairs, guilt clawing through her chest. *That's not true.* Of course she would have left. She would have done what she needed to do. That was how they stayed alive. She reached out and tapped Jared's knee as Clara disappeared from view. "Go with her, please," she said. "I'll be there in a minute."

She couldn't fall apart yet, not when there were so many other things to think about first.

Ava slid into the cockpit as Jared followed Clara downstairs, and she did her best to ignore the tension rolling off Shane in waves. "Where are we going?" she asked.

Shane shook his head. "Somewhere far away."

Her fingernails were coated in red. Ava didn't think she'd ever get it off. She took another breath and said, "I think we should go home."

"Too risky."

"It's been a month, Shane," Ava murmured. "We destroyed their supplies. The least we can do is tide them over a few more weeks."

It was a low blow, using their families to guilt him into going where she wanted, but Ava was long past caring. She didn't particularly care about the fate of West Rama, either. She would be perfectly happy to take her mother and never set foot on that planet again, but for some reason, Shane still felt compelled to go back. For all his talk of getting off Nakara, of leaving West Rama and his family's farm behind, he had never been able to do it for long.

He flinched, expression shuttering as the truth sank in. "Fine. You want the usual spot?"

Ava fought to keep her voice light. "Let's do Whitby Field. We haven't been there before."

"One night." Shane held up a finger. "Nothing more. We'll refuel and figure out where to intercept the next Opian ship."

Because they always had to intercept another ship. It was the extent of what they could do, and it was like trying to hold sand.

Without a way to destroy the dreadnoughts blocking Nakaran airwaves or show anyone the armed Opian warships in their airspace, their only chance was to destroy their equipment before it made its way to the surface. The strategy wouldn't work forever. It was barely working now, but they had yet to find a more permanent solution to removing the Opians entirely. Maybe Cyrus really did have an answer. Or maybe he'd kill her and save them the trouble.

Anything was better than this frustrating limbo.

"You're bleeding."

Ava looked up and found Shane staring at her arm. Only then did she remember the second Opian soldier, the flash of pain as the bullet grazed her shoulder. "Oh."

She didn't know if the pressure building in her throat was laughter or tears. She couldn't stop seeing the crumpled bodies. *So many.* She had killed *so many* people. And she'd do it every day if it meant getting them out alive. Ava ran a hand over her face, and when she finally looked up, Shane was still watching her. "That could have been any of us," she whispered.

He didn't move. Ava felt the silence between them sink into the pit of her stomach. They used to be able to sit like this for hours, a familiar shield from the outside world. Now the quiet felt like a trap. Because she looked at Shane and all she wanted to do was reach over and wipe the blood from his face. She wanted to wrap her arms around his neck and breathe in the fact that he was still here. She wanted him to do the same to her.

There had been a time she thought he wanted that, too.

Ava twisted her fingers in her lap as the silence stretched. Sometimes she wondered who she would be if she had never gone to that party, if she'd never let Shane walk her home. That felt like a different girl, a different life. Another bad decision gone wrong.

Maybe that was all she was good for—bad decision after bad decision until there was nothing left. But even now, Ava thought she'd rather shoot her way out of a hundred Opian ships than sit alone on a dying planet, another faceless girl in a crowd of *nothing*. It was an unavoidable truth, an inevitability she had accepted the first night Shane said her name.

Ava closed her eyes as the stars blurred together outside the windows. *Another bad decision.*

And they were a long way from home.

CHAPTER EIGHTEEN

***

There was a headache building behind Cyrus's eyes, thrumming louder with each erratic heartbeat. It had started when he landed on the satellite base yesterday morning, and now it flared and faded with each step, a constant reminder of what he was about to do.

Meet me west of Whitby Field two days from now. If you make it, maybe we'll talk.

Cyrus pushed the thought away, straightening the cuffs of his uniform as he walked.

The satellite base floated somewhere between Opia and Veritas, a halfway point for ships returning from the far corners of the system. Cyrus knew it was practical, an ideal location, but the whole place made him uncomfortable. The winding steel corridors reminded him of the supply ship, like any second he would stumble over another body or go up in flames.

"It doesn't look that bad, Cy."

Cyrus looked up and found Cornelia sitting cross-legged on a bench outside the base's armory, a half-eaten sandwich in one hand. She fell into step beside him and reached up to examine the jagged cut on his forehead.

"Really," she added. "You look like a dashing romantic lead with a very dark secret."

Cyrus looked away. He was lucky to be alive. Half his team

hadn't made it back, and the ones who did had needed more than a few stitches. *Your fault.* Another thing to weigh on his conscience. Another thing he was supposed to fix.

Cornelia looped her arm through his. "So, how's Lark?"

"Fine, remarkably," Cyrus said. "Even more insufferable than usual. Did you hear he was *stabbed*, Cornelia? Don't worry, he'll tell you all about it."

She bit back a grin. "I heard he saved your life."

Cyrus wouldn't go that far, but he knew how it must have looked. He could still feel Ava's grip on his throat, see the way her face twisted when she flung her blade in Lark's direction. She had killed half his team without batting an eye and left the rest of them stranded on a burning, sinking ship. Cyrus shivered and pulled Cornelia closer into his side. "Sorry I haven't messaged you," he said. "I've been . . . busy."

"Right." Cornelia nodded. "Busy having council room eye sex with Lark."

Cyrus almost tripped over his own feet. "What? Who said—? No."

"I'm kidding." Cornelia dug her elbow into his ribs. "But you *did* spend last night at his hospital bed."

Cyrus's face heated. "That's nothing. I'd do that for you."

"Well, yeah, I'd be offended if you didn't."

But there really was nothing between him and Lark. Cyrus had only recently stopped fantasizing about strangling him in the middle of the Opian Capitol building. Anything else would be too risky, too distracting, especially when they both had work to do. Especially when Cyrus was standing on the brink of a twisted path he couldn't turn away from.

"I suppose he's tolerable," Cyrus said, turning back to Cornelia. "But we work together. It would be unprofessional."

"Right. And Cyrus Blake wouldn't dare do anything unprofessional." Cornelia looked around, taking in the wide, sweeping corridors of the base's administrative sector. "Where are you going, anyway?"

Cyrus's stomach twisted. He'd been trying not to think about it. "We have a meeting."

"Now? About what?"

Probably so General Noth could ask him how he managed to fail so miserably, how he lost so many people on their own ship. Or maybe she knew exactly what he'd walked onto that supply ship to do, what he'd talked about, and where he was considering going even now. It didn't matter if he trusted Ava or not; Noth was lying about her involvement on Nakara. Cyrus might not know the extent of her orders, but he knew what Opian warships looked like. They had passed more than one on their way to stake out the supply ship, and if Noth was lying about sending armed forces to Nakara after Derian told her not to, that meant Shane Mannix had been telling the truth. A partial truth, maybe, but a truth nonetheless.

Before Cyrus could answer Cornelia's question, Lark limped around the corner, braced between two slim crutches. "Oh no." Cyrus stepped forward, trying to block Cornelia's view, but she had already seen.

"Oh *yes*!" She raised a hand in Lark's direction, eyes sparkling. "Hello, Larksarid, always a pleasure."

Lark's gaze flicked back and forth between them before he settled himself on a crutch. His face was pale, but despite the bandages wrapped around his thigh and what Cyrus knew was an outrageous amount of painkillers, there still wasn't a hair out of place. "Cornelia," he said. "What a surprise. Did you hear I got stabbed?"

"I told you," Cyrus muttered. "You didn't even have to ask." Then he nodded down the hall. "Come on. We're going to be late."

He wanted to get away before Cornelia embarrassed him further, but she trailed after them anyway. Cyrus was fairly certain Lark wasn't supposed to be walking yet, let alone taking meetings, and he could still see the tension in the stiff lines of Lark's mouth, the rapid rise and fall of his chest. *Ava did that.*

"Stop it," Lark said. "I can feel you worrying."

Cyrus looked away. "I didn't say anything."

"You're looking at me like I'm dying."

But he nearly had. Lark hadn't been fully conscious on the flight to the satellite base, but Cyrus remembered everything in cold, pristine detail. The clammy press of Lark's skin, the sweat gleaming in the hollow of his throat, the way his eyelids fluttered in the muted starlight.

"Hey." Lark's hand brushed Cyrus's leg as they walked. "It's fine. We're okay."

He stiffened at the touch, heat roaring in his ears as Cornelia let out a dry chuckle. "It's a miracle no one's put you two on probation yet."

"And it's a miracle no one's shot you out of the sky," Lark snapped, turning as best he could on his crutches.

There was a moment of silence where Cyrus genuinely considered throwing himself out the air lock before Cornelia grinned. "I missed you, too, Lark. Who are you meeting?" she asked. "I thought at-patrol were the only officers here this week."

"No, Noth's here." Lark grimaced. "She messaged us this

morning asking if we had time for 'a quick chat,' which obviously means we're about to get fired."

"I don't think that's what that means." Cornelia's tone was light, but Cyrus watched her expression tighten at the mention of Noth's name.

"It's my fault," he said. "If she's firing anyone, it's me."

Lark took another limping step. "You did everything you could. No one else wanted to talk them down; you tried your best. They didn't leave us much choice."

Right. Cyrus swallowed hard. That was what he was supposed to do on the supply ship—talk them down. Instead, he'd taken one look at Ava Castor and promised her help he didn't think he could give.

The three of them came to a stop next to Noth's temporary offices. It was quieter here, especially without the sound of Lark's crutches against the floor. The satellite bases weren't heavily staffed, but Cyrus thought this one was almost eerie. They'd been walking for ten minutes and had yet to encounter a single soldier. Shouldn't there be more security, especially when Opian ships were blasted out of the sky every other day?

Cornelia swayed back and forth on the balls of her feet as they waited. Cyrus could tell she was wavering on something big, and sure enough, she looked over both shoulders before lowering her voice. "Can I ask you something? As friends?"

"We're not friends," Lark said. "Let's start there."

But Cyrus knew what she meant. She meant off the record, not as soldiers. But that didn't seem like a great idea. Not here, on a base surrounded by people who would happily take Cyrus down if they knew what he'd done.

"I don't think—" he began, but Cornelia interrupted before he could finish.

"Did you notice anything strange while you were out?" she asked. "About the supply ships or . . . any other vessels we're deploying?"

Lark tapped his chin. "Actually, now that you mention it, I saw a bunch of Nakaran insurgents robbing their own supply shipment. Oh! And one of them stabbed me."

"That's not what I meant."

"Then what *do* you mean, Cornelia dearest, because I'm unable to read your mind."

"I'm just wondering why at-patrol has orders to deploy armed warships after Derian specifically told us not to," Cornelia said, glancing pointedly from Cyrus to Lark. "We're not getting Nakaran comms, either—which, to be fair, isn't that unusual; they're pretty far out—but you're the only two I know who've been up recently. Are there really warships?"

Every word was measured, deliberate, but there was something frosty behind her gaze. Cyrus wished Cornelia wasn't so good at her job. He wished she wasn't this smart. Because she was right, but he didn't have proof to give her, nothing besides the word of criminals and convicts. He glanced over his shoulder, suddenly certain they were being watched. A hundred eyes in a hundred places, waiting for him to make one fatal mistake.

Lark shrugged, oblivious to the tension rising around them. "Maybe Derian changed her orders."

"Is that a yes?"

"That's a *mind your own business*, Cornelia. Not everything concerns you. Come on." Lark braced himself on a crutch and motioned Cyrus forward. "We're already late."

Cyrus could feel Cornelia's eyes on him, burning against the back of his neck. He shook his head, avoiding her gaze as he opened the door to Noth's office. "Sorry. I didn't see anything."

He was a terrible liar; she would see through it immediately, but he didn't know what else to do. One of them had to make it through this, and the further he walked along this path, the less Cyrus thought it would be him. The door closed behind him before she could respond.

It took too long for Cyrus to quiet his nerves, to force himself back into the body of the Academy graduate as he and Lark took their seats in front of Noth's desk. He knew these offices were temporary. She was probably leaving to fly back to the capital tonight, but the emptiness unnerved him. Opia was always loud, always moving. Cyrus hadn't realized how much he craved the distraction until now.

Noth didn't look up right away. She kept sorting through paperwork as Cyrus twisted his hands in his lap. No one could have known he spoke to Ava on the supply ship or what else he had promised her. This was a routine meeting—nothing more. But when Noth finished filing her papers and looked up, Cyrus almost forgot his composure. She was smiling, an expression so familiar and warm that he immediately relaxed. Perhaps he'd made a mistake. This wasn't the face of someone who threatened and terrorized planets for personal gain or disobeyed the planetary leader's orders on a whim.

"Lieutenant Belle." Noth glanced at Lark's leg. "How do you feel?"

Cyrus thought it took most of Lark's self-control not to immediately mention that he'd been stabbed.

"Better. I can be back in the field next week. Full recovery."

That was definitely pushing it. Cyrus still didn't think Lark should be walking now, but Noth nodded. "Good. How about you, Blake? You look worried."

Cyrus bit the inside of his cheek and forced his expression to clear. He was pretty sure Noth could smell fear, and he didn't want to test that theory now. "Just glad to be back."

Pull it together. If this really was a mistake, he'd be fine. He'd forget about Ava, he'd forget about Nakara, and he'd go back to his job. He'd tell Cornelia there was nothing to worry about, and no one would know about his moment of weakness on the supply ship.

"You're both indispensable soldiers," Noth said, glancing between him and Lark. "I hope you know that. You risked your lives this week, and you did it without question."

Because that was how everything happened around here. *Without question.* It was supposed to be a compliment.

"You've also earned the right to honesty." Noth's expression turned distant the longer they sat. "And I have to admit, I'm worried. We've underestimated this insurgency group for too long, and we're still outgunned with no idea of their true numbers. I truly fear the day they come to Opia."

"You think they will?" Lark leaned forward, excitement dripping from every word.

"I hope not. The planet is well guarded, yes, but if they came here? If they attacked another satellite base? We have no idea what they want, and when I leave in three days, this place will be defenseless. The data they could make off with from this base alone . . ."

She trailed off, expression glazed, but Cyrus saw something

twitch at the corner of her mouth. He couldn't place the expression until it happened again, and then the realization landed like a stone in the pit of his stomach. *This is an act.* Cyrus knew Noth well enough to know that she didn't get worried, and if for some reason she was now, she wouldn't admit it to two junior officers. No, she wanted him and Lark to think she was vulnerable.

"What sort of data?" Lark asked. "What are they looking for?"

Noth sighed. "They're looking for a reaction, and unfortunately, they're getting it." Then she shook her head like she'd said too much. "Enough of this. I'm sorry. You're not here to worry. That's my job. I called you in here to make sure you have everything you need, especially after this week. Do you need more resources? Soldiers?"

She looked back and forth between them, and Cyrus wished more than anything he could let his suspicions go. Here he was, on the precipice of everything he had worked for, and he still couldn't shake the feeling that this entire meeting was a lie. If Noth truly wanted to give them more soldiers, she could have written the order from her desk. If she wanted to talk strategy, they could do it during the council meetings. But she had made a point of telling them she was concerned, and Cyrus was beginning to wonder if it was so that when Derian learned about the unauthorized warships she was sending to Nakara, she could play it off like a preemptive necessity instead of the invasion that it was.

Cyrus took a deep breath. "Actually, General, I heard something while we were on the supply ship."

Lark's head snapped toward him, but Cyrus kept looking at

Noth. Her eyebrows lifted ever so slightly. "Yes?"

There was a way to balance the truth here—enough to satisfy her and to turn any suspicion away from him. "Ava Castor said they were heading back to Nakara. They talked about meeting some allies in the desert near West Rama. I'd like to go after them again, and I'd like to bring them back before anyone else gets hurt."

That much was true at least.

Noth nodded. "Next week, after Lieutenant Belle is healed, you can both—"

"No." Cyrus flinched at the interruption but forced himself to continue. "They'll be long gone by then. They might be gone now, for all I know, but if I leave tonight, there's a good chance I could intercept them tomorrow. It doesn't have to be a whole team," he added when Lark started to protest. "I can get the information we need, find out exactly how many of them there are, and we can take it from there. They won't catch us off guard again."

Noth was quiet for so long Cyrus thought she'd refuse. He thought she was going to call him on every lie he'd ever told. He could feel Lark's indignation growing as the three of them sat in brittle silence until Noth inclined her chin.

"Very well," she said. "You can leave tonight. Was there anything else?"

Cyrus shook his head, exhaling as his muscles unwound for the first time in days. "No, General. Thank you."

"Of course." Noth looked from him to Lark, who was still slumped and scowling in his chair. "Don't worry, Lieutenant, you'll be back in action soon enough. We don't want to lose you." Her gaze landed on Cyrus once more, piercing and hollow all at once. "We don't want to lose either of you."

Lark was still fuming when they left the meeting half an hour later.

"*Nakara*, Blake?" he snapped before Cyrus could say anything. "You want to go back? Who's going to pull you out of the desert this time?"

Cyrus ignored him, quickening his pace as he turned a corner, but Lark followed, crutches clanging against the floor with every step. "I can't believe you're leaving me here."

"You're supposed to be resting," Cyrus reminded him.

"I don't care. I'm bored!" Lark hesitated too long before adding, "If you get a chance with them, you have to take it. You know that, right? I don't know what they want or what they think they're doing, but if they can be stopped . . ."

Cyrus didn't need him to finish. He knew what Lark meant, but hearing it out loud felt different. Another rule not meant to be broken. He could probably do whatever he wanted on Nakara, kill whoever crossed his path. If he brought Noth what she wanted, she would protect him from any consequences, regardless of what Derian said.

"They stabbed me, remember?" Lark put a hand on Cyrus's arm, his touch lingering as they stood together in the hall.

"Did they really?"

"And I don't want to attend your funeral because—"

"—because you look terrible in black," Cyrus finished. "I remember."

The corner of Lark's mouth curled as he ran a finger down the length of Cyrus's sleeve. The electricity in his veins wasn't uncomfortable, exactly, but Cyrus still thought it was distracting. It wormed its way under his skin, made him feel like he was perched on the spiral edge of a faraway galaxy. Any second they would tip into perilous, uncharted territory. It was an effort to pull away.

"I don't want to attend your funeral, either," he muttered.

It was the closest he could get to telling Lark the truth. That he didn't want anyone else to die. That he couldn't watch his friends leave and wonder who was next. And even though Cyrus knew the likely outcome was that *he* would be, he couldn't stop this momentum. He wasn't entirely convinced he was in charge of his own fate anymore. Maybe he'd dumped it in Ava Castor's hands on that supply ship. Maybe he'd signed it away long ago, for a military contract and a uniform.

Either way, Cyrus was certain this was something he couldn't stop, an inevitability crashing forward with or without him. He wanted to pull everyone out of the path of destruction before it was too late. Before they all ended up like him.

CHAPTER NINETEEN

✳ ✳ ✳

Ava woke to the sound of a radio and Jared's voice in the back of the ship.

She had fallen asleep in the cockpit, and her back ached as she pushed herself up. Jared was leaning over the hastily assembled radio, twisting a spare wire around one finger. "Strange weather we're having," he said, and there was a long pause before someone on the other line answered.

"Can't complain. Dry air is good for the crops as long as the wind stays low."

Glen. Ava had only met Shane's brother once, but he was always the one who answered. Jared had figured out how to slip a lone signal through a crack in the Opian blockade weeks ago, but even his skill had limits. The coded exchange was supposed to sound innocent to anyone listening in, but Ava thought it felt like a warning. She listened to Jared confirm the meeting location with Glen, and Shane gave a stiff nod of confirmation.

He hadn't moved from the pilot's seat, stopping the ship only for fuel as they flew across the system at a punishing speed. Tension carved the lines of his shoulders, and he didn't look at her as she stood, brushing past him into the back. The flight had been unusually rough, rattling their meager belongings with every turn. It drove Ares downstairs on the first day. Ava didn't mind his absence, but Clara had stayed away, too, shut in one of the smaller rooms and ignoring every knock. She'd only emerged that morning and had spent the last few hours sitting in the back, knees drawn against her chest. She still hadn't said a word, but when Ava sat next to her and extended a hand, Clara took it.

Because at the end of the day, they had to keep moving, even when the world cracked open and the stars blinked out. Because they weren't allowed to stop.

Shane took the north detour to avoid spilling out of hyper speed in front of the Opian ships that lurked right outside Nakaran airspace, forming a threatening army Planetary Leader Cordova had done nothing to disperse. All he'd done was slap a price on Shane's head and flash Ava's wanted picture around the planet. Like they were the problem.

Like he wasn't the one who sold them out.

Ava watched Rama's dome shimmer as they descended. Each time they came back, Ava noticed something else was missing. The diner where she'd worked. The library. The elementary school. She had spent years wishing someone would wipe this town clean, but now every loss felt like a knife in her ribs. It was one thing to want to be free of a place, but it was another to watch someone else wipe it out. She didn't breathe normally until Shane brought them down behind a dune, right outside Whitby Field. Only then did she push those thoughts away and stand. There were other things she needed to do tonight. More fate to tempt.

"You go ahead," she said as Shane opened the doors. She glanced toward Clara and added, "We'll be right there."

Shane hesitated a second too long before nodding and nudging Jared across the sand. Ares stalked in their wake, and Ava waited until the three of them vanished over the next dune before she pushed herself up. Silence fell over the desert, broken only by the sound of Clara shifting forward in her seat. "What are you doing?" she asked.

Ava wished she knew. "Don't worry about it. I'll be back."

"Absolutely not." Clara stood. "I'm coming with you."

"No, you're not."

"Am I just supposed to sit here and be your alibi?"

You're supposed to stay safe. The last thing Ava wanted was to drag Clara into another interaction with an Opian soldier, but Clara was glaring down at her now, steely-eyed and fierce against the open desert, and Ava didn't think she was going to stop.

"Fine," she sighed. "But whatever happens stays between us, understand? Not a word."

Clara's eyebrows lifted. "Who would I tell?"

Fair point. Ava lowered herself to the sand. It piled around her ankles, cool and smooth, and she was halfway to the next dune before she realized she couldn't remember the last time she'd stood on solid ground. She and Clara moved one step at a time, hands clasped together against the biting wind. Ava felt it catch in her dress, in Clara's hair, and when she looked over her shoulder, eyes stinging from the cold, the Lincoln had vanished over the horizon.

If Cyrus sold them out and sent a legion of Opian soldiers to collect her body, Ava wanted to be as far away from the others as possible. It wasn't until she ducked around the next dune, heart a rapid rhythm in her throat, that she noticed the subtle change in the air. Clara's fingers tightened around hers, forcing them to stop as the shadows slid across the sand. They came closer and closer until a lone figure emerged from the other side of the hill, and Ava exhaled when she caught the gleam of his ship in the distance—a single-pilot fighter. No Catapults. No warships.

"Ava . . ."

Clara's voice might have been the beginning of a warning, but Ava wasn't listening. She pulled out of the girl's grip and watched Cyrus stop several feet away, rubbing his arms in a vain attempt to ward off the chill.

"I'm here," he muttered. "You said if I made it, we could talk."

Ava nodded. She was currently regretting that act of mercy. What help could he possibly offer? What motive could he have? The smartest thing would be to put a knife through his ribs now, before anyone else ended up dead. She folded her arms. "Okay. Talk."

Cyrus pulled his coat tighter, like he was gathering his courage. "You killed half my team, you know. No one was supposed to die up there."

Ava didn't know what she'd expected him to lead with, but it certainly wasn't that. Next to her, Clara let out a low laugh. "Are you serious?"

"I get it," Cyrus said, continuing like she hadn't spoken. "I know she's sending dreadnoughts. I know she's not supposed to, and I'd be angry, too, but you have to stop. People are getting hurt."

The words sparked a molten fury in Ava's chest. Was this

JENNA VORIS

the real reason he came? To lecture her about the blood on her hands as if she didn't already know? "Is that all you think she's doing? You think we're upset that she sent a couple ships to hang out in our atmosphere?"

"Yes! I mean . . ." Cyrus shook his head. "No. Maybe? Sorry, what is it you want, exactly? What are you trying to do?"

"I want you to leave. All of you. I want you off this planet."

"That's not—"

"Don't tell me it's not possible." Ava advanced toward him. "The undomed cities are barely getting enough supplies to make it through the week. Opia hasn't been holding up their end of the treaty for months; why should you get to mine our deserts for nothing? You were there that night on the ship. We told you exactly what she was doing, and you still went back. Do you think you're safe here? Do you think we're friends? Let me tell you something, Lieutenant: no one cares when kids go missing in the desert. It doesn't matter whose colors they wear. You couldn't even send a distress signal from here. You're *nothing.*"

There was something pounding inside her skull now, the same drive she had felt picking up Shane's gun on the supply ship. Ava hated the Opian blockade with every fiber of her being, but she'd take advantage of the silence now if it meant no one would notice her leaving this boy bleeding and broken in the sand.

"What do you mean?" Cyrus asked. "Why couldn't I send a signal?"

Ava seized the collar of his jacket, forcing him to look at her. "You're the one blocking our airwaves; why don't you tell me."

"I . . ." Cyrus blinked, mouth falling open as his face turned the color of the sand. When he spoke again, it was with slowly dawning realization. "It's purposeful," he murmured. "Cornelia said she wasn't getting Nakaran comms, but it's not because of the distance; it's because Noth is blocking your airwaves so no one sees she's sending unauthorized warships. Because she couldn't get away with breaking your trade agreement if everyone knew." He pulled out of her grip, and Ava let him go, watching as he paced a slow circle. "That's what you want, then? You're trying to get the other planets' attention. You want to lift the blockade so they know what's happening?"

Despite everything, the question sounded genuine. Ava glanced at Clara, who was still standing with her arms folded and lip curled as she watched Cyrus waver on the sand. "We can't," she said carefully. "Trust me, we've tried. We can take on supply ships and mining vessels, but we don't have the crew to hack a dreadnought."

There it was. The limit. They could pick off Opian ships, slow them down one by one, but a permanent solution? One that could stop all this? It was just out of reach, a morning star on a distant horizon. Ava knew it was what kept Shane awake at night, searching for cracks in Opia's impenetrable armor. Maybe if they had a bigger crew. If Cordova had stood his ground instead of selling them out. If anyone had cared.

If . . .

"What if . . ." Cyrus's face twisted, moonlight catching in his dark hair. "What if there was another way to get a message out?"

Ava glanced at Clara and saw her own surprise echoed on the girl's face. "What do you mean?"

"You want the other planets to know what's happening,

right?" Cyrus rubbed his hands together as he paced. "You don't need to take out the dreadnoughts for that; you need proof of what's happening here to get leaked—shipping manifests, flight orders, anything that proves Noth's sending armed troops to Nakara against orders. And not just Derian's orders, this is against, like, a dozen interplanetary bylaws. You could send that information from anywhere, even if the blockade isn't lifted."

The words tripped over each other, like he couldn't get them out fast enough. Clara lifted her chin. "Where would we find information like that?"

There was something warring on Cyrus's face. Ava watched it rise and fall with every breath. She didn't understand how people could still look as open as he did right now, earnest and torn, like he was genuinely weighing the cost of every outcome.

"There's a satellite base halfway between Opia and Veritas," he whispered. "It's mostly for at-patrol—no one's ever there— but I know we keep digital backups on those servers. Noth goes back to the planet the day after tomorrow. She'd be gone and you would just have to get in and out. The proof—everything you need, if it's real—would be right there."

Silence settled over the sand. Ava blinked, trying to wrap her head around what he was saying, what this meant for all of them. "You just gave up your biggest bargaining chip. You know that, right?"

"Oh." Cyrus's face fell. "Okay, I didn't . . ."

Clara snorted. "Kill him now, before he goes back."

"Wait!" Cyrus held out his hands. "You would need some-one's access codes. They'd shoot your ship out of the sky without proper clearance. You'll never get close."

"Okay." Ava shrugged. "Give me the codes."

"I don't have them."

"Seriously?"

Cyrus folded his arms. "I honestly didn't think I'd make it this far."

He wasn't in the clear yet. *You can't trust the officers.* That was the first rule Ava had learned in West Rama. The second was that when one of them offered her a shiny opportunity on a silver platter, it was always too good to be true.

"What's in it for you?" she asked.

He didn't hesitate. "I want you to stop attacking our ships. I want my friends to stop getting hurt."

"That's not enough. No one risks all this for nothing."

Cyrus lifted his chin, defiance momentarily flashing across his face. "Isn't that what you want? For your families to be safe?"

"Yes, from *you*. So why should I believe a word you say when we're not even supposed to—"

"—to trust the officers," Cyrus finished. "I know. That's the first thing they tell us." His lips curled in a wry smile. "Ironic, isn't it?"

Ava stepped back, watching Cyrus's mouth go thin, like he knew he'd said too much. Nothing about this boy made sense—an Opian soldier willing to stake his career, his livelihood, his life on the word of a runaway convict. But how many times had the Nakaran army tried to recruit her throughout the years? How often had they set up booths on school grounds, waved printed brochures, and promised everyone who passed a future of wealth and glory, far away from West Rama's frigid streets?

Maybe she would have ended up like him if she'd stayed, another kid trapped by hunger and desperation and a distinct lack of options.

She couldn't trust the officers. That much was not negotiable, but maybe she could trust Cyrus. Their crew was crumbling, worn and broken, and there was nothing to show for it. Cordova sat in the capital, back turned to the outside world, and the other planets went about their lives in blissful ignorance as Opian soldiers paced the Nakaran deserts, watching West Rama blink in and out along the horizon.

"Say we listen to you." Ava watched Cyrus closely. "Say we succeed and expose what's happening here to the entire system. What do you think happens next?"

His shoulders tightened. "Noth's gone, I guess. Everyone learns what she did, she's removed, and we go back to normal."

"Normal?" It was such a wistful, naive scenario that Ava couldn't tell if he was joking. "Whose normal are we going back to? Yours?"

"Why not?" Cyrus looked from her to Clara. "Things were fine. We helped you."

Ava laughed. "Sure, with a problem *you* created. Look around, Lieutenant! You think Nakara always looked like this? You think it always felt like this? Your planet never cared about us, and I don't think a change in leadership will fix that."

"No. There are good people there. I—"

"People who take her orders and look away? People who watched this happen for years and did nothing?" Ava could feel herself trembling, on the verge of something dangerous. "Are *you* a good person?"

She was starting to miss the ship heists. At least there, when the shooting started, she knew who the enemy was. They didn't waste time trying to convince her otherwise. But when Cyrus looked up again, his face was set and determined. "I don't know," he said. "But I can get you those codes. I can help you."

Ava knew how traps were laid. Some were a stab in the back, quick and ruthless. Others were gradual, a suffocating wave. She still wasn't sure which one this was. Before she could decide what to do, Clara stepped away from her side and turned to face Cyrus.

"Rowena," she said. "We'll need to refuel before going anywhere. Meet us in Rowena tomorrow night."

"Clara." Ava grabbed her arm. "Maybe we should think about this."

When Clara looked down, half the system was caught in her eyes, shining and brilliant. She leaned in and whispered, "We can't keep dying for nothing, Ava. There has to be a point."

Ava wanted to tell her that sometimes there wasn't a point. People died all the time, caught in the wrong place at the wrong time at the end of someone else's rifle. But right now Clara looked so certain that Ava couldn't bear the thought of breaking her again.

"Fine. Rowena." Then she shoved a finger in Cyrus's chest. "And then I never want to see you again."

Cyrus snorted. "Trust me. The feeling's mutual."

He was halfway to the next dune before Ava remembered the other question burning in the back of her mind. "Hey, Lieutenant?"

She watched him flinch, like she'd shot him in the back, and when he turned, his expression was wary. "Yes?"

"Your friend. The other soldier from the ship. Is he . . . ?"

Ava trailed off, unable to finish the question.

What was one more dead Opian soldier, anyway? It was better like this, safer, but for some reason, the thought of another life gone at her hands was too much right now.

Cyrus's mouth twitched, like he wanted to smile. "He's fine."

That small motion softened his face, and for a minute, he looked like a different boy, one Ava wouldn't mind meeting in another life. She shook back her hair and straightened, watching fear cloud Cyrus's expression once more.

"Good." She flashed him a wicked smile. "Next time, I won't miss."

The others were done eating by the time Ava and Clara made their way back across the desert. Glen noticed them first, and his face broke into a hesitant smile as they crested the final dune. "There you are!" He motioned them forward with barely contained enthusiasm. "We were beginning to think you weren't coming."

Ava kept her voice light as she plucked a roll from his hand. "And miss your cooking? Never."

The bread was cold, but she finished it in two bites. It did nothing to fill the hollow ache in her chest, but it made it easier to face Shane as he shifted forward on his knees.

"What took you so long?" His gaze was sharp, edged with something Ava didn't recognize, but she shook her head and glanced pointedly at Clara. She'd let him draw his own conclusions tonight. Each one was easier than the truth. She nodded to Shane's parents as she passed, ignoring their tight-lipped scowls, and knelt next to her mother on a worn blanket. Ava hugged her longer than she meant to, and for a brief, terrifying second, hot tears clawed up the back of her throat.

"You're cold." Her mother's hands fisted in the back of her dress. "Where's your jacket?"

Ava might have laughed if she hadn't felt like she was coming undone. When she pulled back, she noticed a swirl of fresh radiation burns under her mother's sleeve. *She's worse.* Everyone was worse. She fished in her pocket until she found the bottle of pills she'd stolen off the last supply barge. "Here. You have to remember to take them."

She didn't let go of her mother's hand as Shane's family resumed the conversation, trading stories with forced, steady voices. They coped by pretending things were normal, like their son wasn't the most wanted convict in the system. Ava usually ignored them, but she was grateful for their voices now. Every whisper of wind through the brush was an Opian soldier. Each cricket was a gunshot. Any second now, Cyrus would turn around and finish the job his planet started. He'd save her for last, probably, make her watch as the consequences of her own actions turned the sand red.

"I saw your friend Sayra the other day."

Ava jumped when Glen spoke, and turned in time to catch the sandwich he threw in her direction. "Sayra?"

It felt like years since she'd heard that name.

Glen nodded. "She said to tell you the schools are low on heat lamps and if you could send the next Opian supply ship straight to her—ow!"

His mother elbowed him in the stomach, but it was too late. Shane leaned back on his hands, a smile tugging at the corner of his mouth. "Did she say anything else?"

Ava could feel the satisfaction radiating from him in waves.

They know who you are. The knowledge was always enough to lift the weight from her chest. Because people *knew* them. Not Cordova, not Opian officers. Real people from West Rama whose lives were better because of what they were doing. It wouldn't last forever. Their families would be forced to evacuate if she and Shane failed to stop the invasion. Cordova had no plan for the crisis unfolding in his lap, nowhere for these people to go, but for now, they didn't have to know their time in West Rama was limited. They could live in blissful ignorance for a little while longer, believing whatever they wanted about where Shane got his money.

Glen slid a stack of magazines in her direction as his parents pivoted the conversation away from Opia altogether. "Here. I got these for you."

"Thank you!" Ava snatched the first one, all other thought vanishing as she turned it over in her hands. "I haven't had fresh reading material in months, and Jared never lets me use his screen."

Jared rolled his eyes. "It's annoying."

"*You're* annoying." Ava nudged him with her foot and flipped open the first cover. Her heart skipped a beat as she scanned the headlines.

One Officer Dead, Another Missing.
Authorities Suspect Nakaran Rebels

WANTED FOR MURDER AND ARMED ROBBERY

Lawless Lovers Strike Again:
Shane Mannix, Girl, Kill Nakaran Captain

"Are they serious?" Ava held up the last magazine so Jared could see. "*Girl*? Who do we have to rob to get them to print my name?"

Jared shrugged. "If it makes you feel better, I'm not even mentioned."

It didn't make her feel better. Ava always knew she would make the headlines. She hadn't been sure how, exactly, but here she was, smiling from the inside of every major Nakaran publication. Shane hated it. The first time he saw her picture in a magazine, he crumpled the page in his fist and didn't speak for two days. When Ava finally cornered him in the back of the ship, all he said was, "We have to be more careful."

But Ava didn't understand why he cared, if the majority of the publications couldn't be bothered to print her name. She wanted more. Two months ago, the idea of blasting a foreign vessel out of the sky had been wild and impossible, but now Ava thought everything about them was impossible. A make-shift crew with jagged edges. A boy who could topple empires. And now an Opian soldier with an outstretched hand and a way forward.

This was the furthest from ordinary she'd ever been, and Ava had no intention of going back until they printed her name on every cover in the system.

By the time Shane stood, brushing the sand from his pants, she was ready to leave. Ava watched him slip his father another bag of coins. "See you next time," he said with the kind of certainty only Shane Mannix could have. Then he patted his mother's shoulder before turning his back entirely.

"Make sure she takes her medicine," Ava whispered to Glen,

watching her own mother retreat across the sand.

"Of course." Glen nodded toward Shane. "And keep an eye on him."

That was how they said goodbye, with pacts and promises Ava was never sure how to keep. She always thought Glen knew more than he was letting on, like somewhere deep down he understood that they wouldn't be doing these kinds of jobs if it wasn't completely necessary. But one of these days, a good-bye like this would be their last. Ava wondered if she would know it when it came. She wondered if Henry had known.

They walked back to the ship in silence, Ares leading the way and Clara trailing behind. Shane fell into step beside her as they moved. His feet were light on the sand, but she felt that wall again, heavy and impenetrable steel. Sometimes, she wondered if she'd ever seen Shane without it.

"We need more," he muttered.

Ava looked up. "What?"

"More. You heard what Glen said—people know us. They know what we're doing."

Moonlight caught in his hair as they walked, spreading across his skin, and Ava thought steel wasn't the right word for what Shane was. Tonight he was marble, solid and cold and so beautiful it hurt to look at.

"We could hit something tonight." His eyes were unfocused. "I know we didn't plan it, but I could find another ship. They have so many ships."

Ava shook her head. "When's the last time you slept?"

"I'm fine."

"That's not what I asked."

They came to a stop a few feet from the Lincoln, and for the first time, Ava noticed how truly exhausted he looked. It wasn't just the circles under his eyes; those had never really gone away. It was the way his shoulders curled inward, how every word sounded a breath away from breaking.

If Shane wanted more, she could give it to him. But the only plan she had was signed and stamped with the enemy's golden seal. She lifted a hand, turning Shane's face toward her. "You need sleep."

His lips paled as he pressed them together. "It's fine."

"It's not. What—?"

"I said it's *fine*, Ava." He pulled out of her grip. "Look around. You think I have time for that? We are one missed ship away from an all-out war. There are people waiting for the supplies we blew out of the air. I can't just stop."

Because that was their curse. Always moving but never forward. Always running but never fast enough. They needed a permanent solution.

You have one.

Ava didn't really trust Cyrus. He was a means to an end, a subtle manipulation tactic, but if there was even a chance he was telling the truth, didn't she owe it to this crew to try? Didn't she owe it to Shane? No more warships hovering overhead, no more aching, desperate people held hostage on their own planet. *One more job.* And if they played this right, she'd never have to set foot in West Rama again.

"You're in luck." Ava gripped Shane's arm, and this time, she didn't let him pull away. "I might have a plan."

CHAPTER TWENTY

✳ ✳ ✳

"Okay, explain it to me again."

Shane was sitting with Ava and Jared on the floor of the cockpit, sandwiched between the seats so the dull echo of desert wind masked every word. He had brought the ship behind a pair of dunes, too far out for any patrol to venture through. With Clara down below and Ares shut away in the back, it was almost like old times. The thought of a new mission used to feel like lightning, but Shane could hardly see through the haze of exhaustion. His body hurt, sharp pains and steady aches that never really stopped, and when Ava took a deep breath and started explaining the plan again, he couldn't shake the threads of apprehension tightening around his chest.

"We've been on the defensive for months, right?" Ava looked from him to Jared. "Blowing up Opian ships, kidnapping officers, collapsing mines. It's good, but we've been thinking short term. Destroy the mining equipment before it reaches the surface, make sure West Rama has enough to eat, but that won't work forever. We knew that when we started."

Shane nodded. He was supposed to have figured out a way to hack the Opian dreadnoughts by now, to send distress signals to the other planets, to make everything stop.

"So you found it?" he asked, unable to keep the bitterness

from his voice entirely. "A way to take down the blockade?"

"Not exactly." Ava shifted close enough for Shane to feel the soft press of her knee against his thigh. "The problem is no one knows that Opia broke our treaty, and no one knows they're coming for us. Cordova's useless, we can't get a signal out, and they're not exactly broadcasting their war crimes. But if the other planets *did* know, if they saw the fleets in our atmosphere, the warships, the soldiers . . ." Something hardened behind her eyes. "That's evidence they can't ignore."

"Right." Jared tapped a fingernail against his screen. "If Opia's powerful enough to do it to us, they could do it to the other planets. No one would want to risk being the next target. But you want to go where?"

"An Opian satellite base." Ava's expression didn't change, but Shane thought something about it felt rehearsed. "We'd need hard evidence—files, flight logs, manifests. If we hit the base, we can hook what we find back into their comm towers and send it directly to any Nakaran allies we can reach."

Jared nodded. "Then the other planetary leaders would have to ask why they haven't heard from Cordova in months. And if they looked into that, they'd find the warships . . ."

"And there's our army," Ava finished triumphantly. "They can fight the real battles, I don't care. We just need someone to hear us."

The three of them sat in silence for a moment, and Shane let the plan work its way through his mind. It slipped every time he tried to get a closer look, silk through his fingers.

"Military comm towers are always good," Jared said. His screen cast a soft blue glow across the bottom half of his face.

"I could download what we find to the servers directly. But how long would I have? Government comms are shit to hack."

"Jared!" Ava whacked his knee. "Language!"

"Are you serious?" Jared's mouth dropped open. "I've watched you literally murder people, but I can't say *shit*?"

"You can murder someone when you turn sixteen."

"That's not what I meant!" Jared shuddered, like the thought alone was too much. "Fine. Government servers are *complicated*. How much time would I have?"

Ava's mouth twitched. "Don't worry about it. I'll get us the clearance."

"Really?" Jared's eyes narrowed. "How?"

Shane was wondering the same thing. The idea was good, flashy in a way that reminded him of their old heists. But he couldn't figure out where Ava got it or why she was so confident it would work.

"Look," she said. "I think this is our best option. If you have another suggestion, fine, but we *have* to try something different. We don't have the time."

They really didn't. Even now Shane could feel it dripping through his fingers, pooling in the cracks of the floor. One month from now, it would run out. He imagined turning out of the jump point and finding Nakara already charred and cracked below his feet, the consequences of his failure written out for everyone to see. Ava was right. They had been thinking small for too long. If they were going to do something, it had to be now.

"What's the timeline?" Shane asked. "What do we need?"

Ava glanced at Jared. "I can get us clearance tomorrow night. If

I gave you access codes, could you work on the servers remotely until we land?"

Jared shrugged. "Depends on how complicated they are. And how are you getting—?"

"Don't worry about it."

Ava's voice was a clear dismissal. Jared sighed and pushed himself to his feet. "Fine. Wake me up when we land, and I'll pull the blueprints."

He stifled a yawn as he disappeared into the back of the ship, and Shane heard him trip down the stairs two separate times before reaching the bottom level. Ava watched him go with equal parts amusement and exasperation. "We probably shouldn't let him murder anyone, right?" she asked. "There should be some boundaries?"

Shane shrugged. "We didn't have boundaries."

"Of course. And we're shining examples of good behavior."

Shane wanted to smile in return, but it wouldn't come. It had been a while since they had sat alone like this. He always forgot how little room there was for error next to Ava. He dragged a hand over his face. The nightmares always came in the dark, ghostly figures with cold hands. Sometimes he was back on Chess with the cruel guards and faceless droids. Sometimes, he was standing alone in the desert with the brittle skeleton of a ruined ship.

Henry would be there tonight, if he closed his eyes.

"Shane." Ava slid across the floor, closing the space between them. "Breathe."

He hadn't realized he wasn't. But it always happened like this—a simple thought turned sharp and deadly, the past wrapped around him like a fist. No warning and no release.

Ava slipped a hand under his jacket, warm and steady on the small of his back, and Shane forced himself to open his eyes. "I'm fine."

How many times would he say it before the words stopped biting his tongue? It was habit now, an instinctive response.

Ava nodded and ran her fingers down his back. "Okay."

Shane didn't mean to lean into the touch. He couldn't remember the last time he had stopped or slept, but he wanted to do both now. He always felt the wanting as a dull ache, steady and low in the pit of his stomach. For her. For everything. Maybe he couldn't have both.

He turned his face into the curve of Ava's shoulder, enough to block out the light, and for a second, Shane let himself imagine how it would feel to live without the constant terror that someone was coming for her. All the things they could be with this planet behind them. When he looked up again, Ava's face was closer than he expected, barely a breath away. *Invincible.* He wanted to feel like that again.

Shane leaned toward her and Ava went still. She felt like glass, a statue frozen in the desert, but when his lips ghosted against the underside of her jaw, her skin was warm. She exhaled, somewhere between a gasp and a sigh, and the sound of it set his blood on fire. Shane wanted to chase it down her throat, coax it back into the open so he could hear it again. So he could memorize it now, before everything vanished into the dark. Then her thumb skimmed along the edge of his rib cage, over healing wounds and raised scar tissue Shane had forgotten about. He stiffened.

Would Ava still touch him like this if she knew every twisted thing those guards had done to him on Chess? If she knew everything he did to survive, the bodies he saw when he closed his eyes?

Shane scrambled back, out of her grip, until he hit the opposite wall. "It's late." He could barely get the words out. "I should go."

His face was too hot, but the places Ava touched felt like ice. The empty space between them crackled, and when she spoke, her voice was a hoarse whisper. "You could stay."

Shane couldn't unravel her expression. He didn't know where to begin. "I don't think that's a good idea."

Ava's face darkened and she pushed herself to her feet. "Of course not."

"Wait." Shane rose up on his knees. "That's not—"

"Is it me, Shane?" Ava's hands twisted in her skirt, white-knuckled against the crimson fabric. "Did I do something wrong?"

Shane shook his head, voice caught in his chest. He didn't know how to tell her it was him. That he was terrible and selfish for wanting her this way. That he couldn't breathe when she was around, but the thought of her leaving was unspeakably worse. That he would tear the sky open if she wanted. He would run this ship into the ground for her, and that scared him more than any army.

"Then what?" she asked. "What is it, because I want . . ."

She trailed off and Shane tensed. Here it was. Ava was going to lay everything out in the open, finally confess that whatever they had between them had grown too deep and tangled to ignore. But instead she shook her head and stepped out of the cockpit entirely.

"Never mind. I'm sorry."

Shane reached for her again, but she was too far. "Ava—"

"You should get some sleep." It was too dark to make out her expression, but Shane still felt it burned into the back of his mind. "We have a lot of work to do."

And then she left him kneeling on the floor, with nothing but the open sky for company.

Shane woke to a cool hand on his shoulder and the first shafts of dim morning light. For a terrifying moment, he couldn't remember where he was. He lurched forward, instinctively feeling for his gun.

"Whoa!" Jared tripped back against the wall. "It's me! Sorry!"

Shane gritted his teeth and hauled himself into the front seat as his pulse steadied. He felt like he was still wading through the dark, pulling off sleep as he went. "Don't do that," he muttered. "I could have shot you."

"Sorry!" Jared said again. "I'm sorry. But you wanted to move before midday, right?"

Shane noticed then how much the sky had lightened, the distant sun reflecting off the sand. They had let him sleep all morning. *Irresponsible.* He stood and brushed past Jared without another word. Clara sat in the back, picking through leftovers while Ares stabbed at a sandwich with a little too much force. Ava was nowhere to be seen. That was fine; Shane didn't want to think about their last conversation ever again. He lowered the exit ramp and descended into the sand.

Now that he was awake, Shane could see last night's plan in stunning clarity—how it would work, how they would move. He stretched his arms above his head as the pieces slid into place one by one. It had been a while since he felt like the Shane Mannix from the headlines, the icy convict, ruthless and clever.

Maybe he'd never truly feel like that again, but right now, he wanted to try.

"Get out here!" Shane slapped a hand against the side of the Lincoln. "We have a new job."

It took several minutes for the others to file down the ramp. Ares glowered from the shadows, arms crossed over his leather jacket as Jared and Clara emerged together. Ava was last, and Shane felt his confidence falter at the sight of her. Were they safer here in the light of day? Then she looked at him, and her brows lifted.

"You know how we're getting into Opian airspace."

It wasn't a question. This planet could crack under their feet, force them to opposite sides of a gaping chasm, and she'd still be able to read him through the dark.

Ares whipped around before Shane could speak. "I'm sorry, getting *where*?"

Shane ignored him. He turned, pacing a slow circle as he felt the anticipation build. "We have a new job," he repeated, letting some of his old, casual swagger creep back in. "There's a satellite base not far from here. It's small but a major Opian supply hub."

That last part was a lie, but he didn't care. Let Ares think they were walking into a jackpot bigger than anything they had scored so far. Shane knew he didn't care about Nakara, but he cared about money.

Still, Ares's expression didn't change. "*You're* going to rob an Opian base?"

"Of course." Shane ignored the challenge laced between the words. "That's kind of our thing, Ares."

"It's not what I signed up for."

"Too bad. It's a solid lead, a good job, and Ava's getting us the clearance we need to—"

"She is?" Ares let out an incredulous laugh. "How?"

Ava rolled her eyes. "Don't act so surprised. This ship would literally combust without me."

"I'm not risking my life on an Opian base." Ares glared from her to Shane, shadows cutting deep lines down his face. "Henry is *dead* because of you, and I don't particularly want to join him."

Shane heard Clara draw in a shaky breath over his shoulder and felt his composure slip, just for a second. He knew the attack on the supply ship had rattled them all, but Ares's anger felt calculated, like he'd spent the last two months waiting to set it loose.

"Henry knew the risks of the job he signed up for," Shane said, willing his voice to steady. "So did you."

Ares's hands curled. "You're not qualified for this. You never were, and if you had any sense, you'd hand this ship to someone who is."

Ava laughed, the sound high and cold as the desert wind. "Someone like you? Come on, Ares, we all want the same thing."

"Really?" Ares turned, and Shane tensed as he backed Ava against the side of the ship. "I think we want very different things from him."

Ava's jaw tightened, but she didn't look away. For once, Shane wished she would. "Did you think we'd get rich right away?" she snapped. "That we'd be done by the new year? If you don't like it, you can leave."

"Don't." Ares's voice was a low warning. "I don't take orders from you."

"And I don't care if your feelings are hurt because you weren't included in one planning session! *Stars*, Ares, this is why everyone hates you."

Ares moved so quickly Shane almost didn't see it. One second he was standing in the shadows and the next he'd grabbed Ava's wrist with one hand, the other lingering on his weapon as he leaned in. His voice lowered until it was nothing more than a gravelly whisper.

"You think you're safe with him?"

Shane froze at the thinly veiled threat. He watched Ava's free hand twitch, like she was debating which part of him she was going to break first. "Let go of me."

Ares leaned closer. "You don't tell me what to do. No one does. You—"

Ava ducked under his outstretched arm and drove her elbow into the hollow of his throat. Ares stumbled back, gasping, and Ava yanked herself from his grip. She rubbed at her wrist with her other hand, like she was trying to scrub all traces of him from her skin. "Get out," she hissed. "Now. You're done here."

Ares let out a choked laugh, hand still lingering at his throat, but his expression faltered when he looked at Shane. "I'm not leaving?"

It sounded like a question. Shane clicked the safety off his gun. He remembered thinking that he would run his ship into the ground if Ava asked him to. Now he realized it was more than that. He'd kill Ares right here if she wanted, job or no job. He'd add another face to the nightmare lineup, another body to his rapidly growing list. When he caught Ares's eye again, Shane thought he looked genuinely worried for the first time.

"No." Ares shook his head. "You just lost Henry; you can't do another job without me, you know that."

"But I thought you weren't risking your life on an Opian base." Shane didn't raise his voice. He didn't have to. "I thought I was leading you to ruin. Don't," he added as Ares reached for his own weapon. "Do you want him gone, Ava?"

Ava's eyes were bright, and Shane saw the corner of her mouth lift as she watched them. He knew that look—the thrill of holding someone else's life, knowing how fragile it truly was. It never got old. She nodded, and Shane felt something like pride spread through his chest. This was why he had hired her. This was why he couldn't let her go. Because he had never really been the dangerous one on this ship.

But Ares was right about one thing—the heist on the Opian base would require them all.

Shane flipped his weapon from hand to hand, watching Ares flinch each time it moved. He was very aware of the others—Clara standing with one arm looped protectively around Ava's waist, Jared slowly inching under the ship with his tool bag clutched to his chest.

"I'll give you a choice," Shane said, reveling in Ares's obvious discomfort. It had been a while since he'd felt this powerful. "I can leave you here, if you want. You'd be home, free of us forever."

Alone and unarmed in a Nakaran desert was as good as a death sentence, and Shane let the reality of that option sink in before continuing. "Or you can get back on the ship and do the job you signed up for. I'll even let you take your share and leave afterward, if you want." He took another step forward. "But if you touch her again," Shane whispered, pressing the barrel of his weapon between Ares's ribs. "If you so much as look at her, I will let her break every bone in your body before dumping you out the air lock. Do you understand?"

It wasn't a choice, not really, but Shane had learned that from the Opian general. Offer your enemy two paths. Let them pick. Let them believe it was their idea.

Ares was so still, Shane wasn't sure if he was still breathing. He tightened his grip on the weapon, pushing harder until Ares's face contorted. "Fine," he grunted. "I'll do it. But then it's over for you, Mannix. We're done."

Just what he wanted. Shane returned his weapon to his belt, feeling the familiar weight settle at his side. "Okay," he said. "Let's go."

CHAPTER TWENTY-ONE

***

Cyrus was good at a lot of things, but breaking and entering, it turned out, was not one of them.

Not that walking into his own office on his own planet was technically considered breaking and entering, but something about sneaking through the halls of the Opian Capitol building felt wrong. When had he started thinking of this place as something to fear?

Not fear, Cyrus thought as he tapped his arm against the locks and pushed the door open. He was just being cautious. What was the worst thing Ava could do with the access codes, really? If she was right, she'd have the information necessary to expose General Noth's actions on Nakara. If she was wrong, there'd be nothing to find. He would learn the truth either way. Why did it matter how? He was simply pursuing every possibility before passing judgment, just like the Academy taught him.

They had also taught him to obey his commanding officers without question, to nod and salute and put his planet first, but Cyrus wasn't going to think about that now.

If he did, he'd never leave these rooms again.

He crossed the floor, sidestepped Lark's messy but blessedly empty desk, and tore open his own top drawer, riffling through old files and stacks of forgotten paperwork. *Where is it?* He knew the folder he wanted was here somewhere. It was the entire reason he'd come back. He remembered taking it from Lark the same day Noth handed it over.

"You're going to lose it," Cyrus had said, tucking the file into his bag. "Your desk is like a black hole."

Lark had wrinkled his nose. "No, it's not, I know where everything is."

"Really? You found the book I lent you?"

"Okay, I know where *almost* everything is."

But Lark let him keep it in the end. Which meant it had to be here *somewhere*.

Cyrus opened another drawer, wincing as his elbow knocked against the wall. The sound was too loud, too suspicious when his office was supposed to be empty. *You're not suspicious.*

There was absolutely nothing suspicious about returning several days early from a foreign surveillance mission, stashing his Falcon at the far end of the aircraft hangar, and sneaking up the Capitol's back stairway in the middle of a workday. There was nothing suspicious about conspiring with the very people he'd been chasing for months.

Cyrus's fingers brushed something smooth in the back of his drawer. *There.* He spread the contents of the file across his desk, flipping through page after page as his pulse rattled. It was here somewhere. He remembered seeing it on his initial read-through, remembered asking Lark if it was a mistake. His finger skimmed across lines of neatly printed text. He didn't know what he'd do if this didn't work. He didn't even have an excuse for being back on Opia, and he needed to leave within the hour if he was going to make it back to meet Ava. Her trust felt precarious, a razor-thin blade he'd find lodged between his ribs if he weren't careful.

Why do you want it?

Cyrus didn't know, not after the number of times she'd tried to kill him, not with the amount of Opian soldiers she'd gunned down. He was fairly certain she'd slit his throat next time she saw him, codes or not, and dump his body in a frosty Nakaran alley. It was what his commanding officers would tell him to do to her. But something was wrong. He knew that. And if he ignored it, Cyrus had a feeling he'd become exactly the kind of officer Ava Castor put her knife through.

Cyrus wiped his palms on his shirt and turned another page. This was another thing no one taught at the Academy. No one told him what to do when the enemy looked at him with cold understanding and offered a truce instead of a fight. No one told him where to go when the people he was supposed to serve kept brutal secrets buried in the dark.

A lone pair of footsteps passed too close to the door and Cyrus quickened his pace, tearing through page after page until he found it. There, at the bottom of the second to last piece of paper, stamped beneath General Noth's signature. A long string of letters and numbers.

"This feels classified, right?" Cyrus had asked the first time he saw it, holding the file up so Lark could see. "Should we give it back?"

Lark had shrugged. "I don't think it matters; it's not like we're using them."

Of course not. Cyrus folded the page as many times as he

could and tucked it inside his boot. *Because Cyrus Blake wouldn't dare do anything unprofessional.*

He'd been here long enough for sweat to soak through the collar of his shirt. Sooner or later someone would notice his Falcon. Cyrus closed the file, shoved it back in his drawer, and gave his office one last glance before walking back the way he'd come, pulse hammering with every step. He ducked outside, closing the door as quietly as he could behind him. Perfect. In and out before anyone noticed. This was—

"Cyrus?"

He whirled, hitting the wall so hard the doorknob rattled. Cornelia stood a few feet away, watching him with a mix of apprehension and curiosity. Her uniform was pressed and polished, hair smoothed into a tight braid under her cap. She must have flown in from the satellite base that morning to attend some meeting Cyrus had been excused from. It was probably important, because she never wore the hat unless she had to.

Cyrus ran a hand down the front of his own flight suit as his pulse slowed. It was dirty, damp from sweat and desert ice. Why hadn't he changed? In the tall, arching halls of the Capitol, he stood out worse than he did on Nakara. "Cornelia," he gasped. "What are you doing here?"

"Me?" One of her eyebrows lifted. "Aren't you supposed to be on some secret mission?"

Cyrus nodded. "I am."

"You're very much not."

"No, I mean . . ." He shook his head, easing himself away from the office door. "I mean I was. I am. I'm going back. I just stopped to grab some paperwork."

Cornelia's brows drifted higher, and Cyrus realized that excuse only worked if he had thought to bring paperwork with him. He tucked his empty hands behind his back. Usually he'd be thrilled to see her, but usually, he didn't have General Noth's access codes tucked in his boot. Cornelia was already suspicious of the dreadnoughts and flight orders. If she found out what Cyrus was planning to do, she'd want to help, and that was something he absolutely couldn't allow.

"Great to see you," he said, taking a casual step down the hall. "Really, but I'm heading back out. Now. Sorry. I have to—"

Cornelia caught his arm. "What's wrong?"

Cyrus almost laughed. Where would he even start? With the failed chase through the Nakaran capital all those months ago? Or should he skip right to the high treason? "Nothing! Just tired. About to do another space flight. You know how they are."

Cornelia's grip tightened. Her nails were blue today, digging into his arm as she glanced up and down the hall. Then she nodded toward his office. "Is anyone in there?" When Cyrus shook his head, she shoved him back. "Good. Open it."

It took him too long to fumble with the locks. Cyrus knew he was running out of time. He needed to get back to the hangar, but he couldn't see a way out that didn't lead to more questions he couldn't answer. "What?" he asked, closing the door behind them. "Did you want a tour?"

"No." Cornelia tossed her cap onto his desk. Then she exhaled and unbuttoned her jacket, letting it hang open as she tipped her head back against the wall. "Sorry, I need a minute."

For the first time, Cyrus noticed the sharp set of her mouth, the exhaustion lining her edges. "Are you okay?"

"I had a meeting with my supervisor today," Cornelia said as she loosened her tie. It was another minute before she added, "They kicked me off the security council."

"I . . ." Cyrus blinked. "Wait, *what?*"

For a second, he forgot all about Nakara and the codes tucked in his boot. That wasn't possible. Cornelia didn't get demoted; she was good at her job. She was strong-willed and confident and . . .

And she questioned Noth in front of Derian. She talked about warships in the open halls of the satellite base.

Cyrus looked down as the realization burned through him. Why did this feel like his fault, too?

"They didn't tell me who wanted me gone, but it was clearly an order they couldn't refuse." Cornelia's eyes fluttered shut as her shoulders drooped. "I know it's because of that meeting where I said we shouldn't send people to Chess for stealing ships. I know it's because Noth thinks I'm going to tell Derian she's sending illegal dreadnoughts to Nakara."

Cyrus flexed his toes, feeling for the folded paper. They were sliding too quickly toward a place they couldn't come back from. That was *his* risk, *his* knowledge to bear. "I'm sure it's nothing," he said. "It's not like they fired you. It was probably a misunderstanding."

"But I got *demoted.*" Cornelia folded her arms. "I'm the best pilot they have. You don't think it's a little suspicious?"

"I think you need to be careful. You can't say things like that in public and not expect people to have questions."

"Why not? Why not, if they're true?"

Because there are rules. Because even though Noth didn't

follow them, Cyrus knew the rest of them were expected to. Because this was about power, and power always came at the expense of people like them.

"Because it's not worth it."

Cornelia's face twisted, somewhere between exasperation and fury. "And where have you been? You never told me where you were going."

The change in subject caught Cyrus off guard. It sounded accusatory. "It doesn't matter."

"Since when do you keep things from me?"

"Since when do you get demoted?"

Cornelia's expression hardened, and Cyrus wished more than anything he knew how to explain. He just needed to survive the next few days. That was it. Then the threat would be gone. Cornelia would be rightfully outraged when he told her the truth, but they'd be fine. They were always fine.

"I'm doing surveillance of the outer planets," he said. One slip of truth to hold them together until he was done, but Cornelia's head shot up.

"You're going to Nakara?"

Cyrus hadn't mentioned Nakara, but his face must have given it away. "Only for surveillance."

"So you *have* seen the warships." Cornelia stepped forward, chin tilted so she could still look him in the eye. "You know I'm not making that up. Derian told us invading Nakara wasn't an option, but Noth's doing it anyway. Who do you think benefits from a war like that? Who do you think gets rich from it?"

Cyrus felt the desert chill on the back of his neck. Those were the same dangerous thoughts that had gotten Cornelia shut out in the first place. She didn't know about the secret meetings in Cordova's office or the shredded treaties left in their wake. She thought this was a power play, an act of war taken simply because they could. Because no one was stopping them. Maybe that was all it was, in the end.

But Cornelia was never supposed to pay for his mistakes. If this plan shattered beneath him, Cyrus wanted to be the one left with the consequences.

"I'm not the only one who sees those orders, you know," she whispered. "A lot of us do, but no one questions it because it's *General Noth* and she's in charge. It makes me feel crazy. Tell me." She grabbed his hand, nails digging into the skin around his wrist. "Tell me I'm not crazy, Cyrus. Please."

The truth lodged in his throat. Cyrus could hardly swallow over the aching lump. "It's okay," he managed. It wasn't an answer. "It's fine. We'll figure it out when I get back. We'll . . . I don't know. But you'll be fine. I promise."

Cornelia looked down, and for a moment it was so quiet, Cyrus could hear every beat of his traitorous heart. He traced a thumb over the freckles on the back of her hand, over and over. *She'll understand.* When this was done and he sat her down, Cornelia would understand exactly why it had to happen this way, why this information could never go further than him. Cyrus was so focused on his own breathing that he almost missed what she said next.

"We could leave."

It was a dark whisper. When Cornelia looked up at him through her eyelashes, Cyrus felt the world tip under his boots. "What?"

"We could leave," she repeated. "Right now. We could get in a ship and go. It would just be us, like how it used to be on the roof, remember? Something spectacular? No secret missions, no security council."

"Cornelia . . ." Cyrus shook his head. He couldn't leave, not with everything hanging so precariously. He had made too many promises, started down too many paths. He couldn't leave Lark on a planet rotting from the inside out. He couldn't leave Ava stranded in the desert. He couldn't leave his friends to fight a war they had no right to win. "Cornelia, you can't say that."

Her jaw tightened. "I could if we left! What's stopping us? Honor? Loyalty? Dedication?" She ripped her badge from her jacket and tossed it aside. Cyrus watched it clatter to the floor, glowing in the dim light seeping in from under the door.

"Where would you go?" he asked. "Port City? There's nothing for us there."

"There's nothing for us here, either! I don't think there ever was. I think someone told us the Academy was a way out one day and we believed them."

"Maybe, but there are still things happening here you don't understand!"

Cyrus regretted it the instant the words were out of his mouth. It was too close to the truth, too hard to explain. He watched Cornelia's eyes widen. She tore her hand from his.

"You did know," she whispered. "You knew about the warships this whole time, and you lied to me. What, were you going to let it happen? Were you going to *help* her?" Her voice cracked on the last word.

"No!" Cyrus shook his head. "Cornelia, I—"

"Did you *know*?"

She was close enough for Cyrus to see the color staining her cheeks as she glared up at him. This was it, he realized. A way to keep her out of this a little while longer, a way to keep her safe. He inhaled and forced himself to meet her gaze.

"Yes," he said. "I knew."

Cornelia's chin trembled as she looked away, and Cyrus realized, with a terrible aching jolt, that she was trying not to cry. She'd never hidden her tears from him before; there had never been a reason to. *It's not real,* Cyrus thought desperately. *It's almost over. Trust me.*

"So you're going back to Nakara now?" Her voice was a cold bite. "You're going to fly by all those warships and pretend we have jurisdiction even though you know it's wrong."

"It's not like that. I can't—"

"Can't or won't?"

She had every right to hate him, Cyrus knew that, but the dismissal still stung. They were beyond absolutes, drifting alone in uncharted waters. "I'm sorry," he whispered. "But I really can't."

By the time he looked up again, Cornelia had sealed herself behind something solid and impenetrable. In that moment, she was a mess of contradictions, familiar and foreign all at once. His best friend. A stranger. A soldier. The girl perched on the rooftops. She lingered in the middle of his room a second longer, like she was waiting for something, and Cyrus realized too late she was waiting for him.

We could go. We could go tonight.

But he didn't move. Out of the corner of his eye, he watched her pick up her hat and tuck it under one arm. Then the door swung closed behind her, and Cyrus was alone in his office with stolen paperwork tucked in his shoe and the sinking feeling he'd just made a horrible mistake.

CHAPTER TWENTY-TWO⊙

✳ ✳ ✳

The first time they passed an Opian Falcon, Ava thought she'd imagined it. It wasn't until they flew over three more and an army of uniformed officers that it fully registered. *Opian soldiers patrolling an undomed Nakaran town.*

"Okay." Jared pressed a hand to the window as he scanned the street below. "This could be a problem."

Ava had seen the makeshift army camps in the desert as they flew, the lone Opian vehicle patrolling the sky, but this felt different. A targeted attack designed for intimidation.

Clara leaned over her shoulder, lowering her voice so only Ava could hear. "You think they're looking for us?"

Ava knew immediately what she meant. *He betrayed you.* Cyrus had sold them out. She shrugged, absentmindedly rubbing the rectangular pendant of her necklace with two fingers as they dipped lower. That was the most likely option, one she would pay dearly for if it turned out to be true, but she thought the real answer was simpler. These soldiers were here because they could be. Because Cordova had given up on the undomed cities months ago, so focused on protecting his assets that he forgot how many lives were going to be lost in the balance. Soon, the whole planet would look like this.

Ava shivered as Shane brought their ship down in a narrow side street, out of sight from the main road. She could hear the sound of boots against pavement from here, an unsteady rhythm that caught in her chest. *This was a bad idea.*

"Well, we're here now." Shane released the landing gear, and Ava watched him force a smile through layers of unease. "It'll make more of a scene if we leave. Ava, you're in charge of supplies. Jared and I will switch ships and refuel. Not you," Shane added as Ares pushed himself to his feet. "You're not going anywhere."

Ares had been quiet since his outburst in the desert, but Ava felt the earlier tension crawl across the walls as he stood. He was a full head taller than Shane, broad-shouldered and massive. With both of them outlined in the dim light of the street, Shane should have looked unmatched. But there had always been a wild energy under his skin that reminded Ava of a spring wound too tight, a safety right before someone flicked it off.

Shane let his hand drift toward the weapon at his side, a casual reminder of earlier, and Ares scowled. "Whatever."

He sat, propping his dirty boots against the window, and Ava turned, watching Shane duck out of the ship. "Give me a minute," she muttered, resting a hand on Clara's arm. "I'll be right back."

Clara's fingers tightened over hers, and when Ava looked up, her eyes were soft, the deep black of a desert night. "Be careful."

Ava nodded once and descended toward the sand-slicked cobblestones. An icy blast of wind cut through the alley, and she shivered, hugging her arms around herself as she walked. Once, so many years ago Ava couldn't quite grasp the memory, her mother had told her repeating harmful patterns was a sign of madness. This was after the fourth time Ava made herself sick off stolen chocolates. She always promised not to, swore up and down she was done until the next time the convenience store cashier looked away.

Maybe that was what this was, Ava thought as she ducked under the ship. *Madness.* Because here she was, chasing the same elusive thing she knew would hurt them both in the end.

"You should go." Shane's voice came from somewhere to her left, and Ava squinted until he came into focus, halfway inside the engine panel. "We don't have time to waste."

Ava nodded, watching what she could see of his outline through the shadows. She remembered him in the desert, ruthless and cold. She remembered the brush of his lips against her neck, remembered him on his knees before her in the dark. *Madness.*

"Would you have killed him?" she asked. "Ares, I mean?"

It wasn't the question she wanted to ask, but Shane's answer was quick. "No." He gave something inside the engine one final twist and a mess of wires fell into his outstretched hand. *"You would have killed him."*

Ava almost smiled. "You know you can't let him go, right? Not after everything he's seen?"

"I know."

Maybe Shane never intended to let Ares leave the satellite base alive. And maybe one day Ava would understand how the boy who offered to kill for her was the same as the one standing in front of her now, refusing to meet her gaze.

"The codes." Shane's fingers tapped an erratic beat against the side of his leg. "How are you getting them?"

Ava shook her head. "Don't worry about it."

The same answer she'd given last night. She would tell him eventually, after this job was done and they were safe. She would tell him when they were halfway to a new system, basking in the glow of another impossible success, because that was what he would do. Shane would never put her before a mission. He would never risk a lead for something as trivial and unimportant as her feelings.

One of his hands twitched at his side, like he couldn't decide if he wanted to reach for her or his weapon. Then he slung the cables over one shoulder and nudged the engine panel back into place. "Be back in an hour."

There was that wall again, so icy and solid Ava still didn't know where to start. She stepped back, out from the sheltering curve of the ship. "All right," she said. "An hour."

And then it was easier not to look back.

CHAPTER TWENTY-THREE

✳ ✳ ✳

Cyrus felt the pull of Nakara's dusty surface before he even reentered the airspace.

He flipped on the radio as he descended, sinking into the sudden electric gravity urging him down, away from the memory of Cornelia's wide-eyed accusatory glare. He couldn't stop seeing her—the constellation of freckles across her cheeks, the bright hair coming loose from her braid, the sharp set of her jaw. *We could go tonight.*

The desperate whisper of two kids on a smoggy roof who had no way of knowing which way the world would turn.

Maybe Ava Castor had felt like that once. Maybe someone had offered her a way out, a shiny deal and an empty promise. For Cyrus it had been the sleek pamphlets the army passed around the Port City piers—free housing, free tuition, the chance to be a hero. For a family drowning under never-ending piles of medical bills, it wasn't just an opportunity. It was salvation. How was he supposed to know it would lead to this?

If you get a chance with them, you have to take it.

Lark's words echoed in the back of his mind as Cyrus pushed his Falcon into the final descent. This was his mission; he was in control. It all came down to control in the end. General Noth knew that. It was why she was winning this dark, twisted game even now, and why Cornelia was the one paying the price.

Rowena was a small, undomed town on the opposite side of the planet from West Rama. Cyrus dropped his Falcon into a narrow alley along the main road and released the air lock, but the first breath of Nakaran air was painful enough to make him double over, gasping into the cold. He had barely gone a dozen paces before the sound of armored boots on cobblestones shattered the silence. He peered around the corner, then immediately pulled back at the sight of another Opian Falcon. There were soldiers everywhere, marching down alleys, pushing into shops, filling the streets with crimson. They moved with the practiced ease of people familiar with their territory. Cyrus wouldn't be surprised if that was true. These soldiers could have been here long before Noth cut Cordova a deal, back when their planets were still pretending to be allies.

He inhaled as much as his frozen lungs would allow and slipped into the street, keeping his collar turned into the wind and away from any too-watchful soldiers. The sooner he found Ava, the sooner he could leave. Or the sooner she could kill him and put him out of his misery. It was so *cold*. Cyrus had forgotten how the desert stole his breath that night in the capital, how much worse this planet felt without the protection of the domes. But that had been the desert. This was a town. People lived here.

How long had it taken the rest of the planet to turn their backs on this town so completely that they didn't even notice a foreign army slipping into its streets? Cyrus had a feeling it started when the money ran out, and everyone stopped pretending to care about a city that couldn't give them something else in return.

A flash of bright fabric caught his eye, and Cyrus drew back into the shelter of a nearby alley. It wasn't the dark color of the Opian uniforms, but that shade of red was familiar. *Ava.* But when he stepped into the street again, she was gone. Cyrus hesitated, wavering between the road and the alley. He was about to look again when something shifted in the air over his shoulder. He turned, instinctively reaching for his weapon, but the alley behind him was empty. He eyed the long stretch of pavement until it faded into inky black, heartbeat rattling in his ears. Every instinct was awake, itching across his skin, but it was the Port City voice that whispered, *You are not alone.*

"I didn't think you'd make it, Lieutenant."

Cyrus whirled back toward the street, boots catching in frozen clumps of sand, and there she was.

It had only been a day, but he thought Ava looked thinner. Hungrier. He remembered watching her in the Nakaran capital on that first day and thinking she didn't belong on a planet like this. Now Cyrus couldn't picture her anywhere else. He patted frantically across his chest, where his weapon had been strapped seconds before. Nothing. When he looked up, Ava had his rifle casually tucked under one arm. *Stars, how does she keep doing that?* He reached for the extra gun in his boot.

"Looking for this?"

A second voice floated over his shoulder, and Cyrus's head shot up as another girl peeled herself off the wall. He remembered her from the desert, the girl with dark-brown skin who had watched him with open, unbridled hatred. She hadn't seemed like a threat then, but now her lips twisted into a wicked grin as she tossed his pistol from hand to hand. Cyrus decided it was probably best he'd come alone. Lark would never let him live this down.

He held out a hand. "Give it back."

"Or what?" Ava lifted a brow as she stepped closer. Over his shoulder, Cyrus felt the other girl do the same, trapping him against the wall.

"I . . ."

Ava tossed the rifle in his direction without warning. Cyrus barely got his hands up in time to catch it, and she moved in the split second he looked away, pinning an arm across his throat and slamming him back against the bricks. He gasped, an agonizing breath that froze in his chest as his head cracked against stone. Then there was something cold on his neck.

"Did you bring them here?" Ava's breath caressed the shell of his ear, each word sharper than the new blade in her hand. "These soldiers? Are they here because of you?"

"No!"

If you have the chance with them, you have to take it. Cyrus winced as her elbow dug into the side of his neck, and he adjusted his grip on his rifle, finger reaching for the trigger.

"Don't." The other girl was on him in seconds. She drove the barrel of the pistol between his ribs with more force than Cyrus thought necessary, then reached down and pried his fingers open until his rifle clattered to the cobblestones.

"No," Cyrus tried again, every word straining through gritted teeth. "I didn't say anything."

Ava's grip tightened, pulling his attention back to the knife in her hand. "Don't lie to me. I'll cut your throat right here."

Cyrus could feel his own pulse under her fingers. He believed her. There was something wild behind her fury, so different from the girl in the Nakaran capital who'd laughed and flirted with Lark. So different from the girl he'd spoken to in the desert. This was the Ava Castor from the wanted posters, who'd walked in and out of Chess without a scratch, who'd left her knife buried in Lark's leg.

Everyone was afraid of Shane Mannix, the sharpshooter, the convict, the runaway. Why did no one in the Opian capital have the sense to be terrified of her?

Cyrus felt the blade nick the hollow of his throat. "Why would I come back? If I sold you out, why would I bother?"

Ava's hand wavered. "Then why are they here?" Her voice was quiet, but Cyrus didn't think it was entirely devoid of fear.

He pressed his hand against the bricks, forcing himself to steady. "Those soldiers look like they've been here a while. I think you know that." He hesitated before adding, "When did she say she was coming back?"

Ava's mouth tightened, but it was the other girl who spoke first. "Three months?" Cyrus could still see her out of the corner of his eye. She was taller than Ava, willowy and long, like she could have been a dancer in another life. Then, her eyes narrowed and the illusion shattered. "It's only been two."

Cyrus knew that, but it was one thing to hear it, to feel the uncomfortable truth in the pit of his stomach, and quite another to watch it unfold. This wasn't the dramatic siege of his imagination. It was happening the way things like this always happened—in the dark. One day at a time. Slow enough for people to look away if they wanted.

Cyrus lifted his hands as best he could. "I'm trying to help."

It was all he'd ever done. He didn't have much to show for it.

"Fine." Ava jerked her chin toward the other girl. "Give whatever you brought to Clara."

"How do I know you're not going to kill me?"

"How do I know you brought something real?"

"I don't know," Cyrus snapped. "Maybe you should have thought about that before you invited me to the middle of nowhere."

There were probably smarter things to say when being held at knifepoint on a foreign planet, but Cyrus didn't care. He watched surprise flare briefly across Ava's face, and it was another minute before she released him. He resisted the urge to run a hand over his neck where he could still feel the cold press of metal and instead fumbled in his boot.

"Really?" Clara wrinkled her nose as he drew out the slip of paper and dropped it in her palm. "You couldn't have put it somewhere else?"

Despite himself, Cyrus felt his face heat. "It seemed like a good idea at the time."

Clara muttered something in Nakaran he couldn't understand, but the tone was clear. *She hates you.* That was fine. She could think whatever she wanted as long as she and Ava let him leave this alley in one piece.

Clara unfolded the paper. Ava leaned in and when she looked at him again, something had softened behind her eyes. "You know we can't read this, right? It's in Opian."

"Oh, sorry." Cyrus pointed over her shoulder. "It's those numbers there. You won't need to translate anything else. That gives you clearance to dock at the satellite base, and once you're inside, you'll have access to anything you need. Video evidence, flight orders, direct lines to the other planets. All you have to do is hit send. Just don't use it to, like, wipe everyone's bank

---

accounts or something," he added, realizing too late the full extent of the power he'd passed off.

Clara's mouth twitched. "That's an option?"

Ava scanned the paper again, face shadowed and downcast. It was another minute before she looked up, and Cyrus felt the earlier tension return. "You know these codes are our only option, right? We don't have another choice."

For a second she looked so young Cyrus felt his chest ache. *Seventeen.* He was only a year older. She shouldn't be talking about last chances and long-shot plans. She shouldn't have to weigh the consequences of trusting him against the future of an entire planet.

He nodded. "I know."

"I'm not kidding. If this doesn't work, if this is a lie . . ." She trailed off before adding, "That's it. You win."

Cyrus couldn't think of anything that felt less like a victory. "I know. But this is your best chance." It was the only chance he could give her. He glanced toward the dusty cobblestones. "Okay, I'm going to pick up my rifle now, and I would really appreciate it if you didn't stab me."

He knelt slowly, sliding the weapon across his back, and when he straightened, Ava was much closer than he remembered.

"Why are you doing this?" Her voice was low, but most of the bite was gone. "Really."

Cyrus had wondered the same thing for the last two months. Since their meeting in the desert. There was the simple answer, the one playing in his head even now, but he thought the truth was more complicated. Because he might not know what it felt like to live on a planet like this, but he knew without a shadow of a doubt that if Port City stopped being profitable, if it ever stopped churning out wide-eyed, hopeless kids to fill uniforms and meet quotas, it would end up like this.

"Because it's wrong," Cyrus said eventually. "And when something's wrong, you fix it."

A ghost of a smile flitted across Ava's lips. "And you think you fixed this?"

Sometimes Cyrus thought he was making things worse, but he shrugged and said, "I think I'm trying."

"And you're still going back to them?"

You're going back to Nakara? Even though you know it's wrong. That was what Cornelia had asked him in his office. And for the first time since setting foot in the Academy, Cyrus didn't know what to do. He turned away to avoid answering and held out a hand to Clara, who still clutched his pistol. "Can I have that back?"

"No." She shook her head. "I like this one. I'm keeping it."

Cyrus's stomach sank. The armory was going to revoke every privilege he'd managed to scrape back. They were never going to let him leave the planet again.

Ava grinned. "You should take better care of your things. This is really embarrassing for you." She nodded toward the mouth of the alley. "Get out."

Just like that the edge was back—sharp angles, snapping teeth, the girl from the papers in all her murderous glory. Cyrus took a tentative step.

"You're not even holding it right," he said. "If you're going to rob me, at least pretend to know what you're doing."

"Get *out*, Lieutenant. Now, before I change my mind."

Cyrus exhaled through his teeth, mentally preparing for the punishment awaiting him back home. "Fine. Keep it. It's your loss."

Then he turned and ran straight into the end of someone else's gun.

Cyrus stumbled back as Shane Mannix materialized from the shadows. Somewhere over his shoulder he heard someone inhale, the scrape of boots on stone as they moved.

"Him?" Shane's gaze drifted between Ava and Clara. "He's your contact? This is his plan?"

"No." Ava tucked the piece of paper behind her back. "I mean yes, technically, but—"

"Get back to the ship." Shane's grip tightened, and Cyrus flinched as cold metal dug into his collarbone. "Now, both of you."

No one moved. Cyrus felt Clara's hand on the small of his back as the tension closed around them inch by inch. Her voice was a cool whisper in his ear. "This isn't a fight you can win, Lieutenant." Her fingers twisted in the back of his jacket and she yanked him away from Shane, shoving him toward the opposite end of the alley. "Go!"

The first bullet whipped overhead, so close Cyrus felt the wind from it ruffle his hair. The second cracked into the wall, scattering pieces of brick across his path. He skidded along the icy stones, fumbling for his weapon with numb fingers, but it was the dark that saved him. He slipped into it as someone shouted and another bullet whizzed past his ear. Panic slid down his spine—the same urgency he'd felt when he leaped from his burning Falcon. The same desperation that had never failed to keep him alive.

Cyrus tucked the feeling into his chest and ran, blocking out everything but his own heartbeat and the rapidly fading sound of gunfire.

CHAPTER TWENTY-FOUR

✳ ✳ ✳

A va had seen Shane angry plenty of times. When a job fell through, when their ship broke down, when Jared spilled an entire bottle of rootwine in the cockpit. When he stared Ares down in the desert and threatened to put a bullet through his skull. But as they walked back to the ship in razor-sharp silence, collars turned against the wind, Ava couldn't remember a time she'd seen him look like *this*.

Uncharted. Unreachable.

She should have killed Cyrus the second he gave her those codes, and she should have known Shane didn't trust her. Not as much as he claimed, anyway. For some reason, that realization hurt the most. Ava tucked her arm through Clara's as they turned another corner, shivering at the next icy gale. When they reached the Lincoln, Shane stalked inside without a backward glance, stepping over Jared on his way to the front of the ship.

Jared flinched, glancing over his shoulder as Ava and Clara followed. "What's going on?"

"Nothing." Ava handed him the folded-up piece of paper. "Here's the clearance for the satellite job. Think you can work with this?"

Jared's apprehension vanished as he scanned the lines of code. "Whoa," he murmured, eyes widening under his tangled mop of curls. "This is *good*."

The ship roared to life under their feet before Ava could respond. Jared braced himself against her legs at the first acceleration, and Ares stood to look out the window as the street fell away, but Shane still didn't speak. Ava wondered if she had crossed some unspoken line, shattered something not even they could put back together.

But Shane had no right to be angry, not when they had been living job to job for the last two months. He had no idea how to hack the Opian dreadnoughts or bring down the blockade. He couldn't stop the impending invasion, but Ava had found a chance. If this was it, a way to end it, to put Opia back in its place and finally *leave*, wasn't it worth the risk?

They flew low and fast across the desert, cutting through dusty clouds. For the first time since leaving that alley, Ava wondered where they were going. They had a plan, a job laid out in pristine detail, but they were heading further into the desert. When Shane switched to autopilot without taking them through the atmosphere, she felt her stomach hollow.

Would he really abandon this job just to punish her? Would he really risk Nakara now, after everything they'd done?

He moved through the back of the ship like a ghost. Ava knew that look. The pilot who drove through sandstorms, the convict who shot his way out of Chess. The boy willing to do whatever it took. "We'll leave the surface in the morning," he said without looking up. He disappeared downstairs before anyone could speak, and Ava heard one of the bedroom doors slam. The silence stretched a second longer before Clara blew out a breath and pushed herself off the wall.

"Well, that was very dramatic. Come on, I need a drink."

She rummaged through one of the storage bins until she

found a bottle of wine, but Ava didn't move. There had been something else under Shane's voice, a thin ripple she barely recognized. She sighed and started for the stairs. "I'll be right back."

Clara snorted, lifting the wine in her direction. "Good luck. I'll save you a glass."

Ava was pretty sure she'd need the whole bottle.

The bottom half of the ship was always warmer than the other decks. She felt the hum of the engine echo in her bones with every step down the metal stairs. She couldn't decide what annoyed her more—Shane's dismissal or the fact that she was right and he didn't even care. By the time she knocked on his door, the engine's steady pulse had grown to a roar, pounding in her ears. He didn't get to shut her out, not anymore. After the third knock, Ava pushed the door open without waiting for a response.

Shane was sitting on the edge of the worn mattress, head hung low as he watched the starlight flicker across the floor. He stood when she entered, turning his back on the door. "Get out."

Ava could feel the heat from the engines working its way through her feet. She shut the door behind her. "We're not going to talk about this?"

"What is there to talk about?"

She could only see Shane's back, the sharp line of his shoulders. She shouldn't be surprised; this was how things worked with him. Seal it up before anything got out, turn away before it got too real, but she was tired of it. Ava crossed the room, stopping on the other side of the bed.

"You know this is a good plan," she said. "We don't have another choice; this is our only shot."

"You're right." Shane rounded on her, color staining the sharp ridges of his cheekbones. "We have one shot. *One.* And you based everything off the word of an Opian soldier. *Stars,* Ava, what am I supposed to do with that?"

He was moving now, pacing restless circles across the cramped space. Ava was used to his silence, but this set her teeth on edge. He felt like the end of a lit fuse.

"It's the same plan," Ava said. "You liked it. You agreed to it. Nothing's different."

"Everything's different! You really trust him?"

"No, but I think he's telling the truth."

Shane laughed, a low sound deep in his throat. "We don't have time for this. *They* don't have time for this."

He meant Nakara. He meant their families, and somehow the reminder of everything they had to lose sawed at Ava's already fraying nerves. "You think I don't know that? I live here, too, Shane! That's my family."

"Don't." Shane closed the distance between them in two strides. "You never wanted anything to do with that place."

"Neither did you!"

"But you left." His face twisted, somewhere between hurt and anger. "You wanted out the first night we met; that's why you took my offer. You never would have gone back if I didn't want to, so why are you still here?"

Why are you still here? The question stung. Maybe Shane had been asking himself that same thing for months. Maybe every moment they'd shared had been another lie, a careful manipulation to keep her close, doing his dirty work.

"You think I want to be here?" Ava asked. "You think I like

risking my life for a planet that never cared about us? Of course I don't! I hate it! I hate watching people die and I hate living in this ship and I hate that it's never going to stop. This isn't what I signed up for."

Every word burned on the way out, a toxic secret she'd kept hidden for too long. Shane's eyes widened, and for a second, Ava thought she caught a glimpse of him under the fury, real and raw. But it was too late to stop.

"We're not the only ones who could do this, you know. A lot of people could and they'd do it better than us, but they aren't. Because nobody cares. We're the only chance these people have and it's not fair. I'm supposed to believe that you actually want to be here?"

Shane nodded. "Yes."

Sometimes, his eyes were so dark, Ava felt like she was drowning in them. Right now, she was certain he could see every traitorous thought that had ever crossed her mind, every time she secretly wished West Rama would disappear, every selfish desire tucked inside her chest. He took a step closer, and when he leaned down, Ava felt his breath against the side of her face. "Why are you still here?"

He was too close. She could still feel the anger, the frantic pulse in her veins, but something about the way Shane was looking at her spilled a different kind of heat across her skin.

"Because of you," she whispered. Then, because that was too close to the truth, she added, "Because of my mother. Because of Jared and Clara. Because we're supposed to be the ones who got out. Stars, Shane, do you even want me here?"

"I don't know." Shane ran a hand through his hair. "I *don't know*."

Ava felt the words echo through her, each one landing harder than the last. So there it was. The truth. Shane's eyes widened, like he realized too late what he'd said.

"No, wait, that's not what I meant."

"I know what you meant." She needed to get out of this room before it burned her up. She needed to get off this planet.

Shane exhaled through his teeth, a rough, frustrated sound. "Ava."

Ava shook her head, ignoring how the sound of her name on his lips still sent fire racing under her skin. "It's fine. I get it."

"No." Shane caught her wrist, drew her back into the room. "You *don't*."

Then he slid his other hand into her hair, pulled her close, and kissed her.

Ava remembered their kiss on Chess as quick and careless, a means to an end in a place that didn't allow for anything more. She had thought about it several times since, of course she had. How it might have felt to linger in that moment, for Shane to kiss her back, for him to mean it. But those imagined kisses were always sweet and warm and wonderful. *Cinematic.* This one was harder. Because Shane kissed the same way he did everything else—like he had something to prove.

He released her almost immediately, stumbling back across the floor, and Ava pressed a hand over her chest. There was air somewhere in this room; there had to be. "Oh."

Oh.

Shane sank onto the mattress, elbows braced against his knees as he buried his face in his hands. "I'm sorry."

But Ava couldn't move. She also couldn't stay still. There was something molten in her chest, pooling in her stomach, and she wanted more, no matter how much it burned. "What . . ." She could barely get the words out, but she needed to know, before Shane locked himself away for good. "What *is* this?"

She stepped forward, right between his knees, and when Shane looked up, his eyes were damp. The sight of it sliced through her, and Ava tried to remember if she'd ever seen him cry, if he'd ever let her.

"They're coming for me," he whispered. "We could win this whole thing tomorrow, and they'd still come for me. You shouldn't be here when they do."

"Why?"

"Because I know what they do. I know what they'd do to you, to Jared. I can't—"

"But you're not going back," Ava interrupted. That much she was certain of. "You're not going back, and I'm not going anywhere, so what are you so afraid of?"

Shane let out a ragged laugh. "Everything! This job. Opia. You."

"Me?" Ava leaned down until they were barely a breath apart. She could still feel the press of his lips against hers, the pull of his fingers through her hair. "Why are you afraid of me?"

Shane ducked his head, and Ava felt one of his hands slide up her leg, gripping the back of her thigh. She shivered, and when he spoke again, it was so soft she almost missed it. "Because I'd stop right now if you asked me to. I'd leave all of this and go."

A thrill sparked through her at the thought—the two of them on a different planet, a different system where no one knew their names. Ava imagined opening her window to sunlight each morning, wandering the streets without the constant threat of discovery, kissing Shane whenever she liked. *We're not the only ones who could do this, you know.* Maybe someone else could try. Maybe someone else would win. But Ava had lived on the edge of the system her entire life. Nobody had come for them before.

She reached out and caught Shane's face between her hands, brushing a thumb over his cheekbone. He was going to fall apart one of these days, right there in her hands. "I'm not going anywhere," she whispered. "Neither are you."

Shane closed his eyes and Ava watched his throat bob as he swallowed. It took him three tries to get the words out. "Don't let me ruin you. Please, Ava, it's not worth it."

Of course it was. She might not have signed up for an Opian power grab, but she had signed up for him. For the strange, terrible boy who found her in a crowded room, who offered to kill anyone she asked, who faced down the full might of the Opian army again and again. Who kissed her like it was their last night in the world. Somewhere in the back of her mind, Ava felt the familiar flare of caution, but she was too close to ignore how much she wanted him. She leaned forward again and let Shane pull her onto his lap. "This is worth it," she breathed. "You're worth it."

Shane's exhale was hitched and shallow, and when Ava kissed him again, his face was wet. His hands were always steady on the trigger of a gun or the controls of a stolen ship, but Ava felt them shake now, tangled in the hem of her dress. The air was cool against her bare skin, but Shane's mouth was hot, ravenous, and Ava couldn't remember why she'd ever wanted to do anything other than kiss him. She dragged her hands down his chest and he groaned, low in the back of his throat.

"Ava."

Had her name always sounded like that, raw and biting and desperate? She used to sneak people up to her room in West Rama, let them take her apart piece by piece just to feel something, but Shane didn't feel like coming apart. He felt like coming home, and when he shifted his hips against hers, Ava forgot about everything else entirely. The ship. The job. The thousands of lives hanging from her hand. *Dangerous.*

That's what this whole thing was, reckless and careless and so very dangerous. Because they were never supposed to last. Maybe that was why Ava couldn't stop.

She gasped as Shane slid a hand along the inside of her thigh, soft and hesitant. She wanted to touch him everywhere at once. She wanted to know that he was here and this was real. She gripped the bottom of his shirt with trembling fingers, then stopped, remembering how he'd pulled away last time, the thick knots of scar tissue slashed across his back. She sat up.

Shane blinked, and despite herself, despite everything, Ava almost laughed. She'd never seen him like this before, flushed and rumpled, leaning back on his elbows on a bed that wasn't theirs. It made him look younger, less like the convict from the papers. She tugged at his shirt again. "Can I?"

"Yes." Shane's answer was immediate, rough with desire. "Please."

He ducked his head free, hooking an arm around her waist as Ava pressed a kiss to his bare shoulder. He was beautiful, unmasked and unraveled in her hands, and she thought if someone told her she and Shane were the only two people in the system right now, she would believe them.

They had always walked a fragile line, toeing the edge of some deep, unending chasm. She could ignore it if she had to, but it was always there, begging her to fall. Ava felt it open now as Shane fumbled with the buttons on her dress. Starlight painted his hair silver, gathering in the sharp crevices of his torso, and when he kissed her again, deep and open and full of unsaid promises, she closed her eyes and let it pull her over the edge.

CHAPTER TWENTY-FIVE

* * *

Cyrus flew back to Opia in a ship that felt like a closed fist
and tried to remember the last time he had felt this uncertain about anything.

CHAPTER TWENTY-SIX

✳ ✳ ✳

"You don't have to test everything. You know that, right?"

Shane glanced over his shoulder as the lights in the air lock flickered again, glinting off rows of armed Opian warships. Jared jumped and tucked his hands behind his back, but not before Shane watched him type another command into his screen.

"I don't know what you're talking about."

It wasn't even a convincing lie. Ever since they'd landed, Jared had been testing the limits of the access codes in his arm: opening doors, closing the air lock, turning off lights. Shane couldn't even blame him. It was a power not even he had felt before, the kind people like them weren't expected to have. They weren't supposed to be standing in the middle of an empty Opian base, and they weren't supposed to make it this far.

Clara rolled her eyes. "If you're going to mess around, at least open a vent. It's hot in here."

"Agreed." Ava fanned herself with one hand. "Let's get this over with."

Shane cast one last look over his shoulder. He had parked the Lincoln among the Opian warships, far enough back in the hangar that any officers passing by wouldn't immediately notice the civilian model, but his stomach twisted as he turned back to the door. This could be the last job they ever worked, the one thing standing between him and the elusive, intangible freedom he'd sought for years. *So close.*

He forced the thought away and rapped his knuckles against the door. "Jared?"

It didn't take long. With the access codes already loaded in his screen, all Jared had to do was tap his arm against the locks and the door slid back, revealing the curving hallway beyond.

Ava sighed and pushed herself off the wall. "It was more fun to guess the password."

"I know." Jared grinned. "I hope RevengeDaddy3000 is doing well."

Shane released a breath at the comforting familiarity of it all. The light banter before a job, the way Ava reached down to ruffle Jared's hair as she passed. This was just another supply ship, another job to check off the list. Ava slipped her hand into his as they walked and Shane held it close.

He had woken that morning to her curled against him in the dark, so warm and wonderful that it took him several minutes before he could move. The bubble of peace was small, one he knew would disappear as soon as he got out of bed, but it still felt too rare and precious to lose. Not even these empty corridors could chase the feeling of it away completely.

Ares stopped at the first corner, pressing himself against the wall as he peered into the hallway beyond. He motioned them forward with a sharp wave, and Shane pulled himself out of Ava's grip to take the lead. He didn't trust Ares in a place like this. It was too easy to remember what happened last time, all the different ways it had gone so terribly wrong. There couldn't be any slips tonight. They were close enough to Opia that if anyone noticed their presence and called for backup, the army would be there in minutes. They would never make it back in the air.

By the time they filed into the server room, Shane's pulse was pounding in his ears. There was an energy to this place now, different from the quiet of the supply ships or the restless void of open space. It rose and fell, humming with life and light and blinking computer screens, but Shane didn't think it was any less sinister. It was the quiet of people sure in their own power, confident enough to leave their assets unguarded and alone. Because who would dare take it?

He nodded toward Ares. "Watch the door."

For once Ares listened. Clara ducked around the edge of another computer tower, weapon outstretched as she scanned the room, and Ava gave Shane one last look before following, circling the perimeter with quiet steps. They didn't need to bother securing anything else. There was only one way in and out of the room. Shane swallowed and extended a hand. "You ready, Jared?"

Jared nodded, but all humor had vanished from his face. He stepped forward, lifting the control panel on the nearest computer tower with pale, trembling fingers. "This is . . . a lot."

"I know." Shane squeezed his arm as Jared linked his skin screen to the wires waiting below. "You can do it."

But there was a very real possibility he couldn't. Jared might not be able to pull the evidence they needed. The servers might not be powerful enough to broadcast what they found to the other planets. But there was another fear playing at the back of

Shane's mind, the realization that they could successfully share proof of Opia's crimes to the entire system and everyone might still choose to collectively turn their backs.

Jared's fingers trembled as he entered the code again, one character at a time. The password box blinked mockingly down from the screen, blue-tinted light spreading across the floor like sand. There was a brief moment of panic when the entire screen flashed black. Then it opened, loading file after file as everything popped up at once.

"Yes!" Jared leaned forward, and Shane felt himself go limp with relief.

He stepped back as Jared got to work, and took in the rest of the server room. The walls were rounded like the rest of the base, so tall he couldn't see to the top. What else could he find here? What other information could he take for himself? Bank accounts? Government savings? If Opia was here at his fingertips, Shane wanted to make them hurt, make them pay.

"How long do you need?" he asked, glancing over his shoulder at Jared.

Jared's brow furrowed as he clicked through screen after screen. "I don't know. There's a lot here, I can—"

A voice sounded from the hall before he could finish, then there was a series of pattering footsteps. Shane whirled as a group of four Opian soldiers turned into the server room. They stumbled to a halt when they saw Jared, and there was a sickening silent moment where nobody moved. Then Ares melted out of the shadows, weapon raised, and clicked the safety off.

"No." Ava knocked his hand aside. "Are you trying to tell everyone where we are?" She turned her own weapon on the officers instead and steered them toward the center of the room. "On the ground," she added in the system language. "Now."

She forced them to their knees, one by one, and Shane's breath caught at the sight of the weapons hanging from their sides. How many more still patrolled the halls? They'd come looking for their friends eventually.

"Jared."

"I'm working on it." Jared's eyes blurred. "There's so much here, I don't really know where to start."

Fine. That was something Shane could fix.

He strode across the floor and grabbed the first officer he saw. The man was sweating, his glasses slipping to the end of his nose, and he let out a choked gasp as Shane hauled him to his feet. He shoved the end of his gun into the man's stomach.

"I want information on Nakara," he whispered, in the cold, dangerous voice he knew people feared. "Where do you keep those files?"

The man's throat bobbed as he swallowed. "I don't know! I'm not usually stationed here. I just fly!"

Next to him, Jared tapped away at his screen, eyes unfocused and glassy as he shifted through files. He was right; there were too many. They couldn't linger like this, especially if someone was going to notice these soldiers' absence.

Shane's grip tightened on the trigger. "Who does?"

"I don't know!" The man shook his head. "I'm not supposed to—"

Shane drove an elbow into his throat and shoved him aside. The officer fell back, dazed and choking, but Shane was already reaching for someone else. He gripped the back of the second soldier's jacket and yanked him to his feet, away from where Clara and Ava still held the others at gunpoint. He would go through them all if he had to.

"Let's try this again. I want information on the Nakaran mines. Where do I find it?"

The officer shook his head. "I can't."

He couldn't be much older than them, with cropped red hair and a round face, but Shane didn't care. He gripped the officer's jacket and slammed him against the wall. "That wasn't a suggestion," he hissed. "We'll take it all, then. What else is here? Battle plans? Weapons inventory? Other things you don't want me to have?"

He'd do it. He'd tear them apart from the inside out, bring the entire Opian empire crashing to the ground.

"Shane."

It was Jared's voice that brought him back. When he turned, Jared was still standing in front of the screens, but his hands had gone very still. "What?"

Jared swiped through a folder, closed it, then opened another. When he looked up, all the color had drained from his face. "They're empty."

Shane wondered if it was possible to drown in silence. *They're empty.* No, they couldn't be. This was the place. This was the plan. They had gotten this far, won the battle, shot their way out of every fight so they could make it here.

To a room in the heart of Opian territory, with one way in and one way out.

Shane shook his head. "What do you mean?"

"I mean they're gone." Jared swiped through screen after

screen. "The folders are here, everything looks fine, but . . ."

Vaguely, Shane was aware of Ava watching him as she held the other soldiers at gunpoint, of Clara's brittle frown and Ares's hulking glare. *In and out.* It was supposed to be easy.

Shane rounded on the red-haired soldier again. "Where are the files?"

He shook his head, jaw set, but Shane was done. He drew his weapon and fired two shots into the boy's ribs. He fell back with a strangled cry, and Shane planted the heel of his boot in the center of his chest, leaning forward until he could smell the blood creeping across the floor. "Where are they?"

The boy's face was the color of ash. "You don't have time," he gasped. "You're too late."

Fear curled in Shane's stomach, and he fired again. The shot was reckless—the sound could give away their position, but if there was a fight coming, he wanted it now. The boy crumpled to the floor and didn't move again.

"Wait." Jared tilted his head as he started working again, eyes darting back and forth across the screen. "There's something here, I think . . ."

The first officer was still hunched on the ground, rubbing his throat, but as Shane turned, momentarily distracted by Jared, he launched himself forward. The movement caught Shane by surprise, and dull pain thudded through him as they both crashed to the floor. Jared jumped, and Shane had enough time to yell "Keep going!" before the soldier's hands closed around his neck.

The panic set in before the pain, a drowning rush cascading down the length of his spine. If Shane had the breath, he might have laughed, because this was how he'd killed that man on Chess, so long ago it felt like a different life. He dug his nails into the backs of the officer's hands as his vision dipped. He could feel the blood under his fingers, hear his own pulse in his ears, slowing with every passing second.

The pressure fell away as suddenly as it had started, and Shane rolled over, gasping for breath. Ava stood above him, her gaze pure fury as she fired. The officer slumped forward, motionless on the ground. There were stars in her hair; Shane wanted to touch one, to hold it in his hand. Then he blinked and realized there were stars everywhere, dancing on the edge of his vision. He let Ava help him to his feet and tried frantically to pull himself together.

"Let's go," she whispered. "This was a bad idea. Let's leave."

She was right. Shane thought of their ship parked at the opposite end of the base and wondered how many other traps stood between him and freedom. *Will it ever stop?* But they wouldn't get this chance again, and Shane wasn't going to die on an Opian base without taking a few more officers with him.

He pulled out of Ava's grip. "What's going on, Jared?"

Jared's eyes darted back and forth as he tapped at the computer. His face was flushed, like it always was when he downloaded large swaths of information. For the first time, Shane wondered how much was really on these servers. Enough to overload the memory processors buried in Jared's skin?

"I don't think the information is gone," Jared muttered. "Hold on, there's something here. I think someone else is inside."

Shane's fingers tightened around his weapon. So that was it—Cyrus had sold them out, betrayed them to the first person who asked. Maybe that had been his plan all along. The panic was flowing fast now, dripping in from every corner of the room. Two soldiers were dead. Across the room, Clara held the other two at gunpoint. She glanced over her shoulder, mouth opening in a silent question, and Shane realized her mistake the same time the officers did.

"Clara!"

Ava whirled, but it was too late. One of them lunged, smacking the gun from Clara's hand, and she didn't even have time to cry out before he knocked her to the ground. Her body hit the cement with a sickening *thud*. Ares threw himself behind a pillar as the officer picked up Clara's gun and fired over his shoulder. The bullets nicked a computer monitor, exactly where Ares's head had been seconds before. Then the officer turned and dashed for the wall.

The alarm.

Shane let out a strangled cry, but Ava was already moving. She fired, and the first man went down. Jared's head shot up at the noise, concentration momentarily breaking, but Shane waved him away.

"Keep going!"

He took aim at the last officer. He would have made it if he hadn't still been dizzy from lack of oxygen, if his hands weren't shaking, if he hadn't been distracted by the trap they had stumbled into.

If . . .

Instead, he missed by an inch, and the shot shattered a screen next to the man's arm. He swore and aimed again. This time, he caught the soldier between the shoulder blades, but not before his hand had slammed through the alarm's protective casing.

The siren blared, and the world shattered.

"Go!" Shane pushed Ava toward the door, slipping on the blood under his feet. "Get out, now!"

Footsteps pounded in the halls outside, and there it was again, the unmistakable feeling of a trap snapping shut. The two remaining officers were stirring, injured but reaching for their weapons as the alarm howled overhead.

"Jared!"

Shane ducked as one of them fired, and before he could take aim, the man rolled behind another bank of computers. Shane would take the two-to-one odds any day, but now the room was closing in.

Jared's shoulders tensed as he worked. "I'm almost done."

But the sirens were grating and insistent, burrowing into his head with razor-tipped claws. Shane had never heard anything like it. It made his pulse jump and rattle. It made him afraid. More shots from behind the barricade. Ares fired back, but Shane couldn't tell where the other officer had taken cover. "Jared . . ."

"I got it!"

Jared ripped the wires from his arms, and the screens flickered black. He swayed on his feet, expression dazed, but Shane couldn't wait for him to adjust. He dragged Jared across the floor, bursting into the hall as Ares fired over his shoulder, over and over again.

The emergency lights pulsed, relentless and blaring. One second the halls were blazing with violent red light, the next it was so dark Shane couldn't see his own hands, couldn't tell which way to go. Where had they come from? The halls twisted together, a maze of death, another trap.

"This way!" Jared tugged at his sleeve, pointing down a hall.

There was a rough screech of metal on metal as a door separating their hallway from the rest of the base started lowering from the ceiling, inch by inch. Each pulse of the lights brought it closer to the ground and Shane pushed himself faster, ignoring the sharp pain in his chest. They couldn't be on the other side when it closed.

Vaguely he was aware of Clara at his side, of Ava firing into another hallway as they ran. Shane couldn't tell where the footsteps were coming from, if anyone was firing back or if it was just the echo of their own panic across the walls. He pushed Jared under the door and watched him roll out of the way, but Ares grabbed his arm before he could follow.

"Stop. We need to—"

Ares never finished the sentence. An Opian bullet caught him in the ribs, and he went down hard. Clara gasped, slipping on the steel floor as his blood splattered across her legs, but Ava grabbed her arm. She forced Clara under the door and fired into the hall. Shane caught a flash of metal as another soldier went down.

"Ava! Come on!" Shane lowered himself to the ground as a cold hand gripped his ankle. Ares was crawling forward, a slick trail of blood in his wake.

"Help me!" His eyes were wild, voice panicked, but Shane remembered that hand clenched around Ava's wrist.

He lifted his gun. "Nice working with you, Ares."

Shane's aim was good, right between the eyes, and Ares's

head snapped back before he could speak again. He collapsed, lifeless and cold, and Shane slid under the rapidly lowering door. Then he ran.

Clara was already halfway down the hall, sprinting for the hangar. It hadn't seemed far before, but Shane was all turned around. The windows blurred by as he ran, an endless tunnel of stars and twisting constellations. He could hear Jared's wheezing gasps, the insistent hammer of shots coming closer, and he reached behind him for Ava. His fingers closed on empty air.

She wasn't there.

Shane stopped, squinting back toward the server room. Panic, true cold panic, clamped across his chest. "Where's Ava?"

Jared stumbled. "She was behind us, right?"

A thousand thoughts ran through Shane's mind at once, but only one mattered. *Find her.* Jared started to turn, but Shane pushed him back. "No! Get Clara and start the ship!"

The sound of his feet against cold steel drowned out the rest of Jared's protests. Shane didn't look back again. This was what he'd been afraid of, everything he'd tried to prevent. A bullet cut the air over his head, so close Shane felt it ruffle his hair. He tore past room after room as footsteps pounded toward them. He would be trapped here, in this dead-end hallway. He'd have to shoot his way out.

Another shot grazed his thigh, and Shane's leg buckled at the flare of white-hot pain. But there was Ava, pinned underneath the steel-plated door, trying in vain to lift it.

She looked up as Shane stumbled to a stop, eyes widening. "What are you doing?" she gasped. "Get out!"

Something slammed into his arm, and Shane went down,

slipping across the smooth floors. There was blood there, under his hands, streaming down his wrist. Was it his?

"Shane!" Ava reached for him, her voice a strangled sob. "You can't be here!"

But Shane forced himself up, shoving his shoulder under the door. He didn't know how he lifted it, not with the pain coursing through his arm, not with the bullets raining down. He heard Ava gasp as the pressure lifted and she rolled free.

"Come on." Shane pulled her to her feet. "I got you."

He ignored the awkward twist of her ankle. They would think about that later. Right now there was too much smoke, shouting and gunfire that clawed through his head.

The first soldier ducked out of a hallway to their left and Shane fired. Ava took the next one, then the next. Because they always fought their way out. Black spots danced at the edge of his vision, but they were close to the hangar now. He could see the Lincoln among the Opian ships, see its engines firing.

He heard the whistle before he recognized what it was. When Shane looked up, he had a split second to watch the grenade soar over his head, outlined against the sharp steel beams. It flew in slow motion, in pristine detail as it bounced off the ceiling and clattered to the ground. Shane watched it roll under the ship. He watched his own hand extend, like he could snatch it up and pull it back.

The force of the blast knocked them back into the hallway, and Shane caught himself against the side of another ship as hot flames seared the side of his face. Ava might have screamed. Or maybe that was him. He couldn't tell over the sound of their ship crumbling and burning in the middle of the hangar. His knees buckled, but he clutched at the wall with aching fingers.

If he went down now, he wouldn't get back up.

There was a part of his soul so dark Shane never let himself look at it for long. It was where the memories of Chess lived, where he kept each kill. And it was where he shoved every thought in his head now, letting them tumble into the abyss until only one remained.

Get out.

They were surrounded by Opian military vessels. If he couldn't pilot one of them, what use was he?

"No!" Ava twisted in his arms, back toward the smoking wreckage. "We can't!"

But Shane ignored her. He could do this if he had to, if Ava couldn't. Because it wasn't ending like this. He drew his knife and jimmied the lock on the nearest Catapult with numb fingers. The back ramp released in seconds, hissing to the floor as the main cabin depressurized.

Ava took a few limping steps toward the fiery remnants of the Lincoln, but Shane grabbed her around the waist and yanked her into the bay, slamming the air lock behind them. He could feel every action, frigid and robotic. What would the Shane Mannix from the papers do? What would the outlaw risk to get out alive? Who would he sacrifice?

The ship roared to life under his fingers, and an automated voice chirped, *"Welcome, Captain Kaylor."* Shane didn't even fasten his seat belt before slamming the acceleration forward. The Catapult barreled down the launch tunnel and into open space with more force than he'd anticipated, triggering every alarm along the way.

In and out. They were supposed to be in and out.

He could hear Ava sobbing in the back, but Shane shut it out before the dark overwhelmed him, too. *Later.* Right now, they were fine. They were out. They were invincible.

But the word rang hollow and false.

So Shane pushed the Catapult forward as fast as it would go, letting the harsh growl of the engine wash over him as they soared to the first jump point, leaving those twisted thoughts and the smoking wreckage of his life far, far below.

CHAPTER TWENTY-SEVEN

***

If Cyrus hadn't spent the last several days on Nakara, he was certain General Noth would have cracked him on the spot.

Instead, all he had to do was remember the cold bite of the desert, the press of Ava's knife against his skin, and the desolation of each quiet, undomed town. He had survived this long. What was one more lie? What was one more council meeting of forced smiles and easy laughter? Cyrus felt like he'd been faking his way through this job since he first set foot in the Academy. He could hold out a few more days.

The council chambers were only half-full by the time he arrived. He had fallen into bed ten minutes after landing on Opia and woken up the next afternoon to multiple unread messages and meeting requests. A week ago, the thought of letting Noth down or missing a meeting would have eaten him alive, but when Cyrus had searched for the old thread of panic, he found nothing but cold, empty disdain.

But as he scanned himself into the Capitol building, hair still wet from the shower, he felt some of that courage waver. He wouldn't be able to pass this last mission off as a moment of weakness if anyone found out. A conversation in a quiet supply ship was nothing. A meeting in the desert could be ignored, if he tried hard enough, but deliberately passing classified information to the very people he was supposed to kill would be harder to explain. General Noth looked up from the table when he entered, and it took every ounce of Cyrus's willpower not to collapse under the weight of her gaze.

"Lieutenant." It was that same easy smile from days ago. This time, Cyrus felt it crawl across his skin. "So good to have you back. Please, have a seat."

Cyrus sank into the first available chair and silently willed himself to pull it together. He had been expecting the full security council, but instead it was just him, Noth, and a few of her officers he barely knew by name. *Where is everybody?* He had already known Cornelia would be gone, but the sight of her empty seat was still painful to look at. She was probably somewhere in the armory or aircraft hangar, working on her ship and hating him in secret, but where was Lark? For a wild second, Cyrus wondered if he had been demoted, too, if Lark had done something equally reckless in his absence.

The last of the officers filed in, dropping into the open seats by the door, and Cyrus watched surprise flash across the face of the man nearest him. "I didn't know you were back, General," he said. "Didn't you head out this morning?"

Noth waved a hand. "Change of plans. Come on, let's get started. Lieutenant Blake?"

Cyrus inhaled and ignored the apprehension still gnawing at him as he forced himself to straighten. He kept his debrief simple, only inserting details where it felt crucial. It was a story he'd developed on the flight home, an explanation that toed the line between truth and fiction. *The rebels were coming to Opia. They wanted to hit the planet, the capital, the major trade cities. They were upset about the new mines and blamed them for Nakara's destruction. They wanted it to stop. They would do whatever it took.*

He remembered the first time he'd lied to Noth that night in the desert, how the pressure of it built in his stomach. Now he felt nothing. After lying to Cornelia, this was easy. Noth watched him across the table, her eyes never leaving his face, but Cyrus refused to let himself flinch. He was careful and calm, serious and professional. He was a good soldier, the valedictorian cadet, and he had never done anything wrong in his life.

Noth's expression was still guarded when the meeting adjourned, but Cyrus didn't think it was because of him. She would have disposed of him already if she had any suspicions, just tossed him into the Nakaran desert and never looked back. He was sure of it because that was what happened to Cornelia. And Cyrus was more of a liability than she would ever be.

Daylight was fading rapidly, painting the streets under the Capitol windows a dusky orange, but Cyrus didn't head back to his room. He had too much to do, too many thoughts rattling around his head. He kept replaying Ava's words as he walked toward the armory. *Are you a good person?*

Until now, Cyrus would have said yes. He tried to be. He had worked his way out of Port City for his mother. He stayed through the Academy for the tantalizing promise of helping more people on the other side. Even the work he was doing now, the dangerous, illegal work that left a bitter tang in his throat, was for good because Noth was the problem. She was the source. But even as he thought it, Cyrus knew it wasn't true. Hadn't he just spoken to a roomful of officers who had learned about his secret mission to a foreign planet they didn't control without batting an eye? Hadn't they asked questions like it was the most natural thing in the world?

Cyrus's stomach twisted as he wondered how many of those officers knew exactly what Noth was doing, how many saw the dreadnoughts and the unauthorized acts of war and let it slide. How many thought they were good people because they weren't the ones pulling the trigger.

Maybe Ava was right. Maybe there wasn't a way to be a good person in a place like this.

Cyrus made it as far as the last staircase before he heard someone call his name.

"Cyrus! I didn't know you were back."

He turned, the winding corridors of the Capitol building swimming back into focus. Lark was limping toward him, boots marking an uneven rhythm across the floor. He leaned against his crutch, cracking a hesitant smile, and Cyrus felt guilt rise in his chest. Between the panicked flight off Nakara and the thought of confronting Noth again, he had forgotten to tell Lark he'd landed safely. "Sorry," he muttered. "I lost track of time."

Lark's eyebrows lifted. "Lost track of time?"

It was partially true. Cyrus's body still ached from lack of sleep and the long hours of space travel. He barely knew what day it was, but part of him felt like he deserved the discomfort. Like this was the price for trying, and it was only a matter of time before he crashed and burned. Cyrus pushed the thought away and started down the stairs again. "I'm going to the armory."

It was supposed to end the conversation, but Lark followed as best he could, gripping the railing with his free hand as he descended. Like this was normal. Like they got back from illegal missions every day. They walked in silence for a few minutes before Lark spoke again. "So how was it?"

"Fine." Cyrus felt the word catch between his teeth, short and clipped.

"Fine," Lark repeated. "That's it? You were gone for days. What happened?"

The beginnings of a scowl flitted across his forehead, and Cyrus felt his guilt flare again. He knew Lark was frustrated about being grounded, itching to be back in a ship, but Cyrus had just bluffed his way through an entire meeting. He could still feel the grip of it around his shoulders. He had a ship to tune, armory soldiers to beg for forgiveness over another stolen weapon, and he didn't have time to pretend anymore.

"It was a mission." Cyrus shouldered open the door to the courtyard. "I don't know what else you want me to say."

Lark's frustration was impossible to miss. "You were on *Nakara*, Blake, that's not nothing. Did you see them?"

"Yes."

"And?"

"And they're terrible," Cyrus snapped. "They're the worst kind of people, and we can't get them out of the air soon enough. Is that what you want to hear?"

"I want—" Lark winced as he limped around another corner. "Can you slow down? I was stabbed, remember? Last week?"

"Then go *home*, Lark."

Cyrus didn't mean for it to sound like that, but he couldn't lie to anyone else right now. And he certainly couldn't tell the truth. He needed a second alone, to close his eyes, but everything about this city felt so breakable. "I'm sorry," he added as he yanked open the armory door. "I just need to turn in my weapons and find Cornelia. Then I'll be back."

It was supposed to be a peace offering, but Lark's scowl deepened as they stepped into the cool hallway. "Cornelia," he muttered. "Of course, how could I forget?"

"What's that supposed to mean?"

Cyrus turned, folding his arms as Lark stumbled to a stop behind him. It was darker in the armory building, every corridor shaded by opaque glass and thick carpet. Without the constant motion of the Capitol, Cyrus could almost pretend he was alone, back in his Falcon with Lark's voice in his ear. But Lark was here, looking at him with a thinly disguised frustration Cyrus couldn't unpack. With a thrill, he realized it felt like the Lark from the Academy, the adversary, the rival. Color spread across Lark's throat the longer they stood together, inching up from the collar of his uniform. Then he shook his head.

"Nothing. Never mind."

"It's clearly something." Cyrus ran a hand over his face. "I'm sorry you can't fly and I'm sorry I haven't been here, but I really don't have time to deal with your passive-aggressive problem-solving skills right now."

Lark's lip curled. "Of course. You're so important, flying around for the general on interplanetary missions. What would I know about that?"

"That's not—"

"Are you going to tell Cornelia?" Her name came out as a cruel sneer. "Does she get to know about your top-secret missions?"

Cyrus didn't know why it felt like a trick question. "Yes, probably."

"Why? She got demoted from her only Capitol job. What does she know?"

"She's still my friend."

Lark let out a low laugh. "Of course. How could I forget? She's such a good *friend*."

Cyrus was too tired for this. He didn't entirely know what they were fighting about, but he wanted it to stop. "What are you—?"

"The two of you," Lark said before Cyrus could finish. "Are you . . . did you ever . . . ?"

He trailed off, waving one hand wildly in front of his face, and Cyrus thought he looked genuinely flustered for the first time. He realized what Lark meant a second later and choked back an incredulous laugh. "Are you serious?"

That was what he wanted to talk about? Now?

Lark took another step forward. "Well, did you?"

"No! She's my friend, Lark. Why do you care?"

Immediately, Cyrus wished he could take the question back. It felt like a door that shouldn't open. Because he knew what he wanted Lark to say, in the end, and he also knew exactly why neither of them should go anywhere near it. There was something intense behind his gaze, wild and burning, and for a second, all Cyrus could think about was the pink flush spilling across Lark's face and if his skin would feel as warm as it looked. If he could run his thumb along the edge of Lark's cheekbone, just to find out. He could do it quick, before anyone passed them in the hallway. Before either of them could linger on what it might mean.

The piercing screech of the armory alarm sounded before Cyrus could move, high-pitched and wailing. Lark leapt back, gasping as his bad leg took most of his weight, and Cyrus gripped his arm to steady them both. The sound clawed through the corridor, shredding every thought as he pressed against the wall. *Security breach.* That was what the alarm meant.

Cyrus swallowed the terror rising in his throat and fumbled with his sleeve. He knew what he'd find, but the emergency alert still sent panic racing into the pit of his stomach. The words were bright, scrolling across his screen with alarming urgency.

> Security breach on Satellite II. All available
> personnel report to Capitol Armory. Prepare
> for immediate departure.

"Shit." Lark looked up from his own screen, mouth hanging open. "What is this?"

Cyrus shook his head. It wasn't just the alarm pounding through his veins now; it was fear. There weren't supposed to be people on the satellite base. That was why he'd given Ava the access codes, but if the Capitol was calling for available personnel, someone must have found them. There must have been a fight.

What does that mean for you?

Suddenly, Cyrus wished he was alone so he could slip back to his room, curl up under his blankets, and shut everything out. He never meant for it to go this far. He was trying to *fix* things, but Lark was here, looking seconds away from doing something reckless, and Cyrus wasn't ready to lose anyone else today.

"Don't—" he began, but Lark had already tossed his crutch

to the ground and shouldered his way into the armory. Cyrus bit back a curse and followed him through the swinging double doors.

The armory was thrumming with barely contained adrenaline. Around him, soldiers reached for their weapons, strapping on helmets and tactical gear without bothering to check anything out. Most were at-patrol or foot soldiers in casual dress, but Cyrus noticed a few cadets among them, borne forward by the flow of people streaming toward the aircraft hangar. His stomach twisted at their wide-eyed expressions. Did they think this was another simulation? Another test?

He found Lark in the back, leaning forward to shout over the alarms as an at-patrol girl struggled to fasten her helmet. "What is this? Where are you assigning ships?"

Cyrus did a double take at the girl's red hair before she turned and he saw her face. *Not Cornelia.* "Garage seven," she said. "You can follow me." Her voice was muffled, bright with fear, and Cyrus felt the floor rumble under his boots as ships fired up, one by one. She strapped her weapons across her back and motioned them forward. "Did you hear what the alert was for?"

Lark shook his head. "No. Did you?"

The girl's face was pale through her helmet. "It's Mannix. Shots fired on Satellite II."

Lark's eyes widened as she disappeared into the crowd. Then he grinned. Cyrus knew that look. It was the same one he had before taking to the sky in the Nakaran capital, the one that almost left him in pieces on the ground.

"You're hurt," Cyrus reminded him, gripping his arm. "You should stay—"

Lark shoved him away before he could finish. "She *stabbed* me, Cyrus. If she's there, I'm going to kill her."

Then he was gone, caught up in the crowds streaming toward the waiting ships. Cyrus swore again, turning in a circle on the armory floor. If he had any sense, he would stay far away from this mess entirely. He'd let the satellite soldiers sort themselves out and write their reports. He'd never speak of this again. But Lark was here and Lark was reckless, and even though Cyrus hoped Ava was light-years away from the base by the time he showed up, he couldn't risk the option where she wasn't, or where Lark became the kind of officer Cyrus was trying so hard to save them from.

He grabbed a spare helmet from the wall and ran into the crowd. *This is never going to end*, he thought as he pulled himself onto a waiting Catapult. This was never going to stop.

Maybe that was his consequence at last.

CHAPTER TWENTY-EIGHT

✳ ✳ ✳

Asteroid motels were made for fugitives. That was what it always felt like.

The rooms were in constant motion, too difficult to track through open space, and there was so much junk floating around the colonies that no one ever bothered to come looking. Because there was no one out here worth saving.

Ava remembered pacing one of these grimy motel bathrooms the night the Nakaran authorities took Shane to Chess. She had cried in the shower, splashed foul-smelling water on her face, and walked out with a plan. She remembered washing clothes in the rusty sinks, cleaning wounds by flickering lamplight, stitching Jared's hand together after he sliced it on a piece of glass.

She remembered feeling invincible.

Now Ava had to clutch at the wall as her ankle gave out again. She knew it was broken. She'd heard the snap the minute that door came down on top of her. The pain had pulled the air from her lungs in one crushing blow, and the thought that followed was instant and certain. *This is what dying feels like.* Of course it was. What else hurt like that? But here she was on the dusty carpet of some long-forgotten motel, stubbornly, inexplicably alive.

Ava closed her eyes as another sickening wave of nausea crashed overhead. She could see them here, outlined behind her eyelids, bright and burning and painful to look at. Jared, who had been with her since the beginning, who had sat next to her on the floor of their stolen ships during the months they'd been alone. Clara, who had held her hand in the desert, who Ava loved more than she wanted to admit, because admitting it would mean losing someone else.

The thought fractured through her, cruel and sharp. *Clara, Jared, Clara, Jared.* And what did they have to show for it? The information they'd risked everything for died on that base, smothered by gunpowder and smoke and angry blue flame. Nakara would be next.

That's your fault, too.

Ava slammed her fist into the wall, and the cheap plaster cracked around her knuckles.

They weren't supposed to carry hope on jobs like this. She should have abandoned her own years ago, left it buried under the floorboards in West Rama, but she hadn't been able to let it go. She kept it locked under her ribs so that each time the shadows lengthened and the stars blinked out, she could put a hand to her chest and remind herself that they weren't done.

But when Ava reached for it now, her fingers only brushed bare skin and the cold metal bite of her necklace. There was a strange sound echoing in the back of her mind, like air hissing through locked vents. Maybe this motel really was falling apart. Maybe there were Opian soldiers at their door, whispering as they closed ranks. At this point, Ava would let them take her. It wasn't until she felt Shane's hands on her skin, gripping her face, that she realized the sound was coming from her.

Her own ragged breathing, too rapid, too tight.

"Ava."

His voice was far away, floating somewhere in the space over her head. Ava's fingers ached as she gripped the cheap motel carpet. Because this was her fault. Shane was still saying her name, forehead pressed against hers, but Ava felt the touch like she was watching herself from another room.

"*Ava.*"

She drew in another shuddering breath as Shane's fingers slid through her hair again and again. The first sob tore its way up from that place deep in her chest, and Ava lurched forward as the sheer gravity of it slammed into her. Shane caught her before she hit the ground.

Your fault.

For trusting the wrong people. For thinking there was a chance. People like them didn't win wars or topple empires. No one did. Ava's fingers twisted in Shane's shirt as pain sliced through her ankle. Maybe this was how he felt all the time, haunted by demons and ghosts and lost friends he couldn't save.

"It's okay." Shane's voice was low in her ear. "You're fine. I'm fine. We're *fine.*"

The words tasted like ash in her mouth. Docking a stolen ship at an asteroid motel and sneaking into empty rooms used to be a game. Now, crouched together on the floor, it felt hopeless. Shane hadn't even put their usual security measures in place or covered their tracks on the way in. *Let them take me,* Ava thought savagely. Let them string her up as an example of what happened to those who dared challenge Opian power. This was what they wanted, wasn't it? This was what she deserved?

But the deeper she sank, the tighter Shane held. He gripped her shoulders, fingers curled in the back of her dress, and every time she struggled to catch her breath, he pulled her closer, like he was afraid she would vanish if he let go. Ava thought she might.

There wasn't much left to hold on to.

CHAPTER TWENTY-NINE

✳ ✳ ✳

Cyrus saw his first dead body when he was seven, stuffed behind a dumpster in an alley that smelled like rotten fruit.

Back then, no one said the girl died of starvation. The official report probably said exposure, from breathing the smoggy air without a filter for too long. But Cyrus knew what hunger looked like. He'd seen the way the girl's skin stretched over bones that had nowhere left to go. After that, he started noticing where people went to die. Under the highway overpass. Between the school and the library. They became a part of the city's landscape, so common Cyrus forgot there were people who didn't grow up stepping over corpses on their way to class.

During his first year at the Academy, a cadet had smashed his Falcon into the docking station during a test flight. He and Cornelia helped haul him into the air lock, but it was already too late. Cyrus could still picture his classmates' shocked faces, how afraid they all looked as they watched the boy's hand dangle from the smashed window, blood dripping between his fingers.

Like it never occurred to them how easy it would be to die.

But Cyrus hadn't seen anything close to the scene that greeted him when his ship docked at the satellite base.

He saw the bodies as the doors slid open, five of them piled in front of the air lock. Mouths open, uniforms stained red. He swallowed and turned his back, scanning the faces inside his ship instead. He had lost Lark in the chaos and boarded the first Catapult he could find. This one held a few combat soldiers, a pilot, and three cadets he didn't know. They were all looking at him, wide-eyed and expectant, and it took Cyrus too long to realize they were waiting for his orders.

He cleared his throat and pointed at the cadets. "You two, go find a medic. Do what they tell you and don't ask questions. You." He jabbed a thumb at another. "Take a lap. See what's on the other side. I'm going to find a commanding officer."

They nodded, flashed him a quick salute, and jumped to the ground, tracking blood down the hallways as they moved. Cyrus had to take several deep breaths before he steadied himself enough to follow, through halls riddled with bullet holes, past the smoking, burning wreckage of what was once the aircraft hangar. The whole base felt like a dream, like an unrelenting nightmare of his own creation.

Cyrus tried, *really* tried not to look at the ground, but the carnage was impossible to miss. A line of corpses stretched from the air lock toward the server room in the center of the base, a gruesome parade of twisted limbs and frozen faces. *You did this.* He'd sentenced these people to a gruesome fate the second he believed Ava Castor was anything other than a murderous, manipulative liar.

I want my friends to stop getting hurt. That was what he'd said.

It was what she'd promised.

Soldiers moved in every direction, taking inventory, examining bodies. Some were at-patrol, dressed in dark blue, some were foot soldiers, others were dressed in capital colors. For once, the uniforms didn't matter. Even the medics were useless. There was nobody to save.

Cyrus watched a bulb flicker on and off in a smashed window as he stepped over another outstretched corpse. If this was Port City, he'd be making a wish.

He spotted Lark as he turned the next corner, standing with a gloved hand braced against the wall.

Cyrus lurched forward instinctively, hand outstretched, and was surprised when Lark did the same. He didn't realize how much he was shaking until Lark's arms locked around him and all thoughts of their earlier fight vanished.

"Cyrus." Lark's voice was hoarse, breath ruffling the hair against his ear.

Cyrus drew back but didn't let go entirely. "How long have you been here? What—?"

He broke off without finishing the question. It was pointless. He already knew what happened. He knew whose fault it was.

Lark scanned the bodies under their feet, then looked away, face ashen. "They caught us by surprise. Some of the squadrons in the area answered the distress call without knowing what they were flying into, but it was too late. They were . . ." He had to clear his throat twice before finishing. "Outmatched."

It was the first time Cyrus had seen Lark talk about the gang with anything other than hatred and burning revenge. There was something dark filling his stomach, rising in his chest. How many had died here this afternoon? He thought of that first botched flight from the Nakaran capital, the way he'd been so convinced he was *right*, all the times he could have killed Ava where she stood. She had made him believe they were helpless, a small crew incapable of taking on the Opian dreadnoughts, but they had destroyed this place. They had used his weakness to their advantage and fled, like this was a game.

More blood on his hands, more consequences laid at his feet. They were going to crush him one day.

He gripped Lark's arm a second longer before pulling back. "I'm going in," he said. "Meet you back at the ship."

Lark looked like he wanted to say something else but thought better of it. "Be careful."

By the time Cyrus entered the server room, he was starting to wish he'd brought Lark along. Being alone here felt like an admission of guilt. There were soldiers everywhere, running tests on the computers, poring over bodies in every corner. Cyrus focused on his breathing as he walked and forced himself to memorize every detail.

The sound of a faded gunshot echoed through the room, and Cyrus flinched. He turned to find two older officers reviewing security footage on a grainy screen. He recognized Ava immediately. She stood over two kneeling soldiers, dark hair flowing down her back as she pointed her weapon between them. The video warped as he watched. When it came back into focus, both soldiers were crumpled on the ground, and Ava was walking away. The next clip was the same. Ava, gun pointed down. The sickening crack of a bullet releasing from its chamber. The *thud* of a body against the floor. One by one, over and over.

Cyrus stumbled back, gripping the wall as the truth hit him, hard and fast as one of those bullets. *She killed them.* She had killed them all after promising she wouldn't. With a single shot to the head so every Opian soldier had time to watch as death came to claim them, just like she had on the supply ship, and it was his fault. Ava could have slit his throat anytime, but she had always been saving him for this. So he could watch the destruction of his own people at her hands, a sick revenge for the power General Noth took from their planet.

"Capital soldier?"

Cyrus blinked and turned to find one of the other officers staring him down. "What?"

"You're from the capital, yes?" she asked, nodding toward his uniform.

Cyrus looked down. *From the capital.* She probably thought he could help, that he knew what to do. "I . . . Yes."

"Good." The woman jerked her chin toward the hallway. "There's something you should see."

Cyrus followed her out of the server room, around a corridor that curved toward the east end of the base. There weren't as many bodies over here, but the smell of smoke still lingered. Cyrus did a double take as an at-patrol soldier shouldered past them. *Cornelia.* Cyrus hadn't thought of her since he boarded that ship, but he would find her after this, regardless of whether she wanted to see him or not. No one should be alone here.

He followed the officer down another quiet hallway, and it wasn't until she turned, sweeping out an arm, that Cyrus realized why they needed privacy.

Two figures sat bound and gagged against the wall, hunched and shaking in the harsh light of the base—Clara and the Nakaran boy who had held him at gunpoint that first night on the ship. Both were dirty, coated in dust and debris. The boy flinched at the sight of them, and a flash of light caught Cyrus's eye. He looked down at the pane of glass embedded in the boy's pale forearm. *A skin screen.*

So he was the hacker, the mysterious figure terrorizing the Nakaran military. He was barely a kid.

Neither of them spoke as Cyrus came to a stop, but he could feel Clara watching him. He forced his expression to remain neutral as the officer nudged the boy with the toe of her boot.

"They haven't said anything," she muttered. "We found them in the air lock, and Noth wants them in the capital tonight. You have room on your ship?"

Cyrus felt like he was coming undone, but he forced himself to sort through the information piece by piece. He was the closest thing to a capital authority here, the closest person to General Noth. Of course she wanted these two in custody. This was her breakthrough, her moment, but they still didn't have the proper jurisdiction. Despite everything, they should still be turned over to Nakara's authorities for punishment. But General Noth always did whatever she wanted. Cyrus wondered if she ever faced the consequences of her own actions.

"Yes," he choked out. "There's room on the Catapult I came on. You can take them there."

Better him than someone else.

The officer nodded and hauled the two prisoners to their feet. "I'll meet you at the ship."

Cyrus looked away as Clara's eyes narrowed, and it took every ounce of willpower to avoid sinking to his knees as he watched the three of them vanish around the corner. As soon as they were out of sight, he sagged against the wall, running a hand through his hair as his thoughts spiraled. This was too much. This wasn't what he signed up for.

It is, though, the Port City voice whispered. *This is exactly what you signed up for. You knew it from the beginning.*

Cyrus took his time walking back to his ship. He wanted to remember every face, every prone body, every twisted limb. He kept coming back to the hands as he walked, still caught in the memory of that first cadet's mangled fingers. There were young hands, fresh out of the Academy. Old ones, veiny and twisted. Hands still gripping weapons or clutching the front of someone else's shirt. A hand with chipped, blue nail polish, just like the kind Cornelia wore.

Just like Cornelia.

Cyrus had never been cold on Opia or any of its bases, but there was ice in his veins now. It felt like a warning, and he knew before he touched the palm, before he felt the scar on the back of her hand. He knew before he shifted the bodies and saw her face. *Cornelia.*

She could have been sleeping. Her eyes were closed, hair swept in a careless wave around her head. A trickle of blood dripped from the wound in the center of her forehead, the only sign anything was wrong.

Cornelia.

Brave, fearless, reckless Cornelia, his first friend, his second half, who made spectacular plans on rooftops and whispered secrets in the dark. *We could go. We could go tonight.*

Cyrus released her hand and stumbled back. Now he was the one who couldn't breathe. He was frozen, and they were the only two people in the world. Except Cornelia wasn't here. A cry bubbled in his throat, and he tilted his head toward one of the cracked windows and the void beyond.

She did this.

And in that moment, Cyrus didn't know if he meant Ava or General Noth, because if one of them had pulled the trigger, the other had loaded the gun and placed it in enemy hands. But his second thought was worse. *You did this.*

These were supposed to be his consequences to bear. He was supposed to *save* her.

Cyrus took another step and felt the soft cushion of skin beneath his feet. He whirled, chest tight, and stumbled over the twisted corpse of another at-patrol soldier. Death. Carnage. *Cornelia.*

Your fault.

Cyrus's knees buckled, and he fell to the ground, hand slipping on a stagnant puddle of blood. It was still hot.

PART THREE:
One Last Shot

Some day they'll go down together
they'll bury them side by side.
To few it'll be grief,
to the law a relief
but it's death for Bonnie and Clyde.

—Bonnie Parker,
"The Trail's End"

CHAPTER THIRTY

***

Shane dreamed of open space and cold hands, faces blurring together too fast to see. *Henry. Ares. Jared. Clara.* Countless Opian officers and Nakaran soldiers. The man he had murdered on Chess. They laughed as they descended, ghostly figures against the stars.

Henry ran an icy hand down Shane's face. *You killed me,* he whispered. Then he vanished, and Ares took his place. *You killed us both.*

Shane was never cold, not even on Nakara, but he couldn't stop shaking now. He closed his eyes as Clara wrapped her long fingers around his throat and whispered, *You left me,* in a voice dry as the desert wind. Shane tried to shout, but the abyss closed over his head, pulled the sound from his lips. He couldn't speak. The pain around his neck was unbearable.

You thought you could save them? It was the voice of the Opian general, the woman with eyes like steel. *You thought you could win?*

The figures swarmed together, the frozen tail of a passing comet. Jared's eyes were pure longing. *You killed me. You killed us all.*

But the ghost who took his place was worse. It was Ava, gaze edged with glittering, cruel frost. Shane's knees buckled as she leaned down and cupped his face. *You killed me. I trusted you, and you killed me.*

Shane shook his head. *Not real.* She was alive. She was safe. But those eyes . . .

The others joined in, a haunting chorus of voices, and Ava let him fall back into the dark.

Shane.

She might have said his name, but he was too far gone, falling down, down, down into the void.

"Shane." Ava's voice again, louder this time. Then a touch on his arm.

Shane jolted awake. He reached for her instinctively as the world sank in a fraction at a time. The dim motel, the dusty air, the cold, empty sheets. *She's gone. You're alone, you're—*

"I'm right here."

Ava sat on the edge of the mattress. She reached back, and Shane tensed, momentarily expecting the burning cold from his dream. But no, she was real, and the fingers on his skin were warm. He sagged forward without thinking, pulling her into his arms, and Ava gasped as he knocked her injured leg.

"Sorry!" Shane released her immediately, wincing at the rough scrape of his words. When he brought a hand to his throat, the skin still felt bruised and tender. "I'm sorry. How do you feel?"

Shane realized too late what an absurd question it was.

Ava had dug three different bullets out of him last night, just let them clatter to the floor before wrapping his injuries as best she could. He'd tried his best to bind her ankle, working with what he could find around the room, but it wasn't enough, and

Shane could tell from the light sheen of sweat on her forehead that she was still in pain. They both needed real medical care sooner rather than later. Ava didn't answer him. Instead, she turned and pointed across the room with a trembling finger. "Look."

Shane squinted at the wall screen as the pain from his own injuries edged in. Ava had left the sound off the news program, but he translated the text scrolling across the bottom in the system language.

Nakaran Insurgency Group Massacres
Opian Soldiers: Over Fifty Dead

He had to read it three times before the words sank in. *Fifty?* No, he must be translating something wrong. Shane remembered being surrounded. He remembered shooting his way out, like he always did, but neither of them had time to murder fifty people. He barely had time to save one. *And you lost two.*

Shane couldn't hear what the reporters were saying, but the images sliding behind them didn't require an explanation. Bodies piled in the halls of the satellite base. Blood running between cracks in the floor. Limp hands and open mouths and glassy eyes. Some of the photos had been censored for broadcast, but it wasn't hard to fill in the blanks. *A massacre.* Shane pressed both hands over his face.

He couldn't match his memories with what he was seeing on-screen. It hadn't been like that. It wasn't possible. But every time he tried to push the thoughts away, they dug their claws in deeper. Maybe he had fractured somewhere along the way, lost it enough to not remember murdering fifty soldiers.

"Why does it look like that?"

He looked up at the sound of Ava's voice. There was a video playing behind the anchors now, grainy and warped, like it had been taken from a security camera. It showed Ava standing over two Opian soldiers, weapon in hand. The video blurred, bathed in static, and when it cleared they lay sprawled on the ground as Ava walked away, gun extended like she was ready for her next victim.

Shane's head spun as he tried to place the video. There had been so much happening, people running, gunfire, flames. Ava had probably stood over someone like that at one point, maybe she shot them, too, but the context was wrong. Where were the others? Where was the chaos?

Why was she alone?

Shane couldn't help it; he turned the volume up as the program cut back, and he flinched at the sight of the Opian general sitting beside the anchors in the studio, head bowed as if in mourning. She looked as cool and collected as she had in the Nakaran capital, haunting as the ghost in his dream.

One of the news anchors turned to face her. "Can you explain what this footage means, General Noth?"

He spoke the system language so anyone watching would be able to understand, but his accent was Opian.

"Of course." The general answered in the same language. "That video is appalling, isn't it? Ava Castor—one of the Nakaran insurgents we've been tracking for the last two months— executed Opian soldiers while the rest of her group robbed us blind. She showed no mercy."

Next to him, Shane felt Ava release a shuddering breath and on-screen, the other anchor nodded, like that made perfect sense. Like she always thought it would end like this.

"Can you tell us what exactly was stolen?"

Noth shook her head. "That's largely classified, but I can tell you they made off with several dozen military-grade weapons and a decent amount of sensitive information—the location of our at-patrol teams and ground soldiers, for example."

"Exactly how much does that endanger Opian troops?"

"More than I can express." General Noth's face was grave as she turned to look directly into the camera. "Ava Castor executed dozens of soldiers on an Opian base. Shane Mannix killed countless more. They've destroyed our ships, our property, and endangered every one of our troops. This story that they're rebel kids in over their heads . . ." She trailed off before adding, "I wanted to believe that for a long time. But make no mistake, those two are threats, and if Nakara can't stop them, we certainly will."

Shane had heard enough. He turned the screen off before the story could continue, but the silence that settled over the room was almost worse. So this had been the general's plan all along. Set them up, lead them into a trap, frame them for a crime they didn't commit, and use their fall as an excuse to invade Nakara on her terms.

Ava was twisting her necklace between her fingers, pulling at the chain until her knuckles went white. "Who killed those people?" she breathed. "Why? Why is she doing this?"

Shane didn't know. It was possible no one was dead. He couldn't tell the lies apart anymore. Maybe the Opian general's secret deals were making her rich. Maybe she enjoyed the thrill of tearing Nakara apart from the inside out, of letting Ava take the fall for her crimes.

When the nightmares first came, Shane would close his eyes

and tell himself that Chess wasn't an option for her, not really. People liked the idea of her more than they liked him. They might lock her in a Nakaran prison for a while, but she was *Ava Castor*. She'd get out eventually, and every magazine in the system would clamor for an exclusive with the girl who ran with convicts and lived to tell the tale. Now Shane couldn't think of anyone who'd jump to profile a killer. He had accepted his fate long ago, but General Noth had just handed Ava a death sentence.

He reached out, wrapping a hand around Ava's knee. *Not an option.* He'd kill every person in this system before he let them take her.

"It's fine," he said. One day, it would be true. "We'll try again. There's still time. We'll find another base, hack a different system."

But you don't have a hacker, a voice whispered in the back of his head. *You don't even have a crew.*

Ava looked like she was thinking the same thing. "No one cares, Shane. No one has ever cared."

"I care." Shane pointed toward the screen, where the general had been seconds before. "It's her, right? *She's* doing this. Everything we needed was on those servers. Why can't we try again?"

"Because it's gone," Ava whispered. "I failed. Who knows if it existed in the first place? She's not some random Nakaran officer. We're nothing to her. We have no proof."

Shane shook his head. "We're the proof. She's not hiding. The fleets, the meetings with Cordova? She's colonizing Nakara right now. If we could lift the blockade, the other planets would see it, too."

He couldn't remember the last time he'd talked like this. The plans had been his, yes, but the hope, the drive, the unwavering belief that they were going to *make it* had always been Ava's. He could hope for them both, if he had to. Just this once. Just enough to finish it.

But Ava's eyes were still wet. "They won't believe us. Especially *now*. Not when I'm . . ."

She trailed off, but Shane didn't let her linger. He had momentum now, a feeling that had eluded him for months. "We don't need them to believe us. Isn't that what you said? We just need them to hear. Let's go back to Nakara and—"

"Shane, the whole system is looking for us! Especially Nakara."

"Exactly why they won't expect us." Shane could feel the current of desperation running under every word and forced it away. "No one knows how we get in or out. I'm the only one who can drive through the jump point."

Ava looked away, and Shane shifted toward her across the bed. They didn't have a choice. They didn't have *time*. They were bruised and broken and bereft, but every second wasted here was another closer to Nakara's destruction. Maybe they were the only people left in the whole system who could stop it.

"We can fix this," he insisted. "We're close, Ava, and once we do, we'll go somewhere nice. Just the two of us."

"Shane . . ."

"We'll figure it out! We'll leave the system, just like you wanted. There's—"

"*Stop!*" Ava buried her face in her hands. "Stop it, Shane. This is my fault. I did this. Stop acting like we're going to be fine. You don't know that!"

Her voice was glass shattering in the air between them, scattering across Shane's lap. When Ava looked up, there were tears caught in her lashes. He reached out and swept one away with his thumb, letting his hand linger against the side of her neck. There was something still nagging at the back of his mind. About the satellite base. About Jared's realization seconds before they fell apart. Someone had known about their arrival, but despite everything, Shane didn't know if it was because of Cyrus. It had been too precise, too calculated.

"We *will* be fine," he said. "I know it. And I know it's not fair, I know we didn't ask for this, but they're never going to stop. That's not on you. They're going to take what they want, and Cordova's going to let them, but our *families* . . ."

His voice wavered, and Shane had to squeeze his eyes shut to keep his composure intact. *It's not fair.* That was what Ava said that night on the ship. She was right. They had been at a disadvantage since the day Opian forces landed in the desert centuries ago. Ava ran a hand down his arm, threading her fingers through his as he struggled to catch his breath.

"I know it's not fair," she said, almost too quiet to hear. "But I don't think we're the heroes of this story."

No. Shane was starting to think they never had been. He squeezed her hand anyway. "Maybe, but this is not how it ends. Not here. We can't stay in an asteroid motel forever."

The corner of Ava's mouth twitched, and Shane's chest loosened at the sight. It wasn't a smile, not really, but it was close. "I wish we could."

"Me too."

Ava's hands slid along his forearms, up and down in slow, leisurely strokes. Shane shivered at the touch.

"Remember when you said I could tell you to stop and you'd

do it?" Ava asked. She didn't meet his gaze, but Shane could feel her trembling. "What if I told you to leave me here?"

"No." Shane shook his head. "Absolutely not."

"I can't help you," Ava said. "I can't even walk. You want to find a new crew and hit another base in the next two weeks? Fine. If anyone can do it, it's you, but I'm a liability. We both know it."

"No."

Shane was surprised by the conviction in his voice. He had no doubt Ava could take out every Opian soldier she needed to, even on one leg, but the thought of leaving her here, leaving her *anywhere* made panic blank out every thought. All Shane knew was that if the clock ran out tomorrow and they returned to find Nakara a crumbling mess of broken rock, he wanted Ava by his side, no matter what.

He leaned forward and slipped his hand around the back of her neck. "No," he said again, firmer this time. "I'm not leaving you."

Ava's eyes fluttered shut. "There are people counting on us to finish this."

"I know. We'll do it together."

"We might not have a choice, Shane."

Shane tightened his grip, weaving his fingers into her hair. "When I got out I was going to dump everyone and run, you know. I was going to take our money and go, but I couldn't leave you. Even then, I knew I wanted you with me."

Ava let out a frustrated sound that was half groan, half sigh. "But why—?"

"Because I love you!" The words hissed out between clenched

teeth. "Because I don't care what happens to that planet if you're not on it, and I don't see the point in fighting for something you wouldn't get to see."

Shane closed his eyes as a wave of dizzying terror swept through him. Those weren't the kind of thoughts he was supposed to share, and it was too late to take them back now. Too late to pretend it was anything other than the wild, unbridled truth. When he opened his eyes again, Ava looked momentarily stunned, mouth half-open as she blinked. "You *love* me?"

Shane ducked his head, ignoring the heat racing under his skin. "Well . . . yeah."

"Don't say it like that." Ava smacked his arm. "You have threatened to leave me in a remote location multiple times, Shane Mannix. You weren't exactly obvious." Then she leaned forward and kissed him, and Shane could feel her smile, timid and tremulous under her tears. "I love you, too."

The relief was instant. Shane choked out a rough laugh as he slid his fingers into her hair again. "Good. That would have been really embarrassing otherwise." He hesitated before adding, "We're finishing this together, Ava. All of it. I'm not leaving you here."

She nodded. "Okay. Together."

Outside, the abyss of open space roared. Not long ago, Shane wouldn't have been able to resist the call of adventure, the beckoning promise of a better world. But now, in this cheap motel room with its stained carpet and dirty sheets, he couldn't remember why he'd cared.

He was already holding the world in his arms.

CHAPTER THIRTY-ONE

✳ ✳ ✳

Cornelia looked like her aunt. Cyrus had never seen the resemblance before, but it was all he thought about now, as he watched her family sit together on the opposite end of the courtyard. But maybe he was seeing things. If he squinted, he could still see her perched along the brick wall. He could see her in the trembling blades of grass, in the open expanse of sky, in every glittering window. But there weren't enough wishes in the world for this kind of pain.

Cyrus managed to keep it together for most of the funeral, only making eye contact when necessary, half listening to speeches about other soldiers he barely remembered, letting Cornelia's aunt pull him into a single, bone-crushing hug. His skin felt alive when he stepped back, itching with things he couldn't begin to unravel, so he didn't try. He just shoved everything down as far as it would go until he stopped feeling altogether.

It was easier that way.

Because people like Cornelia shouldn't be able to die. She was too vibrant, too important, too real. She was spectacular, and Cyrus kept expecting to see her everywhere he went. Laughing in the dining hall, skipping through the aircraft hangars, jumping out of a Falcon. He hadn't said goodbye. That was the worst part. He had flown off on another mission, desperate to right some wrong that didn't matter anymore.

It wasn't until he watched Cornelia's family pick up the sleek, black jar of her remains that something inside him cracked. It looked too small in their hands, too fragile, and that couldn't be all that was left. Cyrus clutched at the bench in front of him as the ground tipped dangerously under his feet.

Breathe in. Cornelia racing him to the simulation pods. *Breathe out.* Helping her pick an outfit for their first Academy party. *In.* Cornelia on the rooftops of Port City, etched against the sky like an oil painting, hand outstretched in his direction. *Out.* That same hand sticking out of a mountain of corpses.

He didn't realize he was crying until Lark squeezed his hand.

"It's okay," he whispered. "It's okay, you're fine."

You're not supposed to show emotion in uniform.

Cyrus shrugged out of Lark's grip. He wasn't supposed to cry in uniform, and Cornelia wasn't supposed to be dead.

Maybe some rules were meant to be broken.

He spent the rest of the day flitting between security briefings. Somehow, the real world kept moving, even though Cyrus's own had collapsed. Precautions had to be taken. He kept his head down, listening as the older officers debated what to do next, how to prepare if the Nakarans came to the capital. At this point, Cyrus didn't care.

Every file on the satellite base had been wiped clean. It was only a matter of time before the gang released the stolen information and used it to bring an army of their own to Opian soil. The thought should have been reassuring, but Cyrus couldn't remember why it had been so important.

Was this what Cornelia had died for?

Through it all, General Noth handled the situation with a poise that Cyrus hated with every fiber of his being. Already, she was restocking weapons, reimbursing the base for its losses, making sure at-patrol was on alert for another attack. Even Planetary Leader Derian was taking action, giving clean, concise interviews to every media outlet who wanted a sound bite, stressing how dangerous the group was, how important it was to find them, how Nakara had failed the system time and time again.

Noth ran every council meeting with an ease Cyrus hadn't seen in weeks. It didn't make sense. A foreign insurgency group had infiltrated her airspace, stolen her property, massacred her people, and it wasn't until the next meeting that Cyrus realized why she was so relaxed. She was a victim now. She didn't need jurisdiction on her side. Her warships were justified. Her soldiers on a foreign planet were warranted. If she captured Ava or Shane, if she killed them even, there were dozens of dead soldiers that said they were hers for the taking.

It was exactly the opportunity she had been waiting for, and Cyrus had dropped it right into her lap.

Next to him, the at-patrol representative who had replaced Cornelia shifted in his seat. General Noth glanced toward him and the man looked down, clearly uncomfortable with the attention. "Forgive me, General," he said. "It's just . . . You still want them alive, right? They're so young. Are we supposed to shoot them out of the sky if they don't surrender?"

Honestly, Cyrus didn't want to shoot anybody ever again. He'd had enough violence to last a lifetime. But he watched the other officers nod and knew the answer before anyone spoke. *Yes.*

Planetary Leader Derian held up her hands. "No," she said. "We're not shooting anyone if we can help it; we're better than that. But I shouldn't have to remind you what they've done here. Fifty people are dead; it doesn't matter how young they are."

The at-patrol officer nodded, but Cyrus could see the hesitation in the hard set of his jaw. He should learn to hide that now, before someone decided his sympathy was a problem.

"You know." Lark leaned forward, elbows braced on the table. "I bet we could get them both alive if we timed it right. Use their families, lure them out."

Another at-patrol soldier scoffed. "And how many more of us would they kill in the process? No, we need to take them out now. Maybe a long-range silent missile? If we can get Mannix by surprise, then—"

"You really want to shoot them without a chance to surrender?" The words were out before Cyrus could stop them. He felt the entire room turn to look at him.

Under the table, Lark's hand settled on his knee, a gentle warning. "That's what they do, isn't it?" he asked. "That's what they did on the base?"

Cyrus flinched. He could still feel Cornelia's blood on his hands. *Your fault, your fault, your fault.* He should want to end this, by whatever means necessary, but they weren't even *pretending* anymore. He used to think the Opian military was the pinnacle of respect, that they lived by their motto of honor, loyalty, and dedication. Had that ever been true? Or was it just another lie to get kids like him to pick up a gun?

Sometime between Cornelia's funeral and now, his shock had hardened into something deep and cold. As the meeting carried on around him, Cyrus realized he was furious. At Noth for continuing like everything was fine when she was the reason they were falling apart. At Derian for sitting in her office and doing nothing. At Cornelia for leaving him here alone. At Ava for not cutting his throat when she had the chance.

"I'm sorry," Lark whispered when the meeting adjourned. "I didn't mean it like that."

"I know what you meant." Cyrus didn't recognize his voice. It was low and simmering. *Hide that now, before someone decides it's a problem.* He shook his head. "Never mind. Sorry, it's fine."

"Good." Lark exhaled, standing and slinging his bag over one shoulder. "You know it's for the best right? We need them gone, and if Cornelia—"

"Don't." Cyrus stood so fast his chair scraped across the tile. Briefly, some buried self-preserving instinct reminded him to calm down and not make a scene like this in public. But he couldn't help it. The sound of Cornelia's name on someone else's lips was too painful. "Don't," he said again. "I'm tired, Lark."

That might have been the first honest thing he'd said in days. His thoughts were a thousand fractured stars, a hundred disjointed constellations. *We could go. We could go tonight.*

He should let General Noth and the gang destroy themselves, claw each other to pieces until there was nothing left. Maybe they would tear the whole system apart in the process.

Lark looked like he wanted to say something else, but he froze, gaze snapping to something over Cyrus's shoulder. Cyrus turned and found General Noth walking around the table in their direction. Most of the other officers had left, and when Cyrus felt her gaze linger on him, he forced himself not to look away.

"Good morning, Lieutenants," she said. "Would you care to join me?"

Cyrus didn't care if she was offering the entire system; he had nothing left to give. But Lark raised an eyebrow, curiosity sparking in his eyes. "Where?"

Noth grinned. "I think it's time to give our prisoners a proper welcome."

There had been times over the years when Cyrus had been certain he'd reached the limit of what someone could reasonably be expected to endure.

When his father died mid-shift at an Opian factory and the officers fined his mother for lost production hours. When he learned his own general lied with ease and abandon so she could hoard entire planets for herself. When his friends didn't question increasingly violent missions or obviously skirted jurisdiction laws. When he found Cornelia's body in the mountain of corpses.

But Cyrus had learned to control that unease, to shove it away so anyone looking would see the polished soldier, the valedictorian cadet. He could push this feeling away now if he tried, standing in the narrow hallway of the capital prison. He wouldn't look at the blood on his shoes. He wouldn't watch the casual way General Noth wiped her fingers with a handkerchief. He would just take all of this and put it away.

"They have to know something," Lark said, and Cyrus flinched, yanked back to reality by the rough scrape of his voice. "Mannix could be in another system by now."

"Give it a minute." Noth tucked her handkerchief back in her pocket. "Let them feel it. What do you have so far?"

Lark's brow furrowed as he scrolled through his skin screen. "Not much. I got a name from an old yearbook—Jared Hamilton. But if he was good enough to defect from the Nakaran army, he probably wiped everything relevant." He paused before adding, "You think he's the hacker? The one getting into our ships?"

Noth's mouth thinned, but she didn't answer the question. "Anything on the girl?"

Lark shook his head. "Nothing. What about you?"

It took Cyrus a minute to realize Lark was talking to him. He jumped and pretended to scroll through his own screen. "Nothing."

Noth held his gaze a second too long before giving a small shrug. "Not a problem. They'll give in eventually."

They always do.

She didn't have to say the last part out loud. Cyrus wondered if she'd ever tell the Nakaran planetary leader about her prisoners. Maybe she would kill them in secret and pretend they had perished at the satellite base. The lie would be easy to craft, easy to believe.

Noth made them wait ten more minutes before opening the cell door again, and Cyrus searched for the familiar refrain as he followed, the comforting thought that this was *just another job*. But every job he worked had ended with people dead.

Another thing the Academy brochures neglected to mention.

Clara was crouched on the floor of the cell, adjusting the makeshift bandage she'd tied around Jared's arm. Cyrus looked away as the coppery scent of blood hit him. Earlier, Noth had taken one look at Jared's skin screen and pried it out with her knife, leaving nothing but a gaping hole and a few sparking wires behind. Now he watched fear slide across Jared's face as the door slammed shut. Cyrus knew how it must look. Three officers outlined in the murky glow of the lamps, stone-faced and scowling, weapons strapped to their sides. Cyrus used to avoid people who looked like that. He used to run.

Lark inhaled, stealing one last glance over his shoulder at Noth, and Cyrus watched him lock any lingering doubt behind a wall of thick, icy contempt. Clara pushed herself to her feet as he approached, shoving Jared into the corner behind her, but Lark didn't hesitate. Wordlessly, he wrapped one gloved hand around her arm and shoved her in Cyrus's direction.

Cyrus caught her before she fell, but Clara yanked herself out of his grip. He remembered her in the alley pressing his own gun between his ribs. He remembered her careful smile, how she put herself between him and Shane to give him the chance to escape, and he stumbled as General Noth pushed past him into the cell.

"Get out of the way if you're not going to be useful, Lieutenant."

She caught Clara's chin in one hand, and Cyrus felt his stomach drop. He wanted to shout. He wanted to tell Clara to run, to get out, but there was nowhere to go.

"Such a pity," Noth whispered. She turned Clara's face from side to side. "Everything you did for them, and they left you on a foreign base. How sad." Clara tensed, like she could sense the trap before it closed. Noth's grip tightened, voice lowering as she pulled Clara toward her. "Where are they?"

There was panic coursing through Cyrus's veins now, a trembling terror he couldn't pack away. Clara shook her head and Noth sighed, brushing a piece of the girl's hair behind her ear with gentle, deliberate fingers. "I'm trying to help," she murmured. "Those two used you, strung you along and dumped you as soon as it was convenient. You don't want to die for them." She paused again, letting the words sink in before adding, "Tell me where they are."

"No." Clara yanked herself free, gaze darting between Lark and Noth until it landed on Cyrus. Her face twisted. "You're a coward," she hissed. Cyrus felt each word latch in his chest. "You're a traitor and a coward. I hope you die here."

"*Enough!*" Lark stepped forward. "Where did they go? Where's Mannix?"

"I don't know."

Lark's hands fisted at his sides. He wavered, and when he glanced over his shoulder, Cyrus couldn't tell if he was looking for salvation or permission. General Noth made the choice for him. "Well?" she asked, one eyebrow lifting. "What are you waiting for?"

Silently, Cyrus willed him to wait, to look at him, to *stop*, but when Lark turned, all remaining traces of doubt had vanished, buried under years of high-level combat training.

Clara started to say something else, but Lark moved first. His fist slammed into her face, and Cyrus heard her nose crunch as her head snapped back against the bricks. Lark asked another question, then another, but Cyrus couldn't hear it over the roar in his ears. In the end, it was Ava's voice that found him. *Are you a good person?*

"Stop!" He stepped forward, catching Lark's wrist in midair. "This isn't helping, Lark!"

Clara's knees buckled, and she sank to the ground, eyes fluttering behind bruised lids. Lark tugged his hand away. He wouldn't look up, wouldn't meet Cyrus's eye as the silence stretched. For a minute, the only sound was Clara's ragged breathing. Then Noth stepped forward, lips curled as she unsheathed her knife.

"I didn't realize how deeply you cared for her, Lieutenant." She extended the blade, hilt up. "That's sweet. Do you want to ask him instead?"

Her gaze landed on Jared, and Cyrus swallowed the next swell of panic. He didn't want to ask anyone. He wanted to leave. But Noth was standing between them and the door, knife in hand, and Cyrus knew someone would have to take it. It should be him. This was his fault, his consequence to bear, but the thought of wrapping his fingers around that particular hilt was too much. *You're a coward.*

That was what Clara had said. As Cyrus watched Lark draw in another steadying breath and reach for Noth's blade, he knew she was right.

"Where are they?" Lark yanked Jared to his feet, letting the tip of the knife rest directly beneath the boy's chin. "Where did they go?"

Jared let out a terrified whimper, and Cyrus opened his mouth again. This time, nothing came out. He was too aware of Noth standing over his shoulder. *What is the point?* What was the point of exposing Noth's crimes and pushing her out if *this* was what she had already created? How far back did it go, this culture of fear and violence and death? How could he fix something like this?

You can't.

There was blood running down the side of Jared's neck now, darkening the collar of his shirt. Lark leaned in. "Where *are* *they*? Tell me, or I swear I'll cut her throat right here."

Cyrus tensed as Lark jammed a finger in Clara's direction. It was an empty threat. It had to be. Lark would never kill someone like that, but Jared's eyes widened all the same. "What would you do with them?" he choked. "Why do you want them here?"

His Nakaran accent was heavy on every word, and Cyrus wondered for the first time if Jared had any real idea what was at stake. Clara seemed to realize the same thing. She pushed herself to her feet, both hands braced against the wall.

Lark hesitated. "What do you mean?"

"I mean . . . you would bring them in?" Jared glanced from Lark to Cyrus. "Here? For prison?"

"No, Jared," Clara began. "Don't listen—"

"Of course they'd come here." General Noth cut in before Clara could finish. "I'm really trying to help you, Jared. Would the Nakaran government do that? You think they won't shoot your friends out of the sky the first chance they get?"

Jared swallowed, face contorting with pain as Lark's grip tightened on the knife. "You won't hurt them, then?" His voice broke on the last word. "If I tell you where they went, you'll bring them here?"

Noth nodded, a smooth, cool movement that sent Cyrus's pulse rattling. She pushed Lark's hand aside until he lowered his weapon, until it was just her and Jared standing against the wall. "You miss your friends, don't you?" she asked in the same soothing tone she had tried on Clara. "I get it. I would, too, and I promise if your information leads to their arrest, you have nothing to worry about. You'll all be together again."

Jared closed his eyes, and when he opened them again, he looked pained. "Nakara," he said. "They'll go to Nakara."

"No!" Clara lurched forward. "Jared, don't!"

But Noth drove her elbow into Clara's face before she could reach them. Cyrus caught her as she fell, and they were both shaking as he lowered her to the ground. *Nakara.* The answer was too obvious, too easy. Why would they go back to the one place everyone would expect them to go? Through his own haze of shock, Cyrus wondered if Jared had somehow pulled himself together enough to lie, if maybe there was still a way out of this for everyone.

General Noth must have been thinking the same thing, because she leaned forward, one hand still resting on her weapon. "Don't lie to me, Jared. You know what happens to people who lie to me."

"I'm not!" Jared insisted. "There's a crack in the jump point at the southern hemisphere. I don't think anyone knows it exists, but Shane does. They'll go home."

The silence was absolute. Cyrus felt it crawl up the walls, over the stones. Lark hesitated, the general's knife still clutched in one hand. "They'd never risk it."

"It's not a risk! Not for them. I can tell you how to find it. It would be an easy capture. No trouble."

Jared was talking fast now, like he was afraid Noth would

change her mind and cut his throat before he could finish. For a horrible second, Cyrus thought she might. Then she nodded and stepped back.

"All right. I want us in the air in ten."

"Ten?" Lark glanced at Cyrus. "You want us, too?"

Standing at the entrance to the cell, outlined in the dim light from the hallway, General Noth looked like she belonged on the battlefield. "I want your entire team. Especially you, Blake." Cyrus's throat went dry as her hand closed over his shoulder, a warning that sat heavy in his stomach even before she let go. "I think it's time for a reunion."

CHAPTER THIRTY-TWO

✳ ✳ ✳

The radio was dead, and Ava didn't know what else to try.

She had watched Jared do this dozens of times: detangling wires, assembling parts, patching them into the nearest comm system. It was the only way to slip a signal to Glen without setting off the Opian blockade, but Ava couldn't remember the specifics. Jared had always been quick and certain and . . .

And you're not Jared.

That was the problem.

Ava dropped the radio to the floor and closed her eyes as another wave of pain rolled through her. They were never getting off this asteroid. They were never getting back to Nakara, and she was going to die in an Opian ship. Shane had disabled the tracking mechanisms during that first frantic flight from the base, but the feeling of being watched lingered. Ava felt it now, sliding down her spine. Like the walls were alive and any second the forgotten souls of everyone she'd ever killed would claw their way up through the floor.

She glanced back at the broken radio, turning the hunk of metal over in her lap. She just needed a minute. One minute to contact Glen or someone else on the ground, one minute to guide them home. She didn't usually think of West Rama like that. Home. But right now, it felt like the only place left in the system. She twisted the radio dial with more force than necessary as she keyed in the call sign again, listening for a breath of static, anything to pull them through the dark, but it remained lifeless and still in her lap.

"Come on!"

Ava flung the radio across the bay. It hit the opposite wall with a loud clatter before falling to the floor, and there was a moment of silence before she heard the familiar dial tone at last.

"Hello?" The voice on the other end was hesitant but familiar. Ava dove across the ship, ignoring the painful twist in her ankle.

"Glen," she gasped. "It's me!"

She was so relieved to hear his voice that she forgot their usual coded exchange. The pause that followed was so long Ava thought she had lost the connection. Then Glen blew out a breath. "What did you do?"

There was a rough edge to his voice. It made him sound like Shane. Ava's vision narrowed on the radio as the ship contracted around her, walls bearing down from every direction. *What did you do?* Had the entire system seen that edited broadcast? Had everyone collectively decided what kind of person she was?

"No, I didn't . . ."

But Ava felt the words die in her throat. She didn't what? People were still dead because of her. Vaguely, she was aware of Shane climbing into the ship next to her, a grease-stained cloth slung over one shoulder.

"You can't." Glen's voice was fading, cutting in and out through the static. ". . . don't . . . it's dangerous . . . I'm sorry . . ."

"Wait!" Ava's hand ached from clutching the radio, cheap parts creaking under her grip. "My mother. Let me talk to her. Let me explain. Please."

She didn't realize she was crying until Shane took the radio and held it up to his own ear. "Where can we land?" he asked. "No, Glen, listen."

Ava buried her face in her hands as his voice lowered. She had been mistaken to think of West Rama as her home. There was nowhere in the system left to run. They weren't going to make it back. They weren't going to win. They weren't even going to leave this asteroid.

"Where can we land, Glen?" Shane asked again, louder this time.

There was another pause, and Ava thought Glen wasn't going to answer at all. When he spoke again, the words were resigned. "North of Bakers Field."

"Okay." Shane nodded. "It's supposed to be nice tomorrow afternoon. I'll see you then." He bit his lip, and Ava watched his shoulders tense before he added, "Bring her mother, Glen. Make sure she's there."

Glen muttered something Ava couldn't hear and the connection cut out. She ran a hand over her face as Shane started disassembling the radio. "I'm sorry," she whispered. "I'm fine."

"I know." Shane knelt, looping an arm around her waist so he could pull her to her feet. Ava swayed against him, unsteady on one leg, and Shane let out a small gasp as he braced himself against the wall. He had waved her off when she tried to check his bandages that morning, and she didn't think it was because he had magically healed over the last few days. As she leaned her head against his shoulder, Ava could hear his breathing, ragged with exhaustion.

If only the papers could see them now.

The pain had been worse last night. She had drifted in and out of sleep, caught in a sickening swirl of nightmares. She was back on the base, frozen as a horde of Opian soldiers swarmed from the sky. She was in West Rama, kissing Shane in the front of a stolen ship, driving with Jared through the junkyards. She was in the Lincoln with Clara, curled together across the seats.

Ava had tried to hold on to that one, gritting her teeth against the ache threatening to rip her apart, but when she pulled back, it wasn't Clara at all. Just a charred skeleton with broken fingers and wide, unseeing eyes.

Was that how everyone would remember her at the end of this? The girl who killed Opian soldiers and left the bones of her friends behind on a foreign base?

Ava turned and buried her face against the curve of Shane's neck. "Tell me the plan," she whispered. "Tell me how we're going to win."

Shane's answer was immediate. "We're going back to Nakara. We'll lie low in the desert for a day or two, find someone to set your ankle, and then we'll build another crew. We did it before; it'll be easier this time."

Ava nodded, and even though it felt impossible now, the idea of having a goal, a purpose, sparked something inside her chest. Not hope exactly, but it was close. "And then?"

"And then we bring Opia to its knees." Shane pressed a kiss to her forehead, and Ava wanted to bottle the feeling of it on her skin. "And then you get your picture in the paper. Front page."

He helped her into the copilot seat, and Ava remembered

the intoxicating feeling of seeing her face on the news for the first time, cutting out magazine covers and poring over articles. She had been famous. She didn't know if she wanted people to remember this—the girl who abandoned her planet, who only wanted to save it because a boy with sharp eyes and wild plans said her name like it was something important. She didn't know if she wanted them to remember the bad decisions, but she wanted someone out there to remember *her*.

Ava tilted her head so she could watch Shane detach from the motel air lock and guide the ship forward. "Do you think they'll print my name this time?"

"Of course." The corner of Shane's mouth lifted. "You're a star. There." He pointed into the void and Ava followed the line of his finger until she found the star he was looking at, brilliant and burning in the distance. "That's you."

She shook her head, unable to stop her own grin from spreading as they slipped into the first jump point. "That doesn't make any sense."

"Sure it does. Now pick one for me."

Ava didn't know how to tell him that there weren't enough stars in the system to do him justice, that the world could explode into a thousand glittering suns and she'd still only want to look at him. The stars were blurring by now, too fast to track as they flew between jumps. She watched the light pattern across the dashboard, falling into her lap, and reached out, sliding a hand over Shane's so they rested together on the controls.

Nakara might not feel like home, but he did. If the two of them were stars, they would be a supernova. They would be spectacular.

Ava was still looking at him when they took the first turn

into Nakaran airspace, her free hand gripping her seat as the turbulence rattled the ship. She was still looking at him when the twisting tunnel of space dust cleared and the stormy surface of the planet spread out below them like an oil spill.

And she was still looking at him when an Opian dreadnought melted out of the dark, crimson Falcons at its side and twelve different weapons systems locked and pointed in their direction.

CHAPTER THIRTY-THREE

✳ ✳ ✳

Cyrus was good at waiting. It was something the Academy had drilled into him from day one, the overwhelming expectation that he'd always have to wait for something. An assignment. An explanation. A way out. But now, perched in a Falcon several hundred miles above Nakara's surface, he couldn't sit still.

The rest of the strike team floated outside his window, forming a semicircle of armored Falcons around the coordinates Jared had supplied. Cyrus kept squinting, trying to find the supposed crack in the jump point, but there was nothing but wide, unending black.

"All wings report in."

General Noth's voice crackled over Cyrus's headset. Her massive dreadnought loomed behind the front line, cannons loaded and ready. He lifted a finger to his ear. "Ursa One, standing by."

He could sound like her, too, if he tried. He could lie.

"Ursa Two, standing by."

Lark's voice was cool and snappy in his ear. It was the first time he'd been in the air since the supply ship raid, and despite the earlier tension in the basement, Cyrus could hear the anticipation shivering through every syllable. The rest of their team checked in one by one, and there was a moment of trembling silence before Noth spoke again.

"I shouldn't have to remind you that this group is considered armed and extremely dangerous. We still don't know how many we're dealing with."

Her voice faded and Cyrus's hands tightened on the controls as she went over the plan again. As soon as the gang appeared, Noth would hail them over the radio to demand surrender. His team would escort their ship to the dreadnought's loading bay, and it would be over. It would be done.

No, it won't.

Cyrus didn't know what, exactly, Noth planned to do with them next, but he had a feeling this night wasn't the end of anything.

The seconds stretched into minutes, then to hours. Cyrus's legs cramped under the controls, and still he couldn't stop moving, tapping his fingers against the side of his seat, foot bouncing up and down on the floor. Maybe they were too late, maybe Ava and Shane had already reached Nakara's surface.

Maybe Jared had lied.

Cyrus had the strangest desire to laugh. Here was General Noth and a squadron of her best pilots sitting in the middle of open space as far from Opia as they could get. If Mannix wanted them gone, if Ava wanted to kill him the same way she had killed Cornelia, now would be the perfect time.

Before Cyrus could consider the possibility, a small burst of light cracked the open space in front of them. It was like it came from nothing, an invisible opening in the jump point that he still couldn't quite see. The air rippled and hummed and there it was—a lone ship in the dark, several yards away. He leaned forward, watching the stolen Catapult swerve at the sight of Noth's dreadnought, but the attempt was useless. There was nowhere for them to go. By the time it stopped, trapped in the semicircle of Opian Falcons, Cyrus was close enough to watch the smile fade from Ava's lips.

Shane had thought about death so many times that it should have felt like facing an old friend. But for all his wondering and all his close calls, he'd never actually considered what it would feel like to die.

He heard Ava inhale next to him, a sound that shattered through his chest with crushing finality. They weren't supposed to die here, surrounded by stars and dust and the vast, open void of space. They weren't supposed to die at all.

Shane reached for her, eyes darting between the waiting Falcons. There was a way out of this, there had to be. *Invincible.*

But maybe it had always been more like inevitable.

Cyrus watched Shane's eyes widen, pale and cold. He remembered standing at the end of Shane's gun in a frozen Nakaran alley, remembered picking his way through bodies on the satellite base. What was the difference, really?

Two boys who could shoot and fly and kill. Two boys from opposite ends of the system, who fought their way out of different kinds of prisons.

Cyrus tensed at the hum of static in his ear, and he remembered the other ships at last. Any second now, Noth would order Shane to surrender. Any second, they'd close in. He almost glanced back to see what was taking so long. But he didn't.

So Cyrus didn't see the shot until it was too late.

Ava wasn't lost for words often, but she couldn't find them now. They floated out of reach, hanging around the cluster of Opian

Falcons. All the things she never said. All the things she would never get to say. Only one remained.

"Shane."

It was barely a whisper. Ava knew he only looked at her for a second, but in that moment, it was absolute. She felt everything. His hand in hers, his lips on her skin, all the whispered secrets and stolen moments and private promises. When he spoke, his voice was fragile as the dusty edges of a dying star.

"I'm sorry."

Then the sky exploded. For an instant, it was like the flash of a camera.

It was like a supernova.

Fire looked different in space, a perfect circle of deep blue. Cyrus tried to remember if he had known that before now.

He didn't know who shot first, but the heat was instant as the rest of his team followed suit. It felt like he was watching through a wall screen, a simulation. He might have cried out. Or maybe he wasn't making a sound at all. That was another thing about space—no one talked about how quiet it was, so utterly still that even though the scene outside his window was brilliant and deadly, Cyrus couldn't hear anything except his own ragged breathing.

It took him a second to realize everything had stopped. The stolen Catapult floated, momentarily suspended between the stars. Then it tilted and fell, glass scattering across the dark. Vaguely, Cyrus was aware of General Noth's voice in his ear, coursing with triumph, but he only caught pieces.

"Recover the ship . . ."

". . . Time to go home."

". . . Congratulations."

Congratulations.

That snapped the final threads of his resolve. Cyrus tore off his helmet, sucking in a painful breath as a few of the other pilots soared toward the Catapult. Someone cheered, the sound too sharp in his ear, and he fumbled with his comm until it went silent. This was supposed to be a capture. This was supposed to be protocol. He flinched as someone else fired a celebratory shot into the distance. The surface of Nakara spread below them, and Cyrus wondered if anyone down there had noticed the ambush. If they wondered what happened. In the dark, the lone shots from the Opian fighters looked like shooting stars.

Maybe, somewhere down below, someone was making a wish.

When they landed back on Opia, the Ursa Team descended on General Noth's dreadnought like it was the last fuel cell in a drought. Cyrus watched the trapdoors under the ship open, slowly lowering the Catapult back to solid ground, and he had to grip the side of his Falcon as the ground swayed under his feet.

"Whoa." Lark's hand closed around his arm. "You okay?"

Cyrus couldn't answer. Everyone was scrambling forward, shouting and laughing, reaching through the Catapult's shattered windows. His stomach clenched at the thought of those prying fingers caressing the dead.

She killed Cornelia.

Ava and Shane had killed more people than he cared to

think about, but so had he. So had General Noth.

"Yeah." He straightened, pulling out of Lark's grip. "Sorry, I'm fine."

Lark didn't look convinced. His face was pale, worn under his helmet, and when he tugged it off, his usually perfect hair was rumpled and messy. Some part of Cyrus had always known he wasn't cut out for the things this job demanded, but the idea that this place and these missions could also tear apart someone as confident and committed as Lark was worse.

The doors of Noth's dreadnought slid open behind them, and Cyrus turned in time to watch two soldiers lead Jared down the ramp. He moved like his legs were made of water, broken and unsteady at every turn. Cyrus closed his eyes as the room swam again. He didn't know Noth had brought Jared. He didn't know she had made him watch. No one reprimanded the officers surrounding the stolen Catapult, and Noth made no move to dispel the growing crowd as she passed. Why would she? She was their champion, and those bodies were her prize, an assurance that no one would question her command again.

There were a lot of things Cyrus had chalked up to Opian politics over the last few months, things he shoved down to hide his unease, but something bitter slid up the back of his throat now.

Are you a good person?

"Cyrus." Lark was still watching him, hand hovering in the open space between them. "What's wrong?"

Cyrus couldn't help the laugh that escaped him then. The sound was too loud, too wild, but the question felt so ridiculous. "What's *wrong*? People are dead. We killed them." Then another thought struck him, chilling and electrifying all at once. "Did you know, Lark?" he whispered. "Did you know what we were going up there to do?"

"No!" Lark's eyes widened. "Of course not. But we had to, Cyrus. They were *bad* people. They killed—"

"I know who they killed, but that doesn't mean . . . I wanted us to be . . ."

Cyrus trailed off, a hundred possibilities slipping through his mind. *Good. Right. Better.* But those ideas didn't exist here, not when the very foundation of this planet was built on exploitation and fear. Cyrus didn't wait for Lark to answer. He didn't care what anyone had to say right now. He just grabbed his helmet from the front seat and stormed into the locker room, leaving the clamoring scene behind.

When he returned hours later to finish docking his ship, most of the crowd had dispersed. The Catapult still sat in the middle of the garage, but this time, Cyrus hesitated as he watched the remaining onlookers crane their necks to peer inside. He didn't want to gloat, but there was a part of him that wanted to know it was done. He wanted to see the girl who'd used him, who promised him peace then turned around and killed his best friend. It wouldn't bring Cornelia back, but it might bring something else. Certainty. Closure. Calm.

Cyrus drew in a steadying breath, slid through the waning crowd, and glanced inside the ship. He immediately wished he hadn't.

The sight of Ava slumped against the ruined seats shattered through him, more painful than he'd expected because he had *just* seen her alive. He had felt the warmth of her breath on his face, watched her eyes soften as they stared at each other across the alley. But her eyes were closed now, head resting against Shane's shoulder. The dark sweep of her hair almost hid the bullet wound in her neck, but the two on her forehead were more obvious. There was blood caught in Shane's hair, too, drying on the seat between them. His face was turned the opposite direction, but he still clutched Ava's hand in both of his.

Where are the others?

Cyrus stood on his toes to peer into the back. It was too dark to see the rest of the ship, but he knew there should be more. There was supposed to be an entire gang here, enough people to overtake the base and slaughter Cornelia's squadron. That was how General Noth had justified her actions. That was what Cyrus had thought, too, because two people wouldn't have been able to do that alone.

As he pulled back, something glinted up at him from the edge of Ava's seat, caught in the fiery fabric of her skirt. Cyrus reached for it instinctively and knew what it was before his fingers brushed the faded metal. His old badge, the one she had stolen from him on Nakara months ago. It had been more than a badge then. It was a symbol of everything he had worked for— honor, loyalty, dedication. Now Cyrus wanted to laugh. Those were pretty words they told cadets.

Under the surface, this entire place was as grimy as Port City.

His badge came up tangled with a thin, silver chain, a necklace glittering in the harsh light of the hangar. Cyrus ran a thumb over the rectangular charm and remembered it resting against Ava's throat in the desert. They must have gotten wrapped together in her pocket, thrown free in the ambush, but he couldn't untie the chain. Someone bumped his shoulder from behind, another too-eager onlooker, and Cyrus pocketed the necklace with his badge as he stepped away from the ship.

He used to think Port City was a prison, with its smoggy walls and constant gloom, but the capital was more of a cage than anywhere he'd ever been. Here, he was bound by orders and oaths and Opian diplomacy. *We could go. We could go tonight.*

If Cornelia asked him to leave right now, Cyrus knew he'd say yes. He'd take her hand and board any ship she wanted.

Somehow, in a city surrounded by parties and celebrations and hundreds of his fellow soldiers, Cyrus was still alone.

CHAPTER THIRTY-FOUR

***

The debrief that followed was more of a party than anything Cyrus had attended at the Academy.

Those had all been secret—stolen alcohol and closeted meetings in the upperclassmen dorms. Now cadets and captains alike crowded together, watching images of the ambush flicker by too fast for Cyrus to track.

The Ursa Team members were guests of honor. He lost count of how many younger pilots asked him to recap what happened, how often he parroted the story back, trying to distance himself from the memory of the brilliant sky and bloodstained clothes. By the time he managed to shrug off the last request and collapse in a corner, his exhaustion felt like a second skin. He blocked out as much of the debrief as he could, but every once in a while, a phrase slipped through.

We fired in self-defense. They were already reaching for their weapons. We can rest easy knowing Opia is safe.

The words felt like ash. Cyrus knew Noth hadn't fired in self-defense, and he knew the rest of his team hadn't joined in because they were scared. She had done it to cover up her invasion of Nakara, to tie up loose ends and quiet the last remaining people who knew the truth, and here they were, letting the lie weave itself into the very fabric of this city. Cyrus didn't know which was worse—the idea that he was the only one who knew what she was doing, or the possibility that everyone else did too and no one was saying anything about it.

He clutched his old badge, letting the cool metal keep him grounded as the videos on-screen looped and played again. This time, it was grainy dashcam footage, short memorial clips of the at-patrol soldiers mid-flight the day of the satellite base attack. When Cornelia's face popped up, Cyrus almost forgot how to breathe. The quality wasn't great, but he could tell she was grinning under her helmet, and his jaw ached as the date and time scrolled along the bottom of the screen. 23:00, just before midnight. She was still alive in this video, on the screens in every corner of the room.

We could go tonight.

Cyrus pushed himself out of his chair. A few of the officers exchanged confused glances, and Lark reached for his sleeve as he passed, but Cyrus didn't stop. He couldn't sit with the secrets and the lies, the knowledge that Cornelia was never going to exist outside of a screen.

He tugged at Ava's necklace as he walked, fingers trembling as he tried to untangle it from his badge, to free some small part of his life from her clutches. Eventually, the chain snapped and the pendant slid into his cupped hand. The charm was simple, smooth silver surrounding a raised black circle, almost like the eye of a camera. A small, portable, stealthy camera.

Cyrus opened his fingers one by one, then held the broken chain up to the light. He worked his fingernail around the edges, digging into every groove until the bottom half of the charm popped back, revealing two paper-thin prongs.

It's a flash drive.

A thrill sparked in his stomach, cutting through the dull haze that had shadowed him since the satellite base. Was this the information he had helped them steal? Cyrus quickened his step as the charm burned into the palm of his hand. If Ava never had the chance to release the evidence of Noth's crimes to the other planets, maybe he still could. He didn't want to owe her anything. He didn't want to think about her, but if there was a way to really, truly end this, he wanted to try.

He was sweating by the time he made it to his room. It felt strange, like he'd been gone years instead of a night, but Cyrus ignored the insistent pull of sleep and switched on his wall screen instead. He slid the flash drive into the back port, and for a long moment, nothing happened. Then a muted, dusty-colored video expanded across the glass.

He flinched at the first glimpse of Ava Castor sitting cross-legged in front of a rumpled bed. The sight was jarring, nothing like the hollow corpse he'd left in the garage. She didn't look like the girl from the alley, either. Here, she was young, vibrant, full of life. She was somewhere on Nakara. That much was obvious from the spluttering fuel lamp over her shoulder. She was speaking Nakaran as well, too fast for Cyrus to piece together with his limited knowledge of the language, but the date in the bottom corner of the screen was clear. *Over a year ago.*

Not from the satellite base, then. Cyrus's fingers shook as he paused the video. He felt like he'd invited a ghost into his room, but if there was anything important on this drive, he had to know. Ava had kept it for a reason. After another minute of hesitation, he pulled up the translation software and started again.

This time, when the video played, he could understand her.

"My mother gave me this last year," Ava said, nodding toward the camera. "She knows I like movies and she said it was to record my exciting adventures, but honestly, the most exciting thing that's ever happened around here was when animal control took Sophia DeRise's cat away because it wouldn't stop biting the children. Which was objectively hilarious, but not exactly film worthy, you know what I mean?"

Cyrus thought it was strange to hear her speaking Opian, in the same silky voice that had threatened him in the alley. Ava ran a hand through her hair, expression souring as she looked away.

"It's so embarrassing. Nothing happens here and nothing happens to me, so this was just an accessory. But something exciting might have happened tonight. Or someone. And I don't know what it means, exactly, but I do know it was nice to have someone look at me like I mattered. And he offered me a job. *Shane Mannix.*" Ava said his name like it was honey. Then she shrugged. "I don't know. I don't know him, but if he ends up murdering me in the back of his ship, it'll probably make the news. I'm worth two weeks of coverage at least."

She hesitated a second longer before reaching out and switching the camera off completely. The screen went black, then faded in on a new video, dated a few days later. *It's a diary*, Cyrus realized. All the more reason to turn it off, but he couldn't move.

"My mother says I make bad choices to feel like I'm in control of something," Ava said. She was back in her room, knees drawn against her chest. "My teacher says it's because I'm impulsive and selfish, but maybe they're both right. I'm going to take that job offer because the thought of staying in West Rama makes me feel like I'm drowning, and if I'm going to leave anyway, I might as well leave doing something that makes me rich." She propped her chin in one hand, and Cyrus leaned forward despite himself.

"I used to climb the dunes when I was bored," she said. "I would stand at the top and look because I could see all of Rama from up there. The ships, the dome, the people. And every time, without fail, I'd look down and wonder what it would feel like to jump. Not because I wanted to hurt myself, but because this town feels like a cage most days, and if I jumped, I think it would be like flying."

Cyrus could feel it all. The gritty sand, the wind, the wild, burning desire to be somewhere else. He remembered sitting on the Port City rooftops, squinting through stinging, acidic rain, and counting the days until he could leave.

Ava's lips twisted and Cyrus had the uneasy feeling she was looking directly at him as she said, "I want to be someone, you know? I want to do something real, something spectacular."

It was like she reached through the screen and closed an icy fist over his lungs. For a second, it was Cornelia next to him, leaning into his shoulder, watching the factories belch smoke into the darkening sky. *Spectacular.*

The next video was dated several weeks later. Cyrus watched Ava settle herself on the lid of a dirty toilet, crouched next to a sink in a dimly lit bathroom. Her face was close to the camera and she kept glancing over her shoulder.

"This one has to be quick," she whispered. "But I feel like if

I'm using this, I should include the parts that are actually excit-ing, right? Like right now, we're in an asteroid motel. They look better in the movies, but I don't even care. This is so much bet-ter than West Rama. I think I'm supposed to feel worse about leaving, but when you come from a town like that, and then you see these places that have everything? It's not fair. And I think Shane has this fear of ending up like his family. He doesn't talk about them much, but he always visits. They've worked that farm for years with nothing to show for it, and I think he looks at his father and sees all this wasted potential."

There was a sharp knock on the bathroom door and Ava stood. "One second! That's Jared," she added to the camera. "We picked him up last week, and he still hasn't learned how to share. I have no idea where Shane found a kid with a screen, but it's nice having someone else to talk to. It was . . ." She trailed off, and Cyrus watched color rise in her cheeks before she spoke again. "It was overwhelming when it was just me and Shane. Usually, I think he's joking when he talks about the things we'll do when we have enough money and all the places he'll take me, but sometimes he looks at me and it feels so real. And I don't think I'd mind if it was."

The video cut out again, before fading in on another cramped hotel room. The next few entries were short, mostly Ava show-ing off her increasingly nicer clothes and bags of money while laughing and posing for the camera. Cyrus half expected to see Jared or Shane make an appearance, but she was always alone. In a bathroom, in a corner, in the front seat of a stolen ship. He watched the months on the run carve hollows into her cheeks until she looked more like the girl he remembered. Leaner, hungrier. Eventually, Cyrus paused on a clip from a few months ago. It was darker than anything he'd seen, and he realized Ava was sitting in the ruined air lock of the Lincoln he had chased from the Nakaran capital.

"I don't think I'm ever getting out of here." She had her hand propped on one knee, face close to the camera as she stared through the ruined floor. Cyrus could hardly hear her over the wind. "This was supposed to be our last job for a while. We were supposed to leave, but I guess if anyone was going to trap me here, it would be the Opian army. We're a commodity to them; that's nothing new. Shane's going to fight, because that's the kind of person he is, so I'm staying, too. Not because of him," she added hastily. "He's made his priorities abundantly clear, but I think he and Jared might literally die without me. And if anyone's going to disrupt the interplanetary trade market, it's going to be me, and I'm going to look amazing doing it."

Cyrus shivered as he clicked through the rest of the videos, hours narrating supply ship heists and narrow escapes and life on the run. In each clip, Ava looked older, cheekbones sharp under her skin, hair dull and tangled. He paused on a video of another dirty motel bathroom. Ava sat on the floor, dress torn against her bruised skin. She wiped the back of her hand across her face, and Cyrus glanced at the time stamp in the corner. It was late, about an hour before midnight. When Ava spoke again, her voice was hoarse, like she'd been screaming.

"I never thought this would last forever," she said. "I knew one day this would catch up to us, and I used to think about death a lot because when really important people died back home, they got their picture in the paper. Even then, there were ways for people to notice you, but . . ." She took a shuddering breath and a single tear snaked down her cheek. "My friends died today, and this is the first time when I really think I'm next."

When she looked into the camera, Cyrus caught his breath. It was a stark contrast to the brilliant, burning girl from the beginning of the tapes. *You did that.*

"Sometimes I feel like a dying star." Ava whispered. She swallowed, and even that small movement looked like it hurt. "Like there's no other way for this to end, but at least when we go out, it'll be spectacular. The kind of explosion that lingers in the sky for years. And I just hope whatever forms from our dust is stronger than we were. I hope they'll finish this if we can't."

Her hand hovered in midair, fingers trembling, and then she shut off the camera.

Cyrus stared at his reflection in the screen for a solid minute before realizing that was the last entry. The end. And he couldn't shake the uneasy feeling that Ava had been speaking directly to him. *I hope they'll finish this if we can't.*

He shuddered and turned off the monitor. The evening light was fading outside his window, and Cyrus realized with a jolt how late it was. Everyone was probably still celebrating their glorious victory, but he couldn't move. There were too many thoughts swirling through his head, forming galaxies, breaking apart. He couldn't catch anything long enough to hold it.

Ava was a good storyteller, but she had conveniently left out the part where she slaughtered dozens of Opian soldiers. Still, her last video was haunting. Cyrus could see it etched behind his eyelids as he buried his face in his hands. Her cold, helpless expression, her broken voice, and the time stamp in the corner.

The time stamp.

Cyrus sat up so fast he almost tipped back in his chair. Ava had recorded that last video an hour before midnight—23:00 on the day of the satellite base attack. The same time on Cornelia's log from earlier. Her squadron had been on their way to the base at the same time Ava had been making a video in the bathroom of some dirty asteroid motel, light-years away.

Was it possible to drown in something like this, for the lies to pull him down for good? They had built up gradually over the years, one by one.

Because, Cyrus realized, fist tight over the flash drive. *Because if Ava Castor and Shane Mannix didn't kill Cornelia's squadron, who did?*

CHAPTER THIRTY-FIVE

*** *** ***

Lark wasn't in his room when Cyrus knocked on the door the next morning. He wasn't in the garage, either.

The Capitol building was deserted as he made his way through the halls, daylight cracking over the horizon with every step. The fog that had settled around him at Cornelia's funeral was still there, cloaked across his shoulders, but it felt different this morning. Cyrus brushed his knuckles against the necklace in his pocket. Two girls from two different sides of the system, waiting with their hands outstretched. He was finally ready to take them. He just needed to find Lark first.

There was no longer a way forward here, and Cyrus was certain that if he told Lark everything, if he laid the evidence out in front of them, he could convince Lark to leave with him, too. He had lost too many people to this city. Another one would ruin him. He turned the corner as a door opened to his left and General Noth stepped out of her office, glowing golden in the light of the sun. Her lips curled at the sight of him.

"Good morning, Lieutenant."

Cyrus wondered if she had developed the ability to read minds now, too, if she already knew exactly how he was planning to desert his post. He inclined his head, every movement stiff. "General."

Noth opened her door, stepping back to wave him inside. "Do you have a minute?"

No. Cyrus never wanted to be in the same room with her again, but this didn't feel like an accidental meeting. The undertones were too sinister. Even now, in the Capitol building of his own planet, it felt like a trap. But what choice did he have, really? By the time he sat down on the other side of her desk, his jaw ached and every muscle was tense and trembling. General Noth folded her hands, and when she spoke, it was with the same measured calm she'd used during their first meeting on the satellite base.

"You know what concerns me the most about the attack, Lieutenant?"

Cyrus didn't trust himself to speak. He knew her concern was an act, but he couldn't help sinking back into it now. What would it feel like to believe her again, to wind everything back to the moment before things went so terribly wrong? Noth continued without waiting for an answer.

"The Nakarans were able to break into our airspace. They were in possession of classified information no one had access to. They used my personal clearance codes to land." She hesitated, and before Cyrus could gather his thoughts, before he could even start to build a defense, she asked, "Has Lieutenant Belle said anything to you about the attack?"

"What?" Cyrus looked up. "Lark?"

Noth nodded. "He was always so eager to pursue them. Ever since that day in the Nakaran capital, do you remember?"

"No." Cyrus could feel his pulse in his ears, drowning out all rational thought. "I mean *yes*, but he would never compromise classified information. Not even accidentally."

"That's what I thought, too. Until I found this."

Noth opened one of the files on her desk, and Cyrus's stomach dropped at the sight of the familiar cover. It was the one she'd given Lark all those weeks ago, the one Cyrus took for safekeeping. The one whose page he'd passed to Ava in that Nakaran alley.

"Here." Noth slid the file in his direction. "There's a page missing toward the back, the page with my personal access codes. I gave Lieutenant Belle this file myself, and my staff recovered it from your shared office this morning."

Cyrus couldn't look at her. He couldn't breathe. Why had he thought his crimes would go unnoticed, that General Noth wouldn't retrace every step in her search for answers? That he was somehow invincible for doing the right thing? His next inhale caught in his throat. "It wasn't Lark."

"This is difficult for me, too, but we need to face the facts. Lieutenant Belle was in possession of classified information— the same information that ended up in the hands of Nakaran insurgents." She rubbed a hand over her forehead before muttering, half to herself, "He'll have to be brought in, of course. If he doesn't confess, we can always stick him in the basement for a while. We were persuasive enough last time, don't you think?"

"No." Cyrus's stomach lurched at the thought of Lark, chained and bloody downstairs, trapped where no one would find him. "You can't."

"Lieutenant, I—"

"It wasn't Lark," Cyrus said, louder this time. He could feel the bite of his nails through his pants, digging into his thighs. "It was me. I did it. I took that file. I told them to come to the base."

The words hung between them, and Cyrus braced himself for their inevitable break, for the moment when they took him down for good. Then Noth sat back in her seat.

"There it is."

Cool amusement lined her gaze, and Cyrus realized, with a shock of pure panic, that she already knew. Maybe she had known the whole time, since the night she pulled him out of the desert.

Noth tapped a fingernail against the desk, a rapid click that echoed the uneven rhythm of his heart. "Why?" she asked.

Cyrus gripped the arms of his chair. He felt like he was sinking, pulling apart into open air. There was no point in lying. "Because you're sending warships to Nakara," he whispered. "Because it's not yours to take. They came to the satellite base to send proof to their allies, to ask for help."

"No." Noth's expression was pure venom. "They came to the satellite base because I told you to bring them there."

Cyrus opened his mouth, then closed it. It had been his idea, his plan. But then again, hadn't he gotten it from Noth in the first place? Her fake concern, her panic, her fear for the base's security. He'd fed that weakness straight to Ava, never stopping to question the source.

"Really, Cyrus." Noth crossed one leg over the other, a victor surveying her prey. "You have a tracking device in your arm. Did you really think I didn't know where you were at all times? Who you were talking to?"

Cyrus drew back. "Then why am I still here?"

"Because." General Noth leaned forward, and in this moment, she looked dressed for battle. "You needed to see what happens to people who defy Opian power. They lose."

They lose.

Ava and Shane had tried to stand against Noth's army and failed. Cornelia had tried to warn him, and she was gone, too. But Cyrus was still here. He was still breathing, and if Noth wanted him to think he was powerless, she should never have let him walk out of the air lock after the ambush. Slowly, Cyrus reached into his pocket, fingers brushing Ava's necklace. He ran a thumb across the back until he found the power button and flicked it on.

"So that was it?" he asked. "You wanted to win?"

"I was always going to win, Lieutenant."

Noth said it so casually, like the lost lives had never even been a consideration. It ignited the long simmering fury in Cyrus's chest, the anger that had been growing since the day his father died a painful, preventable death in a Port City factory.

"Was it a win to murder Nakaran citizens in their own airspace?" he asked through gritted teeth. He was running on adrenaline and panic and two hours of sleep, but if Noth was going to kill him now, he wanted to know everything. "Are you going to tell Cordova you're imprisoning his people? Will Derian ever know you're colonizing Nakara against her orders?"

Noth waved a hand. "We gave Cordova a statement. It's the same one we'll read at tonight's press conference. After the attack on the base, we formed our own strike team. We found the insurgency group before Nakara did and we had every intention of bringing them home. We would have succeeded if they hadn't opened fire. We acted in self-defense."

"That's a lie."

"Says who? Every other member of the Ursa Team will corroborate that story." Noth reached across the desk and pressed the back of her hand to Cyrus's forehead. Her skin was like ice. "Are you sure you know what you saw, Lieutenant? Didn't you just lose your best friend? Multiple members of your team? Was that not traumatic for you?"

Cyrus pulled away. He knew exactly what he saw. "Does Derian know about any of this?"

"Of course not. The planetary leader has no idea what she's doing. She's the reason we had to take it this far in the first place. All she knows is that her strategy of neutrality didn't work. I don't think she'll challenge me again."

"And what was your strategy, exactly?" Cyrus asked. "Why bring them to the base? Why did you use me? Why—?" He stopped abruptly as realization dawned. "Those soldiers," he whispered. "Cornelia's at-patrol squadron. You sent them to the base. You . . ."

He couldn't finish the sentence. The truth sat in his stomach like a black hole, too horrible, too wrong.

Noth shrugged, like the mountain of corpses was an inconvenience she had already forgotten about. "The Capricorn Team was dispensable. At-patrol can have the new round of Academy cadets. It's not like we have a shortage."

"You killed fifty people."

"And how many would we have lost if I let this continue?"

Cyrus remembered Cornelia's body, the single bullet wound in the center of her forehead. *One by one, so they could see death coming to claim them.* It was what he had thought Ava did, but the last thing Cornelia had seen was her own general pressing a gun to her head.

"But *why?*"

The question finally snapped her patience and Noth stood,

hands planted on the desk. "Because those two got *out*," she hissed. "Because they escaped again, and it was supposed to end in the cargo bay of that supply ship. We needed a reason to pursue them, so I made one. That squadron died as heroes."

"But they still died. You murdered them. Some of them were kids."

"They were soldiers. You all are."

Because we can only be one or the other. Cyrus clenched his numb fingers as he glared across the table. General Noth was the reason they grew up so fast in the first place, the reason he still felt like a stranger here. Cornelia was dead because of a political power game she never asked to be a part of, and Ava had been right.

There was no way to be a good person here, no matter how much he wanted to be, because the good people died.

"There's a press conference tonight." Noth sat back down, returning to her notes like he wasn't there, like she hadn't torn the very foundation of his world apart. "Nakara can't say anything without sounding defensive. You can't say anything without being discredited. The Ursa Team will go down in history and the Capricorn team was appropriately honored. They'll be replaced in a few months and everyone will move on. It's done."

Cyrus shook his head. "You have Nakaran prisoners in your basement. You have fleets on a foreign planet. You started a war you can't win, and your strategy was so fragile it was threatened by a few rebels in a stolen spaceship. Two of them almost stopped you; what do you think happens when the other planets get involved?"

"Enough!"

Noth slammed her palm on the desk, the sound cracking against her icy exterior. But Cyrus could tell he'd unnerved her. Maybe those were her consequences at last, to know that even if she turned around and won this whole thing tomorrow, it had been two kids from a planet she had written off who almost brought her down. Noth straightened the cuffs of her jacket as she walked around the desk with slow, deliberate strides.

"What would you even tell the other planets?" she asked. "I know exactly what those two were trying to steal from the base. You think that information still exists? You think anyone's going to believe you? No one cares about Nakara."

Cyrus closed his eyes as the truth of that statement sank in. He hadn't truly believed it until now, but Noth's confession was a complete betrayal of everything he had tried to be. This was the organization that promised him freedom, the same one lying to hundreds of kids right now, luring them in with blood-splattered pamphlets. How many others were like him? How many regretted this and couldn't see a way out?

How many died because they trusted the wrong person?

Noth's hand landed on his shoulder, nails wicked and sharp against his collarbone. "It's over, Lieutenant. There's nothing you can do. You have nothing left."

Cyrus barely felt her. "Why don't you just kill me?"

"Oh, I don't think you'll do something like this again." Noth leaned down until her lips hovered an inch above his ear. "Who might end up in the wrong place next? Lieutenant Belle, maybe? Your mother? She's all alone in that big city; accidents happen." She straightened, patting his shoulder one last time as she turned to go. "See you at the party."

It was several minutes before Cyrus was able to move. Noth would do it. She would march into Port City herself if she had to. To prove a point. It took him a long time to remember the necklace in his pocket. He clicked the camera off and drew it out with trembling fingers. How much of that had he gotten? How much could be heard?

Cyrus didn't remember leaving the Capitol. One minute he was in Noth's office and the next he was spilling out onto a smooth manicured sidewalk. But even in his certainty, he thought there was something comforting about having his worst fears realized. All this time, he had been right. *Never trust the officers.*

He was sweating as he made his way through the streets, palms slick. How could he spin this? How could he make people listen? Because Cornelia had started to figure this out. She had died for this information, and he couldn't just leave it. Cyrus rounded another corner and ran straight into someone coming the opposite way. He grabbed their jacket, and when he straightened, he found himself tangled with Lark.

"Whoa, Cyrus! Where are you going?" Lark's grin was hesitant, and Cyrus remembered their tense exchange in the garage yesterday. It didn't matter. He leaned forward and wrapped his arms around Lark's neck anyway, desperate for something familiar and solid. "Okay." Lark let out a muffled groan. "Love that we're doing this, but remember the time I was stabbed?"

"Sorry." Cyrus stepped back, and in that instant, he almost told Lark everything. But Noth's voice was a bitter echo in his ear. *Who would believe you?*

"It's okay." Lark ran a hand down his arm. "Let's talk at the party tonight. When are you heading over?"

Party. Noth had said something about a party, too, but Cyrus couldn't remember what. "What?"

"There's the press conference tonight, remember?" Lark tilted his head. His hair neatly combed again, glowing gold in the late-morning sun. "Noth invited everyone. Derian, all the ambassadors, a bunch of reporters." Then his voice lowered. "She's executing the prisoners."

Cyrus searched Lark's face for any sign of a joke, but for once, he was remarkably serious. "Executing? Didn't Jared make a deal?"

"I mean, she said she'd show mercy if his information led to an arrest, but they're dead, so technically . . ." Lark shrugged. "I don't know. I guess it's her call to make."

Cyrus's throat tightened. Of course it was. Of course Noth would do it like this—a final power play blasted to every corner of the system. A warning not just for Nakara but for any of the other planets who might have helped.

"And this is tonight?" he asked.

"Tonight." Lark squeezed his arm again, and Cyrus remembered that brief moment in the armory when he thought Lark might be his future. "I have to run," he added. "See you there?"

"Sure."

When he left, Cyrus could still feel the pressure of Lark's fingers on his skin. He had never been good at action. That was Cornelia's thing, but he didn't have the luxury of turning away. Not with Noth's confession tucked in his pocket. He let his fingers curl around the cold, metal charm as he tilted his face up to the sun. But what could he do with it, really? What power did he have?

He could still see Cornelia's expression behind his closed eyelids, the way she looked right before leaving his office for the last time. He hadn't crossed the line then. He hadn't gone with her and hadn't said goodbye.

Can't or won't?

That was what she'd said, and Cyrus hadn't fully understood what it meant until now. His grip tightened around the chain as he inhaled, letting the memory of Cornelia's outstretched hand surround him in the quiet street.

And this time, when she asked, he stepped forward and took it.

CHAPTER THIRTY-SIX

* * *

Cyrus wore his best uniform for his last night in the capital. The party had already started by the time he made it downtown, and Lark was right—everyone was there. Celebrities he recognized in passing, news anchors, every politician, staffer, and assistant. He had never seen this many uniforms in one place. People kept touching his arm, pulling him over to their table, offering him drinks. Because he was also famous now. The Ursa Team would go down in history, bathed in blood and hailed as heroes. Cyrus waved them all off, one hand stuffed in his pocket, where Ava's necklace lay curled next to the replica flash drive he'd made that afternoon.

Lark found him halfway through dinner, and when he threw an arm around his shoulders, Cyrus faltered for the first time all night. Again he remembered that moment in the armory hallway, before the world cracked apart.

"We did it!" Lark's breath was warm against his neck, excitement mixed with almost tangible relief. "We really did it."

"We did." Cyrus was buzzing with unrestrained energy. He felt reckless here, off-balance and drifting. Then Lark pulled back and patted his chest.

"Have a drink, will you?" he said. "You look way too sober for this."

He disappeared into the crowd and Cyrus's hand fell back to his side. He wanted to call him back. He wanted to run his fingers through Lark's hair again. He wanted to tell him goodbye. But that would make what he had to do next impossible, so Cyrus let him go, watching the back of Lark's jacket fade from view as the cameras clicked around him.

He circled the edge of the party as the broadcast kicked off on the steps of the Capitol building. General Noth was already there, standing next to Planetary Leader Derian and a few senior officers Cyrus didn't know. He would be up there soon, smiling for the cameras as Noth pinned a medal to his chest. But right now he made his way to the sound booth, watching as a harried-looking woman manned the controls inside. Cyrus raised a hand in her direction. "Can I make a request?"

"A request?" Her eyes narrowed on his uniform. "For what?"

He took another step forward. "For music?"

"What kind of party do you think this is?"

"One with . . . good music?"

The woman rolled her eyes, and as she turned away, Cyrus took the opportunity to slide the copy of the flash drive into one of the sound ports. "Is that a no, then?" He pretended to reach for the woman's arm, and instead pocketed the remote lying idly on her soundboard. "I really want to hear—"

"Get out of my booth!"

Cyrus didn't make her tell him twice. He ducked back across the lawn and joined his team on the steps of the Capitol. The rest of the party had quieted, everyone's attention turned toward the ceremony, and General Noth took her time shaking hands, adjusting medals on the lapels of every uniform.

"Congratulations, Lieutenant," she said when she reached him. Her voice was soft as she pinned the medal to his chest. "You should be very proud of yourself."

Like the conversation in her office never happened. Cyrus nodded as his finger slid across the remote in his pocket. "Of course. And I want you to know I thought about what you said earlier."

Noth's jaw tensed. "Oh?"

"Yes." Cyrus nodded solemnly. "And you're right. I really have no idea what I saw. I have no one to tell, and even if I did, they wouldn't believe me." He paused for one heart-pounding second as he watched Noth's eyebrows lift, like she couldn't decide where he was going with this. Then he grinned. "But I bet they'll believe you."

Cyrus cranked the volume on the remote all the way up and pushed down. There was a soft, staticky click as the source switched over to the flash drive, then Noth's voice echoed across the lawn.

"The Capricorn Team was dispensable. At-patrol can have the new round of Academy cadets. It's not like we have a shortage."

Noth's eyes widened, head snapping up, and for the first time in his life, Cyrus thought she looked genuinely shocked.

Planetary Leader Derian took a step forward. "What's that?"

"We needed a reason to pursue them, so I made one. That squadron died as heroes."

Noth opened her mouth, but Cyrus stepped back before she could speak. "Congratulations on a successful mission, General." He swept off his hat in a mocking, flourishing salute. "You should be very proud of yourself."

Derian was still looking from him to Noth. "What is this?" she repeated. "General?"

But Cyrus was already gone. He strode across the lawn with a confidence he'd never felt before. Vaguely, he was aware of the woman in the sound booth searching frantically for the source of the noise and of the people in the crowd watching him go. Right before he left the Capitol grounds for the last time, Cyrus plucked a glass of wine from a nearby table.

Lark was right: he was too sober for this.

The streets were mostly deserted as he headed downtown. Everyone was probably inside, watching the chaos at the Capitol building play out in real time, but Cyrus didn't look back again. He tore through the streets, picking up speed until he skidded to a stop in front of the prison. The guards at the entrance nodded as he flashed his badge, but the ones at the bottom of the stairs blocked his path when he tried to enter the high-security wing.

One of them glanced toward the entrance. "Is it time?"

Cyrus knew he meant the execution. He forced his face to clear, taking on the cruel glint of someone drunk off their own power. "Almost. I'm here to escort them, but can I get a moment alone first?"

He said it pointedly, watched the guards' minds run wild with whatever twisted scenario they wanted. Eventually, the one on the end nodded. "Be quick."

It was an effort for Cyrus to swallow his disgust at their non-chalance as he grabbed the keys and started down the hall.

Clara's head snapped up the second he entered the cell. Her nose was still crooked, face a mess of bruises, but Cyrus ignored her and turned to Jared instead. "How did you do that?" he asked, nodding toward the place where the other boy's skin screen used to be. "How did you take out the tracker?"

Jared's eyes widened in obvious terror, but Cyrus didn't have time to waste. "How long does it take?" he demanded. "Can you do it now?"

"I . . ." Jared shook his head. "Thirty minutes?"

"Great." Cyrus unlocked his cuffs. "You have three."

Jared sagged against the wall, cradling his injured arm. "Three? I can't—"

"You can." Cyrus turned out his pockets, scattering a variety of tools across the rough stones. "Do it now."

"My arm," Jared tried again. "I can't move it."

"Tell me what to do, then. I'll be your other hand, but you have to do it now."

Jared hesitated a second longer before picking a long, delicate blade off the floor. He motioned Cyrus forward, then popped the glass plate off his arm and got to work.

"Did you get what you needed from the base?" Cyrus asked, ignoring the sharp jabs of pain as Jared tugged on the wires below his skin. "Was there anything left or had she wiped it all?"

Jared's hands stilled. "I don't know what you're talking about."

"Come on." Cyrus let out a rough sigh of frustration. "It doesn't matter what you tell me now. They're dead."

Immediately, Cyrus wished he hadn't said it like that. Of course Jared knew. He'd been there. He flinched, tangled curls falling in front of his face as he ducked his head. "No," he whispered. "The files were gone. Grab that wire there and pull to your left."

Cyrus obeyed, trying not to look too closely at the inside of his own arm. He bit back another cry of pain as Jared twisted something inside his wrist. "So you didn't broadcast anything?"

Jared shook his head, and Cyrus glanced toward Clara, who had gone very still against the wall. *We can't keep dying for nothing.* That was what she'd said in the desert. Her eyes narrowed on his face, but Cyrus didn't look away until Jared slid his screen back into place and held up a small, square chip.

"There. It's out."

"Thank you." Cyrus's arm was still sore when he reached into his pocket and pulled out Ava's necklace. "There's more footage here. Could you put it on my screen? We should have it in more than one place."

Jared's expression crumpled as he watched the chain catch in the light. "Ava," he breathed. "I didn't . . ."

"Hey!" Cyrus snapped his fingers. "Not now. Can you do it?"

Jared ran a shaky hand over his face. "Why do you want it?"

"To finish this."

Cyrus shivered as the finality of the words rolled through him. There would be no going back if he shared this footage, no slipping into civilian life. The target on his back would be too big. He glanced at Clara. "That's what you wanted, right? To show everyone what was happening here? To make people listen? It's not everything you should have gotten on the base, but it's all I have."

Jared was silent for so long Cyrus thought he wasn't going to speak. Then he sniffed and raised his chin. "I can do it."

"Great. Stay here." Cyrus pushed him back against the wall and walked over to Clara. "I'm sorry," he added as he unchained her from the wall. "I can explain everything, but in a few minutes someone's going to come down here to execute you for a system-wide broadcast."

Clara recoiled so fast she hit the wall, and Cyrus held up his hands, heart hammering at the sudden movement. "Not me!" he hissed. "I'm trying to get you out. You need to trust me."

She looked like she'd rather kill him herself and save Noth the trouble. Footsteps sounded outside in the hall, and Cyrus tensed. They were running out of time. "Please." He glanced between the two of them. "We need to go."

"No." Clara's voice was rough. She folded her arms. "I'm not going with him. Or with you."

"Okay, well, there's not really another option."

"I don't care." Her gaze landed on Jared, and she said something in Nakaran that made him cringe back against the wall.

"Stop!" Cyrus stepped between them, hands outstretched. "You're more than welcome to stay if you want to die in a public execution, but that's not high on my list of fun evening activities."

When Clara looked at him again, her expression was lethal. Cyrus didn't care. She could hate him all she wanted after they were out of the cell. He deserved it. After another moment of tense silence, she extended her hands, wrists bared. It didn't feel like a concession; it felt like strategy. As he cuffed them both again, he couldn't shake the feeling Clara would sooner strangle them both with these chains than follow him anywhere. He slid the cell door back and whispered, "Don't speak," as he led them into the hall.

Clara snorted and said something in Nakaran that was definitely a curse-laced insult. Then the door closed behind them, and Cyrus didn't look back. One of the guards raised his head as they emerged.

"Time for the show?"

Cyrus nodded, willing himself back into the body of the soldier who didn't care. "It'll be a good one."

The officer grinned. "Wish I could watch."

Cyrus had to bite the inside of his cheek to keep from grimacing as he climbed the last of the stairs.

The streets were empty as they made their way toward the aircraft hangar. Cyrus planted himself in the middle of the group, partially because Clara tried to push Jared down the stairs the first time his shoulder accidentally brushed hers and partially because Cyrus hoped that if anyone spotted them, they would see a group of friends on a casual nighttime stroll.

Friends who definitely hadn't just broken out of prison.

For a few blocks, the only sound was the slap of their shoes against cobblestones and Clara's ragged breathing. Then a familiar voice sliced through the gathering night.

"Cyrus!"

Cyrus whirled, already fumbling for his weapon. With one hand, he shoved Clara and Jared around the corner and muttered, "Don't move," before turning in time to watch Lark melt out of the shadows. Now that he was out of the prison, some of Cyrus's adrenaline had faded, giving way to cold panic.

"Lark," he said, fighting to keep his voice steady. "What are you doing here?"

Lark stumbled to a stop. "Me? What are *you* doing? What's happening?"

"Nothing." Cyrus braced an elbow against the wall and tried desperately to look like he wasn't stashing two wanted fugitives a few feet away. "Getting some air. I need to—"

The unmistakable sound of the safety clicking back froze him to the cobblestones. Cyrus turned slowly, every muscle tense, and found himself staring down the barrel of Lark's gun.

"I'm not supposed to let you leave." Lark's voice trembled on the last word, but his jaw was set. "They told me not to let you leave."

Cyrus didn't have time for this. He had a very limited window to pull off the next part of his plan and the last thing he needed was Lark getting involved. He thought of Clara and Jared on the other side of the wall, how exposed they all were out in the streets. He lifted both hands. "We were wrong, Lark. You know we were wrong, right?"

Lark's finger tightened on the trigger. "It doesn't matter."

"It *does*." Cyrus stepped forward. "None of this had to happen. General Noth killed Cornelia." The words stuck in his throat like a rusty blade, but he forced them out anyway. "She killed them all. She's invading Nakara against Derian's orders, and I don't care if it makes me a bad soldier, I won't do that. I won't lie for her."

"Don't." Lark's hands shook as Cyrus took another step. He was breathing fast now, chest rising and falling in short, quick bursts. "Where will you go?"

"I don't know."

"Please." Lark's voice was barely a whisper. "Cyrus . . ."

They were so close Cyrus could see the trio of freckles on Lark's cheek. He reached out, cupping a hand against the warm curve of his face, and felt Lark go still, a crystallized statue warm to the touch. "Come with me."

The same wild idea Cornelia had whispered to him in the dark. Cyrus hadn't been able to save her, but maybe he could do this. Lark's breath was a rough exhale between his teeth. He lifted his chin as Cyrus brushed a thumb over his cheekbone, just like he'd wanted to do that day in the armory.

"Cyrus." Lark said his name like it was an anchor. "I don't know how to do anything else. My family . . . I can't."

"Can't or won't?"

Lark's free hand splayed across Cyrus's chest, firm and unyielding. He made a sound of frustration, low in the back of his throat, then his fingers curled in the collar of Cyrus's jacket and he closed the distance between them.

Cyrus had spent four years thinking Lark was nothing but sharp edges and hidden corners, but now he was enticing and open. He was insistent and warm, all things Cyrus never would have guessed if Lark's lips hadn't been parting under his. His fingers caught in Lark's hair, and for the first time, Cyrus understood the hammering, pulsing heat that had been building since the day they had landed on Nakara. It was desire, and right now, it drowned out everything else.

Then Lark pushed him away, so hard they both stumbled. He dragged the back of his hand across his mouth. "Go."

Cyrus blinked, still trying to catch his breath. "What?"

"I said *go!*" The words cut across the quiet streets, a dagger through flesh. Lark waved a hand as his expression hardened. "Get out."

"You can't stay here." Cyrus could feel his own desperation

heavy in every word, but he didn't care. "Please. She'll kill you."

"Get *out.*"

Lark's shot was purposefully wide, but Cyrus still felt the bullet pass dangerously close to his head. It cracked through the night, embedding itself into the wall to his left, and when Lark lowered his weapon, he had shifted back into the body of a capital soldier. "Go," he said. "I won't tell you again."

Cyrus didn't make him. He didn't think they'd survive it. With one last glance in Lark's direction, he turned and sprinted around the corner.

Cadets were still patrolling the floor of the aircraft hangar when they arrived, weaving between ships, blocking their only means of escape. Cyrus let out a breathless curse and steered Jared and Clara into the first empty office he saw. He had planned on this place being mostly deserted, everyone's attention turned toward the events unfolding at the Capitol. Sooner or later, someone would come for them. Someone would realize the prison was empty, but now that he was here, the full extent of what he was doing hit him for the first time. His chest tightened and, to his horror, Cyrus felt hot tears rise in the back of his throat. He forced them back.

"This is fine," he muttered as he unlocked Jared's and Clara's cuffs. "This is fine. I'm fine. We're fine."

Outside the office window, he could see every ship lining the garage. Catapults, Falcons, supply barges. All they had to do was cross the floor and open the roof. That was it. They were out. Cyrus paced the office, unable to keep still. He couldn't stop seeing Lark's frosty glare, the way his voice had trembled in time with his hands. *I don't know how to do anything else.*

Lark had grown up in this world of secrets and lies. He'd been born for it. If anyone could survive here a little while longer, it was him.

Cyrus scrubbed both hands down his face. When he turned again, he found Clara and Jared watching him warily, and he realized for the first time how absolutely unhinged he must look. "I'm sorry." He extended a hand in Jared's direction. "I'm Cyrus."

Jared started to reach out, but Clara slapped his hand away. That was fair. She probably still thought he'd betrayed them at the satellite base. "I'm sorry," he said again. "I promise I can explain everything, but we have to get out of here first. I have to make things right. I have to try, at least, and I can't do that here."

Clara's throat bobbed. "So it's true, then?" she asked. "They're really . . . ?"

Cyrus knew what she meant. He looked down. "I'm sorry."

It was all he could say.

She shook her head. "You didn't give them a chance to surrender."

"It was—" Cyrus began, but Clara interrupted.

"No, I'm telling you. You didn't give them a chance, because he would never have let her go down with him like that. That was always the line. He would *never* . . ." Her voice broke, and Cyrus felt the words fracture through his chest, one at a time. He reached into his pocket, fingers closing around Ava's necklace.

"Here." He held it toward her. "You should have this."

Clara closed her eyes, and when she opened them again, her expression was steady.

Cyrus took a breath and turned back to the hangar. They had been standing here too long. This city was swarming with armed officers; any second the capital would slam into lock-down and they really would be trapped. "You two have been fugitives before," he said, scanning the options outside the office window. "Tell me which ship does best in open space."

Jared tilted his head. "Well, that's complicated. You have to consider the factors, because I personally don't think it's worth taking anything without thermal insulation and—"

"You haven't done anything wrong in your life, have you, Lieutenant?" Clara interrupted before Jared could finish, and Cyrus thought he saw the corner of her mouth lift.

He folded his arms, suddenly self-conscious. "I committed treason for you."

"Doing the right thing doesn't count as treason." Clara held his gaze for a second longer before glancing at the ships. "You really want us to pick?"

Cyrus nodded, and when she hesitated, he felt the last several years flash before his eyes in stunning clarity. Sitting on his hands during his first day at the Academy. The nervous anticipation on graduation day. Kissing Lark on a darkened street corner, watching Cornelia slip through his fingers, General Noth's hand on his arm. Shane's steady, pale gaze. Ava's brilliant smile.

I just hope whatever forms from our dust is stronger than we are. I hope they'll finish this if we can't.

Clara pointed to a bulky Cruiser at the opposite end of the hangar. "I like that one."

"Really?" Cyrus wavered. "You . . . want to escape from the Opian government in a Cruiser?"

She turned on him, and for a second, the fire from the desert was back in her eyes. "You literally just asked my opinion, Lieutenant dearest. Do you want it or not?"

She still had Ava's necklace clutched between her fingers. Cyrus could almost feel the heat radiating from the pendant. It was all there, everything they needed. Jared stepped forward, nodding at the Cruiser, and for the first time since leaving Port City, Cyrus felt a part of his soul relax.

"Well." He exhaled, already imagining what that ship could do, how fast they could disappear into the night. "Clara darling, I think that's an excellent choice."

ACKNOWLEDGMENTS

* * *

People told me that writing the acknowledgments for their debut was harder than writing the actual book, but what they fail to realize is that I would routinely practice my award show acceptance speech in front of the mirror as a child like a glamorous Hollywood starlet, so not only do I feel completely prepared for this moment, but I also intend to be as annoying as possible about it the entire time.

Still, I don't think there's a way to fully express how grateful I am to everyone who made this book a reality—not only for making all of my sparkly, not-exactly-Hollywood-but-close-enough dreams come true but also for supporting me endlessly through the process.

To Claire Friedman. Please know that I spend at least one minute every day thinking about how lucky I am to have you in my corner. There were multiple times where I thought this book would never happen, but even then, I never really doubted that I would have some sort of career, and that's mostly because of you. Thank you for championing this book from the beginning, for answering every panicked email in two seconds, and for offering rep the day Taylor Swift released *folklore* so I could pretend everyone was celebrating me.

To Maggie Rosenthal, editor extraordinaire. I really can't

believe a version of this book ever existed without you! You somehow knew exactly what I was trying to say before I knew how to say it, and I'm not entirely convinced you don't have magical literary superpowers. I still don't know why you believed in me or that first draft, but I'm so proud of what we turned this book into. Thank you for all the guidance and support and for loving Ava, Shane, and Cyrus as much as I do.

A huge thank-you to the entire team at Viking for making this story come to life. To Jessica Jenkins, Taj Francis, and Lucia Baez for designing the book of my dreams. I want to hang every piece of it on my wall so I can stare at it for hours! To Felicity Vallence, Shannon Spann, Jordana Kulak, and the entire marketing/publicity teams for helping get this book from my brain into readers' hands. To everyone in managing and production editorial, both in-house and freelance—Gaby Corzo, Krista Ahlberg, Sola Akinlana, Marinda Valenti, Heidi Ward, and Kaitlin Severini for all your hard work. I still don't know how to properly use a semicolon, but thanks to you, no one else needs to know that. And special thanks to Fadwa for reading early and providing such thoughtful, insightful feedback.

To Mary E. Roach. I am once again asking how I got such a wonderful, brilliant genius for a mentor. You were the very first person to believe in this book and me, and I wouldn't be writing these acknowledgments without you. Thank you for your incredible edit letters, for telling me to make everyone worse, and for the reassurance that yes, a little murder *is* okay as long as you look sexy doing it. And to Brit, my OG mentee sibling. I'm grateful every day that Mary brought us together and that I get to exist in the same world as you and your books.

I would trust you to be my getaway driver any day.

To Serena Kaylor and Sophia DeRise. You were the very first people I ever sent my writing to and I can't believe I somehow tricked you both into becoming my real-life friends! Serena—I wouldn't want to drink wine and scream-sing Taylor Swift on a Charleston rooftop with anyone else. I'm so glad I've had you by my side for every step of this weird, wonderful publishing journey. Sophia—you have read every iteration of this book since the summer I first sent it to you chapter by chapter, and I couldn't be more grateful for your encouragement, excitement, and friendship. The next one is for you.

To the Author Mentor Match program for giving me some of my favorite people. Jo Fenning, thank you for reminding me to plot and letting me spiral in the group chat. You are truly a magical human and friend with a better grasp on story structure than I'll ever possess. Morgan Spraker, Libby Kennedy, and Katie Bender, your talent inspires me every day, and I can't wait for our Hot Mean Space Ladies to share a shelf together and plot their crimes. To Monica, Jenna, Natalie, SJ, Andy, Leah, Melody, Mallory, Michelle, Nina, and Crystal—what a team! Everyone says to find a writing group that keeps you sane, but I found one that sent anonymous Cinnabon delivery to my door the day I signed with my agent and decorated our retreat Airbnb with Halloween skeletons, so I think I win.

To the 2019 BCT Intern class who had the pleasure of living with me while I wrote the first draft of this book—specifically to Paul, who, when he found out I was writing YA, reminded me every night that "liking John Green is not a personality trait," and to Ares, who happened to be in the wrong place at the wrong time when I needed a name in act two. I promise to make it up to you one day.

To my family, who taught me to love reading before I learned to talk. Mom, you were the first person to put a book in my hands and tell me I was a writer, which was honestly rude, now that I think about it, because writing books isn't as easy as you made me believe. Dad, thank you for reading my earliest attempts at writing fiction. You can read this one if you want; I think it's a bit better. Josie and Jessy, sorry for cutting all the sisters out of this book. It's not personal, but it is a little funny.

To all of my friends who put up with my writing for years before I ever knew where I wanted these stories to go. Alexis, thank you for watching a (totally legal) bootleg of the Bonnie and Clyde musical with me senior year and being one of the first people to know about this idea. Caysi, you are a sweet baby angel with impeccable style and even more impeccable taste in books. Thanks for always being my cheerleader. Chelsea, you read more than anyone I know; I hope you like this one. Carissa, thank you for reading one of the earliest drafts of this book and texting me in the middle of the night to tell me that your only note was "less Shane, more Jared." That was a hot take, but I hope you enjoy all the Quality Jared Content that came to be because of it. Maria (and Athena), you both deserve an entire book of thanks for living with me while I wrote, revised, subbed, revised again, copyedited, promoted, and finally debuted (!!!) this book. You know way too many publishing secrets to ever be allowed to leave, so I'm sorry; you're stuck with me forever.

To Sarina Allison. I cried to you at Coney Island one night because I was afraid I would never write anything good enough and you said that was a lie, but even if it wasn't, you would still love me anyway. And then you told me to never drag you all the way to Coney Island after dark again because that's how people get murdered. I didn't fully realize how much this book was about friendship and family when I started writing it, but fortunately for me, you feel like both. Thank you for always being my biggest champion, my first reader, and my best friend.

And lastly, to Jeremy Jordan. You will literally never see this, but please know that this book exists partially because of how you sing the last chorus of "Raise a Little Hell."